Kane fell into infinity

It wasn't exactly a fall—more as if he had tripped and soared headlong down a black staircase stretching to the very edge of eternity.

Before him a coiling nebula glowed with a pure, blinding radiance. With eyes that should not have been able to see, ears that should not have heard, he saw the light take form and speak with a voice that vibrated to the core of his soul.

The light was a woman, sculpted from wheeling constellations, her eyes a pair of blazing stars. He could see her clearly and she was too beautiful to bear, but he couldn't tear his eyes away.

The language she spoke was new, yet not new...sounds from out of his desperate dreams. "You have not changed overmuch, Cuchulainn, my darling Ka'in."

She reached out a hand for him and whispered sadly, "Time is a river that twists on itself. Past, present and future are its waters. The fluid of time is life. When life, the spirit, ceases to exist, time becomes meaningless. I am overjoyed your spirit lives...."

Then she was gone, lost among the black gulfs of infinity.

Other titles in this series:

JAMES AXLER

OUTLANDERS™

SAVAGE SUN

A GOLD EAGLE BOOK FROM
WORLDWIDE®

TORONTO • NEW YORK • LONDON
AMSTERDAM • PARIS • SYDNEY • HAMBURG
STOCKHOLM • ATHENS • TOKYO • MILAN
MADRID • WARSAW • BUDAPEST • AUCKLAND

To Mark and Marian Wood, Publican Mike Smith and everyone in Rathcoole who makes Eire one of the few places where strangers are still welcome.

First edition December 1997
ISBN 0-373-63816-7

SAVAGE SUN

Special thanks to Mark Ellis for his contribution to the Outlanders concept, developed for Gold Eagle Books.

Some would call this spirit a devil,
Watching all their life's work undone.
All the creatures it bore reeked of evil
Spawned 'neath a savage sun.
> —*The Voyage of Maelduin*,
> fourth-century Irish ballad

The Road to Outlands—
From Secret Government Files to the Future

Almost two hundred years after the global holocaust, Kane, a former Magistrate of Cobaltville, often thought the world had been lucky to survive at all after a nuclear device detonated in the Russian embassy in Washington, D.C. The aftermath—forever known as skydark—reshaped continents and turned civilization into ashes.

Nearly depopulated, America became the Deathlands—poisoned by radiation, home to chaos and mutated life forms. Feudal rule reappeared in the form of baronies, while remote outposts clung to a brutish existence.

What eventually helped shape this wasteland were the redoubts, the secret preholocaust military installations with stores of weapons, and the home of gateways, the locational matter-transfer facilities. Some of the redoubts hid clues that had once fed wild theories of government cover-ups and alien visitations.

Rearmed from redoubt stockpiles, the barons consolidated their power and reclaimed technology for the villes. Their power, supported by some invisible authority, extended beyond their fortified walls to what was now called the Outlands. It was here that the rootstock of humanity survived, living with hellzones and chemical storms, hounded by Magistrates.

In the villes, rigid laws were enforced—to atone for the sins of the past and prepare the way for a better future. That was the barons' public credo and their right-to-rule.

Kane, along with friend and fellow Magistrate Grant, had upheld that claim until a fateful Outlands expedition. A displaced piece of technology…a question to a keeper of the archives…a vague clue about alien masters—and their world shifted radically. Suddenly, Brigid

Baptiste, the archivist, faced summary execution, and Grant a quick termination. For Kane there was forgiveness if he pledged his unquestioning allegiance to Baron Cobalt and his unkown masters and abandoned his friends.

But that allegiance would make him support a mysterious and alien power and deny loyalty and friends. Then what else was there?

Kane had been brought up solely to serve the ville. Brigid's only link with her family was her mother's red-gold hair, green eyes and supple form. Grant's clues to his lineage were his ebony skin and powerful physique. But Domi, she of the white hair, was an Outlander pressed into sexual servitude in Cobaltville. She at least knew her roots and was a reminder to the exiles that the outcasts belonged in the human family.

Parents, friends, community—the very rootedness of humanity was denied. With no continuity, there was no forward momentum to the future. And that was the crux—when Kane began to wonder if there *was* a future.

For Kane, it wouldn't do. So the only way was out—way, way out.

After their escape, they found shelter at the forgotten Cerberus redoubt headed by Lakesh, a scientist, Cobaltville's head archivist, and secret opponent of the barons.

With their past turned into a lie, their future threatened, only one thing was left to give meaning to the outcasts. The hunger for freedom, the will to resist the hostile influences. And perhaps, by opposing, end them.

Prologue

The day before doomsday.
Great Skellig, the southwest coast of Ireland.

From scrolling leaden clouds snow flurries drifted over the snarling surf. The eighteen-foot motor launch pitched and rocked on the relentless combers, white spray flying from the cresting waves.

Inside the pilot housing, Brother Morn wrestled with the wheel and mumbled softly to himself, *"Manannan' Mac Lir doras riaroh har oseails' ceann eile."* It was both a curse and a prayer.

A squat man with the stocky build of a pipe fitter, his mass of silver hair was swept back above a high forehead and a ruddy, weather-beaten face. There were only two specks of color about the man—a pair of cold, vivid blue eyes and the spotless white rectangle of a cleric's collar at his throat. His strangely small, delicate hands gripped the wheel tightly.

Peering through the droplets of water sliding across the windshield, Morn saw only the sea. The wipers droned steadily, but they were unable to keep the glass clear for more than an instant at a time. Waves continually crashed over the prow of the launch.

The hatch covering on the deck slid aside, and Karabatos struggled up from below. He was tall and gaunt, his leanness was accentuated by his black, impeccably

tailored Armani suit, white silk shirt and black necktie.
Though the lighting inside the cabin was dim, he wore
mirrored sunglasses. His short, close-cropped hair was
a dark blond, his pallid face furrowed and deeply
seamed.

"And how is our passenger holding up?" Morn
asked casually over his shoulder.

Karabatos stumbled as the craft yawed to port. "Still
sleeping. God knows how in this shit."

Morn smiled sadly. "Ah, God Almighty has little to
do with this journey, does He?"

Karabatos didn't answer. From inside his coat, he
took a package of cigarettes and shook one out. Without
looking at him, Morn announced, "This is a no-
smoking voyage. We're damned enough as it. We'll be
smoking aplenty by this time tomorrow."

Placing the filter tip between his lips, Karabatos
mumbled around it, "Speak for yourself, Paddy."

As Karabatos patted his pockets impatiently, Morn
produced a Ronson lighter and thumbed a flame into
life. Extending it toward Karabatos, he said, "Allow
me, old son."

Inscribed on the burnished-steel surface of the lighter
were glyphs resembling two scalene triangles flanking
an isosceles. The points of the three triangles were
topped by small circles. Karabatos leaned forward, setting his cigarette alight. Morn snapped shut the lighter
and slipped it back into a pocket.

Exhaling a wreath of smoke, Karabatos inquired, "A
little obvious, isn't it, to advertise the Priory that way?"

Morn chuckled. "And what do yer people do to recognize one another—secret handshakes? A certain floral
print on your undershorts?"

Karabatos didn't respond.

Conversationally Morn said, "I love ye bloody American spooks, I really do. Ye and yer secret-society barbecues and projects and lodge meetings and stock options in the future. What part of the coming wasteland have ye reserved for yerself, may I ask?"

Karabatos let smoke dribble out of his mouth. "You've got your orders. Shut up and drive."

Brother Morn gave the wheel a half spin and laughed. It was a harsh, bitter sound. "I've got me orders, true enough. To observe the Pact and betray an innocent. Who are *ye* betrayin'? The CIA? The NSA? Yer President? Yer children? Yer god?"

Karabatos stiffened. He transferred the cigarette to his left hand as his right slid inside his coat. It came out fisting a dull gray, compact Colt Delta 10 mm automatic. Training it on Morn's back, he said grimly, "One more word and I'll blow your goddamn brains out and complete the transaction myself."

"An' keep me from missin' humanity's final curtain? That *would* be a bloody shame, wouldn't it?"

Morn laughed uproariously, with genuine, scornful humor, though a note of barely contained hysteria undercut it. "I'm Armageddon outta here!"

Karabatos stared at him blankly, eyes masked by the lenses of his glasses. "You're crazy."

Morn shrieked, "Aye, I'm crazy! That Archon Directive's crazy...*yer* crazy! The whole bloody, godforsaken world is crazy! Until tomorrow at noon—then it won't be crazy anymore, will it? It'll simply be *gone!*"

His eyes glimmered with tears, doubling the difficulty of gazing out of the water-splotched windscreen. His hands tightened on the varnished wood of the wheel, the knuckles standing out like ivory knobs.

Quietly, grimly he said, "Go ahead an' blow me head off, you *gruagach* spook."

Karabatos said nothing. He returned the Colt to its shoulder holster. Morn swiped a hand over his face, clearing his vision of tears. Dead ahead the black triangle of Great Skellig reared out of the sea. A massive spire of rock and castellated walls, it loomed seven hundred feet above the North Atlantic, a dark silhouette thrusting up and piercing the sky. Misty clouds wrapped its sharp summit. Thundering waves crashed and broke on the bare rock, foaming spray flying in all directions.

Morn steered the launch on a parallel course with a vertical stone slab, following it into a small, straight-walled inlet protected on three sides from the open ocean. He guided the craft toward a concrete dock extending from one corner. A paved footpath cut into bare rock led away and up from it.

Karabatos remained silent, not wanting to distract Brother Morn from piloting the boat close to the quay. Even inside the tiny harbor, the sea was turbulent and a swell could easily pile the vessel up on the rocks.

Morn expertly aligned the boat with the outer edge of the dock and cut the motor. Tersely he said, "Make us fast."

Karabatos swiftly left the cabin, staggering a bit on the pitching, slippery deck. He knotted a hawser around a rusty cleat embedded in the concrete quay. Despite his lack of a topcoat, he didn't seem to feel the icy lash of the January wind.

Morn watched the American, grudgingly admiring the man's deft, efficient movements. Even though snow sprinkled on his head, he didn't brush it away. Probably too cold-blooded to notice the chill.

Brother Morn stepped into the open hatchway, down

a short ladder to the cabins below. Sliding open one of
the wood-jalousied doors, he wasn't too surprised to see
Sister Fand standing beside the bunk. Her almost in-
humanly large dark blue eyes were ringed with the
shadows of fatigue and glassy with the long effort of
fighting the barbiturates in her system.

Masses of flaxen yellow hair tumbled about her high-
planed face. The black habit she wore contrasted
sharply with her milky white complexion. Tall she was,
two inches taller than Morn. The shapeless garment she
wore did little to conceal the ripe figure swelling beneath.

Fand tugged at the steel cuff encircling her unnaturally long and slender wrist. A chain stretched from it
to a bracket bolted in the cabin wall. She glared dazedly
at him and demanded, *"Cad ta' ar siull agat?"* Her
voice was a rich contralto.

"Tell her to speak English," said Karabatos from the
passageway.

Morn glanced over his shoulder. "Ye object to the
tongue of yer masters, d'ye?"

"What?"

"Gaelic is derived from Sanskrit, and Sanskrit is derived from the language of the Archons." He stared at
the American keenly, mockery dancing in his eyes.
"That's common knowledge among the Priory."

Karabatos grunted his disinterest and stepped into the
cabin. "She should still be asleep."

In a sharp, sneering tone, the woman said, "Ye can
pump me so full of yer damn juice it comes out me
nose, I'll still not give ye what ye want."

Karabatos took a swift forward step, whipped out his
open right hand and slapped her full force across the
face. She sprawled over the bunk, nearly sliding to the

deck. Her fall was brought up short by the chain on her wrist.

Morn hissed in anger as Karabatos stood over the woman, snatching her left wrist and pushing her face down against the mattress. Skillfully he unlocked the steel circlet from the wall bracket, captured her flailing right hand and pinned both wrists behind the small of her back. He cuffed her hands and stepped back, not even breathing hard.

Sister Fand shouldered herself to a sitting position, the red imprint of the American's hand spreading over her face. In Gaelic she snarled, *"D'anam don diabhal amadan'!"*

"What did she say?" Karabatos asked.

"You don't want to know," muttered Morn, moving to the woman's side and helping her to her feet. She tried to wrench herself away from his touch, but he held her firmly.

He whispered to her soothingly in Gaelic, "There is no point in resisting, Sister. This is your fate. When you took your vows to the Priory, you swore unquestioning obedience."

"My vows included chastity," she snapped.

"And a virgin you will remain—for all intents and purposes."

Karabatos led the way from the cabin, down the short gangway and up to the pilot housing. He allowed Morn to guide Sister Fand to the deck. She didn't resist, but didn't give her full cooperation, either. From a cabinet, Karabatos took a leather satchel, slinging the strap over his shoulder. Peeling back a shirt cuff, he glanced at his wristwatch.

"We're off schedule." He fixed his gaze on Sister Fand. "If you try to delay us, I'll knock you unconscious and drag you to the top. My orders were to escort you here. The choice of whether you arrive intact or not is up to you.''

Fand said nothing, but her blue eyes were sapphire hard.

The three of them went out on the rocking deck. Morn handed the woman to Karabatos on the quay. They walked to the paved footpath as it ascended and curled around Great Skellig's almost perpendicular south side. The black peaks reared above them like vast, permanent shadows.

The path terminated in a weather-eroded stairway, chipped out of the rock face by monks a thousand years before. Six hundred steps of differing widths led up the sheer black cliff. The three people scaled the crude, time-pitted notches, picking their way carefully. In some places the steps were slippery with lichens and sea campions.

Fand, still dizzy from the drugs, breathed heavily and had to stop from time to time. Karabatos waited impatiently, drumming his fingers on the leather pouch.

'' 'Forward, forward let us range,' '' Morn quoted wryly. '' 'Let the great world spin forever down the ringing grooves of change.' ''

''What are you gibbering about now?'' Karabatos demanded.

''Tennyson,'' answered Morn. ''Are you utterly without learning?''

''I'm a soldier and a scientist,'' Karabatos replied. ''Not one of your country's fairy poets.''

''Neither was Tennyson, as I recall,'' said Morn. He tugged on Sister Fand's arm.

She whispered breathlessly, '' 'The fairy tales of science and the long result of Time.' ''

The stairway led into a tunnel under a retaining wall. They made their way up the steep slant, shoes slipping and sliding on the wet stones. They climbed through the passage and onto a rock-strewed plateau. It leveled off in a series of narrow terraces. A flagstone path wound among a cluster of little beehive-shaped stone huts, constructed of flat, interlocking rocks.

The path widened into a miniature walled plaza, lined by leaning tombstones topped by Celtic crosses. Their inscriptions had long ago been effaced into illegibility by the harsh wind and the merciless hand of centuries.

They passed through the plaza and stopped in a clearing among the stones. No lichen, grass or moss grew on the earth. In the center of the bare patch rose a stele, a stone column with a crosspiece of two blunted knobs. The weathered carvings formed swirling geometric abstractions.

Karabatos, Brother Morn and Sister Fand stood and stared. The silence atop Great Skellig was unbroken except for the wail of the chill wind and distant crash of the surf.

Softly the American asked, "Now what? They know we're here...don't they?"

The carved column of rock suddenly quivered, and a circular crack split the naked ground around it in a disquieting symmetrical pattern. Slowly, smoothly the stele began to rise, like a single finger at the end of a fist. Dirt and grit sifted down as the sepulchre pushed its way from below.

The air seemed to pulse about the cube of brooding black metal. Dimly came the sound of buried machinery, gears, chains and the prolonged hissing squeak of hydraulics.

Morn and Sister Fand, who had seen the process before, still gazed at the rising structure in something like awe. Karabatos rested his hand on the butt of his Colt, waiting for the sepulchre's slow ascent to stop.

When it did, a perfectly rectangular seam appeared in the featureless cube. By degrees, it widened and enlarged and opened. A figure wearing a black hooded cassock stepped out onto the windswept plateau. A sliver chain girded his waist, and from it dangled a small charm, a talisman fashioned in the shape of three circle-topped triangles.

Brother Morn ducked his head reverentially. "Father Bran. I ask admittance into the Priory."

The priest tugged back his hood, revealed a bearded, blunt-jawed face and bright, questioning green eyes. The wind plucked at his red hair. In a quiet voice, he asked, *"Cad e' seo?"*

"Speak English," growled Karabatos.

Father Bran's eyes flicked toward him. *"An Americeanach thu?"*

"Aye, he's an American," Morn said. "He is here as representative of the Archon Directorate, to enforce the pact."

Bran's eyes widened, then narrowed. "The pact?"

"Between the Directorate and the Priory of Awen." Karabatos's cold voice ghosted over the plateau.

"The time is not yet nigh."

"Truly, that is the terrible thing, Father," said Morn. "It *is* nigh. Judgment Day is upon us. And now the pact struck by Saint Patrick and the Na Fferyllt must be consummated."

Bran's face went the color of the sky. He stumbled back a pace as if he had been a dealt a blow. He fixed his unblinking gaze on Sister Fand. "It cannot be," he said haltingly. "The blood of the Danaan flows in her veins. To mingle it with the blood of the Na Fferyllt is an unspeakable sin.''

"Fuck this,'' Karabatos grated, and drew his Colt. "It's the *pact*, you sanctimonious asshole. You knew one day you'd be called to account, or you wouldn't have sent him—'' he jerked his head toward Morn "—to act as your liaison. He's abiding by it and so will you.''

"Please, Father,'' Morn said in a voice thick with emotion. "The Directive made their choice. Sister Fand has the purest blood, the cleanest line of descent.''

Bran shook his head in horror, in disbelief. "No. I will not allow this...*blasphemy*. Saint Patrick did not envision the pact this way.''

"Ireland was to be free of the Na Fferyllt until Judgment Day,'' Morn responded bitterly. "It is now at hand. The Priory of Awen was formed to protect humanity from the knowledge of the pact. If it is broken now, then our brotherhood's work over the past thousand years is as smoke. A lie.''

Bran inhaled an unsteady breath. "A pact with liars is no pact at all. Saint Patrick would have never agreed had he known.''

Karabatos laughed. "Take it up with Patrick when you see him.''

He squeezed the trigger of the Colt. The crack smothered the wail of the wind, replacing it with a rolling cannonade that echoed over the high plateau.

The steel-jacketed round struck the priest just above his right eye, drilling a dark, neat hole. The back of the cowl billowed out as a chunk of skull exploded in jagged fragments. A halo of red mist surrounded his head.

Father Bran sprang back, his expression holding more surprise than fear or pain. He hit the side of the black cube spread-eagled, blood and gray matter splattering the smooth surface. He fell forward on his face, the silver triangle ornament ringing a tinkling, feeble chime when it struck the flagstones.

Sister Fand and Brother Morn screamed in wordless fury. Morn lunged toward Karabatos, his fingers clawing for the man's face. He managed to snatch away the sunglasses right before the American raked the barrel of the automatic across the bridge of his nose. The blade sight tore flesh, crushed cartilage and blood sprang out in rivulets.

Clapping his hands to his face, Morn stumbled and fell to one knee. Sister Fand made a move toward Karabatos but backed away when he pointed the gun in her direction. Prodding Morn with a foot, he said calmly, "Get up."

Slowly, biting back groans of pain, Morn stumbled erect, hand to his face, crimson streaming from between his fingers. His white cleric's collar slowly turned red as it absorbed the blood like blotting paper. He stepped unsteadily into the cube. Karabatos gathered a handful of Sister Fand's habit and pushed her forward.

The interior of the sepulchre was as blank and featureless as the exterior, except for two buttons protruding from one wall. With the barrel of the Colt, Karabatos depressed one. With a hiss, the cube sealed and began to drop, slowly and without a lurch.

Morn tried to catch Sister Fand's gaze. "I'm sorry," he said in Gaelic, his voice muffled beneath his hand.

She refused to meet his eyes.

The cube sighed to a stop. Karabatos placed his left hand inside the pouch. The automatic doors hissed back, and he stepped out quickly into a large, low-ceilinged room. It was filled with computer terminals and electronic communications equipment. Console and panel lights flashed and blinked purposefully. A bank of closed-circuit monitor screens ran the length of the far wall. Most of them showed images of the rough Atlantic seas.

Six people were seated before the consoles, three men and three women. All wore black cassocks with the silver-triangle ornament dangling from their waists. They whirled when the doors rolled open, their faces masks of fear, shock and rage.

From Karabatos's hands leaped a pair of small metal cylinders. They bounced in a jerky, zigzag fashion on the smooth floor before white smoke exploded from them in a thick pall.

The priests and nuns cried out in terror as the CS powder penetrated their nostrils and eyes. They reeled about the room, slamming into one another, stumbling and falling.

The Colt Delta in Karabatos's fist cracked and cracked, and at each shot, a black-robed figure dropped to the floor, kicking and jerking. After the sixth shot, a shroud of utter silence draped the room. Karabatos, Sister Fand and Morn waited in the lift cube until the air-recycling system cleared the room of the chemical fog.

The American spared the fresh corpses a single, impassive glance, then stepped out into the room. He gestured with the automatic. "Move."

Sister Fand said with great conviction, "You will burn in the deepest pit of Hell for what you have done."

Karabatos grinned. "By noon tomorrow, I'll have plenty of company. Take me to the crypt. Now."

Brother Morn saw no further point in hesitating or arguing. Leading Sister Fand by the elbow, he crossed the room, careful not to tread in the pools of blood. He pushed open and entered a cold gray corridor lit by fluorescent strips glowing on the ceiling. An overpowering sense of overlapping layers of history emanated from the stonework of the floor and walls.

The corridor opened up after a few yards, and at its end stood an immense carved stone door with serpentine, spiraling Tal Tene designs incised across it. With narrowed eyes, Karabatos studied the ornate lintel, the threshold and the jambs.

"Open it."

Brother Morn's tongue touched his dry, blood-speckled lips. He stepped to the door. His hands pushed at the stone molding in several places, pressed certain points in certain ways. Then, very slowly the great carved slab of stone began to tilt inward at the top. It was precisely balanced on oiled pivots. The aperture beyond was black with a darkness that was almost solid. A musty odor poured forth like invisible smoke.

"Enter," said Karabatos.

Sister Fand glanced up, her eyes flashing with scorn. "Do not presume to give us, a brother and sister of the Priory, commands. You are not in authority here."

Karabatos sighed very quietly, almost sadly. He grabbed Sister Fand, spun her around and propelled her into the blackness beyond the portal. Morn followed her. The light from the corridor barely penetrated into the murk as they walked slowly along the passage past half a dozen openings. The walls were covered with barely discernible straight-line inscriptions in ogham, the ancient Celtic form of writing. Faded banners depicting incidents in the lives of various saints and warriors hung from pegs. Brother Morn found it painful to look at them. Blood dripped onto his black coat, spattering it with an artless red pattern.

With Karabatos treading almost on his heels, Morn turned a hairpin corner and descended irregular stairs hewed out of rock. Ahead and below glowed a dim light. At the foot of the stairs was a gallery, a natural, bowl-shaped cavern. The light shone from a dozen copper braziers placed in a circle around the curving rock walls.

Painted on the cavern floor in greens and reds was a large cup-and-ring glyph, a semicircular spiral designed to entrap and destroy malignant entities. Morn and Sister Fand stepped across it, careful not to tread on the intricate labyrinth of lines. Shapes loomed in the shadows, objects and artifacts concealed by linen coverings.

In a shallow recess sat two life-size images crafted out of stone. The right-hand statue squatted crosslegged in an attitude of meditation. It wore a cassock much like Father Bran's.

Eyeing the stone effigy, Karabatos murmured, "Saint Patrick, founder of the Priory of Awen."

The left-hand statue was of a brawny, half-naked man, wearing a diadem of grinning human skulls above a grim, clean-shaved face. The right hand gripped a sword, but the point of the blade branched into the stylized image of three triangles. A pair of huge hounds crouched between his widespread legs, stone lips curled in vicious, fanged snarls.

"Cuchulainn, the most savage yet deeply mystical warrior in Celtic legend," said Karabatos with a smile. "Patrick and Cuchulainn. Peace and war. Yin and yang."

Between the effigies rose an oblong pedestal, four feet tall. Four small pyramids crafted from pale golden alloy were placed at equidistant points around it. Resting on their points was a smooth, crystalline ovoid, around eight feet long. It seemed filled with a cloudy, smokelike substance. Behind it bulked the cylindrical outlines of two cryo units.

Karabatos holstered his weapon and approached the pedestal cautiously. He put out a tentative hand toward the crystal surface. At his touch, the vapor within the ovoid immediately cleared, and he recoiled, hissing, "Jesus."

Within lay a very tall, almost skeletally thin figure. Morn, who had always known it existed here, deep in the Priory crypt, found himself cringing back. Sister Fand bit back a gasp of shock and horror.

It was human shaped, but by no means human. Its cadaverous, excessively slender frame and narrow, elongated skull were completely hairless. The pale, brownish gray skin, wrinkled and tough, stretched over protruding brow arches and jutting cheekbones. There was a suggestion of scaliness about it.

A central ridge dipped down from the top of the domed head to the bridge of the flattened nose. Four long fingers, tipped with razor-sharp spurs of bone, were laced together on the creature's motionless chest. The large, almond-shaped eyes stared blindly, black vertical slits centered in the golden, opalescent irises.

The eyes were the worst.

In a voice hushed and thick with awe, Karabatos whispered, "No myth, then. Enlil, the last of the Serpent Kings, held hostage here since 432 A.D. The basis of the legends of Patrick driving the snakes from Ireland."

In a husky, trembling tone, Fand quoted, "'By the

power of his word he drove the whole pestilent swarm from the precipice, headlong into the ocean.'"

Karabatos barked out a derisive laugh. "Now we know he had a little help. Yet another of history's dirty little secrets."

He stooped, extending a groping hand beneath the crystal ovoid, fingers exploring the underside of the pedestal. A distinct click sounded in the chamber. The transparent sheath suddenly split in two, the halves sliding apart and down into almost invisible slots. There was a protracted hiss, like air pouring into a vacuum. An aroma wafted from the crystalline cocoon, reminiscent of old, moldy leaves.

Morn and Sister Fand watched as a sudden spasm of movement shook the lean form. Its lipless mouth opened slightly, and from it issued a prolonged, liquidy rasp. The repulsive noise was repeated several times, then it changed to a rhythmic burble. Sister Fand and Morn knew it was the thing's laughter. Enlil was happy, gleefully, terribly happy.

It turned its head, and for the first time Sister Fand and Morn accepted it was a living creature, breathing, stirring, aware of its surroundings. Its gold-and-black eyes swept over the people, then fixed and focused on Sister Fand. They stared straight into her soul.

A stream of syllables poured from its mouth. "Tuatha De Danaan."

The voice shocked them all—oily, deep and touched with a note of triumphant realization that a long-ago debt was about to be collected.

Karabatos glanced over his shoulder at the woman. "He recognizes you."

Sister Fand shrank back, face contorting. Karabatos reached for her, securing an armlock on her bound wrists. "Since you two like quotes so much, here's an appropriate one from the Book of Enoch. 'When the evil angels descended and beheld the daughters of man, they began to corrupt themselves with them.'"

He jerked Fand forward, toward the pedestal. Enlil still lay prone. Flesh stirred and slid at the juncture of its thighs. A wrinkle of scaled skin folded back, allowing a thin stalk to push its way up, like the budless stem of a flower.

Sister Fand dug in her heels and screamed, Gaelic words mixing with English in a crazed tumble.

"No!" Morn's shout vibrated with horror. "Not this way! This isn't science! No offspring can be conceived this way!"

"How do you know?" Karabatos asked, struggling with the woman. "There's got to be some reason for their extreme interest in human sexuality. Aren't you curious? I am."

With a hissing grunt of effort, Enlil sat up, then stood. It was very tall, towering at least a foot over Karabatos. With a heave of his arms and shoulders, the American shoved Sister Fand toward Enlil. It caught her in its arms and with one slash of claw-tipped fingers, stripped the habit from her body. She wore nothing underneath, and blood sprang in crimson lines along her back and shoulder blades, shockingly bright against the milky hue of her skin.

Enlil whirled her around like a dancer, bending her half across the open cocoon. It stretched its frame over her. Through eyes half-blinded by tears, Morn saw Enlil possessed no discernable buttocks. Rather, a short, vestigial tail dangled from the base of its spine.

As it forced open her thrashing legs, Sister Fand shrieked, not in fear, but in maddened fury, voice throbbing with the murderous passion of the enraged and outraged Celt.

"You've broken the pact, and whatever issue springs from me will not swear fealty to your kind! Nothing will come from this union but generations of enemies! *That* is the new pact!"

Karabatos laughed. Morn spun away, crossing himself repeatedly. Tears flowed in a flood from his eyes, cutting fresh runnels in the drying blood on his face. He murmured brokenly, "Fand, *go seirbhe Dia dhut.*"

Karabatos slid a mock sympathetic arm around his shaking shoulders. "Yeah, weddings always make me cry, too."

Brother Morn only sobbed. He was still sobbing even as Karabatos shot him once through the head.

Chapter 1

Nearly two hundred years after doomsday.
Southwestern Idaho.

Humankind took the permanence of the earth for granted, and that was its capital mistake.

For thousands of years, the hills, mountains, valleys, plains, rivers and seas seldom altered. The few small, localized changes were noticed only by geologists, whose time perceptions were measured in aeons, not in individual lifetimes.

On January 20, 2001, mountains walked, plains became inland seas, earthquakes and tidal waves resculpted coastal regions. Billions died. For the following generations, nothing was permanent—especially dreams of love, security and a future.

Kane caught those thoughts snaking through his head and tried to chase them out. Too many monotonous hours behind the wheel of the Sandcat had turned his mental meanderings into sour, insipid longings. He remembered the good days in his life, but he could also remember far worse—when everything he had taken for granted sneered in his face and ran over the horizon of lost dreams, never to be seen again.

Kane opened the ob slit wide. An arid wind blew off the Borah Peak and across Hell's Canyon, filling the dusky air with the sound of rustling foliage. He gazed out of the opening, watching the knee-high, unbroken plain of gama grass whisper past the snout of the Sandcat. He felt the faint stirring of the wind as it ruffled his dark brown hair.

Twilight deepened around the vehicle, a sea of russet and indigo flowing down from the western sky. He tightened his hands around the horseshoe-shaped wheel and watched the first faint stars come out. His pointman's sixth sense reacted to the cool yet very dry touch of the breeze. Something was in it, a faint odor of fear.

He glanced over at Domi, slumped and drowsing in the copilot's chair, her white-haired head bowed. In the rearward cargo compartment, Brigid Baptiste and Grant also napped, doing their best to catch up on lost sleep.

Kane inhaled deeply, trying to relax. He sensed a brooding oppressiveness about this stretch of the Outlands, something he normally detected only in a hellzone. He steered the Sandcat slowly through the dusk, the clank and clatter of its metal treads sounding strangely subdued, as did the growl of the 750-horsepower engine. Its gray armored hull plowed through the rippling grass like the blunt prow of a ship.

Like most everything manufactured in the villes, the Sandcat was based on an existing predark framework. Designed as a FAV—Fast Attack Vehicle—for a ground war that was never fought, the Sandcat's lowslung, blocky chassis was supported by a pair of flat, retractable tracks.

The gun turret, concealed within an armored bubble topside, held a pair of USMG-73 heavy machine guns. The hull's armor was composed of a ceramic-armaglass bond, which served as protection from not only projectiles, but went opaque when exposed to energy-based weapons, such as particle-beam emitters.

The interior was the perfect size to comfortably hold four people. At the front of the compartment were the pilot's and copilot's chairs; the rear storage module housed the computer links for the electronic systems. A double row of three jump seats faced each other. The seats could be folded down to make serviceable, narrow bunks. They were folded down now, holding the sleeping Grant and Baptiste.

The Sandcat was one of two all-terrain vehicles in the Cerberus redoubt. Kane had no idea how they had been brought in, since the mat-trans gateway chamber was not large enough to transport them from elsewhere. More than likely the vehicles had been in the installation before the nukecaust, recently refurbished and modified by Lakesh and his refugee staff of tech-heads.

Thinking of Cerberus, Kane turned his thoughts inward again, dwelling on the events of the past week. Lakesh had returned from a week-long sojourn in Cobaltville with a grim report—a new harvest of genetic material was timed to begin in the Outlands. The hybridization timetable that Kane, Grant and Baptiste had overturned in New Mexico nearly five months before was being brought back on schedule.

As usual, the Outlands were the hunting grounds, and the genetic material—human beings—would be harvested from the settlements. The news, though upsetting, was nothing less than any of them expected. Baron Cobalt, as the intermediary of the Archon Directorate, had to abide by the program, as did all the barons comprising the Hybrid Dynasty. The punitive expedition to New Mexico had only delayed the process, not stopped the centuries-old program.

The first settlement earmarked for the harvest was listed on the map as Cuprum, in what was known in predark times as Hell's Canyon National Recreation Area in Idaho. It was also the place Domi called home.

The girl had said nothing when Lakesh related the news, and due to her albinism, no one could tell if she turned pale. She simply withdrew to her quarters. The Cerberus staff sympathized with her, particularly Grant. He more or less owed the half-feral girl his life, but her frequent amorous advances toward him always made him deal with her at arm's length. Though no one had an idea of her true age, Grant assumed he was at least old enough to be her father.

It wasn't until Brigid spoke to her privately that they learned Domi still had family back in Cuprum. Tactically that fact shouldn't have altered the situation. Domi was an outlander, an outrunner, a nonperson by birth. Kane, Brigid and Grant had been reclassified as such in the recent past, with on-sight termination warrants hanging over them. Since their escape from Cobaltville, they had eluded capture simply by staying out of the villes' sphere of influence.

The Cerberus redoubt was the best and, under the circumstances, the only place to remain hidden. A forgotten installation and almost impossibly inaccessible, to leave it and risk apprehension seemed extraordinarily foolish and reckless.

However, the purpose of the small, loosely knit resistance movement based in Cerberus was to oppose the Archon Directorate—something they hadn't actually implemented, despite a recent journey to Asia to investigate Archon presence there. So Kane, Grant and Baptiste volunteered to go to Hell's Canyon with Domi as their guide.

No functioning gateway units were located anywhere near Cuprum. The only option was overland, in the

Sandcat, traversing the treacherous mountain roads high in the Darks. It was a journey no one had undertaken in close to a century.

The gateways were major aspects of the predark scientific project known as the Totality Concept. "Gateway" was the colloquial term for a quantum interphase transducer, otherwise referred to as a mat-trans unit.

Most of the units were buried in subterranean military complexes, known in the remnants of the United States as redoubts. Only a handful of people knew they even existed, and fewer than that knew all their locations. The knowledge had been lost after the nukecaust, rediscovered a century later, then jealously, ruthlessly guarded. There were, however, units in other countries—Japan, England, Canada and Mongolia. The exact purpose of the units and of the Totality Concept itself had vanished when the ultimate nuclear holocaust had destroyed civilization all over the world.

The Darks themselves had once been known as the Bitterroot Range, but the postnukecaust name suited them better—treed with deeply shadowed forests, slashed by ravines, with a sinister mythology that had been ascribed to them for generations.

The road leading down from Cerberus was little more than a twisted asphalt ribbon, skirting yawning chasms and cliffs. Acres of the mountainsides had collapsed during the nuke-triggered earthquakes nearly two centuries ago. It was a tortuous, nerve-racking trek that took nearly an entire day before they reached the foothills.

After that, the trip was relatively speedy and smooth. The weather held, and the instruments in the Sandcat showed tolerable levels of ambient radiation. Only twice did they come near orange, or warm, zones. The far western inland states had, for the most part, been spared direct strikes. Still, the shocks triggered by the Russian ''earthshaker'' bombs had resculpted much of the West Coast.

For five days, the Sandcat rolled steadily along old Interstate 95. They passed piles of overgrown rubble that had once been cities. A few old buildings still rose at the skyline, then broke off with ragged abruptness. They saw very few people and fewer animals.

At the end of the fifth day, following Domi's directions, Kane steered the vehicle off the interstate and onto a vista of unbroken grasslands. The girl, who had spoken very little since the journey began, now said, ''Almost there.''

Kane wondered how she had managed to get from this particular ass-end of nowhere to the Tartarus Pits of Cobaltville, hundreds of miles away in Colorado. In retrospect, it was no great mystery. Wag trains of outlanders often traveled to the network of villes scattered across the rad-blasted face of America, hoping to enter them legally or illegally. Domi had been an illegal, implanted with a bogus ID so she could serve as the personal sex slave of the Pit boss, the late Guana Teague. Domi had seen to his abrupt demise, by dint of a very sharp knife drawn across a very soft and flabby throat.

Kane stole another glance toward her. Domi seemed too childlike to be a woman, yet there was no mistake about it. Her skin was perfectly white and beautiful, like polished porcelain, and her untidy, bone white hair was cropped close to her small, hollow-cheeked face. Her eyes, hidden now by closed lids, were the color of rubies. She wore a red jerkin of some silky stuff, leaving ninety percent of her long, gamine-slim legs bare, and the insolently curved shape beneath it was something to wonder at.

Actually, Kane reflected, it wasn't something to wonder at. Baptiste had admonished Domi more than once for strolling through the vanadium-alloy halls of Cerberus wearing nothing but red stockings. Few of the male residents had lodged objections. Old Lakesh in particular never seemed to mind.

A gully suddenly appeared directly ahead. Kane stamped hard on the brakes, and the Sandcat lurched to a shuddering, clanking halt. The jolt and noise snapped Grant and Baptiste awake.

In a voice sounding like a grouchy lion's, Grant demanded, "What's going on?"

Domi, crimson eyes suddenly open and alert, replied calmly, "We're here."

The terrain appeared perfectly flat, but the gully was wide and cut in clean like a surgical incision, hidden by the high grasses. Only Kane's pointman senses had kept them from driving over the edge. He turned off the engine, and all of them disembarked, walking to the gully's lip.

Pointing eastward, Domi said, "That way, a quarter mile."

Quietly Grant said, "We could be too late, you know."

A very tall, very broad shouldered man, Grant's thick brows were drawn, shadowing his dark eyes. A newly grown, down-sweeping mustache showed jet-black against the coffee brown of his skin. Beneath it, his heavy-jawed face was set in a perpetual scowl. Gray showed at the temples of his short hair, as if sprinkled there by a diffident hand.

"Lakesh said the op was ten days away," replied

Brigid Baptiste. "We're in plenty of time to warn the settlement."

She was tall, full breasted and long limbed. Her willowy, athletic figure reflected an unusual strength without detracting from her undeniable femininity. An unruly mane of long, red-gold hair spilled over her shoulders, framing a smoothly sculpted face with a rosy complexion dusted lightly with freckles across her nose and cheeks. There was a softness in her features that bespoke a deep wellspring of compassion, yet a hint of iron resolve was there, too. The color of emeralds glittered in her big eyes.

Kane glanced toward her, a wry smile crooking his lips. "Or we're in plenty of time to walk into a trap."

An inch over six feet, he was not as tall or as broad as Grant. Every line of his supple, compact body was hard and stripped of excess flesh. He looked like a warrior—from the hawklike set of his head on the corded neck, to the square shoulders and the lean hips and long legs. Kane was built with the savage economy of a gray wolf. His high-planed face, now sporting a five-day growth of beard stubble, held a watchful expression, as did his narrowed gray blue eyes.

Except for Domi, all of them wore drab, neutral-colored clothes, the coarse attire typical of the average outlander.

"Is this just your normal paranoia," asked Grant, "or is it the pointman in you talking?"

Kane shrugged. "Not much difference, is there?"

"Are you suggesting we scrub, after all we went through to get here?" Brigid's tone was crisp and a little challenging.

"No, Baptiste," retorted Kane impatiently, "I'm

suggesting we approach the situation like we would a hellzone.''

Grant sighed wearily. "Tactics?"

"You and Domi stay here while me and Baptiste recce the zone. We'll patch in a comm-link to the Cat."

Grant turned toward the rear of the Sandcat. "Let's get you hard."

He and Kane walked to the back of the vehicle and opened a cargo compartment, wrestling out a medium-sized trunk, finished with leather and cornered by steel. Snapping open the latches, Grant lifted the lid while Kane quickly stripped off his clothes.

From the trunk, Grant removed the one-piece Kevlar undergarment and handed it to Kane. He slipped it on, zipping it up and sealing the wrist and ankle tabs. Next came several oddly shaped jet-black objects. With routine ease, Kane donned the Magistrate armor.

The molded polycarbonate breast and back plates came first. After fastening the side seals, Kane slipped on the ebony arm sheathings, locking them magnetically against the shoulder epaulets. The leggings came next, then the high, thick-soled boots. Grant handed him the gauntlets, and he tugged them on. The only sound was the click and snap of fastenings and couplings.

Grant ran his fingers over the joints of the body armor, making certain all the seals were secure. The armor was close fitting, molded to conform to the biceps, triceps, pectorals and abdomen. Even with its Kevlar undersheathing, the armor was lightweight and provided no loose folds to snag against projections. The only spot of color anywhere on it was the small, disk-shaped badge of office emblazoned on the left pectoral. It depicted, in crimson, a stylized, balanced scales of justice, superimposed over a nine-spoked wheel.

The badge symbolized the Magistrate's oath, of keeping the wheels of justice turning in the nine baronies, but now the only emotional resonances it carried was one of bitter betrayal.

Grant handed Kane his helmet. Like the armor encasing his body, the helmet was made of black polycarbonate, and fitted over the upper half and back of his head, leaving only a portion of the mouth and chin exposed. The slightly concave red-tinted visor served several functions—it protected the eyes from foreign particles, and the electrochemical polymer was connected to a passive night sight that intensified ambient light to permit one-color night vision.

The tiny image-enhancer sensor mounted on the forehead of the helmet did not emit detectable rays, though its range was only twenty-five feet, even on a fairly clear night with strong moonlight.

He slipped the helmet over his head, snapping shut the under-jaw lock guards. He strapped the Sin Eater's holster to his right forearm. A big-bore automatic handblaster, the Sin Eater was less than fourteen inches in length at full extension, the magazine carrying twenty 9 mm rounds. When not in use, the stock folded over the top of the blaster, lying along the frame, reducing its holstered length to ten inches.

When the Sin Eater was needed, Kane would tense his wrist tendons, and sensitive actuators activated a flexible cable in the holster and snapped the weapon smoothly into his waiting hand, the stock unfolding in the same motion. Since the Sin Eater had no trigger guard or safety, the blaster fired immediately upon a touch of his crooked index finger.

Kane lowered his right hand to the familiar handle of the fourteen-inch-long combat knife scabbarded in his boot. Honed to a razor-keen cutting edge, it was also balanced for throwing.

When he walked back to the edge of the gully, Domi and Brigid cast him swift, fearful glances. Kane, the man they knew and with whom they had shared days and nights in cramped quarters, had vanished, replaced by the grim enforcer of the cruel laws of the baronies.

Grant noticed the sudden fear in the eyes of both women and again he realized the Magistrate armor was designed for more than functional, practical reasons. Kane was now a symbol of awe, of fear. He looked bigger somehow. Strong, fierce, implacable.

When a man concealed his face and body beneath the black armor, he became a fearsome figure, the anonymity adding to the mystique. There was another reason for the helmet, the exoskeleton, and it was a reason all Magistrates knew—once a man put on the armor, he symbolically surrendered his identity in order to serve a cause of greater import than a mere individual life.

Grant and Kane's fathers had chosen to smother their identities, as had their fathers before them. All Magistrates followed a patrilineal tradition, assuming the duties and positions of their fathers. They didn't have given names, each taking the surname of the father, as though the first Magistrate to bear the name was the same man as the last.

As Magistrates, the courses their lives followed had been charted before their births. They had exchanged personal hopes, dreams and desires for a life of service. They were destined to live, fight and die, usually violently, as they fulfilled their oaths to impose a degree of order upon the chaos of postnukecaust America.

Kane's life had taken another course, but he learned

later he was following the secret path laid down by his father.

As he joined the women at the edge of the ravine, he said, "Let's get to it."

Brigid nodded, putting on a shoulder rig that held a holstered .32-caliber Mauser. Quietly she asked Domi, "How long has it been since you were here last?"

"A year. Mebbe two."

"How many people lived here when you left?" Grant asked.

Domi shrugged. "A lot."

Kane repressed the urge to sigh in exasperation. The albino girl was essentially illiterate, and he doubted she could count much higher than twenty. There was no point in blaming her for her ignorance. Even the most rudimentary education was available only to a select few. In fact, basic education was actually banned in the Outlands under direct baronial control. Anyone even suspected of possessing knowledge beyond simple survival skills was marked for termination. It was all part of the doctrines expressed by the Unification Program.

The reasons for the antipathy toward education of the masses were simple—human beings were no more than livestock, and if livestock ever realized they were owned, then they might question the whyness of it.

Domi led them about two hundred feet along the edge of the gully, to where it dipped down in a series of broken steps, chipped out of rock. She said, "Safe way down."

Kane nodded, tapping the side of his helmet. To Grant, he said, "Stay in touch. I don't know how long we'll be."

Domi smiled wanly and moved beside Grant. "We wait."

The girl had attached herself to Grant back in Cobalt-ville, and she responded with almost pathetic eagerness to any attention he directed toward her.

She slipped an arm through his, ignoring his uncomfortable shifting of feet. "Take your time," she added.

Chapter 2

The gully floor curved lazily, and the fresh night air acted as a stimulant, driving away the cobwebs of fatigue. Brigid and Kane heard the low, rushing murmur of a river up ahead. Though it was dark, the light enhancer on his helmet made the channel of stone and undergrowth easy to negotiate.

They began seeing signs of human habitation scattered along the path—rusting, gutted husks of old vehicles that had lain there since skydark, overgrown now with vines.

Brigid gestured to one, murmuring, "Domi told me she was born in one of those."

Piles of rotting garbage lined both sides of the gully, heaped so high and narrowing the pass so much they were forced to walk in single file. The gully opened up at the edge of a widely cleared dirt area. Surrounded by brush, it was like a bald spot on top of a hairy man's head. The dirt was hard-packed from the pressure of many feet for many years. In the center of the barren circle was the remains of a communal fire, charred logs crisscrossing at opposing angles.

A path, wide and straight, stretched out from the far edge of the clearing, leading between double rows of huts, shanties and lean-tos. The place looked like it had been abandoned forever. The only sounds they heard were the rush of the river and the lone trilling of a night bird.

Grant's voice whispered in Kane's ear, filtered through the helmet comm-link. "Status."

Into the transceiver in the jaw guard, Kane replied, "Nothing. The place is deserted. We'll keep looking. Stand by."

Kane and Brigid moved to the right, along the edge of the brushline. His black armor and her drab clothing helped them blend with the shifting pattern of moonlight and shadows. He kept the Sin Eater leathered snugly on his forearm, but he drew his combat knife and used it to slash and push aside foliage in their path.

Brigid followed several paces behind him, trying to walk stealthily like Kane. She was very light-footed, but she didn't have his years of experience in penetrating potential killzones.

As Kane crept along the brush-lined perimeter, he peered closely at the ground. He saw the marks of many feet, and twigs stepped on and broken. His sixth sense, which had been observing everything from the back of his mind, suddenly screeched for attention.

He wasn't sure why. In his years as a Mag, he had come across any number of deserted Outland settlements, but the circumstances had easy explanations— famines, incursions of roamer bands or simply dissatisfaction with the territory. Always some sign had been left, or the outlanders would turn up again somewhere else, usually around one of the villes.

If Domi's village had been the target of a Mag hard contact, corpses and burned-out dwellings would be the signals. As a general rule, when Mags cleaned out a settlement for whatever reason, the only negotiation was whether to switch their blasters from semi to full auto.

When Kane paused for a moment in the circuit of the settlement, Brigid whispered, "In 1930, a village of over a thousand Eskimo vanished without a trace. There were no signs of violence, and no bodies, living or dead, were ever found. Even the graves of the cemetery had been opened and the remains removed. A search that covered the whole of Canada turned up nothing."

"Did you learn that while you were an archivist or from the Cerberus database?" Kane asked.

"Does it matter? From the database, if you must know, when I was cross-indexing Archon activities in the century preceding the nukecaust. It was a generalized reference, but I remembered it."

"Is there anything you *don't* remember?"

"No," she answered simply.

Kane knew in advance that would be her answer. As the self-proclaimed possessor of an eidetic memory, she could say nothing else. Besides, it was true. Brigid Baptiste remembered everything she read or saw, and that was how and why she also ended up as an exile. He reminded himself wryly that he had a little something to do with her exile, too.

As soon as the memory registered, the edge of tension that always seemed to pass between him and the woman when they were alone become palpable. He never could understand why it always lurked there. Explaining it away as the natural conflict between their two contrasting personalities—one inclined toward action, one toward cool analysis—was unsatisfactory. It was something deeper, something far more complex and mysterious than a simple personality clash.

A recent mat-trans jump had gone bad. Both he and Baptiste had suffered from jump sickness, the primary symptoms of which were nausea and vivid and frighteningly real nightmares.

In this instance, they had shared the same hallucination, but they were due less to quantum-energy-inspired deliriums than revelations he and Baptiste were somehow joined by spiritual chains, linked to each other and to the same destiny.

Kane didn't possess a metaphysical turn of mind, though he wasn't in the habit of flatly denying the possibility of anything. What he had learned of humanity's secret history saw to that.

Still, the notion that their souls had been together for a thousand years or more seemed absurd. However, it was more than coincidence that caused them to have the same jump nightmare. He knew there had to be a causal factor, and clearly Baptiste did, too. They just didn't want to discuss it.

While recovering from injuries they'd sustained in the Black Gobi, Kane had tried to avoid being alone with Baptiste as much as possible. Fortunately, Cerberus was so vast it wasn't difficult. Grant had told him Baptiste saved his life, coming within a hairbreadth of losing her own in the process.

Kane had yet to thank her, and he didn't know why, except he had the vague feeling it was an action she had been fated to perform, rectifying a mistake made long, long ago—before either one of them had been born.

The whole concept made him feel distinctly uneasy, and therefore he had been distant with Baptiste, dealing with her cordially but formally. If the woman objected to his behavior, she showed no sign of it. In fact, she seemed relieved.

Or she had until now.

Kane walked swiftly to the far side of the settlement's perimeter. A tangled strip of undergrowth sloped sharply down to the bank of the Snake River. Utter silence hung over the riverfront, not even broken by the croaking of frogs. A few yards away was a small bluff. Built at the top of the bluff, extending over it and down was a flume, a chute made of battered tin supported by cross-braced struts of iron and wood. It angled down sharply to the river, following the face of the bank. A few wooden buckets lay scattered beneath it.

"Status?" came Grant's voice again.

"Nothing," Kane responded.

"Lakesh must have picked up bad Intel."

"Or he was fed some," murmured Kane.

Brigid shot him a suspicious glare. "What do you mean?"

"I mean it's possible—if not probable—that Baron Cobalt or Salvo suspects Lakesh of insurgency. This whole op may be a setup and a trap."

Into the helmet transceiver, he said, "Ask Domi if her people would have simply picked up and moved on."

Kane heard Grant muttering, then he announced, "She says no. Her people have been here a very long time and liked it. They wouldn't go on their own."

"Unless," Kane replied, "they were taken already."

"There'd be some sign," Brigid argued. "Houses torn up, blood on the ground. Something."

"We don't know how a harvest is conducted," retorted Kane. "Even Lakesh knows very little about how the Directorate operates." He paused, sighed and added, "We'll keep looking. Stand by."

Kane and Brigid walked swiftly toward the village proper. There was a rustling sound from inside one of the huts, and they spun toward it, hands reaching for their weapons. The Sin Eater filled Kane's hand, and he leveled it, finger lightly touching the trigger, while Brigid still fumbled to draw her Mauser.

An elderly man stepped cautiously out of the hut, holding a yellow plastic washbasin over his head as though it were an oversize sun helmet. His face was deeply seamed, and his straight black hair had long ago turned gray. His skinny body was bare from the waist up. He wore a piece of red terry cloth as a loin cloth.

"Hello," he said in Spanish-accented English. "Sorry I missed you last night."

"Who are you?" Kane demanded.

Grant's agitated voice rasped in his ear. "What's going on?"

"Stand by," snapped Kane. From the old man, he asked, "What's your name?"

"Makayu."

"Says his name is Makayu. Ask Domi if she knows him."

After a murmuring moment, Grant's responded, "She says yeah. Says he's okay. A nice man."

As Kane lowered his autoblaster, he asked, "Where have you been?"

Makayu hooked a thumb over his shoulder, toward the riverbank. "I was asleep when you came last night. Time I woke up, it was too late. You gone already."

"What happened here?" Brigid asked.

Makayu tipped up the edge of the washbasin and glanced around at the tree line before saying, *"Chupahupias."*

"Chupahupias?" Brigid echoed incredulously.

Makayu nodded serenely. "Two of them. They came to the village six, seven times. Always at night. Then, last night they came for the people." Glancing at Kane, he said, "But you know. You rode in their bellies."

"What the hell is a *chupahupia?*"

"Old Spanish slang...loosely translated, it means 'blood-sucking lights,'" Brigid answered, closely studying the old man's dark eyes. Gesturing to Kane, she asked, "You saw men like him, too?"

"Oh, yes," replied Makayu. "They were helping the *chupahupias.*"

"What?" Kane exploded.

"We thought at first they would drive the *chupahupias* away. Instead, when the *chupahupias* appeared and put the sleep-awake spell on everybody—"

"Wait," Kane interrupted. "The sleep-awake spell?"

"The *chupahupias'* eyes shone down. They went like this—" Makayu thrust his head forward and blinked both his eyes very rapidly "—then the people were asleep but awake at the same time. You understand?"

"Yes," said Brigid.

"I don't," Kane growled. "Why didn't they get you?"

"Perhaps I'm blessed," the old man offered thoughtfully. "I'm known as one of the most virtuous of the Cuprum people."

"I think the cataracts on your eyes may have had more to do with it," Brigid observed dryly. "Where did they take the people?"

Makayu waved toward the far end of the village, where the undergrowth was thick and impenetrable. "There. The men in black pushed them. Then the big mother *chupahupia* floated out of the sky."

"What did it look like, the mother?" asked Brigid.

Makayu took off the washbasin and balanced it between his hands. "Like this, only dark and flatter. It called the people, a very sweet song, but it hurt the ears. The people went into the clearing when they were called. The people never came back. Later, all the *chupahupias*, even the babies, fly away."

Kane sighed, ran a hand over his unshaved chin and gestured to the hut. "Get your belongings together, and we'll take you out of here."

Makayu tapped the washbasin. "This is all I need. I'd rather stay here and wait for the people to come back."

"Why don't you lead us to where your people vanished?" asked Brigid.

"Why?" Makayu asked.

"We may be able to find them for you."

He touched a skinny forefinger to the lid of his right eye. "These peepers, they not see so good, especially in the dark."

"We'll be your eyes," Brigid told him kindly.

The old man nodded, pushed between Brigid and Kane, walking toward the thicket at the end of the village.

Scowling after him, Kane demanded, "You don't believe that old fart, do you? Sleep-awake spells, bloodsucking lights in the sky?"

"Ever heard of a process called photic driving?"

"Should I have?" Kane asked dourly.

"I suppose not. When a light source strobes fast enough, the vibratory cycle synchronizes with normal brain-wave patterns. The witnesses lapse into hypnoticlike trances. A form of pseudo-epilepsy occurs. A high-tech way to make zombies."

An uneasy breeze sighed over them. Smells floated with it, like the miasma of a slaughterhouse.

Makayu sniffed the air and murmured, *"Viento de muerte."*

Kane glanced at him quizzically and Brigid translated softly, "'The death wind.'"

The farther they pushed into the shrubbery, the stronger the odor became. Kane's mouth filled with bile. Their path was hemmed in by dense forest on either side. Makayu thrust aside a sapling, then halted so suddenly Brigid nearly trod on his heels. Frozen to the spot, they stared blankly, bleakly at the glade that lay beyond.

Bodies lay everywhere, strewed over the ground in a bizarrely ordered formation. Naked men, women and children, about fifty of them, were shackled together by chains run through loops in metal collars.

Each corpse lay on its back, having been eviscerated and, judging by the uniform waxy pallor of their flesh, drained of all blood. Thoraxes were peeled open, the skin covering the chest and abdominal cavities slit and pulled back. Neither Kane nor Brigid needed to examine the cadavers to know the soft organs had been removed.

The charnel house stench of decomposing flesh was sharp and sickening, like an intangible hook reaching down the throat to yank up the contents of their stomachs. Brigid put a hand over her mouth and tried to bite back the groan of horror working its way past her lips.

Kane said nothing, but nausea leaped and rolled in his belly and bile slid up his throat in an acidy column. He tried not to breathe through his nose. It wasn't that he was unaccustomed to the sight of violent death, but there was a vast divide separating individual corpses and these laid out neatly and clinically, like sides of beef in a butcher shop.

Makayu's shoulders shook in racking shudders, and

he hugged himself, muttering a fervent prayer in Spanish. *"Chupahupias,"* he mumbled.

Breathing shallowly, Kane said, "No flies around the bodies, no predators have touched them. If this happened last night, why is the decay so advanced?"

"Those are all hallmarks of the animal-mutilation phenomena of the twentieth century," Brigid answered. "Some sort of chemical agent may have been used to accelerate the process of decomposition." She cleared her throat, adding lowly, "The people were hypnotized and went meekly to their slaughter. Just like cattle."

"Chupahupias," Kane repeated bitterly. "Lakesh's Intel was wrong. We were too late."

"It's a cold comfort," she replied, "but at least it wasn't a trap."

"Status," demanded Grant's crisp voice.

Before he responded, Kane checked their backtrack. His backward glance showed him a small flash of light, bright against the indigo sky. The light flashed red and green and white. Static suddenly squealed in his ear.

Lunging forward, he grabbed Makayu and Brigid by the arms. He broke into a sprint, running along the edge of the glade. "Run. When we hit the brush, go to ground and don't move."

Brigid swiveled her head up and around and said breathlessly, "Don't look at the lights."

Makayu wrested himself away from Kane's hand, gulped a mouthful of air and started a clumsy, shambling dash toward the thicket, dropping his washbasin hat.

From above, a brilliant blade of light stabbed down and impaled them.

Chapter 3

The light washing over them changed to red, then yellow, and shifted to a greenish violet. The strobing pattern covered the entire spectrum of visible light.

Brigid knew that if either of them glanced back and up, it would be almost impossible to take their eyes away. The flickering, strobing cycle increased in speed and brilliance, accompanied by a high-pitched, undulating whine.

The flashing light played with the colors of the thicket ahead of them. Streaks of green melted into cyan, which instantly brightened to yellow.

Makayu bleated in terror. *"Chupahupia!"* Legs and arms pumping, he twisted his head up and around.

"No!" shouted Brigid, reaching for him.

Her hand clutched empty air as Makayu, blinded by the light, missed his footing and stumbled. He fell heavily, gracelessly to the ground, grunting in pain.

Skidding to a clumsy halt, Kane pivoted at the waist, trying to turn but keep his eyes averted from the light. Makayu, panting and swearing, struggled to his knees. Kane grabbed him beneath his right arm, pulling him to a half-crouching posture.

The old man's arm tensed and stiffened under Kane's hand. He froze motionless, transfixed, glazed, unblinking eyes staring up at the strobing disk hanging in the sky.

Shielding his eyes with one hand, Kane yelled into the man's ear, but Makayu didn't move. Releasing his grip, Kane sprang backward, toward the underbrush, just as a rattling roar tore through the night.

A storm of .50-caliber bullets pounded into Makayu, breaking his chest open amid flowing ribbons of blood. Great gouts of earth exploded all around him.

Kane and Brigid dived headlong into the thicket, glimpsing Makayu's maimed body collapsing on the bullet-chopped ground. They rolled into the foliage as steel-jacketed rain ripped along the edge of the forest, showering them with bullet-sheared leaves and twigs. The brilliant beam of strobing light swung back and forth, probing the darkness for them.

Kane crouched over Brigid, using his armored body as a shield, his arms folded around her. He jerked in reaction to a sharp, jarring impact against his back, but didn't otherwise move. The heavy projectile had only skimmed across the surface of the armor; otherwise, he would have been knocked down, the wind driven from his lungs.

The thudding hammer of autofire ceased, and a steady breeze pressed down the bushes and set the tree limbs to swaying. Kane squinted through the tinted, polarized visor of his helmet, gambling that the sweeping column of light wouldn't reflect from it. He peered upward, out between the broad leaves of a maple tree. He saw what he expected to see.

A Deathbird hovered thirty feet above the corpse-littered glade, so close to the perimeter of the tree line that its spinning vanes nearly slashed through the tips of limbs. The engine and turbines were equipped with noise bafflers, so the only sound was the steady rhythmic swish of wind and a muffled whine.

It was painted a flat, nonreflective black, and though he couldn't see through the smoke-tinted Plexiglas cockpit canopy, he knew the Deathbird could carry only a crew of two—a pilot and a gunner.

Attached to the chopper's nose-sensor array was a photic stroboscope. Beneath it, in the chin turret, Kane saw the M-230 chain gun. Shrike missile pods were deployed on either side of the craft, beneath stub wings. Kane hoped the crew wasn't so desperate to kill them they would risk launching the rockets.

Though it wasn't common knowledge except among the handful of techs and mechanics in the Magistrate Division, the Deathbirds were very old, dating back to the days right before skydark. They were modified AH-64 Apache attack gunships, and most of the ones in the fleet had been reengineered and retrofitted dozens of times.

"I get it now," Brigid said grimly. "The choppers flew escort for a Directorate scout ship."

"Scout ship?"

"I saw one in Mongolia, remember? This one probably came from Dulce, crewed by hybrids. They performed the actual surgery."

"Yeah," Kane replied distractedly. "Mags aren't known for their delicacy of touch."

"But why are they still here?"

Kane turned his face toward her. Because of the visor, she couldn't see the exasperation in his eyes, but she heard it in his voice. "I think that's pretty damn obvious, Baptiste."

Before he could say anything else, the strobing pattern cycled through the spectrum and began again.

Brigid, her voice tight with anxiety, peered through her fingers. "The frequency of the stroboscope is around eighty flashes per second, perfect to induce a hypnagogic state.''

"That's a new piece of ordnance," he replied. "Never heard of such a thing."

"Have you raised Grant and Domi?''

"They've put up a general frequency damper, jamming the carrier wave.''

"What are we going to do?'' she demanded raggedly. "They've got us pinned down here.''

"Let's get ourselves unpinned, then.''

With that, Kane came to his knees, holding the Sin Eater in a two-handed grip. He brought the flickering disk into the pistol's sights and squeezed the trigger. As the deep-throated boom of the big gun sounded, a 9 mm round shattered the stroboscope in an eye-dazzling blaze of multicolored sparks.

The chain gun opened up again, tracer slugs cutting threads of phosphorescence through the murk. Kane knew better than to dig in and return .50-caliber streams of autofire with only a handblaster. Even his body armor wouldn't offer much protection. Multiple impacts could result in hydrostatic shock and stop his heart.

Taking Brigid by the hand, he crawled through the brush while gouts of soil and scraps of foliage erupted all around them. They changed direction twice, heedless of the thorns that scratched her face and the vines that snagged his armor.

The gun fell silent and the chopper ascended, swinging around in a wide circle, hoping to flush them out or see them. Thick as the bush was, there were still open spaces that they had to cross to reach the gully.

At the edge of a small clearing, Brigid and Kane crouched in the shadow of a heavy-boughed tree. They watched the Deathbird swing back and forth above their position. Without a searchlight, the crew had to rely on the illumination of the moon to scan the woods. Deathbirds were normally outfitted with night-vision sensors, and the heat trace of their bodies wouldn't be hard to pinpoint. Grimly, Kane realized their situation would improve if the chopper saturated the area with rocket fire. The heat would overwhelm their own signatures.

Stoically, Kane whispered, "So much for Domi's people. I don't think we'll have the opportunity to bring her back here so she can identify them."

"Yes," Brigid agreed sadly. "Makayu said *chupahupias*, plural. There may be another chopper in the vicinity."

"There's only one way to find out," he replied. "We'll split up. The Birds will come after me."

She swung her head toward him, eyes glowing with a jade flame of worry. "What makes you say that?"

"This is a trap," he said coldly. "That's why Lakesh was fed the Intel, to see if me or Grant would pop our heads into it. We did. If there's another Bird flapping around out there, it's zeroing in on Grant right now."

"That may be true, but you're no more a desirable prize than I am."

Kane's lips quirked in a mirthless smile. "This isn't a popularity contest, Baptiste. The blood warrant on me is personal, remember? You just skipped out on your own execution. I humiliated the baron."

Brigid narrowed her eyes. "Are you deliberately omitting the debt you owe Salvo? If this is a trap, you know he's in one of the choppers."

"I more than know it, Baptiste. I feel it. I'm counting on his fixation with me to allow you the time to get away. As far as he's concerned, I'm the entrée. You're just a mildly appetizing side dish."

"Somehow," she said, with a note of ironic humor in her voice, "that sounds vaguely insulting."

"I didn't mean it to be. Do you understand my reasoning?"

She silently considered the logic of his words for a moment. She nodded brusquely. "Understood."

Kane took a deep breath. "Stay here until you see the Bird alter its course and come after me. Then move out in the opposite direction. Try to work your way back to the Cat."

Again, quietly she said, "Understood."

They looked into each other's face for a long, tense moment. Since they were not lovers, there was no parting embrace, only an aching sense of its absence. Without another word, Kane rose and loped quickly across the clearing and through the overgrowth, keeping always to the concealment of shadows.

He found himself wishing desperately that Salvo would find him. Not so much for the opportunity to chill the bastard, but simply to see him. When he missed his old life as a Magistrate in Cobaltville, contrary to all expectation, he realized he missed his old commanding officer, as well.

There was a bond, a link between Salvo and himself, one that he'd been unaware of until his exile. Baptiste had told him of her private conversation with Salvo shortly after her arrest for sedition.

Salvo had declared his hatred stemmed primarily from the enmity that had existed between his father and Kane's father, and for a Magistrate, family tradition and family honor was all-important. Salvo had told Baptiste that he wanted vindication, revenge for the wrongs he claimed had been compounded upon his family name, his family honor.

Kane had no idea what wrongs his father had visited upon the man's family honor. Only Salvo could tell him that, and he welcomed the chance to finally question him.

Within half a mile, Kane emerged from the trees onto a narrow dirt lane running parallel to the riverbank, very close to the flume. He made a slow visual recce of the area, careful to check his backtrail. In the sky, he saw the flickering pinpoints of the Deathbird's running lights. He gauged the distance at less than quarter of a mile and he came to a snap, almost insane decision— snap because he had no time to weigh reasonable or even semireasonable alternatives, and insane because it was such a huge risk.

At the bottom of the bluff, he inspected the wooden buckets, finally finding a ten-gallon pail that seemed sound all around. He hung the handle onto his belt and carried it to the open end of the flume. He wasn't sure if the bucket was watertight and could thus keep him afloat, but there was only one sure way to find out.

Kane climbed a cross brace, heaving the big bucket onto the outside lip of the flume, and pulled himself one-handed over the curving wall of the chute. He looked back toward the village and swallowed a groan.

The Deathbird made an abrupt figure-eight maneuver and arrowed on a direct heading with his position. Now that he was out in the open, the Bird's crew had spotted him, either visually or with an infrared tracker. It came very fast, altitude dropping.

Kane slammed himself face first and full-length down on the chute and shoved off with his feet, pulling himself down the slant with his hands. A missile flamed from the craft's starboard stub wing. It impacted on the face of the bluff with a thundering shock wave. For an instant, the entire area was illuminated by a ballooning, orange-yellow fireball.

The chain gun opened up behind him. Bullets punched a cross-stitch pattern in the ground, the lines of impact tracking up and striking sparks from the lip of the flume. With his hand on the rims of the flume, Kane slid forward on his belly. He hadn't imagined the ride to be smooth, and his imagination wasn't disappointed. He tobogganed down the chute, bouncing over the welds where sections of the flume had been joined. Behind him, the chain gun hammered steadily.

The .50-caliber rounds pounded into the bluff, chopped out pieces from the wooden cross braces, sending splinters and clods of earth flying into the night. The chute shuddered from multiple strikes. Ricochets and fragments of tin buzzed in all directions.

Kane slid and jolted down the chute, using the toes of his boots as brakes when the speed and momentum seemed likely to bounce him up and out. He managed to snatch a backward glance. The Deathbird swooped in very low, the chin-turret gun still spitting lead and noise and flame. Steel-jacketed slugs pounded the tin barely two yards behind him, smashing and mangling it. Wiry slivers of metal bounced from his armored back. The rattling racket of the impacts was deafening.

Kane raised his arms and lifted his legs, no longer caring about checking his velocity, surfing along on his chest, belly and pelvis. He hit a bump with a bone-jarring, spine-compressing jolt that caused his teeth to clack together, but he was grateful his groin was armored.

The open mouth of the flume yawned ahead and below. He shot toward it. From almost overhead, he heard the faint swishing rhythm of the whirling helicopter vanes. The drumming rattle of the chain gun suddenly stopped.

At the same instant, he struck the open end of the flume and sailed out into open air. The drop to the surface of the river was ten to twelve feet. He tried to align his body into a vertical position so he would enter the river in a dive. Instead, he belly flopped against the surface, and it was all he could do to keep the air in his lungs. Water gushed up his nose and filled his sinus passages, trickling into his throat.

Resisting the impulse to stroke for the surface, Kane allowed the weight of his weapons and armor to pull him down. The current tugged at him, and he kicked and pushed with it, since it was carrying him in the direction he wanted to go. His initial plan had been to float down the river, clinging to the bucket, but since the chopper had got a fix on him, that was no longer viable.

He felt the handle of the bucket tugging at his belt, increasing his buoyancy. He pried it loose and sank deeper. During his Mag training, he used to practice holding his breath under water, and rarely had he managed to exceed four minutes, even when he hyperventilated after the fashion of Polynesian pearl divers. Though he wasn't exerting himself and expending oxygen, his lungs were already aching with the strain.

As he opened his eyes and saw a school of small fish all around him, the silvery moonlight glinting from their delicate scales, he hoped they weren't of a carnivorous mutie variety. The water buffeted him, making him lose all sense of direction and time. He felt like a newborn, expelled into heaven or hell, at the mercy of whatever awaited.

Chapter 4

Rocketing at an astonishingly high rate of speed, holding a course so close to the ground the grasses were flattened by the rotor wash, the Deathbird shot across the plain toward the Sandcat.

Just as Grant spotted it through the ob slit, a hash of static and discordant squawks filled his ear. He swore a blue streak, pulling the headset away, knowing a frequency-inhibiting umbrella had been opened, damping all radio transmissions for miles around.

Grant keyed the vehicle's powerful engine to rumbling life. Through the slit, the Bird swelled larger and blacker. He could see the chin gun and the snouts of the Shrike missiles clamped beneath the stub wings.

"Domi!" he called urgently. "Get to the turret!"

As she clambered out of the copilot's chair, a puff of smoke and a streak of flame flared on the Deathbird's port-side wing. Grant wrenched the wheel, swinging the Sandcat into a wide turn. Domi stumbled, crying out.

The missile exploded on the right, a brilliant red-yellow spout of fire. The wheel fought his hands as the sudden concussion made the vehicle shudder. Clods of turf and shrapnel rattled against the hull. Through the slit, he spied the craft bank to starboard and climb.

Her white legs flashing, Domi heaved herself up into the caged gunner's saddle, bracing herself on the footrests. Grant slapped a button on the console, and microcircuitry engaged, feeding an electric impulse to the chemically treated armaglass turret. It instantly became transparent, and Domi pressed the trigger button of the USMG-73. The blaster hammered rhythmically, the cartridge belt writhed like a coiling snake and spent shell casings spewed smoking from the ejector port. The Deathbird wagged back and forth in a falling-leaf motion, peppered on both sides by balls of white fire marking the tracer tails of the machine gun's armor-piercing rounds.

Domi didn't hit anything, but the backdrop of the night sky lit up with the glowing threads of the tracers. Grant knew she was finding the range and proving to the Deathbird that its intended target had teeth. He steered the vehicle away from the crest of the gully, wondering briefly what Mags were doing here and who they might be.

The Deathbird curved around in a wind-screaming arc, little spear points of orange flame flickering from the chain gun. Fountains of dirt burst in columns right in front of the Sandcat, and then came a series of ear-knocking clangs as .50-caliber rounds struck the front armor. Grant felt their impacts through the thick protection of the bulkhead. The chopper described a swift, strafing circle around the vehicle.

Shrieking a wordless curse, Domi kicked the saddle into a 360-degree rotation around the coaxial turret post, holding down the firing button of the heavy machine gun until it locked. The heavy blaster hosed a continuous stream of slugs, the tracer rounds glowing like light beads on a taut string.

Grant was familiar with the capabilities and limitations of both the Sandcat and the Deathbird. A hi-ex missile scoring a direct hit would certainly disable the wag, nor would its armor stand up to a prolonged pounding of .50-caliber blockbusters. A number of the Shrikes carried incend and hi-ex warheads. A solid strike had the capacity of piercing armor plate to a depth of twelve inches.

On the other hand, as an experienced Bird jockey, he knew the choppers were designed primarily for speed and lightning maneuverability. How fast and how maneuverable depended on the skill, endurance and guts of the pilot. As a Mag, Grant had forced the craft to perform actions in direct violation of the Deathbird's aerodynamic specs. More than once, he had defied inertial stress and directed the choppers at velocities just inside the border of man-killing or machine-wrecking.

From what he had seen so far, whoever was piloting this particular Bird was poking at the safety parameters, but not seriously stretching them.

A Shrike detonated less than two yards away. There was the thunder and shock of the heavy concussion. The Sandcat lurched, slowing down. The instrument lights flickered and came up bright again. Grant steered the vehicle underneath the spreading canopy of smoke, staying near the impact point, knowing the infrared scanners aboard the chopper would be confused by the two conflicting heat signatures.

As he circled the smoldering, flaming crater, Grant shouted, "Another spin, Domi!"

The girl immediately complied, revolving the turret, triggering the machine gun. Bright, relentless sparks darted up into the sky, punching holes in the veil of smoke. The rain of cartridge cases made a steady, semi-musical tinkle on the deck.

The Deathbird sped by, directly overhead. A tracer line touched it, and the craft rocked, a ring of smoke suddenly surrounding the tail-boom assembly. It fought to gain altitude, performing a straining, clumsy pirouette, the Plexiglas port facing the Sandcat.

Missiles burst from both wings, exploding all around. For a moment, all Grant could see were yellow-red eruptions and mushrooming billows of smoke. The thunder of the detonations assaulted his eardrums, and the Sandcat jarred and shook, slamming him hard against the back of the chair. Through the ob slit, he saw misty scraps of crackling flame spew out of the craters and lick at the armored hull.

Lips curled back in a snarl, Grant held the vehicle on a tight, circling course. He winced as the bulk of the Cat tipped onto one treaded track, the return rollers squealing in protest. He gripped the wheel tightly, holding the vehicle to the turn. It bounced and jounced as it settled back down on both tracks, fishtailing for a long moment. The USMG-73 continued to hammer away, the compartment filling with eye-stinging, nostril-searing cordite fumes.

The Deathbird overshot the Sandcat's sudden turn. It banked sharply ninety degrees to the left, and the hail of steel-jacketed hornets pounded into the belly of the craft. The Bird's control cables were sheared away, locking out the horizontal and vertical stabilizers. An oil line burst, and the engine stopped.

Grant caught a fragmented glimpse of an orange puffball erupting from the Deathbird's fuselage. The craft side-slipped to starboard and plummeted straight down, as if it had been dangling from a string and the string had been cut. The rotor blades fanned the air sluggishly even as it plunged toward the ground.

Smoke obscured his vision, but he heard a sound like a rolling, mechanical surf and the ground felt as if it rose and fell beneath the Cat's treads. A huge warm pillow of air squeezed through the slit and smacked him across the face. A shaved sliver of a second later, he was blinded by a hellish blossom of light as the Deathbird's fuel tank ruptured, ignited and exploded. Tongues of flame leaped and lapped in all directions.

Bouncing pieces of machinery rang reverberating chimes on the Sandcat's hull. Fragments of the main rotor blade, pinwheeling at incredible velocities, smashed into the vehicle's frontal armor, actually scoring dents in it. Grant stamped on the brakes, maintaining a steady pressure as he leaned forward and peered through the slit.

The breeze tore enough holes in the pall of smoke so he could see the burning black hulk of the Deathbird, canted on its right side less than twenty feet away. The Plexiglas port was too scorched to discern movement behind it. Sparks corkscrewed into the air, and the thick odor of furnace-heated metal made him want to hold his nose.

"Okay?" Domi called down to him.

"Yeah," he called back. "Okay. Good job."

Grant released his pent-up breath in a long, slow sigh. All his taut muscles and nerves suddenly relaxed. He became aware of an ache in his jaw and he realized he had been clenching his teeth ever since he started the Cat's engine.

Experimentally he opened and closed his mouth several times, muttering, "I'm getting way too old for this shit."

He let up on the brakes, pressing the accelerator, steering around the wreckage before the fire could find the remainder of the missiles and touch them off.

"Come down?" Domi asked. "To celebrate."

"No," he replied. "There may be another chopper out there."

"What to do, then?"

Grant tried raising Kane and Brigid on the two comm-link channels, but once more he heard nothing but static. The frequencies were still jammed.

"What we do?" Domi asked again, peevishly this time.

He downshifted, and the Sandcat crashed through the vegetation bordering the edge of the gully. The front end teetered precariously, tipped and plunged down, carving its own path over the rock face. Grant announced, "We do it the Mag way. Face what's out there head-on."

Chapter 5

Kane bobbed beneath the surface like a cork until the pounding of blood in his temples and the fire in his chest became intolerable. He kicked upward, a little surprised by how much effort it required. His head broke the surface, and he fought the impulse to cough and gasp.

The current carried him around a bend, where the waterway narrowed. He felt his body whipped forward, pushed faster and faster. Through the water-occluded visor, he glimpsed foam glistening white in the moonlight. He shot toward a stretch of white-water rapids, the river swirling and pouring around half-submerged boulders.

Frantically he twisted his body to one side, kicking with his feet, clawing handfuls of water aside. He flailed, sputtering, trying to check his headlong catapult into the roaring cataract.

His head struck the side of a boulder. The helmet cushioned and absorbed the impact, but the visor acquired a crack and the night-sight light enhancer went out. He managed to stroke to the shallows.

Tree limbs, like gnarled fingers, reached down toward the river from the bank. Blinking the water from his eyes, Kane tilted his head up and back, scanning the pale indigo sky. He saw nothing but the moon and a frosty scattering of stars above the tree line. There was no sign of the Deathbird, and though he wanted to believe it had broken off the pursuit, he couldn't convince himself. More than likely, it had flown on downriver, hoping to find him at a stretch of shallows.

He stroked for the bank, reaching up to grasp a low-hanging limb. It occurred to him that a venomous water snake might be coiled around it, but just then the possibility wasn't particularly worrisome.

Using the branch and roots as hand- and footholds, Kane clambered his way up the muddy bank until he reached the top of the bluff. He felt more than justified in sitting down and catching his breath. He unsnapped the under-jaw lock and pulled the helmet off.

With rueful eyes, he examined the notch marring the otherwise smooth forepart. The light-amplification infeed to the visor was smashed, so there was no point in wearing the helmet. His vision would be improved without it. The comm-link circuit was damaged, too, so even if the jamming frequency was deactivated, he wouldn't know it.

He opened a couple of seals in his armor, draining out half a gallon or so of water. Taking off his boots, he emptied them and tugged them back on. Far, far in the distance, he heard faint, booming reports like a series of overlapping thunderclaps.

Craning his neck, he scanned the sky. He glimpsed the pinpoint glow of a Deathbird's running lights as it streaked over the treetops, at an oblique course to his position. As he watched, the lights descended, dropping below the massed tree line and out of sight.

From a pouch on his belt, he withdrew a small compass and spent a minute fixing his position in relation to the gully and the general direction in which the Bird went down. He calculated he was around five miles from the gully, at least a two-hour journey through unfamiliar territory—providing he wasn't forced to play a prolonged game of hide-and-seek with the crew of the Deathbird. Still, it would be nothing compared to the hike he'd made through the rugged Great Sand Dunes hellzone, lugging an injured Grant and suffering from wounds of his own.

He walked inland, knife in hand, Sin Eater holstered at his forearm, moving quietly through the brush. He carried the helmet, though he contemplated leaving it behind. But he was loath to drop any more signs of his presence or jettison more artifacts of his old identity.

Consulting the compass again, he turned a little to the east. Branches overhung his path, sometimes making a murky green tunnel. He didn't need much to prompt his imagination to conjure horrible dangers lurking among the trunks of the oaks and elms. However, he couldn't visualize horrors any worse than he had already witnessed in the past five months.

There were a lot of conflicting and confused stories about Archon activities in centuries past, but the one constant was a standard operating procedure they had employed for thousands of years—establishing a privileged elite dependent upon them, which in turn controlled the masses of humanity on their behalf. Their manipulation of humanity and religions was nearly all-pervasive. However, there was still debate as to whether the Archons were extraterrestrial, interdimensional or pan-terrestrial. According to Lakesh, the Archons claimed they had been on Earth as long or longer than Homo sapiens, and considered themselves native Terrans.

Allegedly it was the Archons who provided the predark governments with the Totality Concept technology and all the spin-off projects, including Operation Chronos, the time-travel process.

Whatever the truth of that, Kane was told the Archons were here, they were in control and all the barons in all the villes were human-Archon hybrids acting as their intermediaries.

Of this, Kane had seen something for himself at least. They claimed they were working for the evolution of humankind. Said evolution was nothing less than a long-range hybridization program, combining the genetic material of humankind with that of their own race—whatever they were—to construct a biological bridge.

Supposedly the program had been instituted hundreds of years ago, long before the nukecaust. Lakesh suspected that the Archons were losing their reproductive vitality and wanted access to fresh gene pools. Since their involvement in human affairs dated back many thousands of years, the nukecaust itself could have been a major component of their program. But clearly, they couldn't freely access the human dimension yet at will.

After the teeming masses of humanity had been culled, then the hybrids would inherit the earth, carrying out the agenda of the Archon Directorate.

Even after all this time and all he had seen, Kane still wasn't sure what or whom to believe. The only thing he could be sure of was that he could be sure of nothing. Yet he kept in mind what Brigid had once told him—*archon* was an ancient Gnostic term used to describe a parahuman, world-governing force that imprisoned the divine spark in human souls. There were even earlier references to them as dark forces battling for man's soul.

Despite it all, sometimes he still awoke in the middle

of the night, scared, sweating and suspicious, positive that he, Baptiste and Grant were victims of some deranged, intricate hoax.

Kane suddenly froze. The sound of a man moving swiftly through the foliage reached him. He immediately sank down to his knees beneath a leafy bush. He tried to penetrate the dark, overgrown tangle with his eyes, searching for any movement. His fingers closed tightly over the hilt of the combat knife in his hand.

Leaves crunched somewhere on the other side of the bush. Holding his breath, he waited for another sound. It came in the next few seconds. A man in a jet-black, multipocketed bodysuit passed by, walking slowly, holding a dark club in both hands. He wore a long-billed black cap, and Kane saw the transceiver unit plugged into his right ear, the stemlike microphone curving around in front of the mouth. A pair of Mag-issue night-vision glasses masked the eyes.

If the bodysuit was a uniform, Kane didn't recognize it, but the man was obviously a member of the Death-bird crew. They had probably gotten an infrared trace fix on him and were backtracking. The best tactic was to lie low and wait until the zone was clear before moving on again. Resisting the flow of anger required all of his willpower. Though he didn't take his eyes off the stalker, he saw only the mutilated and degraded bodies of the outlanders, and simple-minded Makayu lying maimed and murdered. He was only dimly aware of his lips twisting back from his teeth in a grin of fury. His rage was as cold as an arctic night, and as dark. He fisted his knife tightly.

The black-clad man crept to within fifteen feet of him, turning his head to and fro like a foxhound casting for a scent. He moved forward another few steps. Kane lay flat. He had a special technique for silently taking out coldhearts in hellzones and, under other circumstances, he would circle the man's position, come up behind him and slip his knife between the third and fourth ribs, cutting his heart in two.

The man crept away. Kane waited until he was lost in the shadows before moving again. He wormed along on his belly, silently cursing the slight rustle the motion caused. After half a minute, he reached the trunk of a tree and began to rise.

Suddenly something cracked across his right arm. The muscles convulsed and spasmed, and a numbing pain streaked down from shoulder socket to fingertips. Using his elbows and knees as levers, Kane hurled himself to the left in a frantic roll, as if he were on fire, trying to smother the flames.

As he rolled, he received a whirling impression of the black shape behind him, clubbing down with the long baton. The stick hummed and popped as it swept through the air. He was armed with a Shockstick, a device used by Magistrates to control unruly crowds in the Pits. A little under three feet in length, powered by batteries inside the hard, molded plastic grips. The baton delivered a 6000-volt localized shock.

The baton stroked across his rib cage. Streaks of fire lanced up and down his side, and it took every bit of willpower and survival instinct to keep from curling up in a fetal position. If not for the insulating properties of his armor, the kick of the voltage would have incapacitated him.

Kane forced himself to his knees, striking sideways with the blade of the combat knife. The razor-keen edge met and split the Shockstick with a flare and flash of sparks. His opponent snarled in wordless fury.

He didn't use the Sin Eater—the blaster's report was very loud, intentionally so, to intimidate slaggers marked for termination or arrest. With a corkscrew wrench of his body, Kane lunged forward, smashing a shoulder against the man's breastbone.

The man's lungs seized audibly, the air driven from them by the impact. He fell backward into the underbrush. He kept rolling, turning a backward somersault, and bounced to his feet amid a violent rustle of foliage. A standard-issue combat knife sprouted from his fist.

In a thin, aspirated voice, he choked out, "Fuckin' traitor to unity!"

A ville-bred zealot, but also a pro. His training was evident in the fast thrust he made toward Kane's unprotected face.

With a clashing of steel and a small spurt of sparks, Kane parried the thrust, then slashed with his knife across the man's belly, intending to open him up. The double-edged point caught and dragged in the fabric of the bodysuit with a scraping sound. The cloth didn't part, and Kane realized it was a Kevlar and Suprotect2 weave, a special impact-absorbing material.

The two men grappled, securing wristlocks. They strained against each other, faces inches apart. Kane glared into the eyes of the black-clad man. He was a fanatic, all right. He was all hard muscle under the bodysuit, with eyes that matched Kane's for ferocity.

His adversary kicked himself forward, the crown of his head connecting with a teeth-jarring impact against Kane's chin. Reeling backward, Kane felt his fingers loosening, sliding over and snagging briefly on a hard object strapped to the man's right wrist. It came loose, and Kane heard it fall to the ground between their feet.

As he stumbled, trying to maintain his balance, the

black-suited man surged over the ground in a flying, feetfirst arc. Even as a thick-soled boot slammed into his left shoulder, his blade lashed out in a fast thrust, and Kane felt it sink briefly into yielding flesh.

Despite the armor, the force of the kick vibrated through the bones of his upper body, down to the small of his back. He didn't try to resist the force of impact. He allowed himself to fall into the brush, reflexively slapping the ground to absorb the momentum and minimize the chances of having the wind knocked out of him. He rolled and came to his knees, knife still in his fist. The tapered tip gleamed wetly.

The man in the bodysuit thrashed on the ground, plucking at his hamstrung right leg, trying to seal the sliced tendons with slippery fingers. A knife slash might have difficulty penetrating the tough fabric, but not a fast, strong stabbing motion. Between clenched teeth, he hissed into his transceiver, "Fubar! Apprehension is fubar!"

Kane had to give the man credit—consumed by agony, horror struck by the prospect of being crippled, he still didn't scream. He retained the presence to mind to report the apprehension plan was "fucked up beyond all repair." Now he knew for certain he had been expected. Otherwise, the order to neutralize him without killing him would not have been issued.

He watched as blood gushed from the man's severed artery, forming a pool about his twitching body that dully reflected the dim starlight. When he saw eyes glazed over with either unconsciousness or death, Kane toed aside a few leaves and found the small object the man had worn on his wrist.

It was made of molded plastic and stamped metal with an expandable band, the face a liquid-crystal digital-display window. It showed a throbbing green disk. Kane moved a few feet to the left, and the disk shifted slightly in the same direction.

He was both impressed and nonplussed. He had never seen a portable, handheld motion detector before, but he knew they had existed in predark times. He also knew that when some of the Stockpiles were opened up during the Program of Unification and their contents distributed among the nine barons, only a fraction of the tech was made available, even to ville elites. Obviously his stalker had gotten a fix on him, lost it when he froze and went to ground, then reestablished it when he began moving again.

He experimentally punched the small buttons studding the instrument's surface, trying to find the reset function. The green dot faded from the display screen. He pressed another button, but nothing happened.

Kane slid the device over his wrist, picked up his helmet and slipped into the brush, backtrailing the black-clad man.

Chapter 6

Kane had gone about a hundred yards when he heard a faint electronic beep. The motion sensor's screen lit up with a wavery green line.

He stopped and pointed it in front of him, sweeping the device slowly back and forth. The line slid from one side of the screen to the other, formed a dot and froze in a central position. It beeped again.

Scabbarding the knife in his boot sheath, he tensed his wrist tendons, and the Sin Eater filled his hand. He walked straight ahead, consulting the gadget, making sure the dot stayed centered.

He reached the edge of a clearing and peered between the branches of trees. The clearing was manmade, a recently defoliated landing well. The Deathbird sat on its skids in the center, and Brigid stood in front of it. Her arms were stretched out above her head to their fullest extent, her wrists held fast by nylon binders. A rope looped beneath the cuffs and attached to the Bird's main rotor mast had hauled her erect.

Her hair was a disheveled mass, her right eye a bruised slit in her face. Her shirt had been torn open in the struggle to capture her and, with a cynical cruelty, left agape. Her bare flesh gleamed in contrast to the dark sheen of the Deathbird's curving foreport.

It was all Kane could do to suppress the stream of profanity that sprang to his lips. He had been consolidating his gains, confident he could escape the search sweeps, emerge from the forest and get them back to Cerberus intact.

He instantly knew Brigid had been staked out as bait, just as he knew the strategy might as well have been signed, with a flourish, by none other than Salvo. His eyes scanned all the shadows, in and around the chopper. He saw nothing and no one. Swiftly he rifled through his mental index file, reviewing, discarding, considering courses of action. The only one that appeared even marginally sound was to grab Brigid and commandeer the Deathbird.

The only other reasonable tactic was to melt back into the woods and let the woman meet her fate. It was what a Magistrate had been trained to do, to sacrifice anyone in order not to compromise a mission.

But then, he wasn't a Magistrate anymore.

Raising the Sin Eater, he steadied it in a two-handed grip and took a soft, careful step forward. Immediately a faint sound came from behind him, like a short, distant whistle combined with an infant's sneeze. Simultaneously an exquisitely sharp, wicked pain stabbed through the base of his skull, right where it joined his neck, unprotected by the collar of Kevlar protective armor.

His finger jerked in reflexive reaction on the trigger. The autoblaster boomed, and he received a blurred impression of a spiderweb pattern of cracks spreading over the tinted foreport of the Bird. Brigid didn't move, though the bullet must have fanned a puff of cool air on her face.

Kane pivoted on his toes, the Sin Eater questing for a target. At least, that was what his instincts told his body to do. Instead, he achieved a kind of shambling quarter turn, his limbs suddenly feeling as if they were filled with half-frozen mud. The fingers of his left hand explored the side of his neck, found the metal hypodermic dart there and pinched it away.

He tried to curse, but he only croaked. He struggled to stay on his feet, to keep the gun tight in his hand, his nerve centers frantically commanding his arms and legs to do what they were designed to do.

Furious, frustrated, he was dimly aware of sinking to his knees, feeling the cold creep of the drug through his bloodstream. His forehead beaded with sweat, and his right hand, his gun hand, dropped to the ground.

Instantly a black boot came down on his hand, crushing it between the treaded sole and the soft ground. There was no pain, since the drug had evidently scrambled his nervous system, confusing and dissociating tactile stimuli. Strangely, his vision remained clear and he managed to crane his neck and look up.

Salvo smiled down on him genially. The stocky man still kept his dark hair in a short bristle cut. His sallow face had thinned a little since Kane had last seen him. There were a few extra lines etched across his forehead. The lines were bisected by a thin, ragged scar running from his hairline to the inside corner of his left eye.

"You've healed nicely," Kane managed to say. "Not every asshole I've pistol-whipped can say that, you know."

The genial smile didn't waver, nor did the hollow bore of the long compressed-air pistol in Salvo's right hand. "The drug is supposed to be nonlethal, at least in the dosage I just injected into you. Maybe I should give you an extra 20 cc's, just to make sure. Kind of a field test. You know?"

Kane tried to smile, but his facial muscles weren't working. "What is this stuff, anyhow?"

"A new compound," Salvo replied. "A mixture of chlordiazepoxide and carbachol. Damn near an immediate reaction. Makes you feel pretty good, doesn't it? Thought about trying it myself, when I had my anxiety attacks. Trouble is, there are side effects. Hard on the synapses, sometimes causes strokes. If you die, well, hell—just an unforeseen allergic reaction. Even the baron will accept that."

Something very much like shame rushed heat prickles to the back of Kane's neck. "What's he got to do with this?"

A spitting sound of derision passed Salvo's lips. "Did you think he'd forgotten about you, Kane? Did you think *I'd* forgotten about you?"

"I'd have been heartbroken if you had."

Salvo grinned, exposing overlarge, too even teeth. "Still the wise-ass. I'm glad to see some things haven't changed."

"Can't say the same about you. What's with the rig?"

Chuckling, Salvo brushed his fingers across the front of his bodysuit. "Like it? It's the uniform of a very elite, very select task force. Code-named Grudge."

"Grudge?"

"Can you think of a more appropriate designation for an inner circle of Mags assigned exclusively to tracking down traitors like you and your Preservationist whore?"

"Sounds like an awful lot of trouble to go to," Kane observed inanely.

"Not at all. It was my idea, and the baron approved it—enthusiastically." Salvo's brows knitted. "You never should have roughed him up, Kane. If you'd simply cut and run, he probably would have considered you beneath his notice."

"That might have damaged my ego," said Kane. "And that's all this really is about, anyway. Ego."

Salvo raised his boot from Kane's hand and, with his toe, roughly pushed him over onto his side. He drew his knife from a boot, squatted down and used the point to savagely pry the red badge from the breastplate of Kane's armor. His voice rose, high and harsh.

"You're a fucking traitor and you still wear this? I wish I could have shot you full of holes back at the river. But this time you've danced too close to the fire, and I'll gladly be the one to personally char your ass."

He flung the badge away into the shadows.

Limbs leaden, reflexes slumbering, Kane could only watch as Salvo yanked the motion sensor from his wrist, then unstrapped the Sin Eater from his forearm. Under the drug's influence, Kane felt no discomfort, only a pressure now and then.

Salvo casually tossed both the gun and the instrument aside. "What did you do with Grindberg?"

"About what you'd expect. Hope you're not too upset."

One of Salvo's shoulders lifted in a shrug.

"What are you up to here?"

Salvo smiled. "What do you think? The *program*. There's a timetable to observe, schedules to keep, contracts to fulfill." He shook his head sadly. "I missed these chats of ours. Truly."

"Did the baron plan this trap?" Kane demanded, his voice like the grating of chipped pottery.

Salvo wagged in his head in exaggerated negation. "Oh, *please!* This was a scheduled harvest. He has no idea Grudge tagged along." He angled an eyebrow at him. "Of course, I'm exceedingly curious how you knew about it."

"A happy coincidence."

"I won't accept that," Salvo said sharply. "There's no such thing as coincidences, happy or otherwise. I suspected you had access to an Intel pipeline to the ville. Now I'm positive of it. I just don't know who it is."

"But you have suspicions," said Kane dryly.

"Always," Salvo retorted. "But I can't take suspicions to Baron Cobalt. However, I can and will take you and your whore."

Salvo paused a moment, making a theatrical show of ransacking his memory, snapped his fingers and added, "No, wait—the Bird only seats two. Somebody will have to stay behind. I wonder who."

With that, he straightened up and marched toward the chopper. The knife blade glinted in his hand. Kane strained to regain bodily control, his arms and legs flopping like fish stranded on dry land. He opened his mouth to shout.

Salvo slashed through the rope holding Brigid erect against the port. She started to slump, but Salvo bent beneath her. She folded, limp and boneless over his shoulder, her hair hanging down his back.

A wave of relief surged through Kane. She wasn't unconscious, just suffering from the paralytic effects of the same drug that had incapacitated him.

Salvo tramped over and dumped the woman unceremoniously to the ground beside him. Their faces were close together. Faintly, striving for a wry note, Brigid said, "Here I am, Brigid Baptiste, girl hostage."

Her face gleamed with a film of perspiration, and Kane saw the bruises inflicted there. His expression twisted in an ugly display of impotent rage. He locked his gaze on Salvo. In a low monotone, he declared, "You are a dead man."

Salvo bent down beside Brigid. His voice was slurringly soft as he caressed her red-gold mane, as though he were petting a dog. "I don't understand you, Kane. You might have been a key member of the Trust, but no, you threw it all away because you couldn't stomach some plans that have no significance in the future scheme of things. You couldn't understand that sometimes sacrifices are necessary. The philosophy of short-term sacrifices for long-term gains is beyond you."

"I understand the philosophy," Kane said. "But to accept it, I'd have to acquire a taste for losing my own self-respect. That kind of diet tends to disagree with my digestion."

Salvo smirked. "You used to be made of ice, Kane. I know it was this bitch who melted it. What is it about her? It's not sex—you could have had plenty of that as a member of the Trust. Is it her intellect? I admit it's intriguing, but I can't see that as reason enough for you to sacrifice your future to rescue her...and nearly chill me in the bargain."

Kane forced a chuckle. "That really bothers you, doesn't it? The why?"

"Yes, Kane," replied Salvo flatly. "It does. It's a puzzle. What's its solution?"

"It wouldn't be fair to the other players if I told you."

"You don't know yourself, do you?" Salvo challenged. His smiling mask dropped. His eyes slitted, and his hand locked tightly in Brigid's mane of hair. He pulled her head up and savagely shook it. Because of the drug, she felt no pain, but her head wobbled loosely on her neck.

"*She* knows," Salvo hissed. "I should be asking her, not you."

He twisted her head up and around. The muscles of Salvo's face were frozen in an expression of intense hatred, but other emotions lurked there, too—confusion, hurt and even jealousy. Slapping her face, he half shouted, "Why, why, *why?* Tell me why, you whore, you bitch, you rebel, you insurgent. *Why?*"

Kane's body shook and shuddered with a fit of violent trembling. His teeth creaked as he ground them together.

With a snarl, Salvo released her, and she sprawled facedown, panting against the blades of grass. His breathing ragged, he said, "Kane didn't rescue you from your execution, he only managed a stay. I'm authorized to carry out the sentence by any means necessary."

The knife blade pressed against her throat, just at the carotid artery. Kane tried to lurch around, a hoarse cry of rage bursting from his mouth. A spasm shook his entire body. His fingers clawed the ground, uprooting handfuls of grass.

Salvo watched his struggles with amused, mocking eyes. "Oh, settle down, Kane. There's not enough room in the Bird to take both of you back to Cobaltville. Surely you understand my problem here. Sacrifices must be made."

Suddenly heavy-caliber blasterfire ripped overhead, a controlled fusillade that brought down masses of bark, branches and leaves. The air vibrated violently with the staccato roar. Salvo dropped full-length to the ground, yelling his inarticulate shock.

The Sandcat piled at full speed through the woods, the return rollers of the tracks squealing as it bulldozed its way over fallen logs and saplings like matchwood. The tracks caught and churned up heaps of foliage. Branches were flayed of leaves and bark as the armored hull whipped them aside.

The vehicle slewed to a rocking halt, loam cresting from beneath it in a thick wave. The steady autofire from the roof turret ceased at the same time. The driver's hatch popped up, and Grant bounded out, Sin Eater in hand, face set in a ferocious scowl. He sprinted forward.

Salvo moved with the animal swiftness born of desperate fear. His left hand closed convulsively in Brigid's hair, and he pulled her bodily to her knees, crouching behind her, the point of his knife touching her throat.

Grant came to a halt, then took a careful forward step. "Forget it. You know damn well I can shoot around her. This human-shield shit is for Pit slagjackers."

"True on all counts," Salvo replied. "You can shoot around her, but you can only wound me, not chill me. I'll still be able to cut her throat."

"That's true, too," said Grant darkly. "But I'll still be alive and you'll be dead."

Salvo snorted out a laugh. "So will she. I'll take what I can get. But nobody needs to die. You'll allow me to take off. I'll leave her on the ground. At the first hint of a blaster pointed in my direction, I'll chop her to pieces with the chain gun. She and Kane are in no position to dodge. Agreed?"

Grant did not respond.

Digging the point of the knife into soft flesh, Salvo repeated fiercely, *"Agreed?"*

Both Kane and Grant saw the thin thread of blood trickling down the column of Brigid's neck.

"Agreed," Kane snapped.

"Agreed," growled Grant.

Salvo chuckled and began a shuffling, backward duckwalk, one arm hooked under Brigid's arm and around her chest. He dragged her limp body over the ground, the heels of her boots digging twin furrows in the soil. She said nothing, but her eyes were deep green pools of frustrated fury and humiliation.

Reaching the Deathbird, Salvo pulled Brigid erect and held her in front of him as he fumbled with the door panel. When he had it open, he deftly hurled her away and leaped into the pilot's seat. Brigid sprawled on the ground like a bundle of laundry, the multibarreled snout of the chain gun scant inches from her head.

Kane didn't bother trying to raise his face from the ground. He simply lay there and listened. After a moment, he heard the whine of the engine, then the steady hum of spinning rotor blades. The breeze from the rotors blew over him, tossing tree limbs and shaking the underbrush. Then the engine whine and the breeze faded.

When the Deathbird was above the tree line and chopping an easterly course across the sky, Grant ran to Brigid. Domi, a white wraith of motion, left the Sandcat and rushed out to help him. Kane watched as they carried her back, slung between them, and placed her in a sitting position against the bole of a tree. Domi considerately rearranged her torn clothing.

Kane closed his eyes. He didn't want to look at Brigid, at the tears of shame flowing down her face. He felt unbelievably weary, worn and wrung out to the very core of his being.

Grant dragged Kane upright, propping his back against a tree. "Took you long enough," Kane said gruffly. "What'd you do, stop for a cigar along the way?"

"You try inverse phasing a jamming umbrella to turn it into a homing signal," Grant said, his tone a replica of Kane's. "Besides, a little bird laid some eggs on us."

"What happened to it?"

Domi, brushing Brigid's hair from her eyes, piped up, "Clipped its wings big time."

"What's with the outfit Salvo wore?" Grant asked. "What did he do to you two?"

"A drug," Brigid answered unsteadily. "Causes neural paralysis. I hope it's temporary."

Kane concentrated on moving his hands. He almost laughed when his fingers bent and twitched. "It is. As for Salvo's fashion statement, it's the uniform of the day for the Grudge task force."

"Shit," Grant hissed. "I don't need you to tell me why the task force was formed or who it has a grudge against. I expected something like this, sooner than later."

Kane glanced over at Brigid. Tears no longer streamed from her eyes. "How are you doing, Baptiste? You don't look so bad, all things considered."

She didn't reply.

"Did Salvo smack you around?"

"Just what you saw." Her voice was subdued. "Another man jumped me in the woods, used some kind of electric stun-club."

Kane tried to force a smile to his face. "Well, to borrow a phrase of yours, I know it's cold comfort, but he'll never jump anyone again. In fact, he'll never jump again, period."

There was no response from Brigid, and Grant looked around anxiously. "Let's be on our way. Salvo could be screaming for reinforcements right about now."

Kane smiled bleakly. "Unless you want to cart us around like luggage, I don't think we'll be going anywhere for a while. Besides, I have a feeling Salvo doesn't have reinforcements to scream for."

Domi and Grant briskly rubbed Kane's and Brigid's arms, trying to restore circulation. Kane didn't know how long it took, but finally he was able to get to his hands and knees. With Grant supporting him, he pulled himself to his feet. He attempted to take a forward step, but lost his balance and nearly fell. Grant caught him and leaned him back against the tree trunk. He breathed harshly, swaying and listing from side to side.

At Kane's direction, Grant retrieved the motion sensor, helmet, Sin Eater and the red duty badge.

"Leave the badge," Kane ordered.

Grant hesitated, looking uncertain.

"Leave it," repeated Kane, more sharply than he intended.

Grant balanced the disk on his thumb and flipped it into the darkness over his shoulder, like a coin. Kane didn't bother watching where it landed.

Brigid slowly and painfully stood up. When Domi reached out to help her, she waved her away. Her voice detached, she said, "I've been enough of a liability for one night."

Gingerly, as though she walked on a heaving deck, she went toward the Sandcat. Her face was closed, locked in a mask of concentration as she blocked out everything but the necessity to take the next step, and the next, and the next.

As she tottered past Kane, he almost reached out a

hand to support her, thought better of it and dropped it to his side. Softly he said to her, "Forget it, Baptiste. Don't blame yourself."

She didn't pause or even glance his way as she said matter-of-factly, "I don't. I blame you."

Chapter 7

The mountain plateau concealing the Cerberus redoubt was an organized masterpiece of impenetrability. Two centuries before, trained labor and the most advanced technology available had worked hand in glove to ensure that no one—Russian, Red Chinese or ignorant American citizen—might even suspect it existed.

For a handful of years, from the end of one millennium to the beginning of another, it had housed the primary subdivision of the Totality Concept's Overproject Whisper, Project Cerberus.

The Totality Concept was the umbrella designation for American military supersecret researches into many different arcane sciences, from hyperdimensional matter transfer to temporal phasing to a new form of genetics. Most of the separate but related projects had their own hidden installations, like Overproject Excalibur, in a subterranean complex in New Mexico.

The trilevel, thirty-acre Cerberus facility had come through the nukecaust in fairly good shape. As with most of the other redoubts, it had been built according to specifications for maximum impenetrability, short of a direct hit. Its radiation shielding was still intact, and it was powered by nuclear generators, and probably would continue to be for at least another five hundred years.

Lakesh had said that when the redoubt was built, the

plateau had been protected by a force field powered by atomic generators. Sometime over the previous century, the energy screen had been permanently deactivated, so new defenses had to be created. Although they couldn't be noticed from the road, an elaborate system of heat-sensing warning devices, night-vision vid cameras and motion-trigger alarms surrounded the mountain peak. It could be safely assumed that no one or nothing could approach the redoubt undetected. Additionally, on all ville records, the installation was listed as being abandoned nearly two hundred years ago.

The only evidence that it had ever been occupied before Lakesh and his staff of exiles had come to roost was the illustration near the main sec door. Emblazoned on one wall was a large, garishly colored image of a froth-mouthed black hound. Three stylized heads grew out of a single, exaggeratedly muscled neck, their jaws spewing flame and blood between great fangs. Below the image, rendered in an absurdly ornate Gothic script was the word Cerberus.

The ferocious guardian of the gateway to Hades seemed an appropriate totem and code name for the project devoted to ripping open gates in the quantum field.

The vanadium-alloy sec door folded aside accordion fashion. As it opened, a red light flashed and a hooting Klaxon sounded. A half-dozen men and women in white bodysuits flanked the Sandcat as it rumbled over the threshold, past the depiction of the hellhound. They trained spidery SA-80 submachine guns on the vehicle.

It braked to a halt, the engine idling, and Grant popped the hatch. He, Kane, Brigid and Domi stiffly disembarked. All of them looked haggard and exhausted, particularly Domi.

Grant glared at the blaster bores. "It's us. And turn off that goddamn noise."

Auerbach, a big redheaded man stared at him with his good eye. He wore a gauze patch over the left one. It had been injured in a scuffle the month before and was still healing. Crisply he responded, "If it's you, you know the sec protocols."

DeFore stepped forward, a small rad counter in hand. A buxom, stocky woman with dark bronze skin and ash blond hair intricately braided at the back of her head, she served as the redoubt's resident medic.

Consulting the counter, she announced, "Midrange yellow. Not immediately dangerous, but decam is mandatory."

As the sec door rumbled closed, Kane demanded, "Is the old man here?"

DeFore looked him over with a critical eye. He was not a pretty sight—dark-rimmed eyes netted with red, an unshaved face and unwashed body.

"He's here," she answered, "in the center. You need to rest and clean up before you see him."

Without a word, Kane spun on his heel and marched down the twenty-foot-wide corridor made of softly gleaming vanadium alloy.

"Kane!" DeFore's voice carried like the cracking of a whip. "Decam first."

Kane ignored her.

She gestured to Cotta and Farrell, who rushed forward, slinging their subguns over their shoulders by leather straps. They reached out to grasp Kane's arms.

Despite the lack of sleep, Kane's training kicked in automatically, instinctively. He wasn't armed or armored, but he didn't need to be. Gripping Farrell by wrist and shoulder strap, he pivoted and bent at the waist at the same time. The *tai-otoshi* throw smashed him into Cotta, who flanked his left side. The man stumbled, but didn't fall.

Kane let momentum carry him all the way around and, with a kick combining karate with the in-close and unartistic aspects of Pit fighting, disabled Cotta. He fell to the slick floor, clutching at his groin, a cry of agony keening from suddenly gray lips.

Farrell made a motion as if to lift the SA-80, but subsided when Kane cast furious eyes in his direction. Kane stepped over him and continued his measured, deliberate tread down the corridor.

DeFore, watching him go, plucked agitatedly at Grant's arm. "Stop him."

Her anxious gaze met an ironic smile. "*You* stop him, Doc. Of course, if you try, you'll be a living example of Physician, Heal Thyself."

Brigid uttered a murmur of irritation and started down the corridor.

KANE FELT A TWINGE of regret over laying out the two men. Cotta and Farrell had never been anything but cordial to him. Like all the personnel of Cerberus, they were exiles—except for one, and Kane wasn't sure if that particular one qualified as a person.

He strode past the electronically locked door to Balam's cell without looking at it. He had never visited the entity's confinement facility a second time. His initial reaction to the creature had been a xenophobic, mindless urge to kill it.

The door to the control center was up, and Kane stalked beneath it, not even glancing at the consoles of dials, switches, buttons and flickering lights running the length of the walls. Lakesh was seated before a computer station. A dizzying swirl of mathematical formulas and symbols scrolled over the monitor.

Mohandas Lakesh Singh was a lean, wrinkled apparition of a man, with fine hair the color of ash. Thick-lensed spectacles masked his watery blue eyes. A hearing aid was attached to the right earpiece.

He looked very old, like a man from a past age—which he was. As the former overseer of Project Cerberus, he had been allowed the option of surviving the nukecaust in cryogenic stasis. After a century-long slumber, he was revived to serve the Program of Unification. Worn-out body parts were replaced with bionic prosthetics and new organs. Though he looked like a mummy, he was chronologically a shade under 250 years in age. All things considered, he looked fairly spry and healthy. Not that Kane gave much of a damn about the man's health or lack of it.

Lakesh didn't look up when Kane stood behind him. Only when he felt his chair swivel roughly in a 180-degree turn, snatching him away from the keyboard, did he even acknowledge he was no longer alone in the vaulted, high-ceilinged room.

Blinking owlishly, as though roused from a nap, he said in his thin, reedy voice, "Friend Kane. I'm gratified you've returned, apparently safe and somewhat sound."

"No fucking thanks to you," Kane grated. "You sent us into a trap."

Lakesh's reaction wasn't what Kane expected. Instead of shocked surprise or denial, the old man's thin lips compressed tightly. He inclined his head on his wattled neck in a short, resigned nod. "I feared as much."

"*What?*" Brigid's tone was shrill with incredulity.

The two men turned toward her as she entered the

center. "You knew?" she demanded in an uncharacteristically loud voice.

Before Lakesh could respond, Kane declared grimly, "I've been telling you as much for months. He's got his own agenda, and we're nothing but his pawns."

Lakesh made a move as if to rise, but Kane put a firm hand on his shoulder and held him in his chair. "How much did you know?"

Lakesh tried to fling Kane's hand away. His fingers were very cold, as if all human warmth had been leached out of them during his cryonic sleep.

"Take your hand off me," Lakesh snapped. "I won't be manhandled, not by—"

He clamped his lips closed, but Kane finished the man's sentence. "'By the likes of you.'" He glanced over at Brigid. "Hear that, Baptiste? The old arrogance of the ville elite, of the baronial hierarchy. Of the Archon Directorate."

Brigid's face paled. Her eyes shone startlingly bright, disturbingly hard, like polished emeralds. In a strained, unnatural voice, she said, "I trusted you."

Lakesh's seamed face collapsed in a pained network of wrinkles and deep furrows. "I did not betray you."

"Domi's people were already dead, slaughtered, harvested a full day before we arrived." Kane spoke in short, staccato bursts. "Salvo and the Grudge task force were waiting for us. Only sheer luck and timing kept all of us from being chilled."

"*I did not betray you.*" Lakesh's reedy voice was fully of anger and agony. "If that was ever my intent, I could have easily arranged it many times over the last few months."

"Perhaps," said Brigid. "But maybe we had a purpose to fill back then. Now that we've fulfilled it, you see no reason to keep us around."

The scuffling of feet from the doorway caused all three of them to turn their heads. Auerbach, DeFore and Rouch, another tech, rushed in, fingers on the triggers of the subguns, faces taut with anxiety and anger.

Gesturing with her blaster's barrel, DeFore commanded, "Step away from him, Baptiste."

Brigid didn't move. Contemptuously she turned her back on the three Cerberus personnel.

"What are you doing?" Lakesh demanded hoarsely.

"Kane violated the sec protocols," DeFore replied in a clipped, no-nonsense tone. "He attacked Cotta and Farrell. Cotta's on his way to the dispensary. We've got Grant and Domi under guard."

She paused, and added loudly, "Baptiste, get away from Kane. I won't tell you again."

With a surprising surge of strength, Lakesh levered himself out of his chair, slapping aside Kane's restraining hand. His voice was no longer a reedy, quavery piping as he roared, "Lower those bloody guns and stand down! I won't have it, not here, you understand me?"

The redoubt personnel hesitated, gazing with surprised, disconcerted eyes at the old man's sudden and unexpected display of outrage.

"Do as I say!" Lakesh's voice was a strident crash of fury. "Or by God, I'll have all of you transported back to your respective villes, trussed up like turkeys for your barons! I'll even attach compliments-of-the-season cards!"

The blaster bores dropped. Still bellowing, Lakesh ordered, "Remove the guards from Grant and Domi!

And if they want to kick the stuffing out of you for your bad manners, let me know. I'll be happy to help them!''

He stabbed a gnarled finger toward the door. ''Get out of here! Take those guns back to the armory, and never, *ever* touch them without my express permission!''

''Sir,'' Auerbach said defiantly, ''the protocols are—''

''I devised the protocols, and I can dispense with them as I wish. Go!''

The three people backed out of the center. Lakesh's eyes were not owlish or preoccupied now. They burned with wrath, and he turned them onto Kane and Brigid.

''Now, let's return to the topic at hand, shall we?''

Kane stared at him unblinkingly. Then he swiped a hand over his eyes and began to laugh, wearily and bitterly. He found a chair at a console and dropped into it.

''What do you find so amusing, friend Kane?'' Lakesh asked.

''You. Us.'' He gestured to the entire redoubt. ''This little madhouse of ours. I was prepared to believe you were playing your game against the barons, using us as your tools…conspiracy piled atop conspiracy, until the only conspiracy is to make a stupe like me believe in a conspiracy.''

''Quite the conundrum.'' Lakesh was calmer now, almost sad. He shifted his gaze. ''And you, dear Brigid? What had you prepared yourself to believe?''

She shook her head. ''If this is a war, like you've told us, then mistakes and errors of judgment are inevitable.''

''And if it is not a war, but part of the conspiracy?''

"Then nothing is inevitable. Even the errors are factors of the conspiracy."

Lakesh nodded. "A conspiracy dating back thousands of years with an equal number of vectors doesn't look like a conspiracy or a war, does it?"

"No," retorted Brigid coldly. "It looks like chaos."

"And if it *is* chaos, then it cannot be a conspiracy, for where is the plan in chaos?"

"Unless," Brigid said, "the chaos is a planned introduction of random elements, like a diversion."

Kane uttered a loud groan of irritation. "You said something about returning to the topic at hand. Did you or did you not know about a trap?"

"I suspected, which is a different matter entirely. We'll discuss this later, when you've had the chance to eat, clean up and rest. As much as I resent her intrusion, DeFore is correct in insisting upon decam."

Kane was reluctant to let the old man off the hook so easily, but Lakesh was right—Kane was exhausted and he could smell himself. It wasn't pleasant.

He and Brigid walked out into the corridor. "Thanks for backing me up in there," he told her quietly.

"I didn't back you up," she replied evenly. "I had my own questions. You just got to ask yours first."

Chapter 8

In the far stall of the white-tiled shower room, a mixture of warm disinfectant and decontamination fluid sprayed from the nozzle. Brigid stepped beneath it, massaging it all over her body. She eyed the small rad counter on the wall, staying beneath the stream until the needle leaned over into the yellow-green zone. Automatically a jet of cold, clear water gushed down and rinsed the fluid from her body.

Stepping out of the cubicle, Brigid pulled on a long robe, glad to be rid of the coarsely woven outlander garb, and went to her private quarters. Her suite of rooms was a bit larger than the apartment she had lived in at the Enclaves in Cobaltville, but it was just as lacking in frills. More so, actually, because she had been forced to leave behind her few personal belongings and scant collection of mementos.

She had often wondered if her four-room suite had ever been occupied before, and if so, by whom. No record of official Cerberus personnel was extant, even in the database.

From a closet, she withdrew a white bodysuit. The fabric was of better quality and fit better than the bodysuit she'd worn during her years of service in the Historical Division.

As she shucked out of the robe, the slightly ridiculous notion occurred to her that Kane had seen her naked twice. She hadn't been disturbed by it, due to the circumstances, but now the thought made her feel vulnerable.

The return journey from Idaho had been unpleasant in the extreme. All four of them were keyed up and tense. When told of the fates of her people, Domi had scarcely spoken ten words during the entire five days. She and Kane had barely made eye contact and never shared the rear compartment.

The past three days had been the hardest to endure. Their supply of food and water had run low, and they had been forced to go on short rations. Far worse than that, the memory of the humiliating hostage situation was a fresh wound, and the continual close contact with Kane was like salt sprinkled on it.

Stepping into the bodysuit, Brigid angrily zipped it up and adjusted the Velcro tabs on the rubber-soled boot socks. She looked briefly at her reflection in the mirror on the closet door. The swelling around her eye had gone down, but the bruise was still there, like a stamp of her shame.

Her mind flashed back. Instead of making her way back to the Sandcat, she had kept a close eye on the sky. When she'd seen the Deathbird descend, she struck off in that direction, positive that was where Kane would head. She had been rendered a helpless captive with embarrassing ease.

Salvo hadn't abused her—in fact, he had prevented his subordinate from doing so. All he had said after tying her to the Deathbird was, "I'm glad I don't have to dig my own bait."

She would have spit on him, but she had been unable to lift her head.

Six months ago, Brigid Baptiste would not have

thought it possible that the reward for her long career as a midgrade senior archivist in Cobaltville's Historical Division would be a death sentence and exile.

A vast amount of predark historical information had survived the nukecaust, everything from novels and encyclopedias to vid tapes and digitized computer records.

Her primary duty was not to safeguard predark history, but to revise, rewrite and oftentimes completely disguise it. The political causes leading to the nukecaust were well-known. They were major components of ville dogma, the doctrine, the articles of faith, and they had to be accurately recorded for posterity.

Like everyone else born since inception of the Program of Unification, Brigid had believed the responsibility for the nukecaust and its subsequent horrors lay with humankind as a whole. For many years, she had never questioned it. Humanity had been judged guilty, and the sentence carried out forthwith.

As she rose up the ranks in the division, she was allowed greater access to secret predark records and she came across references to something called the Totality Concept, to devices called gateways, to projects bearing the code names of Whisper and Chronos and documents that hinted at phenomena termed "probability wave dysfunctions" and "alternate event horizons."

One day, she was covertly contacted by a faceless group calling itself the Preservationists. Over the following few months, she slowly understood that the Preservationists were archivists like herself, scattered throughout the network of villes. They were devoted to piecing together the unrevised history of not only the predark, but the postholocaust world, as well.

Whoever the Preservationists really were, they had anticipated her initial skepticism and apprehension. To show their good faith, she found an unfamiliar disk in her work area one morning.

On the disk was the journal of one Dr. Mildred Winona Wyeth, a woman born December 17, 1964. A medical doctor, a specialist in cryogenics, she had entered a hospital in late 2000 for minor surgery. An idiosyncratic reaction to the anesthetic left her in a coma, with her vital signs sinking fast. To save her life, the predark whitecoats had her cryonically frozen. She was revived over a century later by the legendary Ryan Cawdor, and she joined his band of warrior survivalists.

Though the *Wyeth Codex* contained her recollections of adventures and wanderings, it dealt in the main with observations, speculations and theories about the environmental conditions of postnukecaust America.

Brigid hadn't known how much of the codex to believe, but the journal began her secret association with the Preservationists. Though she wondered if her supervisor, Lakesh, was the Preservationist intermediary, she never followed up on her suspicions.

When Magistrate Kane brought her a puzzle to solve, an encrypted computer disk found in a hellzone, her illicit delving into predark secrets was no longer an innocent diversion. Though she was able to unlock the disk, the data it held contained far more questions than answers. However, one word, a place name, dominated—Dulce, a secret predark military installation in New Mexico.

Her curiosity aroused, Brigid didn't devote much time to contemplating the consequences of hacking into historical files that had been classified as Above Top Secret for over two centuries. The results of her illegal research yielded frightening data about the Totality

Concept, the mat-trans redoubts and the Archon Directorate.

It also brought her up on charges of sedition, and put her on a collision course with a secret that had damned humanity since the dawn of time. She also found herself embroiled in a strange struggle of wills between Kane and Salvo, his former commanding officer and sponsor.

The dynamic between Salvo and Kane was more than the active hostility between enemies. At this point, the outcome of the bitter test of resolve between two tough and ruthless men could have destructive consequences to everyone at Cerberus.

Brigid had read enough of predark psychological theory to understand the emotional matrix at work—Kane had assumed the role of ideological dopplegänger, or alter ego to Salvo, and both were caught in an interdependent web of vengeance and vindication.

She remembered Salvo's words in her cell in the Administrative Monolith on the eve of her scheduled execution. He was driven by family honor, and it was through Kane he wanted to exact his revenge.

Salvo hadn't explained the tarnish on his name or how Kane's father had put it there. Nor did Kane appear to have any idea of what it was all about, but he accepted the enmity almost gratefully.

Brigid only knew that she violently resented being used as a pawn in a private, childish war of tit-for-tat. It diluted the real work of Cerberus, and she blamed Kane and his blunt-brained Mag's arrogance for playing Salvo's game.

On a deeper level, she knew, albeit reluctantly, that if Kane truly was a blunt-brained Mag, he would have left her for Salvo, not just back in Idaho, but in Cobaltville, as well.

She ran a brush through her heavy mounds of tangled hair. She was an orderly, dedicated, brilliant, almost compulsively tidy woman. On the other hand, Kane wasn't exactly stable. He had the tension, speed and power of a stalking wolf. But unlike a stalking wolf, he had almost no patience at all. One could never tell what Kane would say or do. More than once, he had displayed a reckless disregard for his own life when hers was threatened. Perhaps his unpredictable behavior charted the progress of a man struggling foolishly and bravely toward the light of redemption.

And perhaps she was engaged in that same struggle, only by a different path, which ideally led to the same destination.

During their nightmarish mission in the Black Gobi, she had risked her own life to save his—acting on purely instinctive, almost primal impulses. She had been tortured, incapacitated, in a state of shock. Yet when she saw the Tushe Gun's blade at the helpless Kane's throat, only one emotion motivated her—she would not watch him die again.

The vision she had experienced during the mat-trans jump to Russia, then again in the subterranean chamber beneath Kharo-Khoto, floated through her mind. But it was more than a vision; it was a memory.

She was lashed to the stirrup of a saddle, lying in the muddy track of a road. Men in chain-mail armor laughed and jeered above her, and long black tongues of whips licked out with hisses and cracks. Callused hands fondled her breasts, forced themselves between her legs.

Then she saw a man rushing from a hedgerow lining the road. He was thin and hollow cheeked, perhaps nineteen or twenty years old. His gray blue eyes burned with rage. She knew him, she called out to him, shouting for him to go back, go back....

He knocked men aside to reach her, and a spiked mace rose above his head, poised there for a breathless second, then dropped straight down....

She knew the young man had been Kane, knew it on a level so visceral and soul deep that the intellectual prowess she prided herself upon could never touch it.

As the former overseer of Project Cerberus, Lakesh presumably was familiar with all the side effects of mattrans jumping. Brigid had never told him about her vision of a past life. She feared what he would tell her, not only about herself, but about Kane.

GRANT WAS TIRED. He had driven the last hundred miles back to Cerberus in a state of self-induced hypnosis, his mind asleep yet completely attuned to what the body was doing.

It was a state he referred to as "Mag mind," a technique that emptied the consciousness of the nonessentials and allowed the instincts, honed in hundreds of hellzones over the years, to take over. It left him drained.

Grant had just finished dressing when he heard the faint, timid rap at his door. Half-expecting it to be DeFore bearing an apology, he called, "Come."

Instead of the bronze-skinned, dark-eyed medic, Domi slipped in. As she shut the door behind her, Grant repressed a groan and announced, in a deliberately gruff tone, "You know what you promised."

Domi ducked her head. "I know."

Then she buried her face in her hands and burst into tears, slender shoulders quaking.

Grant gazed at her in silent surprise. Domi was fun

loving, playful, carefree. She had made no secret of her desire to bed him. In fact, she was so blatant about it, Grant had secured a promise from her that her attempts at seduction would stop or he would never speak to her again.

He hadn't seen her shed a tear or ever evince any emotion other than a glib cheeriness that she was away from the Tartarus Pits of Cobaltville. Even while visiting him during his recovery after the Mongolia mission, she had made light of his injuries. Unlike himself, Grant and his companions, the only life path she had abandoned was the marginal existence as an outlander, and later, as Guana Teague's sex slave. Certainly her past had little to make her misty-eyed with nostalgia.

Because Domi had been so quiet on the return trip from Cuprum, Grant had assumed she'd come to terms with the loss of her people, accepting it with the resigned equanimity characteristic of outlanders.

Now, watching her weep, he felt ashamed of his casual assumption that the girl had no past to mourn or the emotional structure to grieve. It was certainly not Domi's first introduction to death and suffering, but it was the deepest.

Grant stepped over to her and hesitantly enfolded her small frame in his big arms. He clumsily patted her shoulder. Domi pressed her face against him, and he noted absently that the crown of her tousled head barely topped his rib cage.

He stroked her head, soothing her, not knowing what to say except a low, crooning refrain of "It's all right. It's all right."

Grant had the suspicion she would move her body against his suggestively, but she didn't. Domi simply wept within the embrace of his arms.

Bleakly he considered that such open displays of human emotions, even honest lust, were becoming more rare with every passing day. True feelings were being bred out of the race, at least those living on the bounty of the barons.

Outlanders, sneered at by the elite of the villes, were possibly the last real human beings on the planet, and they were an endangered species. As a Magistrate, he had chilled dozens of them in the performance of his duty, but he had murdered more than just outlander bodies. He had destroyed their spirits, as well.

Grant felt his throat thicken with guilt. He held Domi tighter, cradling her head. He and Kane had worked as the unaware servants of the Archons, the life haters, the soul stealers.

Guilt, that was the whole gimmick.

For the past ninety years, it was beaten into the descendants of the survivors of the nukecaust that Judgment Day had arrived and humanity was rightly punished. People were encouraged to tolerate, even welcome, a world of unremitting ordeals, conflict and death because humanity had ruined the world, and therefore the punishment was deserved.

Love among humans was the hardest bond to break, so people were conditioned to believe that since humans were intrinsically evil, to love another one was to love evil. That way, all human beings forever remained strangers to one another.

Grant found a bitter chuckle working its way up his throat. He did his best to choke it down, but finally it rose past his lips. Domi lifted her head, tears swimming in her eyes, streaming down her face.

"It makes you...laugh?" Her tone was confused, a bit reproachful.

He stroked her hair and whispered, "It's not true unless it makes you laugh, but you don't understand unless it makes you cry."

RINSING THE LATHER from his face, Kane critically eyed the clean-shaved reflection staring sullenly at him from the mirror. It was a face that had once laughed a lot, and liked adventure and pretty girls and gazed out at the world with prideful eyes.

The face had forgotten all those things now. It was drawn and lined with pain, with a look as when staring out between the bars of a cage.

He toweled his face dry and padded naked to the closet. He hesitated before pulling out one of the bodysuits. Black was more his color. It had been his color for many years, and jumping abruptly to white disoriented him. The pearl gray, high-collared bodysuit he had worn as an off-duty Mag suited him best. Its color accurately reflected his straddling two opposing emotional and ethical poles.

Somewhere in the middle, he said to himself snidely. As usual.

He glanced down at himself before covering his body with the white garment. Violence had left its history, wealed white marks against the smooth, pale bronze. He lifted his hands and inspected them. They were lean, long, sinewy fingers designed for killing, not for loving.

He tried to imagine them running through the sunset color of Baptiste's hair, but the picture refused to form. It was much easier to visualize his fingers knotting around Salvo's neck, crushing flesh and gristle beneath them.

His heart began to pound. His muscles coiled, and a bitter taste was on his tongue. He recognized it as hatred and rage. He filled a glass with water from the faucet and rinsed his mouth out. The taste didn't leave.

Kane sat on the edge of the bed, chin on his fist, memory skittering back to the day, only a few months ago, when he had sat there and contemplated putting the bore of his Sin Eater to his head. Of course, he had been suffering a severe case of shock, having just escaped Cobaltville, learned the backstory of the nukecaust and been introduced to a representative of the Archon Directorate.

Reinvention of the human identity was something that had never occurred to him before. He had been a Magistrate, sanctioned both legally and spiritually to enforce the laws of the barons and arrest the floodtide of chaos by any means necessary.

Though he had often entertained doubts about his life path, his identity seemed inviolate. Now he understood that his identity had derived from his role as a Mag, and both were lost to him forever.

Maybe that was the reason he couldn't put Salvo behind him, couldn't view him strictly as a tactical problem to be dealt with cleanly and dispassionately. Salvo was his anchor to his old self, his former identity—but the connecting chain was tangled up with Baptiste.

He resented her for that, for adding a confusing element to what should be a simple, straightforward blood vendetta. And she, in return, resented him for allowing a personal feud to interfere with the greater war.

Kane felt his lips tug in a mirthless smile. A war that could not be won was no war at all. True, a victory had been scored in Dulce, but only because Baron Cobalt had been taken completely off guard.

Shortly thereafter, he had convened a council of the nine barons. The hybrid intermediaries of the Directorate were smug in the knowledge they must win out. The odds were too great, too improbable for such a small force of seditionists to oppose the combined might of the villes and the Directorate. The barons and their direct progenitors had, after all, cleaned up the horrors of the Deathlands.

In the century following the nukecaust, the barons had warred against one another, each struggling for control and absolute power over territory. Then they realized—or were taught—that greater rewards were possible if unity was achieved, in common purpose and organization.

Territories were redefined, treaties struck among the barons, and their individual city-states became interconnected points in a continent-spanning network. The Program of Unification was ratified and ruthlessly employed. The reconstructed form of government was institutionalized and shared by all the former independent baronies.

Nine baronies survived the long wars over territorial expansion and resources, and control of the continent was divided among them. The pretenders, those who were not part of the original hierarchy but who arrogantly assumed the title to carve out their own little pieces of empire, were overrun, exterminated and their territories absorbed.

Many previously unknown Stockpiles were opened up and their contents distributed evenly among the barons. Though the technologies were restricted for the use of those who held the reins of power, life overall improved for the citizens in and around the villes. Manufacturing industries, totally under the control of the villes, began again.

But it wasn't all the doing of the barons. Someone

or something else was pulling the strings to make humanity dance to a tune of the damned.

Kane massaged his eyes with the heels of his hands. He remembered how his father's face had looked in the cryonic canister in Nightmare Alley, composed and calm in a forever sleep.

He remembered Baron Cobalt's mocking words when he declared he was a hybrid of human and Archon: *At least my human genes spring from very best, carefully selected stock...much of that superior genetic material derives from your father.*

Kane hadn't killed the baron, though the incend grenades he and Grant had employed at the cryogenics crypt more than likely consumed his father's body. He had spared the vampire and slain the victim.

He sighed. Memories could be both friend and foe. He wondered again if Lakesh's war had little or nothing to do with bullets and grenades. It was a wild, wild battle of the human heart, of the human spirit's rage to live.

Chapter 9

Inside Cerberus, time was measured by the controlled dimming and brightening of lights to simulate sunrise and sunset. At 0300, the lights were very dim.

Lakesh met Grant, Brigid and Kane in the control center. The section of vanadium wall was open to reveal the huge Mercator-projection map of the world. Flickers of light shone on almost every continent, connected by glowing threads. The spots of light represented all functioning mat-trans gateway units worldwide. The map also delineated the geophysical alterations caused by the nukecaust.

They took seats around the master monitor screen, a four-foot square of ground glass. Lakesh listened without interruption to Kane's terse details about the Idaho foray. He didn't even raise an eyebrow when Grant displayed the compact motion sensor.

When Kane was done, Lakesh said, "I was unaware of the formation of the task force, though I suspected something like it would emerge from the Council of the Nine. Last month, while you were in Russia, I had a private audience with Baron Cobalt."

Though Lakesh was one of the baron's inner circle, private audiences were rare. Brigid's eyes widened in surprise. "He told you about Grudge?"

Lakesh shook his head. "No, but he indicated that he

considered Kane's apprehension a very personal priority."

"You didn't think that was worth mentioning?" Kane demanded.

Sighing, Lakesh answered, "Keep in mind the condition all three of you were in, friend Kane. You needed time to convalesce without adding more misery to the mix. Ninety percent of the healing process is attitude, you know."

Kane pursed his lips as if he tasted something sour. He reluctantly agreed with Lakesh's opinion. He and Brigid in particular had been grievously wounded, and at the time of their return to Cerberus, not even DeFore knew if the injuries were permanent.

"You'd better stay out of Cobaltville for a while, then," Grant said. "You're the obvious suspect for the leak."

"That I cannot do. If I am a suspect, then a prolonged absence will only serve to further compromise me."

"You don't seem too worried about being fingered," commented Kane.

The old man shrugged. "I've other matters on my mind. My research regarding the origin point of the Archons, for one."

"According to predark classified files," Brigid said, "the speculation was they came from the Zeti Reticuli star system."

"Perhaps they did, many, many aeons ago. Or their forebears did."

"Forebears?" echoed Grant.

"Forebears," Lakesh affirmed. "During my years at Dulce, I read the autopsy reports of Archon bodies recovered from various so-called saucer crashes, particularly the one at Roswell. Forensic and genetic findings indicated they were descended from an unknown reptilian species."

"So what?" asked Kane.

"So, for as long as humanity has kept records, there have been legends of a mysterious serpent folk descending from the heavens to participate in the creation of humankind. Cultures as widespread as those of Sumer, Babylonia, China, Japan and even Central American have myth cycles about these reptilian entities."

"Hmm," Brigid said, clearly interested. "Serpents or dragons signified divine heritage in many Asian countries."

"Exactly," said Lakesh. "Known in ancient codices and texts as the Serpent Folk, a Sumerian tablet calls them the Annunaki. According to a Hebrew document, the *Haggadah*, the Serpent Folk were described as standing upright like humans and in height were 'equal to the camel.' The document mentions their superior mental gifts, despite their possession of 'a visage like a viper.'"

"Did these snake-faces have names?" Grant inquired, a chuckle lurking in the back of his throat.

"Two of them did," answered Lakesh straight-faced. " The Sumerian record calls them Enki and Enlil. The *Haggadah* refers to the king of the folk as Belial, obviously a derivation of Enlil. Enki and Enlil were given the task of creating a labor force on Earth to mine ore. This they did by a process which sounds suspiciously like genetic manipulation of the indigenous species.

"Since we know the Archons have been engaged in a program of crossbreeding for many centuries, perhaps the Serpent Folk did the same to whatever original species the Archons sprang from."

Kane narrowed his eyes. "Are you saying the Archons were Earth's indigenous species?"

Lakesh shook his head. "I am suggesting only that the origins of man are more mysterious than predark science knew. At any rate, the entity called Enlil seems to have been dissatisfied with the way humankind turned out—rebellious, independent and insatiably curious.

"But we're not discussing ancient history here. In the twentieth century, UFO researchers kept stumbling over reports of reptilian creatures working in tandem with the Grays, whom we know as the Archons. Granted, they were reported in a relatively small percentage of abduction cases, less than twenty percent. However, the witnesses in those cases reported that the Grays showed the reptiles a marked deference.

"The last cultural record of the creatures comes from the late 1990s. When the Hale Bopp comet approached our solar system, some fringe astronomers reportedly sighted another celestial object following in its wake. The rumor mill of the time, fueled by paranoia, spread the claim that the object was actually a spaceship, peopled by reptilian beings who were heading this way to enslave humanity, or enlighten it. The rumors reached such a point of persistence that NASA was forced to issue a public statement denying the existence of such an object trailing Comet Hale Bopp."

Grant's dark face locked in a skeptical mask. "If the reptiles were still around in the 1990s, what happened to them?"

Lakesh smiled. "That is the mystery I've been trying to solve. I've reached a provisional hypothesis which at least fits the superficial facts."

"Which are?" Kane asked.

"There was considerable speculation that the Archons were pan-dimensional, a theory to explain how their craft sometimes seemed to simply disappear, and also how the Archons themselves were reported to float through solid objects."

"If they could do that," Grant pressed, "why has Balam been your guest these past three years?"

"Perhaps the Archons can only perform these feats with the aid of their quantum-path technology," Brigid suggested.

"Quite likely," agreed Lakesh. "Removed from its direct influence, Balam is as helpless as any human would be in like circumstances."

"Their technology was the basis for most of the Totality Concept hardware," stated Brigid. "At least as far as the gateways and the time-trawling devices are concerned. Is it possible to modify what we have here to locate their home dimension?"

"Not exactly. However, it is possible to utilize natural vortices that historically possess the same principles as a gateway unit."

Grant, Brigid and Kane gazed at him silently for a long moment. Lakesh waited for the reaction. It was not long in coming. Grant's brown eyes widened until the irises were completely surrounded by the whites, and Brigid's right eyebrow climbed toward her hairline. Kane demanded, "Let me get this straight—*naturally* occurring gateways?"

Lakesh nodded. "Indeed. My pet project for the past few months."

Turning in his chair, he tapped the console's keyboard. Columns of mathematical formulas and twisting geometric shapes appeared on the big VGA screen. Most of them resembled spirals. Brigid put on her former badge of office, a pair of wire-framed, rectangular-lensed spectacles, and squinted at the screen.

"Before the nukecaust," Lakesh intoned in his concise lecturer's tone, "there was a small but growing body of scientific theory that postulated ancient peoples built megalithic structures—such as the dolmans of Newgrange and Stonehenge—deliberately above power points, packets of the quantum field. These antediluvian constructions were expressions of a long-forgotten system of physics, known as 'hyperdimensional mathematics.'

"The theory provided a fundamental connection between the four forces of nature, a connection between uphill and downhill energy flows. For example, an uphill flow would lead to an invisible higher dimension, a downhill to lower one, the dimension in which we live. Evidence has been found that there are many vortex convergences on Earth.

"Some ancient cultures were aware of these vortices and manipulated the energies to open portals into other realms of existence. Personally, I believe this bit of knowledge of our ancestors was all but obliterated with the burning of the Library of Alexandria in the fourth century B.C., an act that may have been due to the Archons."

Brigid pursed her lips. "So you're postulating that by employing hyperdimensional physics, the Archons go back and forth from our world to their own?"

Lakesh indicated the numerical sequences and forms on the monitor screen. "The math checks out. By comparing and cross-indexing my calculations with legends in the historical database, the best chance of finding one of these vortex points is in Ireland."

"*Ireland?*" exploded Grant.

Lakesh smiled blandly. "Also known as Ogyia, Insulara Sacra, Hibernia, Eire, the Emerald Isle—ancient land of magic and mystery."

"How do you know it still exists?" Kane demanded. "It could have been swamped by tidal waves during the nukecaust. It was an island, right?"

"An island still," responded Lakesh smoothly. "I managed to acquire a satellite photo not more than five years old. Ireland remains essentially unchanged, unlike its neighbor and traditional foe, Great Britain."

The fact that Cerberus could uplink with a Vela-class reconnaissance satellite had been a matter of astonishment when they had learned of it. Though all of them were aware that in predark years the upper reaches of the planet's atmosphere had been clogged with orbiting satellites, many designed for spying and surveillance purposes, ville doctrines claimed that all satellites were now simply free-floating scrap metal. According to legend, there were settlements of a kind in space, even on the moon itself.

"Why Ireland?" asked Brigid. "True, there are many megalithic dolmens there, but quite a few in other European countries, as well."

"Unlike Ireland, most of those other countries were devastated during the war. Ireland appears to have remained intact, if not necessarily unscathed. There is more of a chance that the ancient sites survived."

Pausing, Lakesh drew in a deep breath. Solemnly he added, "Besides, there is another reason. In Celtic tradition, tales of an otherworld figured very prominently. Some mysterious law unique to Ireland seemed to bring together the great spaces that divided the domain of the physical with the spiritual. That otherworld impinged and overlapped their reality constantly, as well as the entities allegedly living in it.''

"What kind of entities?" questioned Kane.

"The Tuatha De Danaan, for one."

"The who?" Grant demanded.

Lakesh carefully sounded out each syllable, then explained, "In Gaelic, it translates as 'The folk of the god whose mother is Dana.'"

"What about them?" asked Brigid.

"According to ancient and esoteric tradition, the Danaan wafted into Ireland on a magic city of light and founded four great centers of wisdom and learning. The Danaan brought with them four gifts, which figured in arcane lore for centuries. There was the Lia Fail, or Stone of Destiny, on which the High Kings of Ireland stood when they were crowned and which was supposed to roar when the rightful monarch took his place on it.

"The second treasure of the Danaans was the invincible sword of Lugh the Long Arm. The third was a magic spear, which was popularly supposed to be the Spear of Longius, or the Holy Lance, which pierced Christ's side as he hung on the cross. The fourth gift was the Cauldron of the Dagda, a vessel which could feed a host of people without ever being emptied. The folklore of most Celtic countries is cluttered with just this sort of thing, all of which can be explained in scientific terms."

"And," declared Kane, "you're going to tell us all about the technology on which these magic items were based."

"A pointless exercise," Lakesh said. "It would be sheer speculation, which we don't have the time to indulge in. What is not speculation is that the Tuatha De Danaan reigned in Ireland for many centuries. They were at last overthrown by invaders known as the Children of Miled. This race was represented as coming from Bilé, a term usually describing the underworld.

"But the Danaan did not perish. By their superior art, they cast over themselves a veil of invisibility and withdrew into the hills and mountains, where they rule in an otherworld."

"You believe the Tuatha De Danaan may be Archons?" Brigid asked.

"Or a race very much like them. Consider what I've just told you." Lakesh ticked off the points on his fingers. "One—they arrived in Ireland on a city of light. Two—they can pass between worlds at will. Three—they possess resources that seem magical to humans. Four—they are a race apart. Even in the oldest legends, they are not described as ever being human."

"What's all that have to do with snake people?" inquired Grant, looking interested in spite of himself.

"Druidic shamans often invoked the Na Fferyllt, the beings who maintained the spiritual heat of the land. Their abode was in the Fortress of the High Powers, in the underworld, where they governed the dragons."

"That's quite a stretch," Kane observed.

"There is more, friend Kane."

Grant rolled his eyes. "Doesn't that just figure."

Not reacting to the sarcasm, Lakesh rattled the keyboard again. The screen cleared, and upon it flashed a jumble of symbols, three small circles topping three triangles. The center triangle was a scalene with a pair of isosceles flanking it.

With a wry smile, Lakesh asked, "Does this symbol look familiar?"

"It's very similar to the insignia of Overproject Excalibur,'' answered Brigid. "The division of the Totality Concept's bioengineering researches."

"And the linchpin of the Archon Directorate's hybridization program," Lakesh added.

Kane eyed the symbols on the screen doubtfully. "The insignia we saw in Dulce had the triangles reversed, the points down."

"Yeah," Grant agreed. "So what's that supposed to be—the emblem of another Directorate-sponsored program?''

Lakesh chuckled. "Hardly, friend Grant, though I suspect the Excalibur symbol wasn't chosen at random, and the reversal of it quite intentional. No, this is the emblem adopted by reformed branches of Celtic druidism—and a secret society which flourished from the fourth century A.D. to at least the late 1990s. The Priory of Awen.''

"What's an Awen?" Kane asked.

"In Gaelic it means 'inspiration'…the practitioners, the *awenyddion,* solved problems or looked for hidden information. Celtic seers were believed to be connected with a specific cosmic database of wisdom."

A smile creased Lakesh's face. "In Celtic tradition, the mistress of wisdom was the Danaan goddess Brigid.''

She blinked in surprise, sitting up straighter in her chair.

"You seem to play out your namesake's role here, as well," Lakesh continued. "And I find that something more than a coincidence." He glanced toward Kane. "You may find this edifying, as well, friend Kane. The most legendary warrior of Gaelic lore was named Cuchulainn.''

"So?"

"He embodied the ideals of the Celtic warrior—courage, honor, a deep respect for women, a nonchalant disregard for death and unmatched arrogance. He was well-known for battling 'hostile aerial beings.'"

Impatiently Kane demanded again, "So?"

Lakesh smiled. "He went by several names, too. One of them was a diminutive of Cuchulainn. It was rendered as 'Ka'in.'"

Kane knew Lakesh well enough to recognize the intense glint in his eyes. He was preparing to wax eloquently and endlessly on another metaphysical topic relating to destinies, fate, alternate event horizons and God only knew what else.

Quickly he interjected, "What's the significance of this secret society, the Priory of Awen?"

Lakesh regarded him a bit reproachfully, but answered, "The predark world was full of secret societies, many with religious trappings, though the majority were little more than exclusive social clubs for the elite. The Priory of Awen was one of the exceptions. There is damn little information about it in the databases of government intelligence-gathering agencies.

"I found out this much, though—the Totality Concept's research projects were far-flung and involved many nations and just as many secret societies. Evidently the Priory of Awen was one of them. It was a very small enclave of priests which safeguarded the secrets of pre-Christian Ireland, secrets which flew in the face of accepted religious doctrines. According to an MJ-12 briefing document, the Priory had access to knowledge relating to the root race of the Archons, the Na Fferyllt."

"The snake people," muttered Grant.

Lakesh acknowledged his comment with a short nod.

"The Priory was allegedly founded by Saint Patrick after he had driven the serpents from mainland Ireland. An apocryphal addition to that legend tells of one serpent which was not cast out with the others. Patrick induced it to live on the island of Great Skellig until Judgment Day. The basis of that old myth can be construed to mean the last of the Serpent Folk, perhaps even Enlil himself. And for all intents and purposes, Judgment Day arrived on January 20, 2001.''

Kane, Brigid and Grant gazed at Lakesh contemplatively and quietly. As usual, Kane broke the silence. "Are you aware of how insane all this sounds?''

"Of course,'' Lakesh replied cheerfully. "But is it any more insane than what you've already learned, already experienced?''

Kane created the impression of seriously pondering the question for a moment. In a heavy, ominous tone, he replied, "Yes. Yes, it is.''

Lakesh pushed himself to his feet. "Then allow me to shed a wee bit of the light of sanity upon you. Follow me, children.''

Chapter 10

The workroom adjacent to the armory was deserted. Rows of drafting tables with T-squares hanging from their sides lined one wall. Only a few lights were on, and Brigid, straining her vision in the gloom, could make out electronic circuitry on some of the drawing boards and construction designs on the others.

Lakesh walked to a long, low trestle table and pointed to an object resting on it. It resembled a very squat, broad-based pyramid made of smooth, dark metal. One side was missing and revealed a confusing mass of circuit boards and microprocessors gleaming within it. The pyramid was barely one foot in width, its height not exceeding ten inches.

"Behold the fruits of my labors," Lakesh announced genially, patting the apex of the object.

"What is it?" asked Grant suspiciously.

"A prototype interphaser," the old man replied, a touch of pride in his voice. "In essence, it's a miniaturized version of a mat-trans unit, utilizing much of the same hardware and operating principles." He touched a pair of input ports. "This is for a keyboard, to enter the proper mathematical measurements to effect activation."

"What's it for?" Kane demanded. "Transporting midgets?" He didn't bother to disguise the skepticism and sarcasm in his voice.

Lakesh chuckled. "If only it were that easy. As you know, the gateways function by tapping into the quantum stream, invisible pathways that run outside of our physical space and back again at distant points. In my day, we called these openings wormholes."

Brigid said, "The principle of the mat-trans units is the activation of quantum wormholes, but I thought the transit paths were linear."

"If wormholes can be compared to tunnels," Lakesh replied, "between the relativistic *here* and *there*, it stands to reason there are any number of side tunnels and arteries branching off between the primary entrance and exit points."

"In theory, anyhow," intoned Kane darkly.

Brigid cast him a quick, irritated glance. "If these side tunnels do exist, then your interphaser can activate them?"

Lakesh replied, "As friend Kane commented, in theory. This instrument will interact with a vortex's quantum energy and cause a temporary overlapping of two dimensions that exist on different vibratory continuums.

"The interphaser transmits wavicles, subatomic particles that possess some of the qualities of waves, such as photons and electrons, which have some of the qualities of particles."

Using an index finger, Lakesh traced an X in the air. "The vortex will become an intersection point, a discontinuous quantum jump, beyond relativistic spacetime."

Grant massaged his temples and heaved a deep sigh. "Am I the only one at sea here?"

Lakesh grinned. "As physicist Niels Bohr said many years ago, 'Those who are not shocked when they first come across quantum theory cannot have possibly understood it.'''

"I'll probably regret asking this," said Kane, "but have you located one of these naturally occurring gateways, a vortex point?"

"Of course," retorted Lakesh a bit acidly. "It was the first thing I did when I formulated this plan. The great-chambered tumulus of Newgrange, on the northern bank of the Boyne."

"Why that one?" Brigid asked.

"First, because it was regarded in Irish myth as a dwelling place of the Tuatha De Danaan. Second, it is associated with the ancient Celtic doctrine of transmigration, a gateway to Tir na' Nog, the ancient Irish otherworld...a land, to quote Keating, 'wherein there is neither age nor decay.' Unlike other pagan paradises, Tir na' Nog was believed to be attainable within mortal life."

"How do you propose we get to Ireland?" Grant asked. "Don't tell me there's a gateway unit there."

"There isn't, so I won't," Lakesh stated. "However, there is one in England, though it was not part of the official program. Apparently one of the units was shipped there in modular form and assembled. It took me days of searching the database, but I finally found the transit-initiator code."

Grant's eyes narrowed. He had never made a secret of his violent antipathy toward jumping. "This gateway is fully functional, right, not like that fucked-up one in Russia?"

Kane repressed an involuntary shudder at the memory of that particular jump, of the nausea and the debilitating weakness—and the visions. The Cerberus gateway link had been unable to receive a read on the autosequence initiators on the Russian unit. The matter-stream carrier-wave modulations couldn't be synchronized, which resulted in a severe bout of jump sickness.

"I receive a green signal on the autosequencer," Lakesh said reassuringly. "The quantum-path modulations are in sync. However, once you make the jump, you'll have to find your way across the Irish Sea to Ireland."

"What's the Intel on England?"

"Like most intercontinental locations, fragmentary at best. The only solid, firsthand source of information was derived from the *Wyeth Codex*. She and her companions made a jump there some ninety years ago. The holocaust caused a rift in the land, and the North Sea very nearly divided the entire country. London was completely submerged.

"Dr. Wyeth reported two factions were locked in a battle for supremacy over what was left of Great Britain. One was an agrarian society loosely based on Druidic principles. The other was typical of the pseudo-fascistic baronies that sprang up here.

"In her journal, Dr. Wyeth wrote that the Druidic settlement was attacked and damaged. Since that is where the gateway is located, that is where you will materialize."

Grant glowered at the old man from under ridged brows. "You're not asking for much, are you? Jump to England. Somehow get to Ireland. Hook your doodad up to a quantum vortex, see what happens and then come back. Simple."

"You can pass on it." Lakesh's tone was gentle, understanding. "As friend Kane has pointed out on more than one occasion—"

"A dozen, at least," Kane interposed.

"You're under no obligation to accept these missions. However, as *I've* also pointed out, confrontational tactics against the villes are utterly futile. Considering the news about the task force, it appears a concerted effort will be made against us. Finding both an offensive and defensive weapon takes on added urgency. We cannot afford to wait for Salvo or the Directorate to find us. Therefore, our only chance of survival, much less of victory, is to slip in an unguarded back door."

"That's the snag, isn't it?" Kane snapped. "What if the back door only *looks* unguarded and it slams on us and we can't get out?"

"There's where the concept of sacrifices for the greater good figures into this," commented Brigid wanly.

"Before I make further sacrifices for the greater good, I want some proof that this jolt-brained scheme of yours has some foundation."

Lakesh peered at him over the rims of his spectacles. "How may proof be provided unless you reach your destination?"

Kane took a deep breath, held it, slowly released it. "Let's run it up Balam's flagpole and see if the little bastard salutes."

A CENTURY BEFORE the nukecaust, enlightened minds found it fashionable to speculate that Earth's nearest alien neighbors would be found right next door, on the planet Mars.

A hundred years later, it was discovered that alien neighbors were a lot closer than nineteenth-century scientific theorists ever dreamed. They were right on Earth and had been for a very, very, *very* long time. So long a time, in fact, they felt they had the prior claim.

That fact had been the most difficult for Kane, Grant and Brigid to swallow, much less digest. Kane in particular had demanded hard evidence. The creature called Balam was terrifyingly undeniable. None of the three was anxious to face the creature a second time. On their prior visit to Balam's holding facility, the entity's proximity aroused basic, primitive and disturbing emotions in all their psyches.

Lakesh paused at the door, fingers poised uncertainly over the keypad. "This might be unwise. All the Archons are psi-linked by some hyperspatial mind filament, you know."

"A passive link," Brigid reminded him. "If it was active, Balam would have been sprung a long time ago."

Lakesh nodded in reluctant agreement. "Even though Balam has been prisoner here for three years, we have yet to learn how to open our minds without being manipulated."

Kane smiled coldly. "We have to learn how to manipulate *him.*"

Lakesh tapped in the six-digit code. With a harsh electronic buzz, the lock solenoid slid aside, and he pushed the door inward. Banks, the creature's attendant, was asleep in his own quarters. They stepped into the wide, low-ceilinged room cautiously.

Most of the furnishings consisted of desks and computer terminals. A control console ran the length of the right-hand wall, glass-encased readouts and liquid-crystal displays flickering and flashing. A complicated network of glass tubes, beakers, retorts, bunsen burners and microscopes covered three black-topped lab tables.

Upright panes of glass, beaded with condensation, formed the left wall. A deeply recessed room stretched

on the other side of them. It was dully lit by an overhead
fluorescent strip, glowing a ruddy red. Lakesh had told
them that Balam's optic nerves were very sensitive to
light levels much above twilight.

As they had five months before, they faced the glass
wall. Lakesh stepped up to it and rapped imperiously
with his knobby knuckles. Grant hammered on it with
the side of his fist.

"Wake up in there, hell-spawn," he said loudly. "If
we can't sleep, neither can you."

In a replay of their first visit, shadows shifted in the
ruddy murk. Peering through the swirl of seething mist,
Kane saw the pair of huge tilted eyes flaming out of the
red-hued gloom. Deep in them, he could see the scorn
and the pride of a race so old that the most ancient
civilizations on earth were merely yesterday beside it.

He was prepared for the words that twisted, like
thready, breathy whispers into his, into all of their
minds.

We are old, said the nonvoice. *When your race was
wild and bloody and young, we were already ancient.
Your tribe has passed, and we are invincible. All of the
achievements of man are dust—they are forgotten.*

*We stand, we know, we are. We stalked above man
ere we raised him from the ape. Long was the earth
ours, and now we have reclaimed it. We shall still reign
when man is reduced to the ape again. We stand, we
know, we are.*

The first time those words had insinuated themselves
into his consciousness, Kane had been overwhelmed,
shocked into a brief paralysis. The words and the message aroused panic, fear and despair in those who heard
them. Balam used a powerful psychological persua-
sion—humans cannot win, we are undefeatable, your

side is in the wrong, the fight isn't worth it, bow to the inevitable. Surrender.

This time, Kane managed to shake off the telepathically induced inertia. As the speech began to repeat, he dredged up anger, filled his mind with it and translated it into harsh, disrespectful words. "Fuck you. You're our prisoner, you're at our mercy. There's not a goddamn thing you can do to stop me if I decide to walk in there and break your neck."

We are old. When your race was wild and bloody and young, we were already ancient.

"Yeah, yeah, so you're old, so you're ancient. But the Na Fferyllt are a hell of lot older than you, aren't they?"

Like a voice tape rolling on continuous loop, catching and skipping a beat, Balam's words faded from their minds for an instant.

Kane pounced on that pause like a cat would a mouse. "I hit a nerve, didn't I? Na Fferyllt, the snakes. We're not wasting our time with you little gray bastards anymore. We're going after your daddies."

Your tribe has passed, and we are invincible. All of the achievements of man are dust—they are forgotten.

"We know where you came from," Kane continued, packing every word, every thought with a ruthless conviction. "And we're going there. You're beaten. You can't survive. Surrender."

We stand, we know, we are. We stalked above man ere we raised him from the ape. Long was the earth ours, and now we have reclaimed it.

In a clear, ringing voice, Brigid declared, "You think you know us. But you don't know our potential. You can learn from us, but nothing of value can be forced on us. You've subdued us, not destroyed us."

The mist boiled and billowed, and for a split second it faded altogether, as did the voice in their heads. Kane felt a thrill of savage satisfaction when he caught the briefest glimpse of an unnaturally slim figure, small and compact. For a fraction of a microsecond, he saw a long, pale gray head and a high, hairless cranium. The fog was generated by Balam's mind, a hypnotic screen to conceal his true appearance from the apekin who held him prisoner. For the fog to falter, even for an instant, meant that Balam was shaken, startled, perhaps even afraid.

New words entered their minds, and all of them were struck speechless with surprise.

Humanity must have a purpose, and only a single vision can give it purpose. Only one shared consciousness devoted to this single objective can hope to impose order. Your race was dying of despair. Your race had lost its passion to live and to create. We unified you. We stand, we know, we are—

Kane launched a fierce kick at the pane of glass. It shivered in its expanded metal frame, and the beads of moisture jumped. His voice rose to a hoarse, high pitch of fury. "You little pricks *stole* our passion to live and to create! We want it back! We'll *get* it back, even if we have to burn down your home to get it!"

In a billowing swirl, the mist seemed to recede, absorbed by the thick red shadows. Balam shifted to the far end of the recessed room and out of their sight.

"So much for an open discussion," Grant said grimly.

Lakesh murmured dolefully, "'Humanity must have a purpose.' Probably the closest thing to a statement of Archon Directorate policy we're ever likely to get."

He glanced toward Kane. "My congratulations,

friend Kane. For the first time in three years, Balam deviated from his patented 'we stand, we know, we are' address. Your instincts were sound. You found a chink in his armor of arrogance.''

Kane nodded, wiping away the film of clammy perspiration on his forehead. He suddenly felt numb with weariness.

Softly Brigid said, ''It—*he*—responded to us, interacted with us. Maybe we can open a dialogue with the Directorate and circumvent the barons altogether.''

Grant snorted out a laugh. ''That would be about as rewarding as barnyard animals negotiating for their freedom with the farmer.''

Kane turned his head toward him, a surge of anger beating the hot blood up in his face. His gray blue eyes blazed like the high sky at sunset. ''No,'' he said in a low monotone. ''Not barnyard animals anymore. Wolves. Lions. Tigers. Animals with fangs and claws and a taste for blood. *Predators.* And predators don't negotiate.''

Chapter 11

The following evening, a few minutes shy of midnight, Grant, Domi, Brigid and Kane convened in the ready room adjacent to the jump chamber. Since the intent was to arrive in England around sunrise, the departure had been scheduled for early morning, due to the difference in time zones. Brigid had spent most of the day delving into the database, wringing out every byte and bit of historical information regarding their destination.

Surprisingly, Grant was the only one who didn't question Domi's presence on the op. Responding to an inquiring look from Kane and a comment from Brigid, he said gruffly, "We couldn't have survived Idaho without her." Sotto voce, he added, "The kid needs something to occupy her."

Neither Kane nor Brigid responded, but both of them shared the same opinion—allowing Domi to risk her neck in a dark-territory probe was a curious way of helping her deal with grief.

As was SOP, they had stopped in the armory to select their ordnance. Kane and Grant each chose their usual combination of frag, incend and hi-ex grenades, attaching them to combat harnesses. With their Sin Eaters holstered at their forearms, they donned the long, black Mag-issue Kevlar-weave coats. Other odds and ends of equipment, like Nighthawk microlights, dark-vision glasses, rad counters and the motion sensor were distributed throughout their pockets.

Brigid wore her Mauser in a shoulder holster, beneath an ankle-length coat. Domi had to be talked out of choosing a S&W .357 Combat Magnum. With its long barrel and weight, it was too much pistol for her slight build.

At Grant's urging, she opted for a Detonics .45 Combat Master. A heavy-caliber autoblaster despite its compact size, its recoil could be easily controlled.

Under the long coats were dark, snug-fitting whipcord tunics and trousers. Tough leather boots encased their feet and ankles.

When they entered the ready room, Lakesh was waiting for them. The interphaser and its support systems rested within hollowed-out foam cushions in an aluminum carrying case. It was outfitted with O-ring seals that made it air- and watertight.

Turning to Brigid, he said, "Here is the keyboard and the power source." He flourished a small white card. "This is the equation and initiator sequence."

Brigid gazed steadily at the formula typed upon it.

Within moments, it had impressed itself indelibly on her eidetic memory and she closed the lid, securing the multilatch closure seals.

Lakesh passed a flat, sealed packet to Grant. "Maps, though how much good they will do you nearly two centuries after they were made, I have no idea."

To Domi, he handed a small, square metal box with a shoulder strap attached to it by steel rings. "Survival stores, darling girl. Dehydrated foodstuffs, distilled water, medicines."

They tensed as the jump time drew near. Grant eyed the door to the chamber with building apprehension. As

Kane expected, he mumbled his prejump mantra: "I *hate* those fucking things, I *hate* those fucking things."

Lakesh looked saddened, started to speak, closed his mouth, then opened it again. Very earnestly he declared, "I worry about you. I know I've impressed upon you the importance of this journey, but I'm—"

He broke off, shook his head and resolutely began once more. "I'm endangering your lives to test a theory of mine, but I don't want any more deaths on my conscience. Once you arrive in the British gateway, feel free to employ the LD option at your discretion."

The LD option, or the Last Destination setting, was a fallback device designed to bring mat-trans jumpers back to their point of origin if they materialized either in a hostile environment or not at their programmed destination.

"If you return here," Lakesh continued, "and tell me the risks were too great, not within reason, I won't question you."

Kane almost retorted *The hell you wouldn't,* but simply nodded in acknowledgment. He stepped toward the door. Out of the corner of his eye, he saw Domi lean forward and plant a quick kiss on the old man's seamed cheek.

The four of them went through the anteroom and entered the jump chamber. Right above the keypad was imprinted the notice Entry Absolutely Forbidden To All But B12 Cleared Personnel. Even after all this time, Kane had no idea who the B12 cleared personnel might have been.

Grant pulled the heavy, brown-tinted armaglass door closed on its counterbalanced hinges. The lock mechanism clicked and triggered the automatic initiator. A familiar yet still slightly unnerving hum arose, climbing in pitch to a subsonic whine.

Domi, who had made only one jump before, fearfully stared up and then down at the hexagonal plates on the floor and ceiling. They exuded a shimmering silvery glow that slowly intensified. A fine, faint mist gathered on the floor plates and drifted down from the ceiling. Thready static discharges crackled in the wispy vapor. The mist thickened, curling around to engulf them.

Kane watched the spark-shot fog float before his eyes. He leaned back and fell into infinity.

It wasn't exactly a fall. The sensation was as if he had tripped and soared headlong down a black staircase stretching to the very edge of eternity. He plunged through a multidimensional mural swirling kaleidoscopically across the fabric of space and time. He whirled between ever shifting patterns of colors he couldn't name, somersaulting over a never ending series of contrasting textures, hues and shapes.

Before him a coiling nebula glowed with a pure, blinding radiance. With eyes that should not have been able to see and ears that should not have heard, he saw the light take form and speak with a voice that vibrated to the core of his soul.

The light was a woman, sculpted from wheeling constellations, her eyes a pair of blazing stars. He could see her clearly, and she was too beautiful to bear, but he could not and would not tear his gaze away.

Golden and silver words spilled from her lips. The language she spoke was new yet not new, sounds from long, long before he was born, from out of his desperate dreams. A chaotic montage of images flashed wildly through his rolling consciousness—green hills, clear blue lakes, white surf spraying from bleak black rocks along a fog-shrouded cliff line.

"You have not changed overmuch, Cuchulainn, my darling Ka'in."

For an instant, Kane forgot everything—who he was, where he was from. The goddess with the hair spun from star stuff replaced his memories, gently set aside his identity. He felt a stark terror, then a wild ecstasy of love and lust, which rushed to fill an aching void within him.

"Fand," he called to her, yearning and hungry for the sound of her voice.

She reached out a hand for him, a hand like sparkling motes. He felt her touch, a million electrical impulses bestowing kisses and caresses on every cell, every atom of his being.

She whispered to him, sadly but lovingly, "Time is a river that twists on itself. Past, present and future are its waters. The fluid of time is life. When life, the spirit ceases to exist, time becomes meaningless. I am overjoyed your spirit lives still, Ka'in. There is still meaning."

Then she was gone, lost among the black gulfs of infinity.

"Fand!" He flung himself to where she had floated, diving through a dusting of stars.

The dust cleared and the metal plates beneath him lost their silver shimmer. He realized he lay on his stomach, right arm extended, hand and fingers locked around Brigid's ankle.

Her eyes slightly glassy and dazed, she asked, "What are you doing?"

Kane didn't answer because he didn't know. Even clean jumps left the brain temporarily confused and disoriented. He blinked, grimaced and levered himself into a sitting position, silently enduring the brief wave of vertigo crashing over him.

Grant and Domi stirred, knuckling their eyes and gazing around a bit unfocusedly. "This is different," Grant murmured.

With the exception of the prototype gateway in Dulce, the other mat-trans chambers they had seen all followed a set of general specs. The armaglass walls around them were not tinted, nor were they semiopaque. They were transparent and didn't reach the bottom of the raised platform. Gleaming vanadium alloy comprised half of the circular walls.

"Lakesh said this unit wasn't part of the official program," said Brigid, carefully rising to her feet. She swept a glance over her companions. "Does everyone feel all right?"

"I do," Domi answered, lithely standing up.

"Yeah," replied Grant, pushing himself erect. "A hell of an improvement over that jump to Russia."

Brigid cocked her head quizzically in Kane's direction. "You?"

He had made no move to rise. Frowning slightly, he said, "Physically, yes. Did anybody have jump dreams?"

Negatives were voiced all around. A bit anxiously, Brigid inquired, "Did you?"

Kane hoisted himself to his feet. "I don't know. Something happened, but—"

He broke off, shaking his head impatiently. Silently he cursed himself for an idiot. "Never mind."

Brigid regarded him suspiciously, then turned toward the door and what lay beyond it. A vast room yawned away into gray gloom, like a massive, hollow cylinder.

The convex ceiling was at least thirty feet high, and fluorescent light fixtures provided a feeble, flickering illumination. Banks of computer hardware lined the rounded walls. None of the indicators showed any power.

Kane and Grant slipped on their dark-vision glasses and affixed the microlights to their middle fingers, adjusting the Velcro bands so they fit like rings. Grant handed the motion sensor to Brigid. She set it and secured it around her left wrist, passing the case containing the interphaser to Domi.

Kane heaved up on the staple-shaped door handle, swung open the armaglass-and-alloy portal and stepped out into the chamber. Between the curving walls, the floor was flat, running away into the dimness like an aisle. He tensed his wrist tendons, and the Sin Eater slapped into his waiting palm. The four people fanned out across the room, Kane as always taking the point.

The only furniture was a carved wooden throne positioned at the head of a conference table. Dust thickly filmed both of them. Playing the beams of their lights around, they saw that the floors, walls and ceiling were made of some rough-textured fiber, like wood bark that had been sanded, polished and covered with coatings of lacquer.

"Place like a tunnel hollowed out of a tree root," Domi commented quietly.

Brigid nodded. "According to the *Wyeth Codex*, that's exactly what it is. She was held prisoner here, in the Druidic community of Wildroot."

Kane gave the electronics and computer bank an appraising glance. "Pretty sophisticated gear. Why isn't it working if the gateway is?"

"Separate power sources, probably," Grant said.

"Gateways have self-contained nuke generators, right?"

"Right," confirmed Brigid. She looked toward the far end of the tunnellike chamber, which melded into the shadows. "Dr. Wyeth didn't go into much detail about this place, but she did say it was a labyrinth. The sooner we start looking for a way out of here, the sooner we can figure out how to get to our prime objective."

They walked through the shaft, their feet sending up ghostly echoes as they scraped on the fibrous floor. The cold air smelled faintly of resin. The chamber narrowed into a corridor less than half the width and height of the room. It seemed full of sepulchral silences and haunted by memories of bloody and inhuman deeds. They felt uncomfortably like wraiths themselves.

The corridor didn't bend, but curved to the left and to the right, then back again. Finally it debouched to the right, opening at the mouth of a spiraling stairway that led down into darkness. The steps were carved out of a continuous growth of the fibrous wood, showing no seams or mortise joints. The risers showed smooth spots, worn by years of wear and weight.

The four people stopped, studied the opening, then Kane made a move forward. He halted. From somewhere far below sounded a faint echo—or something like an echo. He strained his hearing, then stepped forward again.

The motion sensor on Brigid's wrist uttered a discordant beep.

Chapter 12

Six green dots marched across the display screen in more or less a straight line. At the bottom edge of the screen, a changing column of digits flickered.

"Six of them," Brigid breathed. "About five—no, four—yards below us."

"How do we play it?" whispered Grant.

"By ear," Kane whispered in return.

Domi and Brigid withdrew into the corridor, fisting their blasters. Grant and Kane took up facing positions on either side of the stairwell opening, their Sin Eaters pointed downward. With hand signals, Brigid informed them of the movement and distance of the bodies below. Her hand froze, index finger extended to indicate one yard.

She gazed steadily at the face of the sensor, then looked up, eyes full of puzzlement and a growing alarm. She mouthed, "They've stopped."

Kane tilted his head toward the opening. He heard nothing, not even a rustle of cloth, a footfall or an intake of breath. A soft, almost apologetic chuff of sound echoed up the stairs.

Kane caught only the briefest impression of a squat metal cylinder arcing up between him and Grant, trailing a banner of smoke. A stunning, painfully loud thunderclap battered them. Solid bolts of hot air pounded into their stomachs, slamming their breath back into their lungs.

Synchronized with the bone-knocking concussion came a nova of white light of such hurtful, blinding intensity that his optic nerves were seared, overwhelmed. The lenses of his dark-vision glasses, treated to enhance ambient light, amplified the blazing flare.

He shouted, but he couldn't hear himself. Deaf and blind, he reeled from the concussive impact, seeing nothing but a triplet of blazing suns.

A numbing blow landed on the back of his neck, delivered with savage accuracy. The glare faded, a swift dissolution as black and still as death. Dimly he felt himself falling and he tried to catch himself by his hands, but they didn't seem to be there anymore.

He didn't lose consciousness, but he hovered at its brink for what felt like a very long time. His dazed brain identified the cylinder as a flash-bang bomb, a combination of a concussion grenade and magnesium flare. It had detonated less than three feet away, almost at head level.

Kane realized he was lying on his side on the hard floor. His ears replayed echoes of the detonation, and his head felt as if it were swelling to pumpkin size. Though his eyes were open, all he could see were swirling, multicolored spheres of light.

He tried to get up, but a boot sole slammed against the back of his head, mashing his face into the floor. Hands groped all over him, snatching away his coat, his Sin Eater and combat harness. They moved swiftly, with a practiced efficiency.

The heavy foot was removed, replaced by the unmistakable pressure of a cold gun barrel. Kane slowly sat up, spitting out bits of fiber. Something cold and hard snapped over his wrists, pinioning them close together. His vision slowly cleared, and he saw a pair of nickel-plated swivel-lock cuffs encircling his wrists. Raising his head, he squinted through the colorful spots swimming across his vision.

The six men were similarly trim, ramrod straight of carriage, brisk of movement and manner. They wore identical dark red uniforms consisting of hip-length leather jackets and berets canted at jaunty angles on their close-cropped hair. The berets bore the same insignia patches—a coiled, bat-winged serpent, bloodred outlined against a black background. Mirrored sunglasses concealed their eyes. All of them were armed with compact H&K MP-5 SD-3 subguns and M-92 Beretta autopistols in shoulder leather. The man looking down impassively at Kane cradled a squat MM-1 Multiround Projectile Launcher in his arms. The spring-powered weapon had obviously fired the flash-bang up the stairwell.

Each man bore strange markings on his face, geometric designs resembling black rectangles, chevrons and circles.

Through the fading roar in his head, Kane heard one of the men speaking in short, clipped sentences. "Yes, milord. Yanks, by the sound of them. Two men, two women. Exceptionally well armed."

A tall, rangy man bearing two black chevrons on his cheek spoke tersely into a comm unit he had pressed against an ear. "At once, milord. Lieutenant Galt out."

The man folded the comm unit and slipped it into a jacket pocket. Addressing one of the redcoats, he said, "Right, Corporal. Let's escort our guests to the compound. We've drilled on this eventuality long enough. Lord's regs, and all that."

The chevron-marked man looked down on Kane. "I am Lieutenant Galt of the Imperial Dragoons. You will accompany us. If you cooperate, you will not be harmed."

Kane swiveled his head around. His companions wore the same kind of cuffs, their hands bound in front of them. Domi kept her eyes screwed up, and tears leaked out of them, but Brigid kept a steadying hand on her left arm. Because of her albinism, the flash of blinding light caused her vision to suffer the worst effects.

Their belongings and equipment were distributed between three men. Galt carried the reinforced case containing the interphaser device. Carefully Kane got to his feet, keeping his expression composed and neutral.

At blasterpoint, the dragoons urged the four of them into the stairwell and down the steps. Galt led the way, backing down the stairs, subgun aimed directly at Kane's midriff.

Fleetingly he contemplated hurling himself forward, as if he had made a misstep, but the men bringing up the rear would no doubt open fire immediately, chopping the others to flesh gobbets.

Besides, the men hadn't offered to harm them. They were cold and professional. Magistrates would have gleefully exploited the opportunity to brutalize interloping outlanders.

The final turn of the stairway brought them into a leaden-skied and chilly dawn. Kane shivered, missing his coat. Breath steaming before his eyes, he took a quick visual circuit of their surroundings.

A gentle early-morning frost glistening on the grass, which slanted down toward a narrow stream. The foundations of long-vanished outbuildings were barely discernible in the ground.

Turning, he saw the mouth of the shaft was indeed a monstrous root, leading back to a tree of mind-staggering proportions. Even the smallest boughs were three times the breadth of Grant's body, the twigs thicker than his thigh. The tree butted up against the base of a grim mountain, looming high above them, the new sun blocked by the peak. The mountainside showed no vegetation whatsoever, stripped of turf and topsoil, showing only the dull gleam of dew-damp rock.

The squad fell into step around them and marched them down the slope to the stream, over a footbridge and toward a fenced-in compound. A dozen identically uniformed and armed men stood sentry duty around a cube-shaped blockhouse.

As Galt approached the door, a sentry stiffened to attention and snapped off a smart salute. Galt returned it. Kane couldn't help but admire the militaristic discipline evident in the soldiers. They kept their eyes straight ahead and they kept their curiosity about the strangers tightly in check.

Inside the blockhouse, men sat before screened consoles, many of them wearing headsets. They maintained a steady stream of brisk chatter in colorless voices. Kane picked up references to checkpoints, weather conditions and New London.

There were no women, and all of the men were of the same physical type, tall, rangy of build, fair-haired and skinned and each bearing a tattoo of some sort on his face.

As they were marched down a wide aisle, Kane managed to take a close look at one of the round-screened monitors and understood how their presence in the tree-tunnel had been detected. The console was linked to a wireless thermal-imaging system that broadcast the sudden difference in temperature to the tech.

Galt led them through a door on the opposite wall of the command post. Parked on a concrete apron was an armored six-wheeled vehicle, very similar to the Hotspur Land Rover in Cerberus.

The rear cargo doors hung open. Inside a pair of hard benches lined the walls and faced each other. Galt gestured. "Inside, please."

Kane didn't move. "Where are you taking us?"

Galt gestured again. "Inside." His omission of *please* was deliberate, a not-so-subtle message that he was not making a request.

Kane climbed up and slid to the far end of the right-hand bench, careful to step over the eyebolts screwed into the metal floorplates. Once his companions had taken seats, Galt climbed aboard, trailing a length of slender chain in one hand. Expertly he looped the chain between all of their cuffed wrists, threaded it through the openings of the eyebolts and padlocked the end to a stanchion near the rear door.

The four of them were forced to sit slightly forward, balanced on the edge of the benches, hands between their knees. The posture wasn't uncomfortable, but it was awkward. Their mobility was limited, and they couldn't even kick without entangling their feet in the chain.

Galt stepped out and slammed the door shut. A weak light filtered in through a small, wire-grilled window backing the driver's cab. For a long moment, no one spoke or even shuffled feet.

Finally Grant said, "These guys could teach Mags a few things about efficiency."

"They didn't even ask us any questions," Brigid remarked in a mystified tone.

"Or feel me up," said Domi.

The front doors clicked open and slammed shut. The engine roared into throbbing life, and with barely a lurch, the vehicle rolled forward. Diesel fumes wafted to them. Craning his neck, Kane peered through the grille. The front ob slits were wide-open, and beyond the hood of the Hotspur, he saw mostly green, rolling hills.

Sitting back as far as he could without putting a strain on his wrists, he looked across to Brigid. "Did the *Wyeth Codex* mention anything about soldiers like these?"

She shook her head. "No. There was a dearth of details in her journal about her experiences here. By her own words, she had so many adventures over a period of time, she couldn't possibly provide a blow-by-blow recounting of all of them. All she said about Wildroot was that its leader intended to release a plague bacteria into the underground water system. He planned to enter cryostasis for a century, then emerge into a world he could rebuild along ancient Celtic principles."

The vehicle took a curve, and Brigid swayed against Domi. "Some sort of revolt and an assault by a militia based in New London put the skids on the scheme."

"The dragoons may be the organizational descendants of that militia," Grant stated. "With that kind of threat in their history, no wonder a permanent garrison was posted there."

"And to guard the gateway," said Kane. "It stands to reason whoever commands the dragoons has knowledge of some aspects of the Totality Concept."

Brigid pursed her lips, nodding. "I'd say that was a

fairly safe assumption, but this time, let's not offer any information about it unless we're specifically asked.''

Grant did a poor job of repressing a smirk, and Kane scowled. Her oblique reference to what she considered his injudicious supply of Intel to Sverdlovosk in Russia was a thinly disguised barb.

He started to say something insulting, but she gave him a wry smile and he forced his scowl into a grin.

"If it makes you feel any better, Baptiste," he said patronizingly, "I'll put everything I know into the vault—including what you look like naked.''

Brigid's smile turned into a scowl.

Chapter 13

The road grew rougher, then progressively got worse. All of them were jolted, jounced and bounced. The vehicle slowed down, but not enough to smooth the ride.

The faint odor of brine crept into the compartment. Brigid sniffed and said, "I've never smelled the ocean, much less seen it, but we must be near Cardigan Bay."

None of them replied, since like the ville-bred Brigid, they had never been within five hundred miles of a sea, either the Cific or the Lantic. Even Domi, raised in the hinterlands outside direct barony control, had not seen a body of water larger than the Snake River.

For a time, after the nukecaust, Utah's Great Salt Lake extended its boundaries and became a true inland sea. Over the past three generations, however, it had receded substantially.

After an hour of being pummeled, the Land Rover turned eastward and the roadbed abruptly and mercifully became smooth. The sound and smell of other internal-combustion wags reached them.

Kane leaned forward to look out of the grille and through the open ob slits. A broad, blacktopped highway led toward a ville. He saw worked stone buildings, a few of them half as tall as the three-hundred-foot-high Administrative Monolith in Cobaltville. A twenty-foot stone wall stretched away from a pair of gateposts.

Glinting strands of razor wire curled along the top of it.

As the Land Rover rolled closer, Kane saw the gate-posts were capped by gun turrets, the hollow bores of 20 mm cannons protruding from them.

A steel latticework formed a barrier at the gate, with a checkpoint cupola standing just outside and to the left of it. Red-coated, bereted men patrolled the outer perimeter, marching in stiff-kneed formation.

The city wasn't as heavily fortified or quite as large as Cobaltville, but it ran a very close second.

The vehicle braked to a stop, and Kane tried to hear the murmured conversation between Galt and the checkpoint guard. The only words he caught were "Yanks" and "Strongbow."

The gate clanked open, and the Land Rover rumbled through it. The vehicle wound through narrow, cobble-stoned streets, past shopfronts and street merchants. The ville looked remarkably clean and fairly well populated. The citizenry, although simply dressed, had a well-scrubbed appearance. However, all the men, women and children seemed subdued, and from Kane's limited perspective, it seemed as if armed dragoons were posted at every intersection.

The Land Rover traversed a number of twisting lanes, then slowed down and braked to a complete halt. Kane saw the stone facade of a sprawling building. It stood tall and dignified, rising three stories above a small, velvet green park. A square stone-block tower extended straight up from the roof. Kane's practiced eye recognized a concealed gun emplacement. The engine of the vehicle was keyed off, the front doors opened.

Kane murmured to his companions, "Wherever we are, we've arrived."

Galt opened the rear door, unlocked the chain from the stanchion and drew it out through the eyebolts. He gestured for them to climb out. The Land Rover was parked at the very foot of a set of wide stone steps that led up to a brass-bound door set inside a deeply recessed, bevel-edged frame. A banner hung from a pole above it, depicting in red on a black background the coiled, winged serpent motif.

Galt lightly ran up the steps and pushed open the big door, indicating with a head nod the prisoners should follow. Kane glanced over his shoulder and saw a pair of the dragoons gazing at him watchfully. He walked up the stairs.

The entrance hall was dim and shadowy, quiet and cold. Curtains masked the tall windows on either wall, allowing only dim cracks of light to peep in. The four people followed Galt up another stone-stepped stairwell, down a short hallway and around a corner.

A carved wooden door rolled back smoothly on floor tracks, and Kane saw a small welcoming committee ready for their arrival. Two people waited inside an office that looked as if it were designed for the use of a baron. The room was wide, solid and almost aggressively masculine. As in the entrance hall, heavy drapes over the windows admitted only a little outside light. A pleasant wood fire blazed in the big hearth and cast wavering orange tones over the bookshelves, polished wood desk and four leather armchairs.

The gaunt man seated behind the desk was old, his long, thin face a parchment of tiny crevices and furrows. His short hair was the color of aged ivory. Gold braid festooned his red, carefully tailored uniform jacket, and the glow from the fireplace struck dancing highlights on shiny metal epaulets. A pair of mirrored sunglasses concealed the shape and color of his eyes.

He looked about seventy, but for some reason Kane guessed him to be older—considerably older. He seemed to radiate the same aura of a past age, another time and place, that Lakesh had about him.

To the right of the desk stood a woman with hair the color of steel, intricately woven into round braids on either side of her head. She was small, not much taller than Domi. Her fair-skinned, heart-shaped face was grave, though agreeably put together, with an impudent snub of a nose and full lips. Her mouth managed to look dainty, disapproving and sensual all at the same time. Her eyes were milky blue with no irises or pupils visible. She was dressed in a dramatic red blouse and bright green leggings, both of which hugged every curve and bulge of her voluptuous figure. Despite the disquieting effect of eyes that clearly lacked sight, Kane thought she was an attractive and colorful addition to the office.

Galt snapped off a salute and announced, "The interlopers, Lord Strongbow."

"Yanks. Americans." The old man's voice, not unexpectedly, was a whispery rustle. However, his lack of an accent was surprising.

Kane nodded. "That's right. You sound like one yourself."

Strongbow gestured to the woman. "Morrigan, suppose you give our guests the full treatment."

Kane and his companions stiffened, but made no other move. They didn't need to see Galt's hand steal toward the butt of his holstered Beretta to know that it had.

Strongbow said smoothly, "A necessary precautionary measure. Part of our regular routine when dealing with uninvited guests."

"We received the impression," muttered Grant, "that you don't get many of them."

No one responded to his comment. Morrigan clasped her hands together at the center of her midriff, drew in a long breath through her nostrils and held it. She stared unblinkingly, blindly at the four intruders. The braids in her hair slowly slid apart, unraveling and untwining, the separate strands stretching out.

Domi made a murmur of dismay, and Grant shifted his feet.

Sharply Strongbow said, "Calm down."

Like everyone else raised in and around the villes, Kane was familiar with the tales of doomies, or doom-seers. Human mutants possessed of a telepathic second sight, they were exceedingly rare in America. Most of them had been exterminated during the Program of Unification, although the rumor mills placed a few of them working secretly for the barons.

Kane clenched his teeth as he hastily tried to empty his mind, visualizing an impregnable brick wall around his memories and store of knowledge. A drill-bit of pain seemed to bore into the cranial bone at the center of his forehead. He cursed softly.

Strongbow spoke again, his husky voice not a request or an entreaty, but a command. "I said to calm down."

The realization that Morrigan could scramble their synapses if they resisted the probe didn't tend to calm Kane, or any of his friends.

A surge of angry fear leaped through him, then vanished, swallowed up in a warm, comforting sea of apathy. He wanted to lie down and rest. He raised his hand to pat back a yawn.

The wave of apathy receded, fell away, leaving in its wake a numbing headache. Kane swallowed his yawn and saw Domi thumbing her eyes, Grant rubbing his forehead and Brigid squinting at Morrigan. He also saw that all of them were seated in the leather armchairs.

Morrigan's hair had rebraided itself. She leaned one ample hip against the edge of Strongbow's desk. Gazing at the old man, Kane said, "Let's get this over with."

The thin lips twitched slightly. "It's over, Magistrate Kane. It's been over some few minutes now. Morrigan kept you asleep so she could tell me what she learned from your minds. Interesting tale. I believe we may be able to help each other."

He levered himself up out his chair and casually walked over to a wooden cabinet near the window. "Allow me to formally welcome you to New London's Ministry of Defense, seat of the Imperium Britannia."

Strongbow removed a crystal beaker full of cloudy amber liquid. As he poured the liquid into goblets, he said, "I know it's a bit early and a break with the tradition of tea, but brandy is a stronger stimulant. You need it to steady your nerves after the probe."

Brigid ventured softly, "What did the probe tell you?"

Strongbow handed her a glass, and she in turn passed it on to Grant. "You're from the Americas. I wondered how long it would take before the baronies dispatched representatives over here to renew old treaties."

Kane couldn't help but cast a swift, startled glance toward Morrigan. She stood motionless, face composed and serene.

"According to what Morrigan learned from you," Strongbow continued, passing around the other goblets, "you're highly placed intelligence officers in—" He faltered, broke off and looked over his shoulder toward Morrigan. "What was the name of that place again?"

In a soft, lilting voice, touched by a trace of an unidentifiable brogue, she answered, "Cobaltville."

Strongbow nodded. "Right. Cobaltville. Quaint. At any rate, that automatically makes you very valuable individuals to New London...indeed, to the entire Imperium."

Kane sipped at the brandy and nodded in appreciation. "Good stuff. From some hidden wine cellar that weathered the nukecaust and the skydark?"

"Synthetic, Magistrate Kane. The nukestorm caused most of the original London and much of southern England to drop into the ocean. Though salvage operations were conducted by survivors and their direct descendants, very little of use was ever recovered. Certainly not fine liquors."

Strongbow took a sip, smacked his lips and declared, "When I arrived here, some thirty years ago, New London was wild, disorganized and anarchic, controlled by the descendants of the original founders. Grubbers, cobbers, scavengers and lowlifes, all."

"And you," inquired Grant, "organized it?"

"Reorganized it, actually, reviving the Anglo-Saxon traditions. Except for New London, the country was divided into separate Celtic states. The old pagan, tribal system had taken root shortly after the holocaust. It required about twenty years, but I was successful in stamping it out—in England, anyway."

"It appears you modeled your city after twentieth-century police states," Brigid said.

Strongbow nodded shortly. "Very perceptive. I'm pleased you noticed. The British are by nature very responsive to regimentation if you strike the right chords of God and country. I struck them.''

"But you're not British,'' Grant argued.

Strongbow regarded him silently for a moment. "Nationalities ceased to have much meaning after January 20, 2001, Magistrate Grant.''

Kane had an idea of the direction Grant's questions might go, and to reroute them, he asked quickly, "In what way are we valuable to you, Lord?''

Strongbow turned toward him, pleased by the deferential, respectful note in Kane's tone. "The Imperium Britannia lives by its trade. We own the largest trading fleet in Europe and have regular routes with France and Germany. We've made inroads to the Mediterranean basin and even some localities in the Balkans. Next year, we may begin negotiations with the Russians, though they appear to have very little worth bartering for.''

Kane and Grant exchanged surreptitious glances. They could have told Strongbow that much.

"Even so,'' the man continued, "the Imperium is no stronger than the quality and quantity of our trade goods.''

Pacing to a window, Strongbow thrust aside a curtain, but the light level in the office didn't rise appreciably. In a quiet voice, he said, "Out there, less than three hours away by ship, lies a treasure trove of natural resources—precious metals, wood, water, cheap labor, all unpolluted and uncontaminated by the nuclear holocaust. And it is out of my reach.''

Strongbow paused meaningfully, and in a tone full of barely controlled frustration, declared, "Ireland.''

Chapter 14

New London's waterfront sprawled for miles along the coast in a broken checkerboard pattern of sooty warehouses, piers, docks and quays. It was so vast, the city proper seemed like an afterthought, a place to house and service the many laborers, longshoremen and sailors prowling the narrow lanes.

All manner of seagoing craft bobbed on their moorings, from diesel-powered barges to freighters to trawlers and even a few three-masted wooden ships.

From the back of the armor-plated touring car, Strongbow said, "Before I established the Imperium, piracy was the primary manner of infusing revenue into New London. Shockingly inefficient."

"You made it efficient?" inquired Brigid.

"By outlawing it. The only long-range result of such depredations was the alienation of other countries. I will concede that I've assigned commissions to certain captains of certain patrol boats. They are authorized to search vessels for contraband and confiscate it, if necessary."

Brigid smiled wryly. "It used to be called privateering. Legalized piracy, if I remember right."

Kane stopped himself from commenting, *No doubt you do.* Instead, he asked, "What about the imperial navy?"

Strongbow leaned back on the soft seat cushions. "That is what I wish to show you."

The touring car was a long, low-slung vehicle, a gleaming silver in color with the bewinged-serpent sigil painted on the hood. Flaring, chrome-lined tail fins rose at sharp angles from the rear end. Galt sat in a separate driver's cockpit, while Strongbow and his guests relaxed in a spacious, plushy passenger compartment.

The man seemed anxious to show off New London, wanting to find out how it compared to the American villes.

"Before the nukecaust," he told them, "a great effort had been put into restoring the quayside, to make it attractive to tourists. A pity all that time and money was wasted."

When Strongbow asked direct questions about the general conditions in America, Kane allowed Brigid to field them. To his mild surprise, she was frank and forthcoming, though she didn't even hint at the Archon Directorate.

Strongbow accepted everything she said, which was another surprise. Kane had the distinct impression he knew the answers beforehand. He doubted Morrigan could have provided him with much more than an overview. As it was, he still wasn't sure if she had deliberately lied to Strongbow about what she had seen in their minds, or if her psi-powers were unreliable.

The vehicle rolled along a lane between the docks and the looming warehouses. Gazing out a side window, Kane sighted a flock of birds, swooping, hovering and diving, black ravens and white seagulls. Several flapped their way toward perches on warehouse roof eaves, clutching small chunks of some substance in their beaks and claws.

Galt steered the car past an open plaza between a pair of the warehouses. Erected in the cobblestoned center was a scaffold. From the crossbar dangled three bodies, nooses cinched tight around broken necks. Squawking birds fluttered around the corpses, pecking and hacking away. There was no way to tell if the bodies had been male or female, but the few strands of hair still clinging to the scalps were red. Judging by their builds and heights, the corpses didn't appear to be those of full-grown adults.

Following Kane's gaze, Strongbow murmured, "Irish spies one of my patrol boats picked up."

"They're kids," replied Kane flatly.

One of Strongbow's shoulders moved in a dismissive shrug. "Another old British practice I've revived. Nits make lice."

It wasn't just an English tradition, Kane reflected fleetingly. During the Program of Unification some eighty years before, it had been an official barony policy of dealing with rebels, muties and stubborn outlanders.

The touring car passed beneath a stone arch, manned on either side by blank-faced dragoons. Galt steered around the base of an observation tower, then braked smoothly to a halt. He climbed out of the driver's compartment and opened the rear doors.

Everyone disembarked, shivering in the dank, raw wind that blew over the swells. Their coats hadn't been returned, and the sea breeze was like a knife. They followed Strongbow down a wide-planked wharf. Black, oily water lapped at splintery pilings.

Tethered by heavy-duty hawsers, rocking gently, was a sleek, sharp-prowed vessel. Painted a flat, sinister black, its streamlined, oddly faceted contours lent it a resemblance to a gigantic knife blade.

Placed amidships, the snouts of three 40 mm cannons jutted out from behind metal deck shielding. Affixed near the bow was a quartet of three-foot-long hollow pipes angled upward at forty-five degrees. A pair of tripod-mounted L7-A1 heavy-caliber machine guns was bolted to the roof of the elevated bridge housing.

Gesturing to the vessel, Strongbow announced proudly, "The *Cromwell.* Corvette class, 114 tons, with over fifty knots maximum speed on smooth seas. Armed with a Bofors deck cannon, an Exocet missile launcher, machine guns and a Limbo antisubmarine depth-charge system. Regenerative gas turbine engines and an emergency diesel-electric drive. She was one of the first ships to apply stealth technology. State-of-the-art, two hundred years ago."

"Antisubmarine?" Grant repeated a trifle doubtfully. "You find much use for that system nowadays?"

Strongbow smiled cryptically. "You'd be surprised."

He walked beside the streamlined corvette, running an affectionate hand along the hull. "The old Royal Navy made only a handful of these beauties. After their war in the Falklands, they found less and less use for them. Warfare had progressed beyond naval engagements."

Strongbow strode to the end of the pier and gazed out across the open sea. Metallic gray clouds scudded low over the roiling waves, seeming to blend in with the dully mirrored surface.

Tucking his hands into his pockets, Kane asked, "With all your other vessels, what use do you find for it?"

"*Her,* Magistrate Kane," Strongbow corrected him sternly.

Kane and Grant exchanged irritated glances. "What

use do you find for *her?*'' Kane asked again, not able to suppress a sarcastic emphasis on the last word.

If Strongbow noticed, he chose to ignore it. "The *Cromwell* is the flagship of an invasion fleet."

"The invasion of Ireland?" Brigid suggested, fingering a wind-tossed strand of hair from her face.

"Exactly. The crowning achievement of my life."

"I figured as much," she replied.

"How so?"

"You provided a few not very subtle clues from the beginning. First of all, there's your name. Richard de Clare was a twelfth-century Norman aristocrat who was known as Strongbow. He led the first completely successful British invasion and occupation of Ireland."

"True. He possessed the ramrod discipline that had made the Roman legions invincible." An edge slipped into his voice. "My namesake with only three thousand soldiers cut through the Irish hordes like grain before a reaper. Ireland was brought under the British heel, a rule which lasted some seven hundred years."

Brigid nodded. "Then, of course, there's your obvious antipathy toward the Celts."

Loathing oozed from Strongbow's every syllable. "The pagan bastards took advantage of a wounded England, still trying to recover its strength after the nuke-caust. They overran the kingdom, breeding like rats. Tree-worshiping savages living like wild animals in the bogs and forests. England could not recover its glory with those parasites sucking away her strength."

Kane had heard the same ruthless creed expressed many times against outlanders. He cast a glance toward Domi to gauge her reaction. She looked bored, picking absently at a flake of paint on the corvette's cleat.

"And then, of course," Brigid continued, "there is

the name you chose to christen this vessel. Oliver Cromwell waged a genocidal war against the Irish in the seventeenth century. Five-sixths of the population perished.''

"Indeed," Strongbow asserted with a smile. "An extraordinary man, he and his legion of ironsides. They swept across the depth and breadth of that damn isle, extirpating the savages by sword and flame."

Squaring his shoulders, he turned to regard all of them impassively. "So you see, we have a common cause. You wish to go to Ireland, and I wish to help you do so."

"Why us?" Grant asked. "With your firepower, why haven't you invaded before now?"

"I've tried. I've failed."

"What kind of defenses do they have?" inquired Kane.

"The kind that firepower, ships and soldiers cannot breach," Strongbow answered. "Unnatural weapons, foul enchantments from the days of the Druids."

"Example," Kane requested.

"A *geas,* a spell cast over the minds of any New Londoner who approaches the coast. The isle always seems hidden by a fog bank which never lifts. Even my finest navigators can't seem to find it, regardless of their reliance on their instruments.

"And there are the selkies…half-human amphibian monstrosities skulking beneath the waves to sabotage my ships and drag my men down to their dooms."

Kane stared at the man, momentarily nonplussed. The last thing he had expected from his thin lips was a spouting of superstition. Trying hard not to smile, he commented, "The fog bank is probably due to mind muties, false perceptions implanted in your sailors. The selkies are other muties, genetically adapted to live in the water.''

"Do you think I could not come up with those self-same inane explanations?'' Strongbow's tone was charged with angry frustration. "You know nothing of the creatures who dwell on that damn island!''

"Tell us, then,'' Brigid urged quietly.

Strongbow took a deep, calming breath. "Thousands of years ago, a nonhuman race settled in Ireland. They've had many names over the course of the centuries—the Sidhe, the Gentry, the Tuatha De Danaan. They came from outside our narrow concepts of space and time, in great numbers and with unknown powers. Their are ethnic legends filled with stories of beings who made themselves known and felt and then vanished. But the Danaan did not disappear. They were only displaced from their position of supremacy. They did not flee, but merely hid. After the nukecaust, they returned to claim the island. Since then, they haven't gone beyond their borders, but they ruthlessly destroy all human vessels venturing inside. About eighty-five years ago, General Graham Adams, Taylor Henstell and a privateer named Johnson set sail with a great fleet to recover Ireland. Not one ship, not one man returned. Until I established the Imperium, all of England shunned the whole Irish Sea as a region accursed.''

Strongbow's face twisted. "There was even a sailor's legend that the souls of drowned Englishmen went to Ireland, to be tortured by the Sidhe for all eternity.''

"*That* you find a superstition, I hope,'' said Grant mildly.

Strongbow gave him a cold look. "Don't patronize me. You are in my service. I am evoking the old treaty of cooperation between the British Empire and the

United States of America. I expect—no, *demand*—the same obedience you would give to your baron.''

Kane quashed the sudden surge of anger. "Why do you want to invade Ireland at all?"

"Because power over the Tuatha De Danaan is only a preliminary step to something far beyond your understanding, a component of a plan stretching back many centuries."

"Who runs things over there?" Brigid asked.

"I have only rumors, pieced together from captured spies. A Danaan sorceress called Fand. The Irish believe she is a goddess, and she exploits that to the fullest. But she is mortal, born of a human mother. She can die."

Kane stiffened with a sudden suspicion. "So what do you want from us?"

"The Celtic people have rallied around her, even those who still live in secret here in the Imperium. Kill her, and they will lose faith in their ancient belief of guardians from a world invisible."

"If you and your fleet couldn't make a beachhead," said Grant, "I doubt that the four of us could."

Strongbow tapped his temple with a long forefinger. "Belief is their strongest weapon. My soldiers, as tightly disciplined as they are, have been weaned on folk tales about the demon-infested isle of Erin. Even the few pockets of Celts existing here are the source of fables. None of you have been exposed to that kind of generational, archetypal conditioning. Morrigan reported to me that you were all excellently trained and accustomed to completing hazardous missions, regardless of the cost."

Brigid fixed her penetrating emerald gaze on the mirrored lenses of the man's glasses. "And did Morrigan happen to mention why we have been dispatched to Ireland?''

"Of course. Otherwise, I would have had all of you executed. You are members of the Trust, a select, baron-approved task force. Your overall mission is to seek out and seal naturally occurring quantum interphase points before they can be used against the Archon Directorate.''

Chapter 15

Strongbow's burst of laughter didn't warm the blood. It was like the rustle of parchment against dry bones.

"Don't look so astonished. Do you think I could have achieved what I have without the help of the Directorate in some fashion?"

Kane realized that with the exception of Domi, his wide-eyed, startled expression was duplicated on the faces of his friends. With effort, he smoothed it away. "Forgive us, sir. In the baronies, knowledge of the Directorate is restricted to such a small few, it didn't occur to us that you might have been briefed."

Strongbow gave a snort of derision. "I was briefed long before any of you were born. I dare say I know more about the Archons and their true history than most of your barons."

The hard note of conviction in the man's voice made doubting his words a distant option. Kane knew Lord Strongbow wasn't simply a territory-grabbing opportunist with dreams of empire, but beyond what Kane had already seen of the man, he was an unknown quantity. A chill of fear spread at the base of Kane's spine.

Strongbow turned away and marched back to the touring car, where Galt stood waiting beside the open rear door.

The drive back to the ministry building was surprisingly short. Galt had evidently followed the scenic route on their way to the waterfront area. When the touring car parked before the entrance, Strongbow said, "Matters of government will occupy me for the rest of the day. Lieutenant Galt will show you to your quarters. Later I will make myself available for your briefing."

The four of them followed Galt through the entrance hall. Kane considered questioning him on a few details, but knew he wouldn't receive satisfactory answers.

They proceeded into a big, high-ceilinged Victorian common room, cozy with overstuffed leather furniture, polished oak tables and tall, crowded bookshelves. A bay window at the far end looked out over a garden. It was barred on the outside. Four doorways lined the facing walls.

Galt said, "You may choose your own bedrooms. The loo is down the hall, to your left. Any questions?"

"Yes," said Grant. "What's a loo?"

"I believe you Yanks call it a bathroom." With that, he backstepped out and closed the door behind him. Kane waited for the click of a lock, but it never came. He heard only Galt's measured footfalls receding down the corridor.

Domi flopped into an armchair and bounced on it, saying, "This place is niiiice."

Kane almost shushed her into silence, but decided to let her babble, if that was what she wanted. Both he and Grant searched the corners and light fixtures for miniature spy-eyes or sound pickups. They found nothing, but that didn't mean they weren't there.

They inspected the bedrooms, which all featured hard mattresses and canopies. Kane chose one at random and immediately stretched out on the bed. Through the doorway, he saw Brigid whispering into Domi's ear, who nodded and began singing in a high, lilting voice. The song was some mindless drivel about a wide river. At least, Kane thought sourly, it wasn't the "Ballad of Ryan Cawdor."

Brigid entered the room and sat down gingerly on the edge of the bed, as far from Kane as she could manage. He whispered, "I don't bite, Baptiste."

Her response was an annoyed slitting of her eyes. "How do you figure he knows about the Directorate? He claims to have arrived here thirty years ago. From where? Not America, or he'd have more knowledge of the baronies."

"Well," Kane said slowly, quietly, "Maybe he knew about the plans for the baronies before they were actually implemented, before they were realities."

Brigid's emerald eyes widened slightly. "And maybe he slept through the unification program. Maybe he slept through skydark."

"And maybe he's a freezie, like Lakesh. Is that what you mean?"

"What do you think?"

"I asked you first."

She sighed. "Until we get some answers, what are we going to do?"

"For the time being, accept the hospitality of the Imperium Britannia."

"Morrigan lied to Strongbow about us, or simply couldn't get an accurate psi-read. If the latter is the case, she might probe us again."

"If the latter is the case," he replied very softly, "then a second probe will be an admission of her failure, something Strongbow probably takes a very dim view of. No, I think she deliberately misled him."

"Why?"

He started to shake his head, remembered the possibility of a spy-eye and said simply, "I don't know. But I know we'll find out."

"Until then," Brigid said, "we've got to keep up the facade of operatives sent from the Directorate."

She winced as Domi hit an off note, wavered, then went on with her song. "It's going to be tough to explain her. She's not exactly operative material."

"Strongbow probably thinks she came along to warm Grant's bed."

Brigid lifted an eyebrow. "Don't expect me to give him that impression about you and me."

Smiling slyly, Kane reached over and patted her leg. In a normal speaking tone, he announced, "Not right now, sweetheart. I have some thinking to do."

She drew back quickly, standing up, lips working as if she might spit at him. In an angry rush, she stalked from the room.

Kane chuckled, but he felt a twinge of shame, too. He shouldn't have teased Brigid, but the temptation to get a rise out of someone who displayed all the sense of humor of his Sin Eater was sometimes just too tempting.

He turned onto his right side and slept an hour or two, soaking the rest into his bones. When he awoke, late-afternoon sunlight slanted in through the bay window in the common room. Finally seeing the sun made him feel better.

Swinging his still booted feet over the edge of the bed, he stood up, stretched and went out into the empty common room. He checked the bedrooms. Everyone, including Domi, napped alone. They had all learned to catch sleep whenever they could, so as to build up a reserve, in case they had to go for long periods without it.

He walked out into the hallway into the bathroom, or loo, as Galt had referred to it. He relieved himself at one of the three urinals, washed his hands and face in the sink. Lifting his head, he glanced briefly into the mirror, froze for a second, then pivoted violently on a heel, droplets of water flying from his face and hands, adrenaline racing through his system. The hairs at the nape of his neck prickled.

Morrigan stood before a toilet-stall door, hands clasped primly behind her back, staring at him blankly.

Angry and embarrassed that he hadn't noticed her presence or entrance earlier, he took a swift step toward her. He put his hands flat against the stall door so that she was prisoned between them. She tilted her chin. Despite her odd, pale eyes, she had a proud, defiant look to her.

"What do you want with me?" Kane demanded.

Softly she answered, "I intend no harm. Neither will I run away."

Kane let his hands drop. Bluntly he asked, "Did you lie to Strongbow about us?"

"Of course. Had I not, you would be hours dead by now."

Kane gave her a slightly mocking smile, though he knew she couldn't see it. He was startled when she returned it. "I thought you were blind."

"Hardly. One does not need eyes to see. I daresay my vision is far greater and deeper than your own. I see nothing but danger for you and your friends."

"Why do you care what happens to us?"

Her tone was slightly scornful. "I care but little for anyone but my people."

"And who are they?"

Morrigan strode deliberately to the sink, leaned forward and breathed heavily on the mirror to fog it. With a finger, she quickly drew three narrow triangles topped by circles.

"The Priory of Awen," Kane said. "Your people?"

"I am a member of that order," she answered somberly. "I glimpsed a vague awareness of us in your minds."

"Then you know of our true mission here."

"Aye, Ka'in, I do."

His breath caught momentarily in his throat. "Why do you call me that?"

A sad, knowing smile touched her lips. "It is your name, or one of them. Your spirit has borne many throughout the long tide of time, as has your *anamchara*."

Kane squinted at her. "My what?"

"Soul friend, she who carried the name of a goddess."

"You mean Baptiste?"

"Brigid, aye. I recognized both of you by your spirits, by your souls' faith in each other. You represent the trinity of soul, heart and mind, which the emblem of my order symbolizes."

Kane paused, not knowing how to respond. He tapped his foot impatiently, then said, "So *you* say. What do you want of us?"

"You and your friends have to get away from here now, while you have the chance. Strongbow lied to you. He will use you and then kill you."

"Why are you with him?"

"I was placed here as a child by the order. Because of my gifts, I am useful to him."

"So you're not British?"

She shook her head. "My mother was a woman of the isle, raped by one of Strongbow's dragoons."

"Just who the hell is he, and what's his real agenda?"

Morrigan wiped the mirror drawing away with a shirtsleeve. "He is a vicious, venal man, no longer truly human. As for his agenda, he has allied himself with dark principalities to avenge a millennia-old humiliation."

"Avenge what? And revenge on whom?"

"The Tuatha De Danaan."

"What do you know of them?"

Morrigan opened her mouth to reply, then closed it, cocking her head to one side. She hissed Kane into silence. With surprising grace and speed, she slipped past him and into the toilet stall, closing the door quietly behind her.

A second later, Kane heard the footfalls in the hallway outside. Galt opened the door wide and peered in.

"Lord Strongbow sent me to fetch you. You are to join the rest of your party in the council room."

He stood expectantly until Kane walked to the door and then he backed out into the hallway. Kane followed him, eyeing his stiff, long-legged gait. A description Grant had once applied to Salvo came to mind: *He walks like a he's got a corncob up his ass.*

Kane chuckled softly. Galt turned his head slightly and regarded him coldly, but all he got was a wide-eyed look of innocence.

They passed the suite of rooms assigned to them, and instead of going up the stairwell, Galt turned a corner, opened a door and went down a wide flight of steps. He managed to keep to the center, and Kane had no choice but to follow in his wake.

The psychological ploy was old, a cheap dominance stratagem. Kane wondered what Galt's reaction would be if he accidentally tripped and fell against him, knocking him down the stairway.

As though he had caught the notion in Kane's mind, Galt stopped at the landing and stared directly at him. His stance showed a sudden awareness that he was in the presence of a dangerous adversary, and it was tactically unwise to allow him to dog his heels.

Side by side, they walked down the rest of the steps. The council room occupied at least half of the building's underground foundation and seemed to stretch on for a mile. Unlike the upper floors of the ministry, the walls and ceiling were made of slick, slightly reflective bluish metal. Kane recognized vanadium alloy, a nearly indestructible sheath around the nerve center of the Imperium Britannia.

Light pulsed here and there, haloing upright glass cases holding mementos of human warfare over the centuries. Reverently mounted in spotlit displays were broadswords, maces, suits of medieval armor, halberds, poleaxes, match- and-flintlock blasters, battle standards from thousand-year-old military campaigns. There was too much to absorb, much less easily identify.

At the far end of the aisle was a conference table, a highly polished, ten-foot-diameter disk of rare and expensive teak. Grant, Brigid, Domi and Strongbow were already seated. Kane took a chair between Grant and Brigid while Galt assumed a parade-rest position behind Strongbow's high-backed chair.

The man sat silently, appearing to think over some weighty decision. He reached down beside his chair and lifted up the metal case containing the interphaser. He slid it across the tabletop toward Brigid. "Open it."

She exchanged a quick, alarmed look with Kane.

"Open it," repeated Strongbow, biting out each word.

Maintaining a neutral demeanor, Brigid undid the intricate system of locks and latches, lifting the lid and turning it around so Strongbow could inspect its contents. He eyed the metal pyramidion, the small battery pack and keypad without altering expression.

"Project Cerberus technology," he said at last.

They all did their best to keep astonishment from registering on their faces.

"I knew they had managed to manufacture the mattrans inducers in modular form, but I had no idea they'd been successful with miniaturization."

Strongbow's tone wasn't suspicious; it was irritated, as if he were miffed about being left out of an Intel loop. Evidently Morrigan had supplied him with the impression that the device was of predark vintage, not the product of Lakesh.

He said, "Power it up."

Hesitantly Brigid replied, "Lord, the instrument is designed to interact and interface with natural quantum vortices. I don't think—"

"I am not requesting your thoughts." Strongbow's dry voice echoed harshly. "I am demanding you follow my orders. Now."

Domi shot him a fierce, red-eyed glare. The imperious tone pricked a layer of that outlander anger toward authority that was under her skin.

Strongbow noticed the hostility and didn't appreciate it. "Girl, you are here as a courtesy and at my sufferance. If you prefer to be ejected and held in irons, Lieutenant Galt will arrange for it."

Grant tensed his leg muscles, fixing his eyes on the

lieutenant, ready for him to make a move toward Domi. An unmistakable tension hung in the air, but Brigid returned all the attention to herself by noisily removing the interphaser and its support systems from the case. The busy clatter focused all eyes on her hands. Deftly she attached the small power unit and plugged in the keypad to the input port.

As she worked, she began a brisk commentary. "As Lord Strongbow is no doubt aware, the pyramidion shape is not arbitrary or for aesthetic purposes. Energy progresses by four different routes, rejoining in a single conclusionary figure at the apex. The energy flows in a helix spiral pattern exactly opposite and of equal frequency, and the intensity on each side of the vortex at any given point triggers a quantum induction shift by vibrational resonance."

Kane listened to her technobabble admiringly. Strongbow nodded impatiently, as though he understood every word and wanted to dispense with explanations. His interest was in results.

Brigid's fingers tapped in a numerical sequence on the keypad. "Like so."

Kane felt the fine hairs in his nostrils, on his arms and legs tingle. At the edges of his hearing, he sensed a distant, muffled roar, a sound he couldn't focus on or even really be sure he heard.

The air in the room seemed to thicken, to swell in the lungs, making respiration labored and difficult. Drawing in a deep, raspy breath, Grant muttered, "What the hell is going on?"

A line of consternation creased Brigid's smooth forehead. She tapped the keys quickly. "Some sort of power fluctuation, almost a surge. I'll take the data infeed off-line."

A softly glowing funnel of light fanned up from the metal apex of the pyramidion. It looked like a diffused veil of flame, with tiny shimmering stars dancing within it. It expanded into a swirling borealis several feet above the table, spreading out along the ceiling.

Heads back, they gaped up as the wreath wavered and billowed and coalesced. Brigid murmured in a strained whisper, "This isn't right—this shouldn't happen!"

Part of the cone of incandescence rippled and bulged as if it were a semisolid membrane and reacted to a force exerted on it from within. The corona shifted and shimmered, and a woman's face formed in the pastel light patterns, a face bearing a nimbus of beauty that was almost heart-wrenching to see. The eyes radiated a too great wisdom, and there was irresistible yet terrifying power in her. The smile on her full lips was subtly cruel and compassionate at the same time.

Kane knew her name, but he couldn't speak it. He stared stupidly, desperately wanting to call to her, but he was frozen in place, struck speechless.

"Fand!"

The shriek burst from Strongbow's lips, erupting from a deeply rooted core of mingled terror and rage. Kane caught a glimpse of him sitting in a stiff and unnatural posture, the aura from the cone of light washing all color from his face and form.

The quality of the light changed, strobing to a deep, searing red. A finger of it stretched out, extending like a shimmering pseudopod. It seared the air viciously toward Strongbow's face. Crying out hoarsely, he flung his arms up over his eyes, lunging backward, his chair tipping over. Galt made a move as if to catch him, but the finger of light formed into a stabbing spear. Adroitly he managed to twist aside to avoid the thrust, but Strongbow and his chair toppled over with a crash and a clatter.

Moving far too quickly for the human eye to follow, the light lanced sideways, hugging the wall of the council room, following a streaking path down the display-case-lined aisle. As it hurtled up the center like a meteor, glass exploded in razor-edged showers. The noise of a dozen glass panes all shattering almost simultaneously made a deafening, nerve-stinging cacophony.

The bolt of energy blazed a 180-degree change of course, arcing around and returning to the funnel of light spreading up from the pyramidion. It disappeared into it like a pebble dropped into a pond. The cascade of light whirled and spun like a diminishing cyclone, shedding sparks and thread-thin static discharges. As quickly as it appeared, the glowing cone vanished, as if it had been sucked back into the tip of the interphaser.

Everyone sat motionless, eyes swimming with multicolored spots, shaken and stunned. The jangling of glass falling from the display case's frames was the only sound in the room.

Strongbow groaned shortly and deeply. Galt helped him to his feet. Though Strongbow's head was bowed, Kane saw the sweat sheening his face. The musty reek of it filled the council room with a repulsive miasma. Years before, he and Grant had stumbled on a snake pit in a hellzone, and Strongbow exuded the same tainted odor of reptilian things slithering in cold dark places.

Strongbow had lost his mirrored sunglasses in the fall and he held them in one hand. Before he slipped them back on, everyone saw his face.

A faint interlocking pattern of scales ringed his brow ridges, extending over and meeting at the bridge of his nose. The deeply socketed eyes were large, almond shaped, with black vertical slits centered in the golden, opalescent irises.

The eyes were the worst.

Chapter 16

The moment Lakesh coalesced from the carrier beam, he knew something wasn't right. Not wrong exactly, but he sensed an overall sensation of nonrightness.

He stood in the gateway chamber, swaying dizzily, waiting for the vertigo to pass and the spark-shot mist to fade. He checked himself over to make sure all his parts, even his green bodysuit with the rainbow insignia of the Historical Division had made the transition.

As one of the very first human beings whose entire molecular structure had been converted to digital information and transmitted along a hyperdimensional path and reassembled into the organic original, Lakesh was inured to the physical side effects. Even before the nukecaust and his century-long cryonic sleep, he knew more about quantum interphase mat-trans inducers than any other person alive.

Now, over two hundred years after his inaugural mat-trans jump, he was the only human who was intimate with all of the devices' maddeningly intricate workings. That specialized knowledge made him a valuable treasure to Baron Cobalt. There were other refugees from predark times scattered throughout the network of villes, scientists and statesmen, but he was the last of the original architects of Project Cerberus, the keystone of the Totality Concept.

And he was also a traitor to the oath he had sworn

two centuries ago, as well as to the one he had taken upon his revival and induction into the Trust.

Turning the handle in a pewter gray armaglass door, Lakesh stepped out of the jump chamber. As usual, the little control complex hidden in a strongroom on Level A of the Administrative Monolith was deserted. Nevertheless, he was back in the world of the baronies, of the villes.

They were all alike—Ragnarville to the extreme north, Sharpeville to the east, Palladiumville to the south. Dedicated to spreading the doctrines of the Archon Directorate, the walled cities with their planned ghettos offered meaning for the elite and a lifetime of thankless servitude for the underclass.

Lakesh hated the villes. In them, the modes of dress, even the thoughts were imposed from without. Only the gateway chamber offered even a temporary escape from the baron's cushioned tyranny.

Knowledge and use of the gateway unit was restricted to the baron, his personal staff and a very few, very select members of the Trust. Only Lakesh enjoyed free and unmonitored access to the chamber. When he reactivated the Cerberus redoubt, he had made certain the unit there possessed no traceable transit-feed connections to any other functioning gateway. Even if someone had the knowledge to replay the computer records of the jumps made from the Cobaltville unit, they would not show his true destination. Rerouting data infeed circuitry had been the work of five minutes.

As he crossed the control room, he reflected on his reservoir of good fortune. So far, his double life hadn't been questioned, and if the Magistrate Division harbored suspicions, they knew better than to voice them.

His role as senior archivist in the Historical Division

was a front. As far as the baron was concerned, his true purpose was to ferret out any and all archivists who stumbled across information regarding humanity's long relationship with the Archons and report them to the proper authorities.

In reality, Lakesh used his position to select likely prospects to join his underground resistance movement. So far, his only real success had been Brigid Baptiste, and even she would have been lost to him if not for the unforseen involvement of Kane.

As a scientist, he was unaccustomed to dealing with visceral emotions. The larger, logical part of his mind knew his tiny enclave of exiles could never overthrow the Directorate or their intermediaries, the barons—certainly not by staging a guerrilla war.

Humankind, at least those who were ville bred, had been beaten into docility long ago. In the Outlands, a fragile, disorganized freedom remained, pockets of roamers, half-feral mutants who had survived the purges and tribes of Amerindians who had returned to their traditional way of life.

But even taken together they represented only a small minority. The population of hybrids swelled even as the few truly human beings on earth were killed and bred and co-opted out of existence.

Lakesh fought back a surge of guilt. It wasn't an emotion he was used to grappling with, and certainly not one he enjoyed. Nevertheless, the guilt was neither neurotic not misplaced. He and other twentieth-century scientists had willingly traded in their human heritage for a shockscape of planet-wide ruin. After all, they had been selected to survive in order to reshape humankind in a nonhuman image.

He reached the door leading to the anteroom and

paused to slip into the persona of a wizened, slightly dotty senior archivist. His shoulders slumped, his liver-spotted hands acquired a slight palsy and his bespectacled eyes took on a vacant look, as if he were staring at some distant point.

So far, his luck at portraying a semisenile favorite of the baron had held, although the odds were it would fail sooner than later. His memory leaped back to New Year's Eve, 2000. He and other members of Project Cerberus had been allowed to leave their subterranean vanadium-alloy tower in Dulce to witness firsthand the arrival of the new millennium.

He had never been to Manhattan before, and the awareness that it would become a radioactive slag-heap in less than a month had added a heart-wrenching poignance to the visit. In the company of fellow scientists and security wardens, he had attended a Broadway show, a revival of an old musical, *Guys and Dolls.*

Lakesh turned the doorknob, humming the opening bars of "Luck Be a Lady."

A member of the Baronial Guard waited for him. His crisp white uniform jacket, red silken trousers and polished black boots were impeccable, without unwanted creases or wrinkles. The man's coffee-colored face bore no particular expression.

Lakesh blinked at him in mild, owlish surprise. Inwardly his heart lurched and his belly performed a cold flip-flop.

"Come with me, sir," the guard stated.

Lakesh made a vague hand gesture. "My duties await—"

"The baron awaits you," he said loftily, as if he had meant to say *God awaits you.*

As far as the Baronial Guard was concerned, there

was no difference. The man turned smartly on a heel and marched forward. There was no need for him to look back to see if Lakesh followed him. The senior archivist had no choice but to shuffle along in the uniformed man's wake.

They walked through a magnificent, chandelier-lit foyer, their footfalls echoing on the gleaming floor. At the far end of the foyer, flanking huge, ivory-and-gold-inlaid double doors, stood two other guards. Faces impassive, they opened the doors, and Lakesh walked between them into a deeply shadowed passageway. The guard who had fetched him stayed behind, assuming that Lakesh knew his destination.

The passageway led into a room through a wide, low arch. Another room lay beyond, and another, all illuminated by the gray glow from an unseen light source. In the fifth and final room, Lakesh joined the semicircle of eight men standing in the center of an enormous Persian carpet.

Lakesh's seamed face didn't register surprise, though it required a terrific effort. The entire membership of the Cobaltville Trust was present. His mind wheeled with conjectures, speculations and fears. He had no idea how the baron knew when he would arrive and thus convene a meeting of the Trust. Since the Dulce strike, the baron hadn't scheduled a meeting of members. Every ville in the network had its own version of the Trust, the only face-to-face contact allowed with the barons.

The oath of the Trust revolved around a single theme—the presence of the Directorate must not be revealed to humanity. If it became known and if the truth behind the nukecaust filtered down to the people, then humankind would no doubt rebel and retaliate, and the

Directorate would be forced to visit another holocaust upon the face of the earth, simply as a measure of self-preservation.

Therefore, maintaining the secrecy of the Directorate and their work was a sacred trust. It was a sworn and solemn duty, offered to very few.

Lakesh glanced casually at the men standing stiffly in the gloom. There was iron-haired and bearded Abrams, the Magistrate administrator. He leaned against a cane in his left hand, to relieve the weight from his right leg, a leg Kane had crippled in Dulce.

Beside him stood Ojaka, a balding Asian and one of the baron's personal staff. Only by a close scrutiny of his face could one see that his nose had been broken in the past few months. Kane's fist was responsible for the breakage.

Small, paunchy Guende bore no visible reminders of his encounter with the rogue Magistrate. Kane had been the most merciful with him during their encounter in the Dulce complex.

The same couldn't be said for Salvo, who stood behind the three men. Kane had broken a couple of his ribs, kicked out his teeth and fractured his skull. Salvo sensed Lakesh's glance, and his dark eyes flicked coldly in his direction. Lakesh met the gaze mildly.

The sudden measured tones of a gong interrupted the brewing eye-wrestling contest. As one, the nine men turned to face a slowly opening door. Behind a filmy gauze curtain, a golden light, suffused in pastel hues slanted down from above. The gong struck thirteen strokes, and the shaft of muted golden light became a painful glare. As the glare faded, a dark figure appeared in the doorway of the arch.

Baron Cobalt said, in a musical voice that was a velvet sheath over chilled steel, "My friends. My *trusted* friends. It has been a while since we've been all together like this."

The baron kept to the shadows, so only brief impressions of his appearance could be glimpsed. He was less than six feet tall, but his arms seemed unusually long and his legs unusually short. His head was long, narrow and completely hairless, the cranium a shade too large and rounded to be completely human.

But then, he wasn't. Lakesh was one of the few members of the Trust who had ever been permitted to see Baron Cobalt without the theatrical trappings to maintain his mystique of semidivinity.

In a fluid contralto, the baron continued, "I recognize and appreciate your devotion and self-sacrifice in an undertaking so instrumental to the destiny of humanity. Together, we have faced enormous adversity, but never have we contended with treachery from our own."

A disconcerted murmuring rippled through the group. Lakesh joined in, but he noticed Salvo smiling, his teeth flashing in the murk with the hungry look of fangs.

"It is with a heartbreaking sadness and deep regret I inform you that the entire structure of the Cobaltville Trust might be compromised by a traitor…a traitor who will stop at nothing to prevent the Directorate from achieving a secure and rewarding future for our world."

Hesitantly but a bit doubtfully, Horan said, "Lord Baron, if you are referring to the renegades, Kane, Grant and Baptiste, they are simply Outland criminals."

Salvo chuckled harshly. "How is it possible for any ville citizen to go renegade without some type of support from within the ville themselves?"

"Do you mean the Preservationists?" Ojaka asked.

Lakesh managed to turn his smirk into a concerned

pursing of the lips. The Preservationists were, to employ a predark term, simply boogeymen. He had exploited the fear of a small cabal of scholars devoted to revealing the truth of man's past and future to divert attention from his own work.

"No," stated Baron Cobalt firmly. "Nor do I refer to random acts of terrorism undertaken by a handful of the disenfranchised. For the past few months, since the Dulce debacle, I and my fellow barons have conducted a very discreet investigation of every member of every Trust in every ville. To this end, I agreed to the formation of a special internal task force, headed by Salvo."

A few eyes shifted toward the man including Lakesh's. He stood straight, shoulders squared, a half smile playing on his lips.

"The mission of the task force is to seek out at least one individual who is unquestionably in the position to weave a web of conspiracy within and without the villes and the Trust."

Lakesh felt his throat close up. Tension coiled in his belly like a length of heavy rope. The moisture in his mouth dried, and the staged quiver in his hands became real. If it hadn't been for the prosthetic joints in his legs, his knees would have buckled.

"And have you found this individual?" demanded Abrams.

The baron's voice dropped to a low, mournful pitch. "I have. You."

Before Abrams could blink, a pair of guards lunged from the shadows and pressed him violently between them. His cane kicked away, he stumbled and sagged, his arms wrenched up and back in hammerlocks.

Abrams's normally basso profundo voice hit a high,

screechy note of terror and outrage. "Lord Baron, this is *impossible*. It is slander! It is an error!"

Baron Cobalt raised his voice without shouting. His words echoed and bounced from the high ceiling of the room. "My reaction exactly, Abrams, until the proof of your perfidy came to me. I shed tears of shock and grief."

Abrams glared madly and tried to struggle. If he had been ten years younger, completely sound of limb, he might have broken free, but even then, he probably wouldn't have gotten far in the Monolith.

The baron spoke in a soft, resonant and very sad tone. "Your long tenure as administrator of the Magistrate Division placed you in the unique position to choose candidates for the conspiracy. You were close to Kane's father, as I recall."

Abrams said bitterly, "I sponsored him into the Trust, yes. And Salvo sponsored his son. In the matter of guilt, he and I shoulder the blame equally for the rogue operatives."

He twisted his head around, staring balefully at Salvo. "But Kane's father didn't try to kill the baron or you or me, Salvo!"

Lakesh fought hard to maintain a staunch, impassive expression, although he noted how Salvo's eyes narrowed speculatively.

"All a cunning ruse, I have determined," declared Baron Cobalt. "Kane could have easily killed you, but he didn't. Secondly, how did he know I would be in Dulce at that date, unless someone told him?"

"*I* didn't!" Abrams half snarled, half shouted the denial. "One of Lakesh's archivists went rogue, too, remember? Why isn't he under suspicion?"

"Two veteran Magistrates who turned renegade to

one midgrade archivist,'' replied the baron. "Two to one, a mathematical law and a solution which leads back to the division under your guidance."

Sweat shone on Abrams's face. He croaked, "This is a setup." He nodded toward Salvo. "If I am removed, he will take my place. Ask yourself who benefits from this? That's the real solution."

Baron Cobalt's voice ghosted in a long sigh. "I have satisfied myself you are guilty and I have decided on the appropriate action. Do not make an untidy scene."

The guards spun Abrams around and lockstepped him away into the gloom. No one spoke until the scuff and clatter of footfalls faded, then the baron broke the silence.

"Greed and ambition," he said softly. "They always degrade humanity. Learn a lesson from this."

The golden light flickered down to a dim glow, and Baron Cobalt stepped back from the arch. Shadows enfolded him.

The remaining members of the Trust stood for a moment on the carpet, silent and shaken, then grimly filed away. Lakesh was the last to leave. He tried to maintain a firm grip on the riot of conflicting emotions seething within him. Confusion, fear, relief and suspicion all battled for dominance in his mind. He contemplated requesting a private audience with the baron so he could review the proof of Abrams's alleged treachery. Baron Cobalt, with his capricious ways, might interpret the request as a questioning of his authority, and that could result in all manners of unpleasantness.

Lakesh reached the small, private elevator shaft, one of three placed throughout A Level. As he stepped inside, onto the disk-shaped floor plate, Salvo smoothly slid in beside him.

The door panel hissed shut automatically, and Salvo punched the button for C Level, the suite of offices, armories and wardrooms housing the Magistrate Division.

As the elevator began its descent, Lakesh eyed him suspiciously. "My destination is B Level, above C. Have you forgotten the layout of the Administrative Monolith, as well as the alphabet?"

Salvo smiled with mock warmth, and a chuckle lurked at the back of his throat. "I haven't forgotten a thing, you double-crossing old prick."

As if by magic, a long-barreled blaster appeared in his right fist. Under other circumstances, Lakesh might have admired the speed and muscular control with which he had drawn it from a concealed holster at the back of his gray bodysuit. He recognized the weapon as a compressed air pistol a microinstant before a wheezy sneeze of sound burst from the bore.

Lakesh looked down at the tiny hypodermic dart embedded in his chest. Quietly he said, "Ouch."

"You have business on C Level," Salvo said. "I need you conscious, but unable to make a fight."

Lakesh reached up to pluck away the dart, but his arm refused to function. His muscles and nerve endings no longer responded. His mind remained entirely clear, but his body was numbed, incapable of movement.

"Abrams," he said, surprised how steady his voice sounded. "A diversion?"

"A necessary one. It fooled him and it fooled the baron."

Lakesh started to sag, and Salvo pushed him against the wall of the car, holding him erect with one hand pressed against his chest. He felt nothing, not even a pressure.

"You're Kane's Intel pipeline," Salvo announced.

Lakesh's tongue moved slowly. "You're deceiving the baron."

Salvo grinned. His eyes, like pools of muddy water, held the same cruel glint of amusement as a cat holding a crippled mouse in its jaws. "And what the baron doesn't know will definitely hurt *you*."

Salvo pulled his supporting hand away, and Lakesh crumpled down into a heap at his feet.

Chapter 17

"You're a hybrid," said Kane with a forced calmness. "Or a mutant."

Brigid stared at Strongbow keenly. "Or both."

"Silence," Strongbow snapped. He jabbed a finger at the interphaser. "Turn that goddamn thing off."

Kane's mind raced with speculations, but he really wasn't deeply shocked. After their return from Dulce, Lakesh had said there was more than one type of hybrid.

Fixing his gaze on Galt, he asked, "What about you, Lieutenant? Is there some reason you and maybe all of the dragoons hide your baby blues?"

"Hold your tongue," Strongbow commanded.

"Blow it out your ass," growled Kane. "You need us to help you, and we need the truth in order to do that."

Out of the corner of his eye, he saw Grant shift, almost imperceptibly, preparing himself to participate in an outbreak of violence. Strongbow focused his mirrored stare on Kane. He met it unblinkingly. Slowly, carefully Strongbow removed his glasses. Kane concentrated on maintaining his steady gaze on those golden, inhuman orbs.

"Lieutenant." Strongbow's tone was soft.

Galt twitched away his sunglasses. His eyes were twins of Strongbow's own, including the faint scaled pattern around them.

"Admirable deduction, Kane," said Strongbow. "And you, too, Baptiste. Yes, I am a hybrid due to a form of mutagenic molecular alteration. As are all of the dragoons."

"A corruption of the word *dragon*, as I recall," Brigid commented.

Strongbow's eyes flicked back and forth across all of the people at the table. "How much do you know about the Archons' program?"

"All of it," stated Kane. "We're operatives of the Trust, upper echelon. We've been told about the Na Fferyllt."

It was impossible for Strongbow to raise an eyebrow, but he performed a fair approximation by wiggling a brow arch. "I wasn't sure if the barons were aware of their true bloodlines. The creatures known as the Archons were not forthcoming about their origins. Certainly they didn't volunteer information about the last king of the Na Fferyllt."

Brigid said, "Enlil, banished by Saint Patrick."

Strongbow glanced at her with new respect in his eyes, though it was difficult to tell exactly what emotion shone in them. "I presume from your reaction, you didn't expect your device to function this way."

"No, I didn't," responded Brigid frankly. "Nothing should have happened, except an invisible change in the magnetic field of this room. It reacted as if it were within the effect radius of a quantum interphase point."

"But something did happen," Strongbow argued. "What was it?"

"You tell us," said Kane sharply. "You seemed to recognize that apparition."

Strongbow shrugged carelessly.

Kane started to bristle at the arrogant dismissal, and

Galt put his hand on the Beretta at his hip. Brigid spoke up quickly. "I can only hypothesize that the energy released by the interphaser interacted with some sort of flow already here. It opened a rift, allowing a synchronized energy pattern to partially penetrate the vibrational barrier."

Strongbow grunted softly. "My thoughts exactly."

Kane demanded, "You expected that to happen?"

"No, but I feared it might."

"Why?" asked Grant.

Strongbow didn't reply. He sat silently for a moment, as if mulling over a complex problem. Then, decisively, he pushed himself to his feet. "Come with me."

They followed him to a small alcove hidden between a pair of display cases. Facing a featureless section of vanadium wall, Strongbow held up his right hand. A tiny circle of light flashed on his skin and a narrow red needle leaped out, touching first his palm then the tips of his fingers. Soundlessly a panel slid upward, revealing only darkness beyond.

Strongbow stepped forward, and lights flickered overhead, a geodesic pattern in precisely regular channels. He led them straight ahead, with Galt bringing up the rear.

After a few feet, the passageway opened into a chamber filled with so many upright glass cases, that the reflection of the overhead lights confused the eye. Unlike the collection in the council room, the artifacts on display weren't reminders of humanity's need to spill blood. It wasn't a museum; it was a shrine and a trophy room. The first case they passed contained what appeared to be a thick column of dark stone, rounded on both ends. Very faint spiral designs were cut into the pitted surface.

"The Stone of Destiny," Strongbow announced. "Also known as the Stone of Scone. A treasured possession of the Danaan, supposedly imbued with their dreams."

Mounted beside it, suspended by a spiderweb of tiny silver wires, was a sword. "The Sword of Lugh the Long Arm, a weapon said to be invincible."

On a pedestal rested an innocuous-looking hollow cylinder, barely three feet tall and a foot in diameter. Like the stone, spiraling, labyrinthine symbols crawled over the exterior. "A grail stone, or Cauldron of Dagda. Throughout the span of centuries, it became confused with the Holy Grail."

Kane inspected and was mystified by the collection of artifacts. "I don't get it. With your hatred of the Celts, why would you go to all the trouble to safeguard their relics?"

Strongbow nodded to Brigid. "Why don't we allow the lovely lady historian to offer a hypothesis?"

She affected not to notice his sardonic tone. "Folklorically speaking, these objects contain the essence of Celtic beliefs. If you deny the Celts access to them, then you deny them access to their spirituality. And, of course, holding the Stone of Destiny makes you, by proxy, the monarch of Ireland."

"Close," Strongbow admitted. "My reasoning for possessing them is a bit more complex, but you're essentially correct."

"If you can't put a foot on Ireland," said Grant, "how did you get your hands on them?"

"I stole them. From a vault buried beneath the island of Great Skellig, off the Irish coast."

Brigid smiled coldly, waving to the collection. "And having them here compromised the vibrational integrity of your headquarters. The interphaser's quantum-effect field reacted to the ambient energy in the relics and opened a rift. A force came through from the other side."

Her smile disappeared. "Who is Fand?"

Kane was desperate to know the answer to that question, too, but he remained silent.

"At this point," Strongbow retorted, "it is more accurate to ask *what* she is. Come with me."

They followed Strongbow deeper into the chamber, past a pair of life-size statues portraying a seated, gentle-faced man in a cassock and a sword-wielding barbarian with a pair of savage hounds at his feet. Strongbow spoke as he strode, and with every step his tone gentled. From his standard aggressive arrogance, the man's attitude softened to an astonishing degree. It was as if he was relieved to break a stifling bond of secrecy, to share his knowledge with people who, if not his equals, were not utter inferiors, either.

"My real name is not Strongbow, as you adducted. It is Lawrence J. Karabatos. I am—*was*—a scientist by training, a soldier by choice. I worked for Overproject Majestic, a subdivision of the Totality Concept. I coordinated Mission Snowbird with Project Sigma, under the aegis of the Archon Directive."

Brigid had memorized an organization chart of the Totality Concept's many spin-off researches. Overproject Majestic was the only one to directly reference the Archon Directive.

As they entered a long corridor, their footsteps ringing hollowly from the floor plates, Strongbow cast them an over-the-shoulder glance. "Do you need me to be more specific?"

"You're a freezie," said Grant, an accusatory note in his voice.

"'Freezie,'" Strongbow repeated disdainfully. "A particularly noisome piece of slang. It reminds me of a frozen confection sold in twenty-four-hour convenience stores to slack-jawed teenagers."

None of them was sure what a twenty-four-hour convenience store was supposed to have been, and at the moment, they were not inclined to ask.

They reached an open doorway with dim lights beyond. If the large room holding the artifacts was a museum, then this small chamber was a mausoleum, or a scientist's notion of one. Pieces of medical equipment lined the right-hand wall, fermentation tanks, microscopes, a centrifuge. They had seen similar instruments in Nightmare Alley. On racks and shelves rested glass jars and a clutter of surgical instruments. A wheeled stainless-steel dissecting table was shoved against the wall. Its gleaming surface reflected the sickly illumination of the ceiling panels.

A long, deep, transparent-walled vat occupied much of the left-hand wall space. Floating in a semisolid gel, curled in a fetal position, was a horribly distorted caricature of a human being. The long arms and legs were drawn up and contracted. The gray brown skin held a faint pattern of scales, and a short tail extended from the base of the spine, tucked between the thighs.

The face consisted mostly of two big opalescent golden eyes set in a hairless, narrow skull. The eyes, duplicates of Strongbow and Galt's, stared straight into eternity.

"Enlil," murmured Strongbow reverently. "The last of the Annunaki, the last king of the Na Fferyllt. The sun source of myth cycles, religious sects and quite possibly humanity's common ancestor.''

Kane felt his lips peel back from his teeth in a grimace of disgust. His wrist tendons reflexively tensed, hand opening to receive the Sin Eater that wasn't there.

Grant reacted similarly, a spasm of primal loathing overwhelming him, a xenophobic cringing from a sight that seemed utterly alien.

Domi swayed, turning away, very nearly retching. The thing in the vat was probably dead, *had* to be dead, but she couldn't look at it.

Brigid forced herself to look, focusing on the body, noting its nonhuman characteristics, her mind functioning in a matrix of horror and detached analysis. The creature was thoroughly dead and had lain in the tank so long that flattened, discolored lesions had formed where the skin pressed against the transparent walls. The twisted rictus on the face made it look as if it had died in extreme pain. The lipless mouth gaped slightly open. Past the neat double rows of serrated teeth, she saw a blue-black tongue. She couldn't tell if it was forked or not.

Strongbow stared at the corpse longingly, almost sadly. He touched the glass with the fingertips of one hand, a gesture that looked like a caress. "Shall I tell you the story, a secret story affecting all mankind, concealed from it and uncovered only by myself?"

No one answered him.

Strongbow cast them a quick glance, and they saw his thin lips briefly curve in a contemptuous smile. "You will be the first people permitted to hear the truth in over two centuries. You should be honored. You *will* be honored."

Brigid's and Kane's eyes met. She shook her head

slightly, touched a finger to her lips and she said, "We are, Lord Strongbow. Very much so."

Kane understood the deference in her voice and her silent warning to him. Strongbow's rigid self-control was a pose. If he hadn't already plunged off the brink into insanity, he was certainly teetering on the edge of it. Trapped unarmed in the bowels of the ministry building, they had plenty of inducement to put a good face to the man's demand. Besides, this was the kind of knowledge they needed, even if they couldn't confirm its veracity.

Strongbow turned around to face them. His face was inscrutable. Visible over his left shoulder was the head of Enlil. The two pairs of staring, monstrous eyes sent a shudder down Kane's spine, tapping into his memories of the creatures in Nightmare Alley.

Taking a couple of deep breaths, Strongbow resolutely began to talk.

Chapter 18

"I tried to warn them, God knows, but they didn't listen to me. My security rating wasn't high enough. They forced me to make a unilateral decision. I survived. They didn't." Strongbow's tone was grim, yet touched with a gloating note of savage satisfaction.

"Warn who?" Grant asked, resisting the urge to avert his eyes from Strongbow's.

"Everybody involved with the agenda, the program."

Strongbow paced restlessly back and forth in front of the vat. "As I said, I was a scientist, what used to be called in the intelligence trade, an omnivore. I dabbled in many fields. For almost twenty-five years I worked as a freelance consultant for the NSA, DARPA, the CIA, the DIA, NRO—"

Kane listened in irritated silence as Strongbow pridefully reeled off a confusing alphabet soup of predark security agencies.

"Most of the projects I worked on were black coded. Everything from microwave mind control to CBW— chemical and biological warfare. Genetically tailored diseases designed to attack humans of a certain racial heritage. That became my specialty."

Brigid and Kane kept quiet, though it wasn't easy. From what they had learned of the years immediately preceding skydark, biowarfare hadn't played a large part in the conflict of 2001.

"I was aware of the Totality Concept projects, of course," continued Strongbow. "I was briefed on their successes and failures though I wasn't officially part of the program. I wanted to be part of it, I wanted a position I felt I had earned during all those years of slaving away in anonymity in military and government labs. In the late nineties I was invited to work for Overproject Majestic, as a liaison officer between Mission Snowbird and Project Sigma.

"In this division—unlike the other subdivisions— Snowbird and Sigma dealt directly with the Archons, or at least one of them. A creature called Balam."

To maintain neutral expressions was very nearly impossible. Brigid, through long practice in years as an archivist, had perfected a poker face, so she didn't even flick an eyelash. Domi's mouth fell open a bit, but fortunately she was partially blocked from direct view by Grant's broad shoulders.

Though their faces didn't reflect them, Kane and Grant shared similar thoughts—during the op in Russia, Sverdlovosk had told them how Balam had been a guest of the Soviets for several years after World War II before being traded to the West.

"I was stationed in Area 51, the Groom Lake proving grounds. My job was to wring every bit if information out of Balam that I could. As an emissary of the Archons and a drafter of the Directive, I wasn't allowed to interrogate him as I would an enemy alien—pun intended. No drugs, no microwave mind controls. Just persistent questioning and research. Hours, days and weeks of reading tedious and little-known historical works to pick up enough clues about his race's involvement with our own. I had to prove to him I knew what I was talking about, you see.

"Balam supplied very few hard specifics about the Archons, but he imparted just enough so I could follow my own line of investigation. I knew, of course, that the Archons had tampered, altered and experimented with human cultures since time immemorial. Their interest in human genetics, reproduction and even sexuality overshadowed almost all of their other activities."

Strongbow prowled impatiently to one side of the tank, then to the other. He spoke faster, snapping out his words in a nervous staccato. "I won't bore you with the details of my researches, but because of my position, I enjoyed access to much suppressed or 'damned' data, material that had been buried and protected since civilization began.

"Sumer, Egypt and many other ancient cultures repeatedly associated gods with serpents. Too much evidence in too many places violated any chance of coincidence or contamination from other civilizations. For instance, in Norse mythology Thor's great enemy was the 'world serpent,' and Set was the eternal foe of Ra in Egypt. Of course, the most ancient symbol of Britain is a red dragon.

"As the centuries passed, the serpents, the dragons receded further into the background and knowledge of their true natures became the province of secret societies—extending back to the mystery cults of Greece and the Masonic builders of Solomon's Temple.

"I focused on the secret societies. In my day, many secret societies were networked with government intelligence agencies—the Knights of Malta, the Order of Thule, the P2 Lodge, even the Jesuits in the Vatican.

Through the Vatican, I found a thread which lead me
to the Priory of Awen.''

Strongbow's face contorted in an indefinable expression. ''A pagan-Christian sect supposedly founded by
Saint Patrick around the fourth century. They were very
wealthy, exceptionally keen on keeping a low profile
and they held the key to the mystery of the Archons'
origins. The Priory had priests placed in important positions in governments all over the world. I made contact with one of them, a pious, drunken fool by the name
of Brother Morn. He led something of a double life as
both a priest and a NATO consultant on religion.

''Needless to say, when I arranged a meeting with
him and asked my questions, he refused to admit that
the Priory even existed, never mind confirm or deny
what I learned about the Annunaki, or the Na Fferyllt,
as the Celts called them. I undertook drastic action. As
a credentialed agent of Overproject Majestic, I had him
abducted and exposed to all the mind-control technology I had helped to develop.''

Strongbow stopped pacing and tilted his head back
slightly, staring at the ceiling lights, at the past. ''I was
obsessed, you see. Not just to fulfill my Overproject
Majestic assignment, but to learn the truth about the
creatures we had allied ourselves with. I felt we needed
some kind of an edge.

''Morn's perspective was limited, but he told me
about the long conflict between Tuatha De Danaan and
the Annunaki. These hostilities were the basis for the
legends about a war in heaven—only this particular
phase of the war was restricted to the disposition of
mankind. The last battleground was Ireland.

According to Priory lore, the Danaan aided Saint Patrick in ridding the island of the Serpent Folk. Embar-

rassed that he had accepted help from creatures he considered hell-spawn, yet grateful to them nevertheless, he founded the Priory of Awen to serve as a philosophical bridge between his own beliefs and those who still viewed the Danaan as akin to gods.''

Pausing, he frowned and shook his head, as if even now, two centuries after the fact, a riddle still perplexed him. ''Even with that explanation, I couldn't understand why a chunk of rock in the north Atlantic was so important. But eventually I learned.

''What the technicians of Project Cerberus and Operation Chronos were trying to achieve through technological means existed naturally in Ireland. It was a seat of naturally occurring hyperdimensional gateways, quantum exit and entrance points to back alleys of space-time. Think of Ireland as a the hub of a wheel in our physical universe, with a multitude of invisible spokes extending into higher dimensional space. Not that this access was automatic, but the basic requirements for it were in place. No wonder wars were fought for possession of it in prehistoric and historic times, why its people continued to cling to a rich tradition of magic long after the rest of the Western world had forgotten such things.''

Strongbow smiled slightly, almost ruefully. ''If that bit of knowledge wasn't startling enough, Morn told me about the pact struck between Saint Patrick and Enlil. Simply driving the Serpent Folk out of Ireland wasn't the entire story. Enlil agreed to be imprisoned until Judgment Day and the members of the Priory of Awen acted as his warders. At that point in time, nearly a thousand years ago, I am certain only a few of the Na Fferyllt still existed on earth. According to Morn, Enlil was safeguarded in some sort of stasis chamber.

"The terms of the pact were simple, though clouded by myth and religious interpretation. On Judgment Day, when Enlil was set free, he was to be provided with a mate, so his race's seed wouldn't vanish forever. The mate was specifically selected. She was to bear the blood of the Tuatha De Danaan."

Strongbow paused to wave away questions or objections that weren't forthcoming. "Yes, if the Danaan now resided in another dimension, how could a mate be supplied? And why? I came up with a provisional hypothesis, which at least fits the facts as I understand them. The creatures we know as the Archons are the products of hybridization themselves, the result of gene-mingling between the Danaan and the Na Fferyllt—with the occasional superior human material added to the mix.

"At first, this process of bioengineering was voluntary, part of some incredibly ancient agreement between the two races. The Danaan reneged, and thus active hostilities broke out.

"It is part of Celtic lore that the Danaan practiced their own program of genetic engineering on humans, mixing their traits with those of the Irish people. It was limited, of course, sometimes seeming like whims. More than likely, this process of hybridization gave rise to the tales of changelings, fairy children born of human parents.

"Over the course of the centuries, the Danaan-human progeny were exalted in legend as mystics, seers and mighty warriors. Merlin is perhaps the most famous example, Saint Brigid is another."

Brigid cleared her throat, which suddenly felt as dry as dust. A chill crept around her heart. She didn't want to be reminded again of the possibility of reincarnation.

Strongbow smiled thinly and continued speaking. "However, the most interesting article of the pact was the apparent willingness of the Priory of Awen to help bring about a new dynasty of Danaan and Na Fferyllt hybrids to populate the earth after Judgment Day. Morn told me the Priory knew which of their members claimed descent from the Danaan, and there was only one female whose bloodline was direct and unbroken. She practiced as a holistic healer and herbalist in County Meath, something of a local celebrity because of her beauty and chastity."

"What was her name?" asked Kane.

"She called herself Sister Fand, evidently taking the name of a Danaan princess she believed was an ancestor."

Grant rubbed his furrowed brow wearily. "She was the woman who came through the rift?"

Strongbow wagged his head. "No. Allow me to continue. Through my own methods, I managed to exploit Morn's basic trusting nature. He came to believe I was a major player in the Totality Concept. Through him, I established an intelligence pipeline between the Priory and Overproject Majestic.

"I was filled with pride and elation at my accomplishments. I had discovered the secrets of the Archons, secrets which if properly played, could give us an advantage over them, or at least level the playing field. I brought my findings to my superiors. I expected to be rewarded with an overseer position. Do you know what they did?"

He didn't wait for a response. In an angry burst, he hissed, "I was relieved of my duties! Rated a security risk! They said I had exceeded my authority, that I had risked offending the Archons, breaching a diplomatic understanding. Oh, I was kept on. Protocol demanded it, security measures demanded it. I knew too much to be fired, and eliminating me was just as chancy. They had no idea if I had sensitive material stashed someplace, to be released upon my death or disappearance. Now, after all my hard work, all my devotion, I was nothing more than a flunky, pushing paper from one nonessential department to another.''

He threw back his head and laughed. His face split in a wide, vulpine grin. Combined with his inhuman eyes and scaled brows, the sudden display of mirth made him look demonic. ''Like so many others in my life—partners, commanding officers, lovers—they had underestimated my resolve. No reduction of rank or responsibility could take that away from me. I was absolutely determined to use what I had learned to my fullest advantage.

''Upon my assignment to Overproject Majestic, I spun a web of informants, contacts and people who owed me favors. I put them to work, called in the favors. Sometimes I resorted to bribery and infrequently, blackmail. Nevertheless, I was always aware of the current status of any Totality Concept project at any given time.''

Strongbow grinned again, with pure pleasure. ''In mid-January, 2001, an ultraclassified document came into my hands. It related to a recent experiment undertaken by Operation Chronos. The future had been peeked into, and it ended, for all intents and purposes, in less than a week. Only a select handful of Totality Concept personnel had been chosen to survive. I, obviously, wasn't among them. I decided to do so, as well as to carve out a piece of the world to come for my very own.''

Strongbow's eyes flashed, and an involuntary shudder shook Kane at the triumphant glint in them.

"I couldn't influence the Archons," Strongbow went on. "But I could and would influence their root race, or the last one on earth. I knew from Morn that the Priory maintained cryonic units in their monastery, just in case the worst ever happened. Their contingency plan was to place a pair of their best members into them, to revive at some future date so their wisdom and knowledge wouldn't vanish from the face of the earth.

"I sought out Morn, and he read the Operation Chronos report. He wasn't hard to convince after that. I played on his conditioning, that the ancient pact must be honored. I managed to persuade him I was operating under sealed orders from the Vatican. I commanded him to acquire Sister Fand and take us to the Priory's monastery. To give him his due, he did object. But in the end, he obeyed."

Strongbow turned toward the corpse in the vat. In an oddly hushed voice, he said, "There, on the day before doomsday, in a vault beneath Great Skellig, the terms of the pact were fulfilled. I revived Enlil and he mated with the woman, impregnating her."

"Impossible," blurted Brigid. "Two such different life-forms conceiving offspring through intercourse? Impossible."

"Don't question me," Strongbow said coldly. He swiveled his head toward her. The ceiling lights threw his face into pallid yellow shadow. His deep-set eyes were smoldering pits of anger. "Don't we all go through an accelerated, encapsulated process of evolution in the womb? What is humanity's common ancestor, after all? Beyond the mammal, there is the gill, the scale, the egg laid in the warm primeval ooze, to the hissing, slithering serpent.''

Not even Brigid could keep all the revulsion she felt from showing on her face, but she said nothing.

Strongbow sighed. "Evidently the exertion of planting his seed was too much for Enlil. It was his last act. He died within moments of consummating the pact. Of course, he was incredibly ancient, on the order of fifty thousand years, I estimate. I returned his body to the stasis unit. Sister Fand and I went into the cryogenic canisters and were revived a century and a half later.''

Sudden bitterness rose in his voice. "Sister Fand escaped me long before giving birth. She struck out in a boat hidden on the island. I tried to pursue her in another boat, but fog hid her from me. I knew she was making for the Irish mainland, and I presumed she drowned in the attempt. As for me, I took as much of the Priory's technology as I could carry and struck out for Britain. I saw a great opportunity in the chaos there and I seized it.

"I appealed to the innate sense of English patriotism, waving the flag and all of that. It wasn't all that difficult, in retrospect, to build an empire in only a few short years. After all, a man named Hitler had once led a nation into thinking it could rule the world simply by making people first dare to think they could. It succeeded, too. And it succeeded here, as well...on a smaller scale, of course.''

Strongbow smiled grimly. "While I built the Imperium, I heard the tales of Ireland, the eternal fog bank and of the fate of the invasion fleet. I knew the Tuatha De Danaan had returned and more than likely had helped Sister Fand escape me. From information wrung from Irish spies, I learned she had birthed a pure hybrid, if there is such a thing, between the Danaan and the Na Fferyllt.

"The girl-child became a spiritual rallying point to the Celtic people. It was a threat to the Imperium to have an unconquered land with a messiah so close to its shores. After driving the Celts into hiding here, in Brittania, it wasn't politically wise to allow Ireland to keep breeding them, but I couldn't oppose the Danaan by conventional military means. I needed an edge against them, so I turned to Enlil, or at least to his preserved remains."

Strongbow shook his head, as if in self-congratulatory awe at his own ingenuity. "The hybrid offspring of Danaan and Na Fferyllt had escaped me. The dynasty the pact was to create would never be realized unless I created a new one. I set out to do that, perforce. Though dead, Enlil possessed all the raw material I needed.

"Traditional gene-splicing methods are a painstaking process, especially without the technology available to, say, the Archons. There is no guarantee of success. Therefore, I created *viral* mixtures from Enlil's nucleic acids, and the virus replicated, infected and transformed my cells. The process nearly killed me, but within a few months my genetic code had successfully melded with that of Enlil's.

"You may wonder what the advantages are. My optic nerves are improved. Though more sensitive to high light levels, I can see into the ultraviolet and infrared ranges. My physical stamina and strength have doubled, not to mention my longevity. I calculate I will live another century barring accidents or assassination."

Strongbow smiled crookedly and said, "After my successful mutagenesis, I fine-tuned the viral reaction. I modified the DNA sequence very precisely and changed the amino-acid structure. Then I exposed volunteers to it.''

Though no one turned around, all of them were suddenly, uncomfortably aware of Galt standing silently behind them.

"There were only a few fatalities," continued Strongbow. "At the end of five years, I had my first contingent of dragoons. And we set about accomplishing our long-range mission."

"Which is?" Kane inquired quietly.

"The pacification of Ireland and control of the forces bottled up there. They work like corrosive winds—constantly and errosively. Mother Fand's daughter is an adult. She has taken her mother's name and she directs these winds. They blow pagan corruption, stripping off the topsoil of the civilized society I have built here. If this trollop controls the vortex points, she controls the fate of the world. I for one will not allow humankind to return to an uncouth, lumbering, barbaric clan, praying to John Barleycorn to make the crops grow. She is the conduit between the hyperdimensional gateways. Until she is killed or subdued, humanity is not safe."

"You make her sound like a witch," Grant rumbled. "Like something out a story to scare kids."

Strongbow made a fierce gesture, drawing a finger across his throat. "If she were a mere witch, she would be less of a threat."

"By your own words," said Kane, "she's a hybrid, maybe with some mutie abilities. That doesn't make her supernatural. Just different."

Strongbow nodded. "I have been considering your earlier comments regarding psi-mutants interfering with my men's ability to navigate the Irish Sea. I confess your theory has a certain degree of merit. Therefore,

Morrigan will accompany you, at least until you reach the coastal waters.''

"And after that?" Brigid asked.

"You will take a skiff to make landfall. The *Cromwell* will weigh anchor and wait for your return. At least for a while.''

Kane didn't like the sound of that. "How long is a while?''

"Whatever I deem is long enough. I will not place an arbitrary time limit on a mission of this import. Lieutenant?''

Galt stepped forward. "Milord?''

"Escort our guests back to their quarters. See to their every comfort. Arrange for a cook to prepare a nourishing supper. That is all.''

Galt heeled smartly around and marched out of the room. After a moment's hesitation, the four companions followed him.

Grant sidemouthed to Kane, "I'm glad he gave us a choice.''

Brigid overheard and murmured, '' We were wondering how to get to Ireland. That problem is solved.''

Kane stole a quick, backward glance. Strongbow still stood before the vat, gazing thoughtfully, speculatively at the corpse of Enlil.

"Yeah," he said dryly. "One problem is solved. Another boatload is getting ready to leave port.''

Chapter 19

Kane leaned on the railing of the foredeck and drew in deep lungfuls of air. Brine and kelp and a wet, wild wind sent shivers of excitement through him. The hull vibrated slightly as the *Cromwell*'s turbines pushed it farther into the open sea.

Although it was very close to dawn, he could see only a gray emptiness stretching to a deeper gray of the horizon. The rising sun was a faint orange smudge in the eastern sky.

He took a slim cigar from an inner pocket of his long coat, comforted by the weight of the Sin Eater holstered on his right forearm. Cupping his hand around the lighter, he set fire to the cigar. He relished the bittersweet smoke mixed with the tang of salt. He stood and puffed on it, letting the restless panorama of rolling waves, the deep rumble of the ship and the thundering strength of the ocean fill him. For a reason he could not identify, he loved it.

Kane looked behind him at the elevated bridge housing. Through the tinted glass, he discerned the outlines of several sailors. Brandt, the helmsman, kept his attention focused on the control console, holding a steady course. Armed guards were posted at stern and bow, clad in the red jackets and berets of the Imperial Dragoons.

His companions were in cabins below, trying to overcome mild cases of seasickness. For some reason, he had been spared. He knew he should be with them, discussing strategies and options, though there was little to discuss. Certainly they had been given no chance to escape, and even if they had, it appeared easier to reach Ireland than the Wildroot gateway. They had to go through with Strongbow's mission—at least until they reached their destination. What would happen after that was a complete unknown.

Exhaling a wreath of smoke, Kane wondered darkly whether he had done the right thing by not telling the others about his mat-trans-dream and his recognition of Fand.

The sky lightened, a pale, weak sun climbing into the sky. A foot sounded on the deck behind him. Moving with an easy, enviable grace, Morrigan padded up to the rail on soft-soled boots. She wore a hooded jacket that shadowed her blue white eyes.

"Good morning to ye, Ka'in," she said politely.

Kane nodded amiably, noting the change in her speech pattern. The proximity of home, he wondered, or the distance from Strongbow? "Do you detect any psionic activity from out there?"

She smiled and shook her head. "If I did, I wouldn't be telling ye. I was conscripted into Strongbow's little navy like ye and yer other friends, but I'm not about to do what he wants me to, not if it could bring harm to me home."

"How long has it been since you've visited Ireland?"

Morrigan smile faltered. "A very long time."

"Then you should be happy to be on this voyage."

"I will not reach Ireland. Nor will this ship." She spoke with a flat assurance.

"Is that a precognitive feeling?" asked Kane.

She shrugged. "One does not need to be clairvoyant to know this attempt will fail as so many others have."

Kane chuckled dryly. "Why do I have the feeling you'll see to it?"

"I do the Priory's bidding," Morrigan replied.

"I got the distinct impression from Strongbow the Priory went up in smoke about two centuries ago."

Morrigan uttered a sneering little laugh. "Enclaves of priests were scattered all over the world. As long as the spirit of Ireland lives, so does the Priory of Awen." Her smile widened and her tone lost some of its hard edge. "I glimpsed in all of your minds thoughts of something called the Preservationists."

"Yes," Kane agreed. "But they don't exist."

"Perhaps not under that particular name, but there are groups who do function in a manner similar to your fictitious Preservationists. They are dedicated to keeping the truth alive and spreading it on the winds. Someday the fires of wisdom will burn through the clouds of ignorance, and there will be peace and justice again. You have hidden allies in your struggle, so do not give in to despair."

Kane said nothing. Her emotion-charged words touched only a cold hollow within him. What meaning and hope could there be in sailing a dark sea of cruel insanity?

Morrigan pushed back her hood. The wind wafted her long, unbound hair in careless streams. The delicate tip of her tongue touched the droplets of water on her lips. Kane's heart suddenly stumbled, then began to race. She's lovely, he thought.

She said quietly, "Thank you."

Kane blinked, startled into laughing. "A simple fact. Not necessarily a compliment."

"Nevertheless, I will accept it as one. I have not heard such comments for longer than I care to remember."

She moved toward him until she was so close he could feel her body heat, even through the tough fabric of his coat. He did not draw back. The rail prevented him. He dropped the cigar at his feet and ground it out. Softly he asked, "Tell me...who is Fand? Who is she really?"

Morrigan placed a hand on his cheek. Despite the chill air, her touch was warm, almost electric. She breathed, "Ah, you loved her once. You fought battles for her. It did not matter to you that she was not human. Your heart saw only your kinship, not your differences."

Haltingly Kane replied, "I don't know what you're talking about."

"Your spirit understands. Fand's spirit understands. You were separated. Great was your sorrow, Ka'in. The Druids gave you a draught of forgetfulness. It is said that Manannan, the sea god who was jealous of their love, spread his cloak between Cuchulainn and Fand, so that they might meet no more throughout eternity."

Kane stared into her sightless eyes, groping for a response. "I'm not this Cuchulainn."

"You are and you are not. But Fand is still Fand. If you meet again, she will kill the part of you which is not Cuchulainn. Not out of malice, but out of love. That is why I told you to flee."

A kaleidoscope of recent memories and fresh hurts wheeled through Kane's mind. He remembered the Kane he had been—prideful, assured, feet firmly planted on a life path. The Kane who had emerged from the old was plagued with self-doubts, with gnawing fears, angers and sometimes even a despondency.

"Maybe," he said very softly, "that might not be such a bad thing."

Morrigan leaned toward him. Her breath carried the scent of fresh flowers and cleansing summer breezes. "It would be a very bad thing. You are a man, a spirit in transition, and the process is painful. You must endure it."

Under their feet the *Cromwell* rocked slightly. Morrigan stumbled, and Kane's arms steadied her. For a long moment, he was aware of nothing but the feeling of her body against his. Looking down into her upturned face, he realized bleakly it was a very long time since he had kissed a woman, and an even longer time since he had wanted to.

He wanted to now.

He bent and touched his lips to hers, first tentatively, then with an urgent, burning passion. She responded hungrily, one hand at the back of his neck forcing his head down.

Kane had no idea how long he stood there and kissed her. Finally his pointman's sixth sense rang a faint alarm, and he reluctantly pushed her away, lifting his face from hers. Through the glass enclosing the bridge, he saw Brigid staring down at them. Though her face held no particular expression, she quickly averted her eyes when their gazes met.

Feeling foolish, and angry because he did, Kane disengaged himself from Morrigan. A tantalizing smile played over the woman's full lips. "She is your *anam-chara*. She will forgive you this dalliance."

More harshly than he intended, he retorted, "There's nothing to forgive."

Morrigan laughed, the gay thrilling of a songbird. "Oh, yes, there is. Between you two, there is much to forgive, much to understand. Much to live through. Always together."

Kane regarded her with slitted eyes, then glanced uneasily up. Grant stood at the window and gestured toward him sharply. Stepping around Morrigan, he said, "We'll continue this dalliance later."

Her heart-shaped face changed in an instant, becoming grave and joyless. "I fear not, Ka'in. A pity, too."

Kane climbed the ladder to the bridge. The instrument lights cast a greenish, unhealthy glow around the room. Domi's face in particular looked remarkably bilious. She gave Kane a disapproving frown as he came in.

Brigid and Grant stood on either side of Brandt at the navigator's station. "We've got a strong sonar hit," Brandt announced. "Bearing zero-zero-point-zero. Dead ahead. Depth of eight fathoms, distance two miles. Speed is around twenty knots."

Kane shouldered in to look at the round sonar screen. The glowing sensor sweep connected with a tiny bead of light, and a warning chime sounded.

"How long until we make visual contact with the Irish coast?" Brigid asked.

"At present speed, less than one minute. However, the fog bank will seriously impair our range of vision."

Kane looked through the window at the open expanse of water, then back to Brandt. "What fog bank?"

The man inclined his bereted head forward. "That one, sir. A real pea-souper, to coin an old phrase."

Kane, Grant, Domi and Brigid all looked again toward the gently heaving ocean surface. Kane asked, "Do any of you see a fog bank?"

Grant shook his head. "Not even a mist."

Brigid said, "No. Nothing."

"Clear as can be," Domi declared.

Brandt said stiffly, "With all due respect, you Yanks must be blind. Or daft."

From a shelf on the bulkhead, Kane took high-powered binoculars. According to what Brandt had told him upon embarking, they had image stabilizers and ultralow dispersion elements in the lenses to allow distortion-free long-distance viewing.

As he peered into the eyepieces, Brigid stated curtly, "It's obvious what's happening. We're entering the so-called *geas* field Strongbow told us about. The four of us are immune to it, like he theorized."

"That's why his psi-mutie is aboard," Grant said. "To help us through it."

"I wouldn't count on much help from her," Kane replied distractedly, continuing to scan the expanse of heaving waters.

He touched a button to increase the magnification. The ocean seemed to swell in size. At the very limit of the binocular's range, dark cliffs climbed steeply from the horizon. Excitement coursed electrically through him. "I see it. Ireland."

He handed the binoculars over to Brigid and pointed out the direction in which she should look.

A rapid series of chimes rang. On the sonar screen glowed a jumble of racing sparks, like a swarm of radioactive bees. Kane asked Brandt, "Do you see that?"

"The selkies," the man answered grimly.

He flipped up a metal cover on the console and thumbed an inset red button. The red-alert Klaxon blared over the intership comm units, an unnerving, ululating electronic wail. Plucking a microphone from the board, he raised it to his lips. "All hands to battle stations. I repeat, all hands to battle stations. Prepare to repel boarders."

Sailors and dragoons ran across the deck in what appeared to be wild confusion, unlimbering subguns and manning weapons positions. In a matter of seconds, all the crew were at their stations and the deck was devoid of movement. Brandt silenced the Klaxon, and the ship was quiet with a kind of quivering anticipation. He replaced the microphone in its clip and touched a pair of levers. The throb of the engines dropped in pitch. All of them felt the ship slow.

"What are you doing?" Grant demanded.

Brandt cast him an exasperated glance. "Cutting back on our speed. We can't see where we're going in this fog."

"There is no fog!" Kane snapped. "Even if there was, you've got your instruments."

"Can't rely on them. If you were a seaman, you'd know you can only trust your own senses."

"Which are being screwed around with," rumbled Grant.

"The closer we get to the coast, the more pronounced the mental interference," Brigid observed.

The sonar screen was alive and alight with tiny, swimming specks.

"Whatever they are, they're globing us," Grant declared.

Kane's hands ached to take the controls away from Brandt, but without training, it would be a useless gesture.

"Contact in about thirty seconds," intoned Grant.

He swept his gaze over the bridge room, then stepped to the fire-control board. He studied its layout quickly, hands poised over the row of buttons and toggle switches. He punched one, flipped another and said, "The antisubmarine system is armed. I've linked it to the sonar."

"We didn't come here to fight." Brigid's voice was terse.

Kane glanced again at the ghostly outlines on the sonar screen. "I don't think we'll have much choice." To Grant, he said, "Give 'em a taste. We might be able to scare them off."

Grant's fingers played over the buttons.

On the deck, the four long, hollow barrels of the Limbo emplacement gouted thunder and smoke. The depth charges splashed into the sea to port, starboard and aft. Scarcely had the ripples begun to spread when columns of water erupted in roaring geysers.

The *Cromwell* rocked from the four nearly simultaneous concussions. Foaming spray splattered over the bridge and drenched the sailors and dragoons on the deck.

The sonar screen blurred and blanked, momentarily overwhelmed by the shock waves. When it flashed back on, Kane scrutinized the readings and snapped, "We tore a hole in the globe, but they're still swimming at us."

He peered through the water streaming over the tinted glass of the window. Less than twenty yards away from the prow of the *Cromwell,* he saw a faint swirl and streak of movement just beneath the ocean surface, darker gray against the sea. He also saw Morrigan, standing serenely at the railing.

Snarling a curse, he snatched the microphone and bellowed into it, "Morrigan, get away from there! Come inside!"

She affected not to hear him, as if she had suddenly become deaf, as well as blind. Kane dropped the microphone, letting it dangle on the floor by its cord, and rushed for the hatchway. Brigid called out after him, something he did not catch. But she sounded angry.

As Kane went down the ladder to the deck, bracing his hands on the slippery handrails and sliding along them, he heard the crew cry out in fear. They gazed with shocked eyes at the shapes leaping across the waves all around them.

A dragoon with the rank insignia of master sergeant tattooed on his face brought the stock of his MP-5 SD-3 to his shoulder. As Kane passed him, he heard him mutter, "If it weren't for this bloody fog, I could have a clean shot."

Kane realized that the fog only the men in Strongbow's service could see blinded them to the real threat racing in from the sea.

"I see something!" a man shouted hoarsely. Overhead, one of the tripod-mounted L7-A1 heavy machine guns began a staccatto jackhammering. Spent cartridge cases clattered down to the deck plates.

Kicking aside a few fish that the depth-charge detonations had deposited on the deck, Kane tensed his wrist tendons and the butt of the Sin Eater slapped into his waiting palm. Even as he ran toward Morrigan, he saw shapes converging on the *Cromwell* from all sides in threshing foam furrows.

A figure sprang from the ocean, seeming to ride atop a cresting wave, water flying from the sleek, dark-furred body. Leathery hands, webbed between the small, talon-tipped fingers, slapped around the rail. Morrigan gazed at it calmly, fearlessly.

Kane's stride nearly faltered. A clutch of panic

stabbed through him. The thing wasn't human, nor did it resemble any mutie he had ever seen.

The selkie was covered by a pelt of smooth fur, like a seal or an otter. Barely five feet tall, the streamlined, missile-shaped body jiggled with a layer of fat. The short, webbed hind feet were held close to the body. The squat, almost nonexistent neck vanished into down-sloping shoulders.

At first glance, the head was earless, but Kane glimpsed small, vestigial flaps folded tight against the sides of the nearly flat skull. The blunt-snouted face showed a mouth grinning with gleaming fangs. The huge, round eyes were dark, alive with intelligence and fury.

It bore no weapons, but it whipped up one clawed hand, fingers curved to rake over Morrigan's face.

She didn't move. She merely stared into the selkie's face. The hand froze in the air, not dropping downward in a maiming slash.

That half instant of hesitation was all Kane needed. The Sin Eater stuttered, flame blooming from the bore. The selkie catapulted backward from the rail, trailing a liquid banner of blood from the cavities punched through its chest. A scream burst from its throat, a dreadful howl of pain holding an echo of a lost humanity.

Morrigan whirled around, face white with outrage. She shrieked something unintelligible and full of fury.

Then the selkies swarmed up from all sides.

Chapter 20

Kane could only guess at what the crew saw. In their eyes, the selkies were the foggiest of outlines, shadows blurring through thick mist, blobs of darkness that leaped onto the deck. Their ears seemed unaffected at least, since they reacted to the barking sounds uttered by the creatures as they swept aboard.

Three dragoons opened fire with their subguns, full-auto bursts that smashed into a pair of creatures, knocking them backward over the larboard rail. The selkies rushed on, swift and agile, their clawed feet clicking against the steel deck plates. A screaming sailor went down beneath the bulk of two sleek bodies, ripped by claws and torn by pointed teeth.

A dragoon staggered from the impact of a webbed hand raking across his face. Blood sprayed from flayed flesh. The selkie wrenched away the man's weapon, and a claw squeezed the trigger. The subgun chattered in a short burst. A sailor spun around on his toes, the top of his skull floating away in a red mist.

Kane opened up with the Sin Eater, the 9 mm rounds driving through the side of the selkie's head, opening up its cranium into a jagged canyon. The creature flopped onto the deck, webbed feet kicking spasmodically.

The decks erupted with blasterfire, screams and shouts. The ship played host to a mindless unleashing of sheer terror and hatred. Steel-jacketed bullets tore ragged holes in furred flesh. Talons caught men, dragged them down, ripping open abdomens and shredding internal organs. The dragoons and the sailors fired wildly, almost blindly. They didn't trust their befogged vision, so some of their own were wounded or killed by indiscriminate hails of lead. A burst from a dragoon's subgun missed a selkie but blasted the head of one of the sailors to flying fragments.

More than once, a slug struck sparks from steel uncomfortably close to Kane. He was forced to dodge and duck instead of finding targets. A heavy, solid weight bowled him off his feet, cannonading him headlong into the railing. Only a last-second, frantic grab at a crossbar kept him from pitching overboard.

Kane sagged to his knees from the impact, trying to drag air into his lungs. As he turned around, the selkie was upon him, towering above him like a storm cloud. It bit, clawed, slashed and clubbed at him all at the same time. The fabric of his coat turned the talons as they raked at him. The smell of brine and seaweed and fish clogged his nostrils.

A webbed paw stretched out to close over his face. Kane managed to bat it aside and lunge forward, hands gripping the creature's slippery sides. He sank his teeth into a roll of fat surrounding the selkie's lower belly. The flabby substance tasted revolting, as did the hot blood that flowed over his tongue.

The selkie squalled in surprised pain and tried to kick itself backward. Kane heard the characteristic thunderclap report of a triggered Sin Eater. The creature's body jerked violently, and Kane opened his jaws.

Even though a fist-sized piece of skull was missing, the selkie still managed to lock its hands around Kane's throat, as though its last conscious wish was to deal death even as it died.

Kane brought the bore of his blaster up under the creature's receding chin and squeezed the trigger. Two rounds exploded through the top of the selkie's head, as if a grenade had detonated within it. The acrid stink of powder-burned flesh replaced the reek of fish. Lifeless fingers slid away from Kane's throat.

As the selkie fell over sideways, Kane saw Grant on the deck, a faint curl of smoke twisting from the barrel of his Sin Eater. Behind him stood Brigid and Domi, faces pinched tight with anxiety, but both fisting their handblasters.

A rush of selkies broke past him and surged over the foredeck, grappling with sailors and dragoons. The creatures fought with a savagery that sickened even Kane, the veteran of dozens of bloody conflicts.

Snapping fangs tore bleeding gobbets of flesh from faces and necks, talons gouged out eyeballs, skulls were pounded and broken against the steel deck plates. In the milling mass of bodies, Kane saw a screaming sailor thrashing crazily underfoot, his neck broken, both eye sockets raw, oozing pits.

A trio of selkies snatched subguns from dead human hands and set up a sporadic fire pattern. They were bad shots, but they exposed themselves to return fire as if they didn't know or care what death was. The creatures courted death to deal death.

Grant opened up with his Sin Eater, and an armed selkie fell heavily, blood spurting from the red-rimmed gouge in its face.

A .32-caliber round from Brigid's Mauser knocked another gun-wielding selkie's short legs out from under it. It squalled as it fell, firing a long burst. Two sailors toppled overboard without a sound.

Kane shifted position, trying to bring the creature into target acquisition. It detected his movement and swung the flaming bore of the blaster in his direction. A quartet of slugs struck Kane's midsection with such a violent jolt he doubled over. Even though the rounds didn't penetrate his coat, nausea flooded through him. On his knees, holding himself up with his left hand, he squeezed off a triburst at the dark, slick body on the deck. Fountains of blood arced from its upper chest and throat, painting the deck plates with crimson streaks.

Back and forth the struggle swayed, blasterfire crashing, human and nonhumans howling. The metal decking streamed with blood. The dead, the wounded, the mutilated were trampled underfoot. The *Cromwell*'s crew backed up to the support framework beneath the bridge. The small killzone was packed and jammed with monsters and men, combatants crushed together chest to chest. When a sailor or a dragoon went down beneath the selkies, he didn't get up from beneath the tramping, slashing feet.

The accuracy of the shots fired by Grant, Kane, Domi and Brigid finally split the selkie ranks. The surge of creatures reluctantly ebbed back toward the rails in a chaotic, confused swirl of rear-guard combat. They retreated fighting stubbornly.

Domi and Grant followed, harrying them, their combined blasterfire ripping holes in furred flesh. Kane scanned the milling press of bodies for any sign of Morrigan. He caught sight of her on the prow, just a second before a dark, dripping arm darted up, clamped around her ankle and yanked. She fell heavily and slid overboard and out of sight.

Kane snarled in frustrated fury, jamming the Sin Eater back into its holster. He shrugged out of his coat and unsheathed his combat knife, lunging to the rail. Brigid raced forward, trying to maintain her balance on the blood-slick deck.

"No...no!" she shouted shrilly. "They'll kill you!"

Sucking in a lungful of air, gripping the knife between his teeth, Kane vaulted over the rail. He splashed feetfirst into shockingly cold water. The icy temperature nearly made him empty his lungs in a gasp. Clamping his mouth tighter around the knife, he dived deep. Beneath the surface, it was a dim gray green. He swam down with smooth, powerful strokes. All around him, he felt the passage of heavy, powerful bodies.

He glimpsed Morrigan's pale, stricken face not ten feet below him, caught in the embrace of sleek furred arms. Kane stroked furiously. The creatures darted around him, bubbles trailing from grinning mouths. Webbed fingers feinted at him playfully. With his knife, he slashed at them.

He felt a great boiling turbulence in the water behind him, like an undersea tornado. He kicked himself around, knife ready to meet an attack.

He saw Brigid, hair floating in a red-gold cloud around her face. A selkie's arms enwrapped her body, and she struggled madly, trying to pry the hands away. Her eyes shone in the gloom, bright with terror and the panic of drowning.

Kane dived toward her. He had no idea if she had jumped overboard after him or been dragged. The selkie's webbed feet churned the water and pulled Brigid out of his reach. It flashed its fangs at him through the screen of her hair, a grin of vicious triumph.

Lungs bursting, on fire, an agonizing pressure building behind his eyes, Kane kept his cold-numbed muscles working. A selkie plowed into him from above and behind. Kane was tossed to and fro, rolling down into the gloom where the feeble sunlight faded away.

Kane strained and threshed and wrestled as arms that were hard as iron beneath a layer of flab encircled his body. He thrust behind him with the knife, feeling the blade sink hilt deep. In a volcanic convulsion, the selkie tumbled backward, rolling, trying to pull the knife from its belly.

Kane rolled with it, brain barely working, hanging on to the hilt like a lifeline, goring, ripping, working the blade through the shuddering bulk. Rage kept him alive and fighting. A thick billow of blood, jet-black in the murk, blinded him.

The heaving mass of the selkie suddenly fell away from him, the knife tearing loose but remaining in Kane's locked fist. He knew he should stroke to the surface, but he had no idea in which direction it lay. Some part of him knew he was dying and that he should simply allow it to happen.

He kicked feebly, shuddered and sank like a dead weight toward the bottom of the Irish Sea.

Chapter 21

Brigid awoke, lying on hard, cold stone, vomiting water. For a long while, all she could focus on was the desperate need to fill her lungs with air, as dank and cloying as it was. She coughed, retched and struggled to draw breath.

When she could more or less breathe and think again, she forced herself to a sitting position. Her temples throbbed, the tissues of her sinuses and throat felt raw and abraded and her eyes stung.

All around her loomed bare stone walls, wet and green slimed, tendrils of mist drifting up under the high ceiling. Faintly she heard the muttering of voices. The only light was a dim blue radiance from fungoid patches growing on the dripping walls, the cold, pale illumination of a drowned corpse. She shivered, her teeth chattering briefly. The smells of fetid sea and fish were very strong.

Slowly she pushed herself erect, staggering slightly on weak, wobbly legs. Her clothes were wet, but not soaked, so she knew some little time had passed since she'd been pulled over the *Cromwell*'s side.

Her coat was missing, as well as her Mauser. Only the wet, stiff, empty shoulder leather remained. She consulted her waterproof wrist chron, thumbing away beads of moisture from the LED display. Four hours had elapsed since the selkies had attacked the ship.

Thinking of the inhuman paw that had dragged her into the sea, she repressed an involuntary shudder.

A noise floated to her from the gloom. She whirled to see a spectral form in a blue robe, shuffle from the murk behind her, making a clicking sound as clawed toes struck stone. The selkie's eyes were like huge black buttons and it lifted webbed, talon-tipped hands in a conciliatory gesture.

"Peace, woman," it said in a voice unmistakably male. The words sounded strange because of the shape of its lips and length of the teeth. "I am Diuran. I mean you no harm."

Brigid forced herself to meet his gaze, staring steadily into the nonhuman yet strangely pleasant face. "What are you?"

"We are called selkies," Diuran answered.

"I know what you're called. I mean, are you mutants or hybrids or what?"

"We are what we are."

Yeah, right, Brigid thought wryly, inspecting the creature as quickly and unobtrusively as she could. Whether the selkies were products of genetic engineering or myths come to life, they obviously were perfectly adapted to an aquatic environment.

The skin was tough, with a layer of fatty tissue for protection against the cold. The big, disk-shaped eyes were modified to see through undersea murk, and the streamlined body shape suggested a strong, flexible spine for sinuous underwater movement.

She demanded, "If you mean me no harm, why did you try to drown me?"

Diuran barked out a thick laugh. "We would not be speaking now if I had that intent. No, I was told to fetch you."

"Told?" she echoed. "By whom?"

"By me." Morrigan glided noiselessly from the dimness. Her hair was unbound, and she wore a blue robe identical to Diuran's. Brigid stared into her face for a silent, appraising moment.

Morrigan smiled faintly. "No need to wonder why your *anam-chara* dived into the sea after me. He turned to rescue you, did he not?"

"You mean Kane?"

Morrigan nodded.

"Where is he?"

"That I do not know at present. A mystery easily solved, however."

"Perhaps," Brigid said, striving for a cool, detached tone. "But you can solve a more difficult one. Kane told me about your affiliation with the Priory of Awen. Was this undertaking part of your plan for us and Strongbow?"

"You will be told what I tell you—no more," answered Morrigan haughtily. "You have me to thank that you're not being eaten by fish at the bottom of the sea right now."

Brigid said nothing.

Morrigan exhaled wearily. "There is a war here that you cannot completely understand—a long-range conflict that has nothing to do with territories or flags."

Brigid truculently knit her brow. "I have a war of my own."

Morrigan's voice became harsh. "You have no concept of a true war. You refuse to think, but respond to ready-made emotional doctrines—a substitute for true thought. What is worse, you try to wrench reality to fit your ideas."

"It's been said reality is in the eye of the beholder,"

said Brigid evenly, refusing to be baited. "And sometimes emotional doctrines are intuition."

Morrigan smiled half contemptuously, half pityingly. "The dynamics of ignorance. Come with us."

Diuran and Morrigan turned and walked into the shadows. Brigid followed, peering between the streamers of mist. She sensed watching eyes, staring at her from the damp dark.

"What is this place?" she asked, unconsciously lowering her voice.

"A monastery," replied Morrigan. "An old Druidic college transformed by the Priory of Awen. Once, arts and sciences were studied here. It was a secret center of knowledge."

"Knowledge? I thought Druidism was a set of pagan beliefs."

"There are many forms of science, of knowledge. Didn't you know early Irish Christianity was as steeped in magical ideas as ever was Druidic paganism?"

Brigid didn't answer, assuming the woman's question to be rhetorical.

They walked through a cavernous chamber, then into an echo-filled tunnel of a corridor, up a long wooden ramp made of massive, square-cut timbers and into a small circular room. Wisps of steam arose from a sunken tub inlaid with colored bits of stone and tile. Brigid inhaled the perfumed vapors gratefully.

"Bathe," directed Morrigan, gesturing to a blue robe folded on the tub's rim. "Then dress. I will fetch you in a few minutes."

She and Diuran left the room, and Brigid speedily stripped off her damp clothing. Even her underclothes were chafing her. She slid into the bath, completely submerging to wash the salt out of her hair. She tried to relax in the soothing heat of the perfumed water, letting the warmth push away the ache of weariness in her lithe arms and legs.

The memory of Kane, his lips pressed against Morrigan's, suddenly flashed through her mind.

She knew she was strong, and she despised softness in others and herself, but she felt tears welling up in her eyes.

Kane...

God only knew what had happened to him in the sea, and she was angry and hurt and ashamed of herself for it. He was her partner, not her lover, not even a friend, really. Their relationship was an alliance of circumstance. Whatever emotional ties bound them to each other were self-imposed, artificial. But—

He had thrown his entire life away in order to save *her* life, and now there was a strong chance he might be dead and lost to her beyond all hope.

Brigid drove the dark, prowling thoughts from her mind and climbed out of the bath. She had just tugged on the blue robe of soft, loosely woven linen when Morrigan entered.

She said simply, "I will repair your ignorance. Come."

She walked off, with Brigid at her heels. They strode through halls of quarried rock, on stones worn smooth by the feet of countless generations. She followed Morrigan into a large chamber where four walls slanted upward to a narrow apex, like a hollow cut in a pyramid.

The room was furnished with a kind of grotesque ornateness—huge tables and chairs carved from oak, mildewy and wilted tapestries, brilliantly colored seashells holding lit candles. A curving harp, the brass frame gleaming, rested in a place of honor on a high niche. The beauty of the furnishings was worn, but still bright. Narrow slits of windows opened on a pale daylight. The boom of surf came through them faintly.

Suddenly Morrigan's manner changed. She stepped carefully, quietly to a point beneath the niche containing the harp. When she spoke her voice was hushed with reverence. *"Nar laga Dia do lamh."*

The language was unknown to Brigid, but it didn't sound alien. Her eyes flicked back and forth, seeking the object of Morrigan's attention. All she saw was a tall slab of ebon stone, like a piece cut from the very stuff of night. On its surface were swirled symbols and glyphs, cup-shaped hollows surrounded by concentric rings. Radial lines stretched out to form the triple-triangle emblem of the Priory of Awen.

Her forehead furrowing in effort, Morrigan spoke again the whispered rituals in Gaelic.

Brigid narrowed her eyes skeptically, trying to dredge up what little she had read of stone worship among the pagan Celts. Suddenly she drew in her breath sharply with surprise when light bloomed from a hollow cut in the stone, a wavering luminescence like a distant candle flame. She sank her teeth into her lower lip, biting back a frightened outcry.

The eerie flare pulsed, expanded, condensed and slowly formed into the outline of a man, hovering just above the stone slab and the harp. A tall man of a vast old age floated there. A long silver cataract of a beard fell from his chin, pouring down the front of the blue robe that hung loosely about his wasted form. Upon the breast of it, worked in silver thread, glittered the insignia of the Priory of Awen.

His skin had the blue-tinge of skim milk. His face was subtly strange, very broad across the cheekbones and pointed and narrow below. Delicate brow ridges arched beneath a very high forehead.

Slanted topaz eyes regarded her with a fixed, penetrating stare, brooding and icy calm.

Brigid tried to meet that stare, stolidly and unblinkingly. The man, a gaunt and ghostly semblance of a human being, lifted his left hand in a greeting. The wrist bone was unnaturally long, and the slender fingers were the length of her entire hand. His movements had a fluid grace to them that was beautiful to watch.

Brigid heard a sudden gasp. Distantly she realized she had made the sound of fear, and she knew why. In ways she couldn't immediately identify, the old man reminded her of the graceful hybrids she had seen and killed in Dulce.

She began a backward step, but a cold force closed about her, a constriction that gripped and held her helpless. The topaz eyes held hers. Though she desperately tried, she couldn't look away, blink or even squint.

A faint, dry whisper sounded in her head. At first it was so distant, she wondered if she actually heard it. It was as if words were spoken from across some incredible distance of space or time. The whisper became louder, easier to comprehend.

"O thou who art sprung from the seed of human, question me not. I am Cascorach, child of the human and Danaan race, minstrel and friend to Patrick."

The lips of Cascorach didn't move. Brigid realized that by some science beyond her understanding, the stone was a telepathic recorder, activated by Morrigan's psionic touch to replay a communication from a time long, long past. Her mind groped through an array of conjectures, pouncing on possibilities other than magic. The most likely explanation was that the patterns cut into the stone were physical manifestations of wavelengths in the electromagnetic spectrum, activated by a combination of telekinesis and ritual.

As if sensing her denial, Morrigan quoted softly, in English, "'I dream the dead into a living presence and shape dead bones into a new design, let speak again the ages' buried voices and so defy the killing power of time.'"

Cascorach's eyes were luminous pools of molten gold, and Brigid felt herself sinking into them, swirling down into an ocean of memory. A combination of words and images churned through her mind, a narrative compressing a hundred thousand years into a handful of seconds, a history shared not only by humanity, but Others.

She saw Earth as it had been in aeons past, the face of the planet covered with throbbing, life-rich seas, fields, deep green forests and jungles. Small, graceful protohumans hunted, lived and loved there.

Then the Others arrived. From where exactly, Brigid couldn't be certain. All she glimpsed was their arrival, first in gleaming disks dropping from the sky and later through glittering archways of fire, portals between far places.

The Others were tall and cold of eye and heart. They weren't evil; they were simply efficient, a highly developed race with a natural gift for organization. They viewed Earth as a vast treasure trove of natural resources. Their technology depended upon it, and labor was their scarcest commodity. The little blue white planet, third from the Sun, provided both in abundance.

Names whirled through Brigid's head—Annunaki, Na Ffleryllt, the Serpent Kings. Whatever their true names, they set about redesigning the earth and its primitive inhabitants into models of maximized potentials.

The images exploding into Brigid's mind were too vast, too complex for easy mental grasp. Across the smoky, sooty sky moved endless shapes—booms swinging in slow circles, black objects crawling along glistening tracks, buildings and factory complexes, the foundations of which stretched deep beneath the surface. The core of the planet was tapped for the generation of pure energy.

Once Earth was modified, the protohumans were remolded. They were graded at rough intellectual levels, classified by physique, agility and dexterity. Once the selection of the best of the best was completed, the process of creating a kindred yet superior species began. The Others unwound the dextrorotary helix, wrapped it around some of their most desirable genetic characteristics, dabbled with the cerebrospinal fluid and rewrote the chromosomal codes.

Brigid saw strange creatures, some slender with wings, some burly and furred, others one-eyed and ugly and some so bizarrely shaped she couldn't even guess at what the bioengineers were hoping to achieve.

The lost races of man, she thought fleetingly. The mistakes, the chimeras that served as the foundation for creatures and monsters of myth.

The first generation of slave labor was only a step above the indigenous hominid species, and the slaves were encouraged to breed so each successive descendant might be superior to the first. Also, children made the best slaves because they knew no other kind of life. The brains improved and technical skills grew. And so did cogent thoughts and the ability to deal with abstract concepts.

Sluggish mental activities increased exponentially in speed and depth, prompting the construction of ideas which eventually led to the formation of the question *why?*

The Others failed to notice this expansion of cognition on the part of their slaves. Nor did they answer their questions. They were essentially a peaceful race primarily because violence was unproductive and a waste of resources. They were exploiters, not conquerors.

Eventually—because revolution is the product of frustration—rebellion came. Earth turned into an unprofitable enterprise, so the Others arranged for a catastrophe to destroy their labor force. The catastrophe was recorded in ancient texts and even cultural memories as the Flood.

As the waters slowly receded, the handful of human survivors bred and multiplied. Centuries passed, nations and empires were built and then fell, many sciences passed down from their former masters were practiced and then were forgotten. Then a new group of Others arrived.

Brigid saw them as the ancient humans saw them— an aristocratic race of scientists, poets and builders fleeing their own home. Names flashed through her mind—the Sidhe, Faylinn, Dei Terreni, Tuatha De Danaan.

This race of Others found a fertile, isolated island and made it their own. They took the tribes living there under their protection and taught them their secrets of art, architecture, mathematics.

"Yes," whispered Cascorach. "We had knowledge. But we didn't share it all, for which we were sometimes hated. Would you give little children the weapons to destroy themselves? We gave men better tools, and if they invented something new, we were happy. But we did not tempt them and burden them with knowledge that was not their own.''

One day the Annunaki, or the Na Fferyllt, returned to reclaim not only their world but their slaves, a hundred generations removed from their progenitors who had survived the submersion of the planet. They were few in number now and they used their wiles to fill the people with jealousy and fear of the Danaan.

"Mankind was content to make war with spear and sword," sighed Cascorach. "They hated and feared and believed, not with reason but because they were told to by creatures they considered gods. We fought them as they invaded on longships, but only to defend ourselves and our cities. We took the war to the Annunaki, ignoring their human pawns."

Mankind became embroiled in this conflict and the conflagration extended even to the outer planets of the solar system, immortalized and much disguised as a war in heaven.

Finally, when it appeared even Eire was threatened with devastation, the war abated under terms. The Danaan and the Annunaki agreed to end it for the sake of all their intertwined futures.

A pact was struck, whereby the two races intermingled to create a new one, to serve as a bridge. Images swam through her mind, of pale-skinned beautiful women with bright eyes and pointed ears birthing large-skulled, black-eyed creatures that did not yet look like Archons.

As for manipulated, foolish humanity, direct communications with the Annunaki and the Danaan continued but were severely curtailed. Both races retreated into realms invisible, demonized by various religions, diminished in stature by fanciful myths. The reign of both had come to an end.

"Yet one last battle on a final battlefield remained to be fought by man, the Annunaki and the Danaan," Cascorach said.

Enlil, one of the original architects of man, refused to go quietly into the other realms. He determined to use the new race to spread his beliefs, his spirit, even his seed throughout the world. He was a leader of genius and he had a vision to unite the planet under one rule—his own. He made his base in the former kingdom of the Danaan.

But the greatness of his people had long passed. He had broken the pact, and none of his own race would come to his aid. They were ancient even when they first arrived on Earth. They feared his ferocity and cunning and were resigned to extinction. The war for possession of the planet now fell to those who had been birthed there—humanity.

"Patrick confronted Enlil. I, Cascorach, helped him. Enlil refused to depart. He feared that his race would die out completely if he quitted the physical realm. A new pact was made. Enlil agreed to sleep until Judgment Day, guarded and watched over by a secret order of Patrick's own devising. You, who are the children of the devoted ones who conceived the Priory, hold the fate of the world within your hands and hearts.

"Hearken well, children of man and Danaan. Honor yet the pact, yet do not permit Enlil to spread his spawn again."

The voice, images and sensations faded. The apparition blurred, flickered and vanished. The light within the stone hollow went out. Brigid felt a spin of vertigo. She felt groggy, thirsty and slightly ill.

"Do you understand now?" Morrigan's voice was hushed and small.

Brigid turned to face her, massaging the sides of her head. "I think so. Some of it. It's not easy to accept...especially the part about the Archons being a mixture of Danaan and Annunaki genetic material."

Though Morrigan's eyes were fathomless as always, a hint of amusement was in her voice. "And you suspect all this may be an Irish trick."

"Half suspect," Brigid corrected. "Some of my questions have been answered, but a little too conveniently to completely believe them."

Morrigan shrugged. "In some ways, the human race is unforgivably ignorant. But not because we haven't learned. It's because we've forgotten. That is why we of the Priory took Danaan names upon our entrance into the order."

Brigid glanced at her wryly, wondering if the psi-mutie knew how incongruous her referral to humanity as a collective "we" sounded.

"Are there living Danaans here and now, like Strongbow suspects?"

Morrigan shook her head. "Not in the flesh-and-blood sense. We have a few of their artifacts, like the harp of Cascorach. Strongbow has most of them, as you saw. Only the shadows of the Danaan walk this island—I am such a one, because I carry their blood, as do the selkies."

"As does the one called Fand, according to Strongbow," Brigid said.

"Yes," Morrigan agreed sadly. "As does the one called Fand. She is the living consequence of a pact that should have never been made. She carries the blood of human, Danaan and Annunaki within her. A trinity, a breathing embodiment of the philosophy of the Awen.''

Morrigan began to say something else, then broke off, shaking her head.

Brigid felt a stirring of fear. ''An embodiment of the philosophy of Awen…and what else?''

Morrigan answered, with a quiet dignity, ''She is also quite mad.''

Chapter 22

Rain and wind came, a lightning-laced squall in which the *Cromwell* wallowed and rolled. The crew stumbled and swore as they unceremoniously dumped the bodies of the slain, comrades and selkies alike, overboard. The downpour washed away much of the blood puddled on the deck.

Within an hour, the storm passed, the sea stilled and the clouds broke up so that the face of the noon sun was clearly visible. A flat calm fell over the waters, rippled by intermittent gusts. To starboard, dark cliffs rose from a foaming surf.

On the bridge, Brandt sighed in relief. "The fog has lifted."

Grant asked, "Now what?"

The man's hands touched the controls. "Now we turn about and return to port."

Domi's eyes widened in angry fear. "No, we'll not leave our friends."

"Young woman, they're dead," Brandt replied in a clipped tone. "Drowned or devoured. Whatever their fates, they're now in the choir celestial."

"Until I see their bodies, we're not jumping to that conclusion." Grant's voice was flat and cold. "The plan was to put us ashore with the interphaser. That hasn't been accomplished."

"We'd have to get closer to the damn place. From our current position, the skiff doesn't have the range."

"Then change our current position. Put us in range."

"And risk being beset by those monsters again?" Brandt challenged. "Or grounding ourselves in the fog? Not bloody likely, mate."

His hands turned the wheel, shifted control levers, and the *Cromwell*'s turbines rumbled as the ship began backing water. Grant watched, aware of the dragoon standing alertly near the hatchway. He heaved a sigh of weary resignation and put his left hand out toward Domi, as if to pat her shoulder.

His right hand clenched, and he drove the back of it against the dragoon's face. He felt the cartilage in the man's nose collapse and warm blood spray his hand.

The dragoon cried out, staggered against the bulkhead and tried to lift his subgun. Brandt whirled away from the console, eyes and mouth both wide in astonishment. Domi closed his mouth, then his right eye with a swift uppercut and a left hook.

Grant's Sin Eater slid into his hand, and he used it as a bludgeon, bringing the barrel down sharply on the crown of the dragoon's head. Metal struck bone with an ugly *chock*.

The man sagged to his knees, still trying to swing his blaster up. Grant kicked him in the face, smashing his mirrored glasses. Consciousness vanished from his opalescent eyes, and he toppled sideways. Quickly Grant snatched away the MP-5 SD-3 and pointed it at the navigator. Brandt leaned against the console, blinking rapidly, dazed by Domi's one-two combination.

"Get us in range," commanded Grant. "Or I'll blow your head off and do it myself."

Brandt gingerly rubbed his chin, touched the swelling

flesh under his right eye, glanced more fearfully at Domi than at the blasters pointed at him and turned to the wheel. He made a few adjustments on the levers and, when Grant was satisfied the ship was on the correct heading, he said to Domi, "Go below and fetch our equipment. Any of the crew tries to stop you, chill 'em."

The girl nodded grimly, drew her Detonics .45 Combat Master and left the bridge. Grant put his back to the bulkhead so he could cover both Brandt and the dragoon with the pair of blasters.

He tried not to think about what had possessed Kane to jump overboard after the mutie. Long ago he had decided it was useless to try to decipher his partner's behavior. He was sometimes impulsive to the point of foolishness. When he had discarded his coat, he had discarded its built-in trans-comm at the same time. The submersion of Brigid's unit had rendered it inoperable, as well.

He deliberately turned his mind away from the high likelihood of Kane's and Brigid's deaths. That was something he refused to seriously consider until he stood over their corpses.

"The damn fog again," Brandt announced angrily.

Grant saw only clear skies and calm seas through the window. "Sonar reading?"

The navigator glanced at the screen, saying, "Clear, for the moment."

By the time Domi returned lugging the cases containing the survival stores and the interphaser, the dragoon had revived sufficiently to sit up. At Grant's order, he scooted into a far corner and sat on his hands. He bared blood-filmed teeth, and the hatred blazing out of his inhuman eyes sparked a momentary desire in Grant to shoot him, just on general principles.

Only the possibility of calling on Strongbow's resources kept him from squeezing the trigger.

While Domi kept her .45 trained on the dragoon, Grant peered through the binoculars. The cliffs were steep and eroded by millennia of water and weather. The sea splashed furiously against the rocks, and through the spray he saw the mouth of a bay.

Brandt cut back on the power, and the rumbling whine of the turbines dropped to a faint mutter. "This is as close as I dare. If the selkies came at us now, we wouldn't last long."

Grant lowered the binoculars. "Get the landing boat ready."

Plucking the microphone from its clip, Brandt barked commands into it. Through the windows, Grant watched sailors scurrying across the deck, raising a hatch cover and allowing a hydraulic hoist and winch to rise from beneath. Cables and grapnels connected it to the gunwales of the skiff. The small craft was barely eight feet long. It reminded Grant of a high-sided bathtub. An outboard motor was clamped to its squared-off stern.

The hoist lowered the boat over the side. When it floated there, still attached to the cables, Domi and Grant backed toward the hatchway. More to the dragoon than to Brandt, Grant growled menacingly, "We'll be leaving now. Anybody who tries to stop us will wish they were still dancing with the selkies."

"Go and be damned," Brandt snapped. "No one will interfere. Nor will we wait."

"Strongbow's orders stated otherwise," Grant reminded him, but Brandt declined to respond.

Out on the deck, Domi and Grant scaled a rope ladder

to the skiff. It rocked slightly on the swells. A number of sailors watched quietly from the rail. After they were seated, Grant started the outboard with a single yank of the pull cord. The grapnel hooks snapped automatically open, and he gunned the engine, the prow riding on a rush of foam.

Domi shivered. "Glad to be away from them."

"Wait till we make landfall before you celebrate," replied Grant dourly.

The wind was raw and biting. Clouds scudded across the sun, and a few drops of icy rain fell. As Grant made for the inlet, domes of water boiled up around the boat.

"Things below," Domi said in a strained whisper, hefting her blaster.

The motion ceased, and the disturbance in the water subsided. Grant cursed softly between his teeth. This wasn't the kind of life he had craved or envisioned. Never in his wildest imaginings had he ever pictured himself spending his middle years this way.

He looked at Domi, sitting alertly in the bow, gazing at the black cliffs as they loomed closer. He had tried to reason with her back in Cerberus, but she chafed at the inactivity of the redoubt. She hadn't said it in so many words, but she thirsted to avenge her people, and if this mission might help her quench that thirst, even by proxy, then she accepted the risks.

It occurred to him that as an outlander she should be accustomed to injustice by now. She had lived her entire life with it, and with the anger that infected entire generations of her kind. In the past, nonconformists had been pioneers, philosophers, artists, explorers. Now they were criminals.

The boat rode the roaring breakers at the mouth of the inlet, rising and falling, rising again. Waves lapped over the sides, drenching them from head to foot, the salt spray stinging their eyes. Grant kept the small craft on course, knowing how easily a swell could pile them up against a boulder.

The violent buffeting ebbed, and an opening stretched before them. Shafts of sunshine broke through the cloud cover, glinting on the rippling waves of the little bay. Gulls and cormorants wheeled and squawked overhead.

Grant steered the skiff slowly to the shallows near the rock-strewn beach. Above them towered dark ramparts. When the hull grated on stone and he cut the engine, Domi climbed nimbly out, waded ashore and made them fast with a rope looped around the base of a pumpkin-size rock.

Grant studied their surroundings, fixing them in his memory. He consulted his compass and, carrying the interphaser, he walked toward the foot of the nearest cliff. The crunch of the slippery rocks under his boots sounded startlingly loud, even over the rhythmic boom of the surf.

He found a rock wall only thirty or so feet high, with a scattering of granite heaped about its base. Turning to Domi, he asked, "Can you climb?"

Domi's teeth flashed in an impudent grin, then she clambered over a pile of stone and up the rock face, agile fingers seizing handholds. Like an albino monkey, she swarmed up the stone wall.

"Come on," she called over a shoulder. "It's easy. Just do what I do."

Grant shook his head in dismay, then passed his web belt through the handle of the interphaser case. Slinging the subgun over his back, he began to climb. Some of the handholds were mere cracks in the sheeted stone, but he wedged his fingers in and pulled himself along.

The muscles in his arms started to burn. He glanced up just as Domi wriggled over the crest. She voiced a short cry, one of triumph, he thought.

Silently he cursed her, cursed Lakesh and the case bumping incessantly against his hip, but most of all he cursed Kane, who had made all this exertion necessary.

As he heaved and scrabbled, he suddenly remembered that his transfer to an administrative position had been only a couple of months away in Cobaltville before Kane's curiosity started the chain of events that made them all wanted fugitives. Instead of looking forward to sitting at a desk and reading requisition reports, he was in a wild and savage land, half a world away from a cozy office in the Magistrate Division.

The flash of anger lent new strength to his limbs, and he clawed his way up the last ten feet and dragged himself over the stone lip. He lay on his stomach, panting, kneading his sore biceps and flexing his stiff fingers. Then his gaze fell on Domi's feet—and another pair, booted in red leather, right behind them.

Grant rolled quickly upright, the Sin Eater filling his hand. Behind Domi, one hand over her mouth, the point of a short sword pricking her throat, stood a grinning man. He had a short beard, and his hair was shaved in a curious fashion, with an upstanding knot at the back of his head. He wore a green tunic and breechclout and red knee boots. His bare arms showed dark blue, spiraling tattoos.

Slowly, with a provocative flourish, he removed the sword from Domi's neck. The long needle of steel inscribed a circle inches from Grant's eyes. Grant kept his face dispassionate. He mentally kicked himself now. What he had interpreted as a cry of triumph from Domi had been one of surprise and warning. He noticed that her holster was empty.

He heard a quick scrape of leather on rock and spun on his heel. A second man, slender and younger and beardless, stood behind him. His flesh was tattooed with the spirals, as well, only not so many. Instead of a sword, he held a long-handled club, a flexible truncheon about two feet long, made of cross-stitched rawhide and probably filled with pebbles.

The bearded man spoke sternly, peremptorily. When Grant made no reply, he spoke again, this time with a harsh emphasis.

"I don't understand you," Grant said.

The younger man, in a voice so thickly blurred with a brogue he was barely comprehensible, said, "He asked if we should expect any more of you."

"Any more of who?"

"English."

Grant shook his head. "We're not English. Who are you?"

"Celts. How do we know you're not English?"

"Do we look like any English you've ever seen?"

The man holding Domi removed his hand from her mouth, turned her and looked her over, up and down. At length, he said, "No."

He lowered his blade, and Grant relaxed a bit. "We're looking for friends of ours. A man and a woman. Their names are Brigid and Kane."

Sudden suspicion slitted the eyes of both men. The bearded Celt motioned with his sword and pushed Domi toward a sloping grade. "You'll come with us."

Grant leveled his blaster. "Do you know what this is, shit-brain?"

The Celt grinned, ducked and weaved playfully, then

a quarter inch of razored steel stabbed through the back of Grant's gun hand. He swore and jerked back reflexively. Three great blows hit him in such rapid succession they seemed to be one. The first was like a lead hammer against his kidneys. Although his coat cushioned it, the second one was like one of the black cliffs toppling on his head. The third blow felt like a caress by comparison.

He came around quickly, though painfully. When he opened his eyes, he saw Domi bending over him, applying salves to his punctured hand and wrapping it with bandages taken from the survival kit. His throbbing head rested on her lap, he realized dimly. Dizzy, nauseated, gritting his teeth against the flares of pain igniting in his lower back, he pushed himself to one knee.

The two Celts regarded him bleakly. The bearded one held his holstered Sin Eater, and Domi's Combat Master was tucked in his belt. The younger of the pair held the subgun and let his leather-encased club dangle from his right hand. He rested a foot on the interphaser case. Grant felt the weight of the gren-laden combat harness, so the Celts hadn't bothered to unbutton his coat to search him thoroughly.

Acidly the younger Celt demanded, "Do you think we're *amadans,* that we don't know what guns are, even if they are forbidden by the Mother?"

In a surprisingly mild tone, the older man asked, "Do you have names?"

"I'm Grant. This is Domi."

The beardless Celt nodded courteously. "I am called Conor. My companion is named Oisin. And in addition to you two being Grant and Domi, you are also our guests."

"Guests?" Domi repeated sourly.

Oisin grinned. "Of course. The Irish are renowned for their hospitality, didn't you know?"

"What if we don't care to accept it?"

"Then we'll make you our prisoners," Conor retorted.

"I figured you'd say that," Grant muttered, pushing himself to his feet. He reeled for a moment, head and back throbbing fiercely.

Conor picked up the case, hefting it by its handle as if trying to guess its weight. "What is this?"

"Nothing to concern you," answered Grant stiffly. "It's not a weapon, if that's what you're worried about."

"Open it."

"No."

Oisin half stepped forward, pointing his sword in a silent threat.

Domi slid between the glittering steel and Grant, glaring venomously, first at Oisin then at Conor. "Touch him again, you rag-assed bastards, and I'll chill you."

Conor and Oisin exchanged baffled glances, then both laughed uproariously. "Look at the wee lass," Oisin exclaimed. "As white as the swans of Lir, no bigger than a minute, yet with the heart of Maeve."

They were marched down the rocky slope, which fell away to a moor rolling in a slight hollow before them. The matted bracken crackled under their feet. Ahead was the dark band of a forest. A breeze bent the high grasses. Oisin took the lead, and Conor brought up the rear, carrying the interphaser. The Celts didn't speak to them or very much to each other except for a few mumbles in their own language.

Grant's hand pained him and swelled, though the medications Domi had applied kept both to a tolerable

minimum and nipped any chance of infection. Still, he
hurt just enough to be in a thoroughly foul humor.

As they tramped across the sward, Grant inspected
their captors. The tattoo designs didn't seem to be rank
insignias, nor did the cup-and-ring spirals appear to be
strictly decorative. He figured they had to be caste
marks of some kind, since the Celts were obviously
tribal.

As they approached the border of the forest, the clean
air grew heavy with the scent of growing things, of
flowers and rich soil. Sunlight warmed him, drying his
clothes. Under other circumstances, he would have enjoyed this little nature walk immensely.

They reached an old, overgrown blacktop road. Grass
sprouted through the cracks in the pavement. Young
trees and shrubs and mounds of leaves cluttered the av-
enue. The four of them strode along it into the forest
until it disappeared beneath a tangle of undergrowth.

The sighing boughs of the great trees shut out almost
all of the sky, and the light beneath them was cool and
green. The air was full of lazy sounds: the far trill of
birds, a hum of insects, the rustle of the breeze. They
walked for half an hour, no one saying anything. The
farther they went down the cathedral aisles of the gargantuan tree trunks, the more they could smell the
aroma of wood smoke and roasting meat. Ahead a spark
of red flickered in the emerald dimness. Oisin quickened
his pace, and Conor urged their captors to do the same.

They strode into a clearing. A roaring blaze fed by
logs burned in the center, with thirty or forty people
sprawled around it, completely at their ease. They wore
a loose uniform of green tunics and red boots. The men
were a rough-looking crew—well-built, some short and
stocky with beards, some clean-shaven and tall with

long limbs. Their hair was of all different colors, lengths and styles. Eye color, however, was predominantly light—blue, gray or green. They were drinking from brown, kidney-shaped leather bags.

There seemed to be an equal number of similarly dressed women, with the same variations of hair and eye color and body types among them.

Domi murmured, "Pretty people."

Grant took a second objective look and realized she spoke the truth. Though they appeared more barbaric than any roamer gang, the people were handsome in a fierce and wild sort of way.

Concentric circles of mud-walled, thatch-roofed huts ringed the clearing, sheltered beneath the boughs of gigantic oak. Children scampered and dashed from open doorways. A rude split-rail corral contained horses, shaggy, squat-bodied animals that reminded him of the Mongol mounts he had seen in the Black Gobi. In the distance, he heard the lowing and bawling of cattle.

Off to one side, some distance away from the outermost circle of huts, stood a tall frame of wickerwork. It bore the general outline of a man, and Grant briefly wondered about its purpose.

A burly man who had been squatting near the fire roasting a squab on the point of a dagger stood up when he caught sight of them. He stood three inches more than six feet, nearly Grant's height, muscular without a spare ounce of flesh. A three-inch brass ring hung from his right ear. He had a hard, bony face, a red spade beard bristling at his chin. He wore a quilted scarlet jerkin over his tunic.

He glanced with only mild curiosity at the approach of the four people, even though the drone of conversation died as they entered the clearing. Oisin spoke to the man in a hurried whisper. As he listened, he tore off a piece of meat with strong white teeth and chewed slowly. His blue eyes flicked between the big black man and the small white girl.

Grant examined the man, too, noting and envying his unstudied ease and indifferent confidence. The other people in the clearing gazed at them carefully, quietly, almost politely. If this were a bunch of roamers in the Outlands, he thought, they'd have been subjected to all sorts of indignities by now. Death by torture the least of it.

The spade-bearded man met Grant's eyes and half smiled. "What is your thought encroaching on the land of Clan mac Trenmor?" His voice was deep, his English fluent.

"We're looking for friends," Grant replied.

The man drew back his lips in a grin. "Friends ye may have found. Or foes. That all depends on who *yer* friends are."

Oisin muttered something into the man's ear, and his grin widened. "Ah, you seek Ka'in and Brigid? Ye just missed 'em…by a few thousand years."

Grant ignored the comment. "Who are you?"

"Phin mac Cumhal mac Trenmor, chieftain of this land."

"Should I call you Mac?"

"Nay," the man answered negligently. "I prick up me ears to Phin. How come ye here?"

"By ship."

"From Britannia."

Grant sensed a tension building among the onlookers. "From America."

Phin spit out a half-masticated piece of meat. "Ballocks. Ye sailed here from Britannia. Me men saw the black ship, flyin' the dragon colors. America, my arse. Place was finely vaporized, it was. Yer in the service of Strongbow, or I'm a hound.''

"Then find a tree and lift a leg," Grant snapped. "Do I sound like I'm British?"

"Nay," admitted Phin reluctantly, combing fingers through his beard. "Ye sound like a great cheeky Yank black fella."

Grant let the observation pass. "America wasn't vaporized. Damn close to it, but it survived. That's where me and my friends came from."

"Then that makes me next question even more barbed."

"Which is?"

"What the fuckin' hell are ye doin' here, with your fancy blasters an' boots an' attitudes? Speak straight, mind, no more shite about lost mates or I'll warm the truth out of ye in the belly of the wicker man."

Grant didn't know what he meant, but knew he didn't like the sound of it, especially when Oisin speculatively eyed the fire, then him.

Conor stepped forward, holding the metal interphaser case out to Phin. He ran a hand over it, then fumbled with the intricate latches and locks. After a few moments, he looked at Grant challengingly. "Open this."

"No."

Phin snorted, reached behind him and drew a broadsword. He used the point to pry at the locks.

"You won't get it open that way," Grant told him pleasantly.

"Why not? Because you think I'm an *amadan?*"

"No, because I think you're a stupe."

Phin's eyes and voice became frosty. "That means

the same thing, black fella. Conor, put it on the ground. I'll get the bloody thing open.''

Conor did as he was told and backed away. Bracing himself on wide-spraddled legs, Phin raised the sword over his head in a double-handed grip.

Grant lunged forward in a bull-like rush, swinging his left fist up from the ground. It was his personal philosophy—strike fast, strike once, then get the hell clear.

But Phin was faster than his punch. He sidestepped so quickly that Grant's fist harmlessly brushed his beard, and he staggered, off balance.

With wild whoops, a number of men leaped to their feet and closed in on him from all sides.

Grant had fought in a lot of places. He'd learned from Mag trainers, Pit slagjackers and even a few cornered outlanders. He used his feet and knees and elbows, the crown of his head and both his hands, flat and fist.

The Celts didn't unsheathe weapons or wield clubs, but they tried to kick his guts loose and knock his brains out through his ears. He heard Domi shrieking in rage and he caught a glimpse of her on Oisin's back, fingers clawing for his eyes, teeth locked on one of his ears.

As outnumbered as he was, Grant should have been beaten to his knees within the first half minute. The fight lasted far longer than that because he knew more dirty tricks and he had no compunction about bringing them into play.

Then his heel struck a loose length of firewood. It rolled, he reeled and Phin caught his jaw with a clean swinging blow. Grant fell backward, and his already tender head slammed against the hard ground. The green-filtered sunlight turned crimson, then darkened. He felt a couple of jarring kicks to his ribs.

A woman's voice shouted stridently, *"Sin e'!"*

With a scutter and scuffle of feet, the men drew away from him. Grant put his hands under him and pushed himself to a sitting position, breath ragged, tasting blood. His face ached dully, and he knew it was swelling. He took a certain satisfaction, though, at the sight of the four men lying moaning on the ground clutching various parts of their anatomies.

He saw a couple of women holding a struggling Domi in armlocks, but he had no eyes for them. He gazed, gaped almost, at the tall woman striding into the clearing.

She walked with a flat-muscled, feline arrogance, her blond hair cropped almost to the scalp except for a lock that curved down over her forehead like a comma. Her eyes were big, blue and hot. She was dressed much like the other women, but her body beneath the loose tunic was magnificent. She carried a long-hafted, vine-wrapped staff over a shoulder.

Her face was translucently pale, her cheeks decorated with the blue spiral tattoos. She marched to within a few feet of Grant, and her cobalt-flame gaze locked on him. She was older than he initially guessed, close to his age. Bitter weariness glinted in her eyes.

Extending her right hand to him, she said, "I never thought to meet a Yank again." Her voice was beautifully melodic, deep and cultured.

Grant clasped the strong, callused hand, and with an astonishing strength, she pulled him effortlessly to his feet. Not releasing her hand, he asked, "Who are you?"

"A good question, and one I've been meaning to find an answer to for many years now."

She turned her head to speak sharply to the women

restraining Domi. They immediately released her. She faced Grant again, a thin smile on her lips. "You may call me Mother Fand."

Chapter 23

Kane fought with the sea as though it were a living thing. He knew it was easier to simply sink, to vanish forever beneath the waves. Who would care—what vacuum would he leave in anyone's life?

He thought of Salvo, of their unfinished business. His death would leave a void in that bastard's miserable life, at least. A bright ball of fury expanded inside of him, forcing his hands and arms to thrash the water. The anger somehow made both legs kick in rhythm with his hands.

His head broke the surface, just as a wave crashed on top of him in a powerful cascade. He sank again, then bobbed up in the wake of a hissing swell.

Riding on the crest of a wave, blinking the stinging brine from his eyes, he gazed around. He saw no sign of selkies, Brigid or Morrigan. The *Cromwell* was far out of the range of his voice, even if he had air enough to shout. The sound of the boat's turbines would smother his cries, at any rate.

Feeling the direction of the wind, he allowed himself to be buffeted by the waves, toward the distant shoreline, husbanding his strength. Though it weighted him down, he didn't consider unstrapping his Sin Eater from his arm. He did, however, struggle out of the gren-laden combat harness and allow it to sink.

Through force of angry will, he floated in the near

freezing waters, the heat of rage warming him, keeping him from succumbing to the cold. He rode the waves, and the flailing of his limbs became a feeble rhythm.

Part of the time he was half-conscious, not knowing where he was or what he was doing. In his imagination, he swam up a limitless liquid treadmill, clawing his way to the top of countless swells, descending into the hollows, rising to the top again.

Somewhere, far off, swathed in a shimmering corona of bright hope, radiantly beautiful, calling to him with a voice of music, was Fand. She sounded like summer suns and small, innocent things being happy.

On the crest of a wave, he swam into her arms. At first he didn't want to remember her, because her sweetness burned away his anger. She kissed him playfully, called him Ka'in and was simply happy to be together again.

Together.

So complete was his happiness by being together it never occurred to him what it would feel like with her gone. But in between the drawing of one breath and the next, Fand disappeared. And Ka'in was gone, too, and he was just Kane again, a drowning, dying exile, splashing and gasping out his life in a cold sea.

A roller wave picked him up and hurled him full-tilt, head over heels, and for a long, long time blackness as deep and as cold as space slid over him.

Then he lay on smooth, water-worn rocks in sodden clothes, spitting out salt and grit, blinded by the sting of spray. The cold wind slashed at him like claws, and he slowly heaved himself to hands and knees and crawled. He fell forward on his face, lay still, and a wave broke over him. He felt the persistent tug of the undertow, dragging him back, trying to reclaim him.

He heaved himself up again, struggling to his feet. The water in his clothes and boots weighed on him like ten men the size of Grant, but he stumbled out of the reach of the tide. When he was well away from the shoreline, he fell down again, breathing deeply, coughing and snorting the sea from his nasal passages.

He knew, as his lids drooped down over his eyes, he was three-quarters dead already. The icy lash of the wind against his sodden clothing would bring about a fatal case of hypothermia. He was too exhausted to worry about it.

Besides, he felt no pain. He didn't feel anything. He was still there, but not attached to anything any longer. It was a good feeling, not to be attached, not to be anywhere. He could sense nothing, he couldn't order his limbs to motion, nor was he aware of any limbs to order.

For a stretched-out span of time, Kane was content to curl up in the womb of nonexistence. Once, he was sure he heard the music of a harp, played softly and dreamily, a half-forgotten tune, but even that went away.

Then pulses of pain scorched up every nerve ending, boring into the marrow of his bones. Wild bursts of sound set fire to the contents of his skull. Intolerably bright white light assaulted his eyes.

He struggled and fought to control his body. He rasped in a breath, and it burned, deep down inside him, like a little fireball exploding in his lungs.

With a tremendous, groaning effort, he wrenched his eyelids open, and the sleet storm of agony stopped, just like that, as though it had never been.

Warm sunlight punctured the leafy boughs nodding above him. He squinted, but not before glimpsing a clear azure sky full of lazy white clouds, like a Maytime dream. The position of the sun told him it was fairly early in the day, but what day he had no idea.

He opened his eyes wider, craning his neck back and up. Above him loomed a carved-stone pillar and he realized he lay in the soft grass right at its foot. Frowning, he moved his head restlessly. His dark clothing was dry and warm. The Sin Eater was still holstered snugly at his right forearm. He looked down his body and saw the woman.

She stood watching him. She smiled as he looked at her. A pulse began to beat in his heart that seemed to spread to other parts of his body.

The woman was tall and sleek and beautiful, with the look of a lioness about her. She wore a sort of green mantle, cinched at the waist by a scarlet sash. Her narrow face was finely chiseled, with high cheekbones and full lips that held a secret, faintly amused smile.

Her skin was of a milky hue, her golden, unbound hair tumbled down past her thighs, like a flaxen waterfall. The silken tresses had been plaited into four strands, and at the end of each hung a little golden ball. He studied the delicate column of her throat, her long wrists and equally long hands, the high, ripe swell of her breasts, the inviting flare of her hips.

She seemed to glow, to sparkle like a fairy thing, a creature of sunshine and meadows and clear, cold water. Her eyes, which never left his, mesmerized him. They were huge, tip-tilted, golden with vertical slit pupils.

The woman held a long staff in her right hand, enwrapped with vines and many turnings of silver wire. An ivory knob, like an oversize egg, topped it.

Her full lips parted, and in a liquid voice, in a language he had never heard but understood, she said,

"You have not changed overmuch, Cuchulainn, my darling Ka'in."

"Fand," he husked out, yearning and hungry for the sound of her voice.

She whispered to him happily, "Time is a river that twists on itself. Past, present and future are its waters. The fluid of time is life. When life, the spirit ceases to exist, time becomes meaningless. I am overjoyed your spirit lives still, Ka'in. There is still meaning."

Then Kane's brain lurched into shattering motion. A naked sense of reality crashed over him, and he understood he was fully conscious, not caught in a gateway transit or delirious in the Irish Sea. His blood ran cold with fear, and his stomach knotted in panic.

The woman spoke again, but this time her words were an incomprehensible garble of noise.

Kane rolled to his left and sprang to his feet. The woman's expression changed, from a fond smile to a bare-toothed grimace of dementia. Her golden eyes burned in hot pools of fury.

Behind her reached a panorama of sun-drenched green slopes, textures of various subtle colors, each texture a meadow or a forest or a lake. Another woman stood nearby, garbed in a flowing red mantle. Her eyes were blue and her hair was like a braided flame falling over her shoulder. She cradled a brass-framed harp in her arms. He tensed his wrist tendons, palm waiting for the butt of the Sin Eater.

The ivory knob of the staff suddenly tapped his chest. Kane felt a numbing jar. Stone pillar, meadows, blue sky, faces became a meaningless jumble. The air seized in his lungs, and his legs felt like logs. He pressed his back against the carved column of rock and tried to keep from falling down.

He managed to drag in enough oxygen to gasp, "Hold it! I'm not who you think I am."

Fand shifted position, a beautifully flowing, disturbingly familiar movement. In lightly accented English, she asked, "Oh?"

He didn't like the way she said that. "My name is Kane."

"I know," came her soft reply, the mad light dimming in her eyes. "My Ka'in."

He pushed against the stone pillar with his back, achieving his full height. "I'm a stranger here, lady. We've never met."

The flame-haired woman said, "He doesn't remember, Fand. He doesn't remember this is the spot where your spirits first loved."

Kane looked around. "How did I get here?" After the initial surge of fear ebbed away, drawing his blaster seemed less important. He hazarded a quick look at his wrist chron, noting that at least eighteen hours had passed since he had last checked it—aboard the *Cromwell.*

Quietly Fand said, "He will remember, Aifa. He will remember and he will aid me and love me again."

The knob of the staff pointed at his chest again. In a sinister tone, she added, "He *will* remember."

A hot anger fountained up within Kane, from a deep well of arrogance and pride. His hand lashed out, closing around the staff. He jerked it, but Fand maintained her grip. She fell against him, staring into his eyes. She was nearly his height, and the bold, molten gaze was steady.

Her eyes poured coolness into his skull. They were like two streams of gold, pouring a calm, golden quiet over the heat of his anger. He felt the proud strength of her pulsing against him. Slowly she released the staff, and her hands slid around his waist.

Fand kissed him, and the touch of her lips blazed through him like white fire. Her kiss was hungry, passionate, yet touched with melancholy.

Aifa stroked the strings of the harp, and a soft, wandering melody floated out of it, the notes seeming to hang in the air. At the sound of it, something that felt like a hand slapped Kane's mind, propelling it down a dark passage, as if it were a baby sliding down the birth canal into the world.

He spun into a tunnel of darkness, so black, so deep it penetrated every neuron and every synapse point and axon membrane that composed his conscious self.

He emerged from the tunnel amid a thunder of hooves, riding a chariot drawn by two fierce steeds, one gray, one ebony. With the reins wrapped around his left hand, he guided the horses through the towering bastions of the great gate of Ulster.

His face was grim and somber under a black tousled mane. From hip to throat, supple molded leather encased him. The overlapping scales of polished steel on the breastplate caught the sun, sparkling and glinting.

A crimson cloak fastened to his shoulders with golden brooches belled out behind him. In his right hand, he gripped the long, slender shaft of Gae Bolg, his war spear. From a leather scabbard at his hip swung a broadsword, the hilt and pommel worked in silver and precious stones.

The people shouted his name, ''Cuchulainn, the Hound of Ulster, Champion of Eire, Cuchulainn, Ka'in—''

Like water sluicing away a picture etched in a dusty

windowpane, the streets of Ulster wavered, faded, changed.

He found himself running through a maze of cool white corridors, panting, sweat crawling between his black polycarbonate armor and his skin. In his ear, he heard Grant's breathless call.

"Kane! Use your head! We're short on time and you're short on brains! Stop and think!"

Kane snapped his head up and back, fetching himself a painful crack on the stone pillar. The landscape tilted around him. His heart pounded wildly in his chest, and his limbs trembled violently. Harp strings gave a thrumming, throbbing sigh and fell silent.

Fand drew back her head, and her huge eyes glimmered wetly. "Strange," she whispered. "So strange. Ka'in, and yet not Ka'in."

Sweat flowed down his face despite the cool touch of the breeze. "What did you do to me?"

"I?" It was impossible for Fand's eyes to widen, but the slightly mocking smile returned to her lips. "I did nothing."

Kane laughed harsh, mirthless laugh. "You bitch. You hybrid, mutie bitch. You got into my brain, planted those delusions to make me doubt my identity. A trick."

Kane half expected her to react with crazed rage again. Instead, she shook her head slowly, but her eyes did not waver from his. She stepped back from him, tugging on his hand. "Come with me."

He resisted. "I'm looking for friends."

She repeated, "Come with me."

"Why should I?"

"What other choice do you have?"

The elegant simplicity of the question couldn't be answered. Kane went, but Morrigan's words burned in his memory: *If you meet again, she will kill the part of you which is not Cuchulainn. Not out of malice, but out of love.*

Chapter 24

Morrigan led Brigid up a long, winding stair chipped and hacked from stone. They were inside a citadel of basalt cliffs rising sheer from the sea. Through the few windows, Brigid saw green fields inland, and beyond, its dark peaks cloaked in wreathy mists, the Mountains of Mohr shouldered skyward.

Morrigan had told her the cliff was hollow, honey-combed with galleries. They passed level after level of caves, some of them open to the sea. "This fortress was created by the Tuatha De Danaan," Morrigan said. "So long ago that even the earliest Druidic records of it were considered to be repetition of folklore. Since the holo-caust, it has served as the primary home of the Priory of Awen and our allies."

Looking through a tall embrasure, Brigid saw family groups of selkies, wading in pools, eating raw fish.

"According to myth," declared Morrigan, "in the beginning, in the Irish Sea, lived a race of amphibious people. After a while, part of this race wanted to remain entirely on land. There was a quarrel, a battle, and some of the people left the sea forever. In time, they got to missing it and wanted to have it both ways—a life on land and on the ocean. Thusly those became selkies."

Lightly Brigid asked, "What's the real story?"

"We don't know very much," Morrigan admitted, "about the original inhabitants of Eire. Whoever they were, they disappeared as a coherent group at least thirty thousand years ago. Perhaps longer.''

"Do you have chronology for the Tuatha De Danaan and their reign?''

"Only guesses. Collective human memory is short. We could be talking about as few as five thousand years or ten times that. Dating in any ancient history is precarious business, but even more so in Eire.''

The stairs ended at a railed platform, overlooking a circular shaft. Directly below the platform, within the shaft, revolved a huge globe made of a softly gleaming alloy. Continents and land masses rose in relief over its curving skin. At least ten feet in diameter, it hung in a supporting web of slender metal girders. Sprouting from its smooth surface were dozens of delicate crystal rods, shimmering, twisting, turning, stretching out, bending in on themselves at right angles. Brigid studied it, trying to discern a pattern in the shapes. If it was a work of art, it left her cold.

"What is it?'' she asked.

"One of the few genuine Danaan artifacts not stolen by Strongbow. According to the first scholars of the Priory, it's a map.''

Brigid tried to make sense out of her explanation. Then she recalled, word for word, what Lakesh had said: *Some mysterious law unique to Ireland seemed to bring together the great spaces which divided the domain of the physical from the spiritual. That otherworld impinged and overlapped their reality constantly, as well as the entities allegedly living in it.*

She said nothing, but Morrigan nodded in assent. "That is essentially correct. The great spaces your Mr. Lakesh referred to are what you call quantum pathways. Interphase points. Thousands of years ago, the Tuatha

De Danaan and the Na Fferyllt mapped them out. For whatever reason, the Danaan bolted into these vortex points and scattered themselves.''

Brigid eyed the confusing crystalline network, trying to focus beyond its physicality. With an almost audible mental click, the puzzle snapped into place. She suddenly understood that the patterns were three-dimensional depictions of the Celtic labyrinthine cup-and-ring markings. She saw their orientation to cardinal points on the globe, the mathematical correlations of land masses and regions. Rather than a crazy patchwork, the geometrics were pristine. She guessed it was a representation of the global grid, connecting all megalithic sites the world over.

Half to herself, she murmured, ''All world mythologies place sacred points which connect the firmament with the worlds of heaven.''

''Exactly.'' Morrigan's tone was slightly relieved. ''Because of the advanced geodetic and geographic science of the Danaan, Eire became the geodetic center of not only the physical world, but the nonphysical, as well. To them, it was 'meridian zero.' The mountain of the gods at the center of the world, to paraphrase Scripture.''

''Lakesh was right. Project Cerberus was only a rediscovery of an ancient system of physics.''

''Exactly,'' said Morrigan again. ''And how those old laws are applied in the here and now, in Ireland, writes the fate of humanity.''

Brigid swiveled her head, staring into Morrigan's face, seeing that she wasn't being melodramatic. ''Explain.''

''To you, from outside, what happens on this little isle is unimportant. But we live in this little world. We die in it, too. And now, what happens here could truly bring about the last days upon the planet.''

Again Brigid said, ''Explain.''

Morrigan sighed in exasperation. ''Do you have a year you can spare? I'll try to give you the broadest idea of what I mean—you came here to open the vortices, hoping to find entry to the home dimension of the entities you call Archons.''

''Yes.''

''Lord Strongbow wants to use them, too. He wishes to forge quantum pathways, points of entry all over Earth, as ingress for invasion forces.''

She gestured to the globe. ''The transfers must take place at very precise points. Each point represents a dimensional coordinate in the space-time continuum.''

''Operation Chronos,'' Brigid blurted, the implications building and piling and almost overwhelming her. ''If the naturally occurring gateways are opened, it's not a simple matter of moving things from place to place, is it?''

Morrigan stated grimly, ''No, it is not. Even your mentor Lakesh does not fully understand the forces flowing within the vortex points. The Project Cerberus technology channels them along very controlled pathways. Without that rigid control, temporal anomalies would erupt throughout the entire track of history, imperiling both the future and the past. Last year and this week could coexist, pushing humanity into meaningless, futile upheavals and chaos without ever knowing the reason. Imagine what is done tomorrow eliminating the civilization of 3998, or conversely, wiping out the world of 1984.''

''Or,'' said Brigid, ''the world of 2001.''

The feelings of dread that had threatened to consume

her in recent days returned. "And what has this to do with Fand?"

"As Strongbow said, she is the key to all the gateways. She has an inborn, biochemically instinctive understanding of their principles. She is human, Danaan and Annunaki. She is the genetic sister of the first Fand, some fifteen hundred generations or more removed.

"She can, through simple focused thought, dilate the matrix points in Eire, and if she so desires, allow elements of the otherworlds to seep into this one. That is how she protects the island from Strongbow's incursions, by slightly altering probabilities."

"Yes," said Brigid musingly. "Lakesh would call it a weak probability wave dysfunction."

"Just so," Morrigan replied. "But Fand has the potential to activate all the vortices simultaneously, triggering a spatial and temporal discontinuity which could engulf the entire planet. The chains of human reason would be broken. Mankind would be plunged into an eternal Dark Age, beside which the horrors of the nukecaust and skydark would be a quaint memory."

"If she possesses these abilities, why hasn't she used them before?"

The girl didn't answer for long moment. She closed her blind eyes as if in pain. Finally she said quietly, "She has not had a reason ere now."

"Morrigan," Brigid urged, "you must tell me everything."

Drawing in a short breath, she said, "Fand's namesake was a Danaan princess who fell in love with the warrior Cuchulainn. He had fallen asleep against a standing stone. When he awoke, he found two Danaan women whipping him with rods while he lay paralyzed by their beauty. Fand was one of them.

"She enlisted his help in battle against her father's enemies in an Otherworld. By historical accounts, Danaan women had a tendency to pick human men of destiny for lovers."

Brigid nodded. "So I've read. The trysts were characterized by many of the same traits as more modern UFO-abduction reports—paralysis, initiation, sex and sometimes even reproduction. So?"

"There is more," Morrigan said. "Even though Cuchulainn's wife was jealous and Fand's husband nearly went to war with him, the two continued their affair. Finally a mantle of forgetfulness was placed over the two lovers. Now, after a thousand years, Fand believes she has found Cuchulainn again."

Brigid stiffened, feeling a rush of heat to her cheeks. "Kane?"

"Ka'in, yes."

"He isn't the reincarnation of Cuchulainn," she said rather desperately. "He—"

Brigid broke off, memories of the mat-trans jump visions flooding her mind.

"That's right," said Morrigan. "You didn't know. That's the misery of it. You don't. Kane doesn't. But Fand does."

"Kane won't cooperate with that delusion," Brigid declared.

"*Delusion?*" Morrigan repeated the word with an angry emphasis. "The doctrine of soul transmigration is the underpinning of Celtic spiritual law. Think about this—my namesake, Morrigan, was an ally of Cuchulainn's."

"And do you have conscious memories of that time?" Brigid challenged.

"No," Morrigan responded. "I only know the legend."

"Then I don't find your thesis of reincarnation particularly relevant. Memories are a subjective phenomena anyway."

"What is the speaking stone of Cascorach but a repository of memory?" asked Morrigan. "The ancient priesthoods of this land knew that stone and metal and crystalline things retain a 'memory'. They can be charged with it, like a storage battery. Quantum theory deals with this electromagnetic effect, though I'm not sure of the exact terminology.

"Fand has tapped into these elemental memories—it all became part of her, or she became part of it. The whole of our history, our legends, living within one body, one mind. She is caught in all the energies which bind Eire in a great, invisible net. She will cast this net over Kane, and it will not matter to him if the memories he experiences are true ones or imposed from without."

Everything she knew or thought she knew about Kane raced fleetingly through Brigid's mind. His depth of naiveté was matched only by his cynicism. His loathing of deliberate hurt and hypocrisy found expression in surliness. Despite his bravado, he had a grace, and though she found it difficult to recognize, an unplumbed depth of passion.

"Yes," Morrigan said, very sadly. "You know that in your soul. And Fand knows it, too."

Despising the sudden quaver in her voice, Brigid asked, "Will she use his passion against him, for her own ends?"

"For *their* own ends. To dilate the continuum, to bathe in the matrix of the past."

Brigid took a deep, calming breath. "This all presupposes Kane can be manipulated or seduced. I can tell you that won't be easy."

"I see in your mind a belief that Kane is too stubborn to be swayed by mere words. Emotions are another matter. Fand will expose him to her mad love, peel away the layers of his identity until she reaches the core of Cuchulainn. Another mantle of forgetfulness will fall over him. He will remember only what Fand wants him to remember. The Kane you know will cease to be."

Brigid looked to the crystal-wrapped globe. "There has to be a way to intervene, to reason with her."

"No." Morrigan's tone was flat. "Do you not think the Priory has tried since she left us?"

"What happened to her mother, the member of your order Strongbow kidnapped?"

"At last report, she lives among the Clan mac Trenmor as a sort of healer, a priestess."

"Can't she reach her own daughter?"

Morrigan visibly tried to repress a shudder. "When her child was six years old, Sister Fand tried to kill her. For that she was banished, cast out. As far as we know, mother and daughter have not met for twenty-five years."

"If she tried to kill her, she must have believed there was a good reason."

"She could not bear the thought of Fand, of the manner in which she was conceived. She felt she had been lied to and betrayed by the Priory."

"Why?"

Morrigan shook her head. "That is not for me to say."

Tersely Brigid said, "Take me to her. Without the interphaser, she's our only hope."

"I can arrange it, but I must warn you—there is little

love between the Clan mac Trenmor and the Priory of Awen.'' Morrigan turned toward the stairs.

Brigid followed, glancing back at the suspended globe and its maze of twisting, turning crystal rods. Portals, gateways, exit and entry points. The whole of Heaven, Hell and the Earth hanging there.

''We are all,'' murmured Morrigan, her voice echoing hollowly, ''children of cosmic waters.''

''Right,'' retorted Brigid darkly. ''And some of us need to be sent upstairs without our suppers for a couple of centuries.''

Chapter 25

In the largest hut, Grant sat on a pile of furs, facing Mother Fand. Between them lay the open interphaser case. The woman inspected the metal pyramidion keenly. He had told her everything about it and his mission.

At a long table across the single room, two young girls pounded meal with stone mortars. At a few Gaelic words from Mother Fand, one of them handed a crockery bowl to Domi. She brought it over to Grant.

"Drink this. They say you'll feel better."

Reluctantly he took the bowl and drank. He winced at the bitter taste but took several swallows. He handed it back and rubbed his aching head. To his surprise, the pain in his skull, hand and lower back almost immediately began to fade.

"What was that?" he asked.

Mother Fand shrugged. "An herbal mixture. Nothing too complicated or arcane. Or toxic."

Grant pulled a cigar from a zipped inner pocket of his coat and set fire to it with his lighter. Seeing Mother Fand looking at it curiously, he drew out another and offered it to her. She accepted it and a light with a murmured word of thanks.

For a moment, they sat and smoked in silence, studying each other through a drifting plane of tobacco smoke. Domi sat down, conspicuously close to Grant.

Mother Fand said, "I was a healer, a practitioner of holistic arts. I had a little second-floor shop and my own weekly radio show."

Grant had no idea of what she was talking about, but he didn't interrupt to ask her.

She smiled wryly and blew a perfect smoke ring. "You couldn't have gotten me to smoke one of these if you put a gun to my head."

"Times change," he said softly.

She sighed, smoke curling from between her open lips. "They do indeed."

Grant could see how life had wounded the woman at every turn. Still, she possessed a sad, graceful dignity.

She lowered her gaze to the interphaser. "How much of your tale should I believe?"

"All of it. None of it. Your call."

Mother Fand raised her eyes and stared into his. "I was just nineteen, you know, when the end times came." She spoke quickly, quietly. "I was selected to join the Priory when I was twelve. They educated me, supported me. Ah, I was so very, very proud of my Danaan blood. I had no notion it would save me from the nukecaust. At least, Karabatos thought it was worth saving."

"He told us the story," Grant replied.

Her eyes flickered with an unreadable emotion. "When I awoke there, in the vault beneath Great Skellig, I thought only a day or two had passed. Imagine my denial when Karabatos told me over 150 years had passed. Nor did I believe I was pregnant. Probably the longest gestation period in the history of the world."

"He said you escaped before you gave birth."

"That I did. It wasn't hard, since he was so preoccupied with his plans to build a power base. I returned here, to Ireland. My home.''

She chuckled bitterly. "A home I did not recognize. It had been spared much of the hell which overtook the rest of the planet, but by no means all of it. Fallout had killed my people by the hundreds of thousands, and since they were never numerous most of Ireland became as it had after the great famine. The wilderness came back to claim much of it again.

"The survivors had enough water, enough food from the sea, but scurvy killed even more of them. They began to raid England, as in the old days. And as in the old days, some of them stayed. The ancient way of the Celt, the Druid, nature magic slowly returned here.

"What you see now is a vast improvement over conditions during the first couple of generations following the nuclear winter, the skydark. All things considered, it was truly the luck of the Irish.''

She took contemplative puff on the cigar. "Imagine my surprise when I found an enclave of the Priory of Awen still in existence. It was they who had drawn on the earth forces to protect Erin from the worst of the nukecaust, and they who managed to destroy an English invasion fleet by invoking the old, old treaty with the sea-peoples.''

"Sea-peoples?" Grant inquired. "You mean the selkies?''

She nodded shortly. "They were delighted to see me, more so when I told them the details of my survival. They wanted me to carry Enlil's offspring to full term, you see.''

Grant stiffened in surprise, even revulsion. "Why?''

"There is a line from the Book of Enoch— 'In those days shall the elect and holy race descend from the upper heavens and their seed shall then be with the sons of men.' They viewed the child in my womb as the fulfillment of ancient prophecy, of the pact of Patrick, the entire reason why the Priory existed.

"They were deaf to my objections that the child had been conceived outside the parameters of the pact. I had been raped, and it had been arranged by Karabatos for his own purposes.

"I told them of the vow I had sworn in Great Skellig. They ignored me. When I told them I would not carry such a hell-spawn, they ignored me. So I left the monastery, and that they did not ignore. They brought me back and held me prisoner until I carried the child to full term."

Mother Fand passed a hand over her eyes. "I don't remember much of the labor, except for the hours upon hours of maddening agony, blood and exhaustion. At last, she was born, the little goddess, the fairy queen, the trinity of human, Annunaki and Danaan."

Grant's voice was hushed. "You didn't look at her in that way?"

"How could I? I knew more than they. Karabatos had told me about his plan."

"Plan?"

"Recessive genes, you see. The Annunaki lived in a kind of mental symbiosis with each other, sharing and utilizing each other's gifts and skills and potentials. That's why they were so efficient and organized."

Grant frowned, recalling Lakesh's description of the Archons: *Each Archon is anchored to another through some kind of hyperspatial filaments of their mind energy, akin to the hive mind of certain insect species.*

He ventured, "A hive mind?"

Mother Fand nodded. "Very much like that. My

daughter, Fand, by a cruel trick of heredity, was born with a brain designed to be one of a community of interdependent minds. That community no longer existed and had not for many thousands of years. From her earliest months of development, that unconscious part of her brain sought that symbiosis. She couldn't find it among humans, but she found it in the flows of energy swirling about Erin.''

A pattern is forming here, thought Grant grimly. A pattern of such intricate evil it made his belly turn a slow, icy flip-flop.

"When she was six," continued Mother Fand, "I knew exactly what she was, though no one in the Priory did. She was their little goddess of the trinity, you see, the living *awenyddion*. So, it fell to me. I stole into her room one fine spring night to kill her."

Mother Fand reached down into her right boot and in an eye-blurring motion whipped out a leaf-bladed knife. "With this. But I did not. I could not. I was a healer, not an assassin. She was tiny and innocent. And damn my soul, I had come to love her."

"What happened then?" asked Grant.

"I was discovered and banished. For a year, I wandered the length and breadth of Ireland, seeking out descendants of my family. I found a few here, in the Clan mac Trenmor. Great-great-grand-nieces and nephews. They accepted me, came to revere me as a witch-warrior, mother of Eire's new guardian. Mother Fand."

Her face creased in a half grin of self-mockery. "It's a far different life than I led before the nuke, but I've lived it longer. It feels right to me now."

"And your daughter?"

"As I feared, the Priory could not control her, especially as she grew older. She left them to rebuild Erin in the image of the old myths, the old legends.''

''And you've not seen her since?''

Mother Fand shook her head, stubbing out the cigar. ''Never. Not even from afar.''

''Why not?''

She sighed, frowning. ''Little point, is there? The Priory, Fand and myself pursue our separate lives when we should all be making common cause. We all fear the Imperium Brittania's designs upon us, but we are too divided to make concerted effort against it.''

Slowly Grant said, ''Usually when there's a three-way deadlock like this, somebody calls for a fourth party to mediate.''

''And who would that be?'' Mother Fand questioned sharply. ''You and your friends from America who were dispatched here by Strongbow?''

Taking a deep breath, Grant asked, ''Did you know that Karabatos—or Strongbow—conducted a gene-splicing program on himself and his dragoons?''

She cocked her head quizzically. ''Gene-splicing?''

''Genetic material from Enlil. He now has Annunaki characteristics. If a hive-mind tendency is part of them, then that would explain how he exerts such control over his dragoons.''

There was no need to voice the rest of it. The rush of horrified realization filled Mother Fand's eyes with tears of shock. She crossed herself, saying in a high, aspirated voice, ''And Fand has those same character-istics.''

Grant nodded. ''That explains his obsession with her. The only Annunaki minds alive—incomplete, not fully formed, touching, wrestling, straining.''

The tears spilled down her cheeks, bisecting the spirals. "No wonder she went mad. And all these years I thought she was a monster."

A moan of pain, of guilt worked its way up her throat. Hugging herself, she began to rock slightly to and fro. "What have I done? Oh, sweet Jesus, Mary and Joseph, what I have done?"

"Stop it," Grant told her sternly. "You've done nothing. And that's the problem. You need to start doing something, to find out what it means."

In a groaning voice, Mother Fand declared, "I know what it means. To gain control of the vortices, he will gain control of my daughter. Then the world itself. The reign of the Serpent Kings will begin anew."

The brassy voice of horn rang through the air. There was a sudden commotion from the open door of the hut. Phin poked his head in, face grim and hard and watchful. He announced, "Mother, we have trespassers in the wood. They fly the banners of the Priory of Awen."

Chapter 26

That morning the dragoons standing before the recessed vanadium double doors were Carter and Woodson. Both were dark-haired and sallow-skinned, and they came swiftly to attention when Lord Strongbow and Lieutenant Galt approached across the polished corridor floor.

Strongbow didn't so much as nod to them. He had raised them up to serve and follow him forever, and their children after them—providing he allowed them to father offspring.

Pressing the stud of the sonic key in his hand, he waited as the doors swung inward on invisible hinges. He and Galt strode forward, past the sentries and into the singularity inversion chamber. The four-ton doors closed silently behind them.

The walls, ceiling and floor of the chamber formed one continuous surface, making a huge, hollow ellipse measuring a hundred feet on the longer diameter, as if they were within the shell of an impossibly gargantuan egg.

From the curving walls of the chamber jutted platforms connected by a series of cage-enclosed lifts and crossed girders. Convection currents danced like translucent, crackling veils from tall Y-shaped induction pylons.

In the exact center of the ellipse, surrounded by a complexity of electronic consoles, relays and snaking power cables, floated a huge orb of absolute, impenetrable blackness. It was like a bubble of burnished obsidian, but its surface reflected no light whatsoever. An eight-foot-high curve of transparent armaglass encircled the black sphere and its support systems.

The singularity floated there, motionless, trapped like a jinni inside of its magnetic bottle, the splash-back of its quantum energies confined and redirected.

Strongbow's yellow eyes swept over the consoles, noting the readings on the indicator gauges. Needles and lights held steady, registering no fluctuations whatsoever.

He was too disciplined to give vent to profanity, especially in front of subordinates, but he did say, "Nothing."

Galt said, "Perhaps it's a bit too early, milord. The *Cromwell*'s last message reported that the black Yank had taken the interphaser ashore. It's rather a long journey by foot to the Boyne."

Strongbow nodded broodily. "Providing he even knows how to reach the Boyne and that he was not set upon and eviscerated by the Celts."

He devoted very little thought to what had happened to the other Americans or even to Morrigan. The selkies had attacked the ship; therefore she had failed him. Her mutant abilities had been a boon on more than one occasion, but as it was, she was Irish and therefore eminently expendable.

He had once, very fleetingly, entertained sexual fantasies about her, but he no longer had the drives or even the genitals of a man. All his emotions and ambitions were represented by the black, floating orb. It symbolized power, and power had no gender.

Followed by Galt, Strongbow crossed the floor to a

lift. He pushed the button to raise them to the second level. He walked along the narrow catwalk that ended at a small, railed platform. It hung directly over the black bubble and held an upright instrument panel, the switching station for the control consoles below.

Every bit of apparatus and equipment in the huge chamber had been fitted into place by him over a period of five years, following the specs laid down by the intellect of the Totality Concept. He had borrowed bits and pieces of the discoveries made by long-dead theoreticians such as Mohandas Lakesh Singh, Stephen Hawking, Torrance Burr and Spiros Marcuse.

There was a certain irony in the fact that much of the equipment had already been built by British scientists under the auspices of Mission Snowbird's SDI program. When thirty of them got too close to the truth, to the real fruit of their labors, Strongbow had arranged for their tragic suicides—but not before confiscating and secretly copying all records of their work. That particular assignment had been code-named "Alternative 3."

Strongbow walked around the armaglass barrier, studying the false impression of three dimensions given off by the orb. *False impression...*

Sometimes he believed that his entire life before the nuke had been nothing but. There were things he had done with the fullest pleasure, confident his actions were for the greater good. That all changed. Instead of a good soldier, a dedicated scientist, he became a man suspected of a breach of security on a secret project. His prior record of service meant nothing. He had learned things that weren't meant to be learned.

Nothing could be conclusively proven, but they had frozen him out. They killed his old life, his old loyalties and created a disenfranchised, lonely man. What woman wanted a man whose reputation had been besmirched?

Strongbow shook his head, pushing the old memories back into a dark corner of his mind. Regardless of his humiliations, one irrefutable fact towered above all others—he had survived, he had thrived, he had power and he would get more of it, far more than the remote physicists of the Totality Concept had ever envisioned.

Physicists and mathematicians were as inbred as a pack of nineteenth-century hillbillies, regardless of the country of their birth. They talked a lot among themselves, and a word here and word there was all it took to build on each other's separate researches.

But even they had never conceived melding their disparate yet similar fields of experimentation in such a fashion as he had done. By combining the working principles of Lakesh's quantum interphase inducers with Burr's temporal displacer capacitors, he had constructed a singularity—for all intents and purposes an artificial black hole.

Hyperdimensional physics depended on the directed acceleration and deceleration of subatomic particles. The singularity was the physical result of the absence of a propagation medium. Powered by a small thermonuclear generator, the singularity was the black maw of eternity, potentially the hub of a wheel to every time, place and person.

The picture of the singularity in its entirety had come quite clearly to him only weeks after his resurrection from the cryo-sleep. The concept of alternative worlds was not new to the theoreticians of Operation Chronos, nor to him once he got his hands on their findings.

When they had drawn the chronon curtain aside and peeked into the nuke-ravaged future, they hadn't pulled it closed and peeked elsewhere. Rather, they had flung it wide. The Archons had decided that particular future best suited humankind and themselves. Although there had been a multitude to choose from, none of the other possible futures offered the opportunity to thin out the herd, to cull the useless eaters from the face of the planet.

Strongbow didn't object to the selection of futures; he only resented not being included in it. Now he looked to another future, one where the world was free of Archon bondage.

Of course, humanity needed to be in bondage, but not to a small, dying group of usurpers and their far larger group of hybridized pawns. Mankind was easy to control. It all came down to numb brains, empty bellies and organization.

The true gift of Enlil and his race had lain in their organizational skills. And though Annunaki genes had been scattered for thirty thousand years or more, their voices still whispered to him, reminding him how certain things might be accomplished, codified, organized.

The singularity had been designed to do all of that, by wringing order from the chaotic flow of the quantum stream, which, of course, only *looked* like chaos. When the energies of the stream were channeled into the singularity, true order could be imposed simply by willing it, as a stone thrown into a pond sends ripples to the farthest shores.

It waited only for the activation of the Americans' interphaser device within a vortex point to set in motion events which hadn't happened, yet any of which could.

But the singularity was quiescent, suspended in its magnetic container, radiating nothing but coldness. He looked over through the window of the ready-room, seeing the heavily armed jump team standing at attention, prepared to respond to their lord's order to leap through the singularity. For the past ten hours, they had waited patiently for the command to invade.

Strongbow's lips tightened at the thought of Fand's arrogant incursion of his sanctum in the ministry. He tried to not hate her, tried not to think about her at all, but it was too late. She sensed him.

For an instant, he saw her again, leaning forward with her hair like a flaxen stream pouring over her shoulders. Her golden eyes were full of mocking laughter. Strongbow heard her quite plainly.

Dream other dreams, goblin-man. Yours are unattainable. You will not have me. I will watch you die, Karabatos-called-Strongbow. I will watch you die and dance in your cold blood.

The image faded in his mind, and he swung around to see if Galt had detected the momentary telepathic touch. If he had, his stony expression showed no sign of it.

It had taken several years for Strongbow to come to grips with the mind-link he shared with Fand. Due to her Danaan ancestry, she was more proficient in its use, injecting the belief in the *geas* field into his mind and he in turn transmitting that same belief to his dragoons. The link was like a virus, intangible yet deadly.

When he thought of the Annunaki-Danaan-human hybrid, he always thought of her mother, the beautiful Sister Fand. He had wanted her, more than any other woman except for Janice.

Janice had mattered to him; she had promised she would stick by him no matter how the investigation into his actions turned out. And suddenly she had vanished from her support position in Overproject Majestic's offices. She had left a note for him. It read: "I'm sorry, Larry. But I can't take it anymore."

He had never seen her again. A lilt of cruel laughter echoed within his skull. He wasn't sure if it was Fand or a memory.

Morrigan had served as something of a psi-shield from the little demon's mental assaults, but the link was always there between them, a haunting presence on the outer edges of his conscious awareness.

Though he knew he was wasting time and effort, he focused on the ebony surface of the singularity and pictured himself and Fand. She lay on an altar stone and he knelt across her naked body, his weight pressed down between her legs. He had her throat between his hands and he watched the blood grow dark in her pale cheeks, watched as the veins stood out on her temples, watched as her tongue protruded past her lips. She fought very little as Strongbow strangled the life from her, even as he planted his seed within her dying body. He crooned a whispering refrain in her small, delicately pointed ear.

"Sir?"

Galt's voice dragged him away from the deep obsidian of the orb, back from his fervent dreams. He glanced toward the Lieutenant, feeling sweat slowly drip from his brow ridges. "Yes?"

"You said something?"

Strongbow palmed away perspiration on his forehead and forced a dry chuckle. "Did I now? What?"

Hesitantly Galt replied, "Something do to with the greater good, I believe."

Strongbow studied his distorted reflection in the mirrored lenses masking Galt's eyes. He smiled at it, a small, thin smile. "I see. Well, that *is* what all this is about, isn't it, Lieutenant?"

Chapter 27

Kane walked with Fand down the grassy slope, Aifa trailing serenely along just behind them. In the broad valley below spread the upper reaches of a forest, but a forest that looked somehow unreal, like colored pictures of an enchanted wood from an old children's book. Beyond, he saw the silver blue loopings of a river.

As they approached the outer rim of the woods, Kane was struck by the delicately curving trunks beneath a maze of glinting leaves and fantastically hued fruit. He stared hard, blinked and for a split second, the trees seemed to become transparent.

Aifa's fingers strummed the strings of the harp, and he felt the sweet notes striking sympathetic vibrations in his ears, then his mind. It wasn't like any sound he had ever heard before. At the same moment, the trees lost their shimmery, semi-unreal appearance and solidified.

Fand turned her head toward him, and he deliberately refused to meet her gaze. Her huge eyes, penetrating and anxious, seemed to be gauging his reaction to the music.

At each finger stroke of the harp, a sensation of lightness grew within him, as though his body were shedding flesh, bone, muscle. The music was beautiful, like something he had heard in a dream.

Aifa began to sing, in a sweet, high voice.

These are the things that were dear to Ka'in,
The din of battle, the banquet's glee,
The bay of his hounds through the rough glen ring-
ing,
And the blackbird singing in gnarled tree,
The shingle grinding along the shore
When they dragged his war boats 'neath a savage
sun,
The dawn wind whistling his spears among,
And the magic song of a victory won.

The forested valley was dim, for all the blaze of the sun overhead. No birds sang in the trees, but Kane glimpsed darting motions in the high boughs, tiny winged forms hovering and peeking through the bright leaves.

He wasn't able to get a straight-on view of whatever they were, but he had the impression they were a pale gold in color, as if covered by phosphorescence.

The harp music became a rippling, racing flood of chords, and the melody wrapped itself around his nerves in a constant shiver of ecstasy. The vibrations grew in him, quivering, stinging, arousing him. A snow-white shape moved in the dappled shadows. It looked like a small horse, but its big blue eyes were wide with innocent wisdom, and a spiraling horn rose from its forehead.

Kane stopped in his tracks, squeezing his eyes shut in desperation. He saw Baptiste, her hair floating around her terror-stricken face, a stream of bubbles spewing from her mouth, which was open in a silent scream. He set his fists against his temples.

"Oh, God," he whispered, "what's the matter with me?"

He opened his eyes, and the magical wood was a solid stretch of thick, ordinary trees and thorny underbrush. No fruit dangled from the branches, and no winged, glowing shapes flitted among them. He saw nothing that he could have even mistaken for a unicorn.

"Do not doubt," came Fand's breathy words. She was very close to him and he felt the heat of her body. *Do not doubt.*

The harp thrummed and throbbed, seguing into a dark and haunting melody that drove a nail of stabbing pain through his head. He flinched, eyes closing in reaction to it. He forced them open and saw the forest as it had been.

The music softened, caressing him, the pain fading. He began walking again, through the beautiful, silent wood. Then the rim of the forest fell away in a sweeping curve. From it stretched an open glade. Dark masses of stone rose from the ground. He knew they were incredibly old, the bones of a civilization that had existed millennia before the age of the pharaohs. But it wasn't dead. Kane felt its faint, ghostly breath.

Built into the face of a knoll, a wide circle of standing stones surrounded a dark entrance. Formed of upright slabs of rock, the portal was some seven feet tall and five wide. A massive ovoid stone lay in the grass before the entrance. It was covered with intricate swirling glyphs. There was something savage in its construction, yet strong and fierce with pride. He gazed at the enigmatic stone spirals, still unblemished by the scars of time.

Kane felt the wind ruffling his hair, and it murmured to him about immortality of the soul.

Fand said softly, "This was the palace of Angus Og'. To my people—the Danaan—it was a doorway."

The Tuatha De Danaan had built something of themselves into this monument, and it was still there, beckoning and calling. The sunlight seemed to coalesce into a shimmering curtain, like a heat wave over a desert at high noon. For one brief instant, he glimpsed an image on the curtain—a fantastically spired and turreted city. Then it was gone.

"Look at me now," whispered Fand. "Look at me now."

Slowly, reluctantly he turned toward her. Her high-boned, delicate face with the arrogant mouth, the eyes as golden as the first rays of dawn and as hot and as proud.

"Now, Ka'in, you will remember."

She leaned toward him, turning her face up, lips parted. For a wild, reeling moment, Kane felt her raw needs, the radiation of a fierce sexual energy. He felt his body respond, and his hands gripped her shoulders. Then he thrust her away from him, holding her out at arm's length.

Speaking quickly, firmly, before the animal passion in her eyes turned to molten rage, he said, "Enough of this. My name is Kane, and I want my questions answered. Where is Baptiste?"

Fand's face twisted, convulsed. "Is she your mate?"

"No, she's—"

"Long ago you were torn between two loves," Fand growled, voice rising to a high, wild pitch. "Your mortal wife, Emer, and myself. I gave you up—I, a high princess of the Danaan race. It was a tumultuous shame within me to be deserted. 'Twill not happen again, Ka'in."

Kane released her. Taking a deep breath, he said very

sincerely, "Lady, you've confused me with somebody else. My name is Kane."

Fand heeled around toward Aifa and screeched a stream of Gaelic words. Aifa's hand immediately struck the hard threads of her harp.

Reverberations leaped out, seized Kane, shook him, hurt him. Screens of fire flared in his eyes, and fiery needles of agony pierced his eardrums. Snarling, he clapped his hands over his ears as Aifa continued to stroke the harp strings.

He had no idea how the musical instrument could have such an effect on him. His only frame of reference was the deadly infrasound wands wielded by the hybrids in Dulce. But this felt different—rather than a physical assault, the harp seemed to batter at his mind, at his psyche.

The notion of shooting the harp out of the woman's hands occurred to him, but before he could act on it, Aifa plucked another series of threads and a wave of exquisite pain crashed through him. He staggered, vision fogging.

Then he turned and ran toward the rock-framed entrance to the tumulus. Bounding over, he raced into the passageway. He thought it would be black as pitch inside, but it wasn't quite. It was full of smoky, yellow-red shadows that shifted all around him as he ran.

The floor rose in a gentle slope. He paid no attention to the intricate carvings and designs on the walls. The incline led to another doorway, and he half stumbled into a central chamber. The ceiling rose to a height of nearly twenty feet, composed of large slabs of stone laid one atop the other. Light peeped in from a small boxlike opening at the apex of the roof.

Nothing appeared to be in the chamber, but Kane's

hair-trigger nerves told him otherwise. It was all gloom and silence, and not even the labored rasp of his breathing echoed from the walls.

The place was older than anything he had ever seen, older even than the Cliff Palace ruins in Mesa Verde canyon, or the city of Kharo-Khoto in the Black Gobi. But this was no ruin. The spiral patterns on the stone walls were slightly blurred, but still identifiable. He reflected on how long ago the rocks had been quarried and went on to reflect it was probably so long ago there wasn't a living memory or even a record of it.

Pacing the circular chamber, Kane saw a shaft of cool golden sunlight fall directly on one of the ornamented stones, highlighting its confusing swirling glyphs. He approached it, seeing that the surface was worn and smooth where an inestimable number of hands had been laid against it over inestimable aeons.

He reached out for the stone, the sun highlighting its design. As his fingers brushed the deep cuts, a low, sweet, mocking laugh came out of the shadows of the passage. Before he could turn, the harp sang. A storm of sensation caught him, wrapped him in layers of invisible flame. He felt as if he were being shaken until all the pieces of himself were scattered over the gulfs of infinity.

A great dark hand clamped on Kane's brain. The breath tore out of his lungs. A sense of suffocation overtook him. His body expanded enormously, his head in the clouds, his feet at the bottom of a chasm. Fand's voice came like a sibilant, delighted whisper in a vast cave.

"Ah, now it begins. Now he will remember."

The harp thrummed, but Kane felt no pain. He had passed beyond all sensation. He relived his life, from newborn infant up through the years, reviewing, reexperiencing, reknowing every detail of his existence, retracing his route from the present to the past. His training in the Magistrate Division loomed up, then his childhood flickered past.

He remembered his little flat in the high-towered Enclaves of Cobaltville, he remembered where he had died, near Slieve Fuad, and how he had bound himself to a tall pillar stone so that he might die standing up and not lying down.

He remembered the battle with the Firbolgs, aboard the flagship of their invasion fleet. He threw his rope, the grapnel hooking into the wooden rail, and he climbed swiftly onto the deck. He saw Fand's naked body bound to the mast with thin, cruelly knotted cords.

She saw him and her mouth opened. She cried out, "Behind you, Ka'in!"

Whirling, he faced a wiry little Firbolg and drove the butt of Gae Bolg into his face. Then he bounded across the deck, engaged two warriors with only his spear. It was a mad whirl of a struggle, hewing at snarling faces that wavered out of the night, slapping down sword thrusts and stabbing for the guts of the enemy. Men fell, and others took their places. He slashed and thrust, feeling the blade of Gae Bolg sink in, and he roared the war cry of his clan, the battle scream of the Ulstermen.

Then he remembered the trysting place with Fand, the Strand of the Yew Tree...

A soft, quick rustle and she stood there in the shaft of sunlight. Her face was as he remembered and loved—proud and fine with a wild, mad strength behind the beauty.

"How you fought," she husked out. "How you fought, beloved!"

Kane looked at his hand splayed out over the incised spiral. It almost seemed to be another man's hand, but the scars on it were from his own battles. He took it away and locked gazes with Fand.

She reached behind her, undid the clasp at the back of her neck and her mantle slid down her body with a silken rustle. She was naked beneath it, her high, firm breasts gleaming like opals, her body slender, catlike, graceful and powerful. The diffused sunlight ran pale gold across her ivory skin, striking sharp shadows under the arching rim of her rib cage and her flat belly. The fine hair at the junction of her smoothly contoured thighs was like spun gold.

Kane stepped to her, and her arms encircled his broad shoulders. He smoothed the long flaxen hair away from her face, and it spilled down her back, nearly to her knees. He kissed her long neck.

She murmured, "Oh, how I have ached for you."

Gently he cupped her breasts, feeling her nipples harden and stiffen at his touch. She gasped and leaned heavily into him, her legs trembling. His fingers explored her face as his lips found hers. She moaned into his mouth. He caressed her throat, then applied pressure to the tiny, racing pulses on either side of her neck.

Fand gasped, jerked, trying to push him away. He maintained, then increased the steady pressure of his fingertips. With a sigh like a baby drifting off to sleep, her body sagged and went slack in his arms. He held her easily, looking down into her upturned face, at the huge eyes closed now in unconsciousness.

"I told you before," he whispered coldly. "My name is *Kane*."

Chapter 28

Brigid and Morrigan rode into the gloom between the gargantuan tree trunks that rose smoothly out of sight into a vast canopy of intertwined boughs and branches.

Brigid sat in the saddle of a dappled gray mare while Morrigan was mounted on a bay. Both horses were well trained, and Brigid's initial trepidation about riding vanished after the first half hour.

Her clothing had been returned, but not her blaster. According to Morrigan, who had it from Diuran, the Mauser was rusting at the bottom of the Irish Sea.

For an hour or more, they had skirted the margin of the forest until they reached a cleft in the overgrown vastness. Morrigan reined her animal to a halt and from a saddlebag produced a folded square of cloth and a slim wooden rod. As she shook the cloth open, Brigid saw it bore the emblem of the Priory of Awen.

"Are you relying on that to ensure us safe passage?" she asked as Morrigan affixed it to the rod.

"Could as likely be a target," she replied. "The Clan mac Trenmor has a very sectarian point of view. They look at the Priory with suspicion, due in the main to Mother Fand's tales of betrayal."

"There's a state of war between you?"

Morrigan shook her head. "Nothing so clear-cut. Some twenty years ago, after Mother Fand fled, we sent emissaries to negotiate with her, so she would return to the Priory of her own accord. The clan protected her, drove the emissaries away. The Priory never tried again.''

The two of them rode into the green depths. They had to go slowly, pushing aside and bending branches as the horses went forward. Dangling creepers caught and snared their heads.

Though they couldn't see it, the sun slowly began its descent and the forest pathways grew dimmer. When, at Brigid's estimation, several miles had rolled past, Morrigan reined her bay sharply to a halt. She cocked her head from one side to the other.

''Listen! Do you hear it?''

Brigid listened for a silent moment, hearing nothing but the sigh and rustle of breeze-touched foliage. ''Hear what?''

''A horn. Way off, like.''

A handful of seconds later, very, very faintly sounded a long note.

''There it is again!'' exclaimed Morrigan. ''Did you hear it?''

''I heard it. What's it mean?''

''It means the clan knows we're here.''

''Is that a good thing?'' Brigid inquired, ''or bad?''

Morrigan heeled her horse into motion again. ''That remains to be seen.''

As they went forward at a walk, they heard the notes of the horn again, this time much closer. The sound faded and was followed a moment later by a whip of blurred motion. An object snagged the banner on Morrigan's saddle and snapped the stick.

Brigid's eyes tried to follow the lightning-swift movement. The banner hung limply against a tree trunk.

From it protruded a ten-inch arrow shaft, a lovely thing of rolled wood with delicately feathered vanes.

There was a gobbling yell, and green-tuniced figures poured out of the overgrowth around them. Brigid caught only fragmented glimpses of swords and bows before her mare reared in fright, forelegs flailing. She fought to rein the animal down, but when she felt herself slipping from the saddle, she kicked herself free of the stirrups and slid backward over the horse's rump.

Alighting lithely on her feet, she was immediately at the hub of a wheel of razor-tipped steel. Tall men in green and red surrounded her, swords in their firm fists. Their faces were grim and hard. Other men clutched at the bridle of Morrigan's bay and dragged her off the saddle.

A red-bearded man looked both women over with calm, unexpressive eyes. A round brass shield embossed with clockwise and counterclockwise spirals was strapped to his left arm. A metal, feather-topped helm encased the top and sides of his head. He detached a polished hunting horn from his belt, set it to his lips and sounded a long, clear blast on it. The call was answered a moment later from somewhere deeper in the forest fastness.

Lowering the horn, he said, "I am Phin, chief of the clan. We need no mummers from the Priory Awen skulking about our wood."

He spoke in English, and Brigid wondered if it was for her benefit.

Morrigan replied, "We seek Mother Fand and three outsiders."

"So," said Phin coolly. "Two outsiders may you find. Mother Fand is a different matter entirely. What is your business with her?"

Before Brigid could ask the names of the outsiders, Morrigan retorted stiffly, haughtily, "That is our affair, not that of a scruffy woodsman."

Anger flashed in Phin's eyes, and Brigid interposed quickly, "It's about her daughter and Lord Strongbow."

The man smiled a little and said playfully, "'Tis an embarrassment of Yanks today. Come, then."

The red-and-green-clad men escorted them along an almost invisible side path, to a secluded glade filled with thatch and mud-wattle huts. Brigid's eyes swept over the bold-eyed faces of the assembled forest dwellers and finally fixed on the sharply contrasting black-and-white features of Grant and Domi. She pulled away from the escort and hurried toward them.

It wasn't much of a reunion. She had barely reached them when a tall, splendidly built woman stepped from a hut, moving with the soundless grace of a hunting cat. She looked past Brigid to Morrigan, a hot blue stare shining out of her tattooed face.

"I am who you seek," she announced. "What does the Priory of Awen wish from me now?"

Morrigan's head inclined in a deferential nod. In a mild, humble tone, she answered, "Only your help, Mother Fand, to redress a long-ago wrong."

"From what I've been told—" Mother Fand gestured to Grant "—events carry us toward a resolution despite our individual wants for privacy."

"True," said Morrigan. "Yet it is still left open to us to find in which direction the events carry us."

Mother Fand's blue stare impaled Brigid. "And you are here to give us that direction?"

Brigid shrugged. "I can but try, though I'm feeling lost myself."

Mother Fand laughed, breezy and freeze. "Let's see if we can't get back on the right route, then." She pointed at the large council hut, and they followed her inside. They ate to repletion on roast fowl, washing it down with a bittersweet brown ale. Afterward Morrigan spoke to Mother Fand of Strongbow, her daughter's unbalanced nature, and of Kane's predicament.

The woman listened without interruption. Brigid judged her to be a wise leader, but weary of sadness and tragedy.

When Morrigan was done, Mother Fand said, "Your fears mirror my own, though the addition of this man Kane into the mix confuses it further."

"His involvement may make no difference," Brigid said. "Strongbow provided us with the means to get here and experiment with our interphaser. The problem we face is whether or not to do it."

"I think," said Morrigan, "the problem is weightier than that."

In an even, self-confident tone, Grant said, "We're not concerned with your politics. We have a mission."

Brigid smiled at him wryly. Grant was still a frontline Magistrate at heart, and he still had that single-minded drive to achieve an objective. He was always confident, never one to take foolish risks with no clear-cut prospect of success. In that, he was completely different from Kane.

"We know that Fand has claimed the region around the Newgrange site as her own," Morrigan went on. "We theorize she channels the vortex energies there in a weak way, enough to alter perceptions of reality, if not alter reality itself. That is why Kane introduces a random element into the flow. There is no telling what she might do."

Phin laughed scornfully. "What is it to us if she thinks he's Cuchulainn come back? 'Tis her life, ye know."

"'Tis your life, as well," Morrigan shot back. "Think you that if Fand unleashes all the forces pent-up on this isle, your little tra-la-la fiefdom in the forest will be spared?"

"Spared what?" Phin demanded impatiently. "This 'spatial discontinuity' shite ye keep jabberin' about?"

Morrigan snapped something at him in Gaelic, and for a long moment the pair snarled at each other unintelligibly.

Mother Fand whipped up her staff and slammed its end down between the two combatants. She shouted, *"Deanfhaidh se' an gno'!"*

The argument instantly ceased, and they both averted their faces from each other.

"Waste no more time. Aye, there is anger between the Priory and ourselves, but we must act on our commonalities, not our differences."

To Morrigan, she said, "You seem to know more about my daughter than I."

Morrigan shook her head. "In actuality, the Priory knows very little. She travels about the land in the company of a woman named Aifa who, as I understand, was a childhood friend."

Mother Fand said, "Yes, I remember her."

"Like myself, Aifa was born with a psi-mind, yet she was enthralled by Fand's visions of the Eire of old."

"How do they live?" Grant asked.

Morrigan lifted a shoulder in a shrug. "On the awe of simple folk primarily. They bring her offerings of food, fabrics. She wants for nothing—except love."

Mother Fand flinched, eyes registering guilt, then accusation. "She would have had that from me, had I not been banished."

"You left of your own free will," Morrigan replied coldly. "And refused to return."

"Aye, what choice did I have? The Priory allowed me no real contribution to her upbringing. They wanted me to act as a wet nurse to divinity. They pampered her, indulged her whims and fantasies, treated her as a goddess instead of what she really was—a poor creature neither human, nor Danaan nor Na Annunaki, yet with the curses of all three ravaging her soul."

"She dissociated, is that what you mean?" Brigid asked.

"Far worse," Mother Fand stated grimly. "Mr. Grant raised a possibility that I never considered, that my daughter is linked on some psychic-genetic level with the man you call Strongbow."

Quickly she repeated what Grant had told her of Strongbow's mutagenesis, splicing the genetic material of Enlil with his own.

Morrigan's face molded itself into a mask of puzzlement, then as the implications sank in, shifted to apprehension. "That explains my inability to read Strongbow's mental patterns. And it also explains why Fand is so uncontrollable by psychic means. 'Tis two minds she has."

"The link has to be broken," said Brigid.

Domi spoke for the first time. "Only one way. Chill Strongbow big time."

"How can we do that," asked Phin, "without taking the battle to him, to Britannia?"

"There's got to be deeper reason behind Strongbow's intense interest in your interphaser device," Morrigan said.

Mother Fand chuckled humorlessly. "His reasons are easy to guess. They are the same ones which drove him to abduct me and mate me with Enlil. Life eternal, the secrets of the universe. All the power denied him in his life before the nuke."

"Activating the interphaser could conceivably give him the means to gaining all of that," Brigid remarked.

"Or give us the means to stopping whatever scheme he's hatched." Grant's tone was gruffly impatient. "We won't know for sure until we do it."

"By then it may be too late," said Morrigan.

Mother Fand sighed heavily. "Regardless of all of this, I need to reach my daughter. She needs my strength, and I need her forgiveness."

Phin said, "We can start out for the Boyne at first light. 'Tis perhaps a half day's ride, less if we push it a bit."

Morrigan blinked at him in surprise. "You now agree we must take action?"

"I fight my own battles," declared Phin. "But here, in Eire. Only here."

They left the council hut and went to the shelters assigned to them. Shortly before dusk, a light rain fell from an overcast sky. Brigid hurried through the drizzle to Grant and Domi's hut. There Domi tended the small fire, throwing lumps of dried peat on the little flames. Aromatic, sweetish smoke curled up from it.

"Where's Grant?"

"Here." He stood on the far side of the hut, staring at the rain and the forest with distant eyes. He didn't turn around. "I guess you want to check over the interphaser?"

"Yes."

He pointed to a corner distractedly. Brigid saw the

gleam of the metal case resting on a heap of furs. She brought it close to the fire, undid the latches and raised the lid. She asked, "Have you tested the systems since you arrived?"

He shook his head. "I've been a little busy."

Normally, Grant was somewhat taciturn, a little short on words, so Brigid didn't immediately pick up on the undercurrent of worry in his voice. She plugged in the keyboard and made sure the power pack was functioning.

"Seems fine."

"Wonderful," Grant replied, still gazing out at the misting rain.

"Are you worried about Kane?" she asked.

He snorted. "Only if he's alive."

"Morrigan seemed pretty certain he is."

Grant finally turned around to face her. The flickering flames cast his features into strange, reddish shadows. "And that might not be good."

Brigid said nothing for a handful of heartbeats. Then she asked, "With all that's happened to him since we escaped Cobaltville, do you think he's still stable?"

"Do you mean do I think he's so fused out he could be put under the spell of this fairy queen, this Fand?"

"Yes."

He considered the question for a moment, then shook his head in frustration. "Even with all that's happened to him—happened to all us—he's still the Kane I've always known."

In a low, dark voice, Brigid said, "That's really the pertinent point, at least at a psychological tangent. He may no longer be the Kane *he* knows."

Chapter 29

Kane tossed the green mantle with his left hand. His right hand was full of his Sin Eater. "Cover yourself up, sweetheart. The Danaan didn't build this place with central heating."

Fand snatched the garment out of the air. Her full breasts rose and fell with emotion. Pure, homicidal fury seethed in her eyes. She spit a few words in hard-edged Gaelic.

Kane smiled without humor. "Speakee English and speakee quietly. If your fairy harpist minces in, I don't want to have to chill her."

With fast, angry motions, Fand slid the mantle over her head, thrusting her arms through the sleeves. "How dare you use me like that, humiliate me in such a fashion?"

Kane's face twisted into something dark and ugly. "How dare you invade my mind, play with my feelings, screw around with my perceptions? What gives you the *right?*" The last word was heavy with a cold, towering rage that dwarfed the fury in her huge, hot eyes.

Urgently, earnestly Fand said, "I sought only to awaken the spirit of Cuchulainn, who I know slumbers within you. Our souls touched, in that borderland between worlds. If only you could remember, really remember our love, like I do—"

Kane cut her off with a sharp, short gesture. "Give

it a rest. I know a little something about psionics. You didn't awaken the spirit of Cuchulainn—you imposed illusions on my mind, no different from that fog *geas*. It's no more than one mind creating impressions on another mind.''

"No," she said raggedly. "The memories I awakened in you were real."

"Even if that's true, so the fuck what? They're in the past. And why are you so positive your memories are genuine and not just old legends you *want* to make real?"

She waved to the stone chamber around them. "The memories here, of this land, of its past, speak to me, sing in my soul. Can't you feel them? I know all the histories of the mighty Danaan race, of their kings, queens, heroes. Their loves, their passions, their tragedies. They live through me, they live on *in* me."

"Memories are all they are, Fand." Kane's voice lost some of its anger and bitterness. "You live in the here and now. You're not a fairy queen—you're a hybrid, the genetic mixture of three races."

Fand glared at him sullenly, lower lip trembling. By degrees, the wild heat in her eyes guttered out, taking on an eerie, remote expression. Kane kept his eyes on hers, shivering slightly. He still felt her power, the swirling, magnetic whirlpool of her unbridled emotions.

"Yes," she said finally in a lost, small voice. "My mother told me the same thing when I was very young. I didn't want to believe her, but I knew she spoke the truth. It became harder and harder to bear it as I grew older. My attendants at the Priory still treated me as if I were indeed a fairy princess."

Kane lowered the Sin Eater and squatted down near her, just out of reach of her long arms and her long, very sharp fingernails. Softly he said, "And so you retreated into fantasy, backing into it one step at a time, further away from reality with every year you lived."

"What would you have done?" Fand asked, her voice tense. "Born with this empathy for this land? Eire may be far older than any civilization on Earth, the most ancient and occult of worlds. I am a bridge between all that lost knowledge and the world of today. I breathe the dust of the vanished and make them live again."

"But I'm not a bridge, Fand. I am myself. I have my own life, my own history, memories of my own. If I ever was this Cuchulainn, it's so long ago it doesn't matter anymore. My spirit has moved on, progressed. As should yours."

She shook her head violently, yellow tresses flying, the gold balls in them clinking and tinkling. "That I cannot do. I was bred as the guardian of Eire's spirit. If I relinquish that role, then my life means nothing, and Eire itself 'twill fall 'neath the heel of an oppressor."

Repressing a smile at her quaint, affected mode of speech, Kane said "You mean Strongbow."

Fury boiled up, white hot in her eyes. Between clenched teeth, she grated out, "Aye, Strongbow! He was the reason I desired you so, Ka'in! With your warrior's heart to augment my own, we could have destroyed him, avenged his crimes against my mother and all Celts."

"Kane," he corrected mildly, as if speaking to a slow-witted child. "There's no denying he's a sick son of a bitch and he has designs on Ireland, but—"

"Don't you understand? He has designs on *me!*" Fand's voice trembled with revulsion. "I know his depraved secrets, his diseased lusts! He could not have my mother, so now he craves power over me. If he cannot rule me, he will kill me. He wants to defile me with his abominable seed!"

The sheer, undiluted horror at the possibility vibrating in her voice shook Kane, triggering a feeling of repulsion in him, as well. He asked, "What do you mean you know his secrets?"

Fand clapped her hands to her head, nails digging into her scalp. Her upper body began rocking back and forth. Despite his warning for her to speak quietly, a keening wail of self-loathing burst from her lips, from the roots of her soul.

"He's in me! I hear his thoughts, vile, depraved, unclean! We are bound, we are joined! Day after day, night after night, I feel his mind nibbling away at mine, groping, probing, *slithering…"*

Her words dissolved in a frenzy of wild sobs. She shook and shuddered and shrieked.

Over the sound, Kane heard a swift scuffle of feet from the passageway opening. In a rush, he came to his feet, leveling his Sin Eater. Aifa appeared, hand poised over the strings of her harp. Her eyes flicked uncertainly from the blaster to the hysterically weeping Fand.

"Drop it," he commanded.

Aifa hesitated, then her fingers reached out for the strings. He squeezed the trigger, the explosive report obscenely loud, the concussion rebounding and ringing from the rock walls and ceiling.

The 9 mm round crashed into the brass frame of the harp, jolting it from her arms with a bone-numbing, bruising shock. She cried out as the instrument bounced, twanging discordantly, over the stone floor of the passage.

Fand lowered her hands from her tear-stained face. She didn't much resemble a fairy princess now, or guardian of much of anything, even her own soul. Tears flowed from her eyes, dripping from her pointed chin, staining the bodice of her mantle. Her hair hung in disarray, and threads of blood from self-inflicted scratches inched their way over her high, pale forehead.

She clutched frantically at Kane, plucking first at his leg, then snatching his left hand. She clung to it with a painful strength.

"Help me," she said in a high, aspirated whisper, half-choked with tears and the intensity of her desperation. *"Dia linn!"*

Kane looked down at her and suddenly felt as old as the stones around him. He thought of Cobaltville and Salvo and the baron. He thought of Baptiste and Grant and Domi and the redoubt and all the desperate people cowering inside of it, waiting fearfully for what the Archon Directorate might do to them, to the rest of humanity.

He said to her quietly, "I will."

Reaching down, Kane urged the woman to her feet. He held her for a long while, cradling the back of her head against his shoulder. Slowly she stopped sobbing, and her body no longer shook and shuddered. He stroked her hair, remembering with an ironic smile how he had tried to soothe Baptiste similarly after rescuing her from execution.

"Let's get out of here," he said into her small, oddly shaped, yet still delicately lovely ear.

By the hand, he led her into the dim passageway, past a staring and dumbfounded Aifa.

When they were out in the sunlight again, they sat down side by side on the massive stone before the entrance. He gazed out toward the belt of the forest and saw, without much surprise, that it looked like another copse of trees he had seen. He saw no sign of winged fairies or unicorns.

Fand leaned her head against his shoulder. "Kane?"

Surprised and gratified she had pronounced his name correctly, without the irritating insertion of the glottal stop, he couldn't help but chuckle. "Yes?"

In a faltering, uncertain tone, she asked, "Could you love me, even if you're not Cuchulainn?"

Kane's quick, evasive retort stuck in his throat. He seriously contemplated the question, but it was difficult to do so, with the heat of the beautiful, elfin woman warming him. He raised his eyes toward the sun, hanging high in the clear blue sky. Aifa had sung something about a savage sun, but it didn't look savage now. It glowed with a friendly, golden fire, reaching down to thaw the ice in his heart.

Turning slightly, he cupped Fand's cheek in his hand and looked into her unsettlingly gorgeous eyes, half-hooded now by her heavy lids and sweeping lashes. He kissed her lips gently. Her arms came up and tightened around his shoulders.

They were still kissing when Kane heard the drumming of hooves.

Chapter 30

There were six of them, all mounted on horses. When Kane saw the sunset glints in Brigid's hair he pulled away from Fand and sprang to his feet, hoping he didn't look as guilty as he felt. His overriding emotion was relief, so powerful that his knees went watery and weak.

Although he was happy to see that Grant, Domi and Morrigan were with her, his eyes were irresistibly drawn to the man and the woman riding out in front. He was a brawny, red-bearded man, like an illustration from an old history text come to life. He carried a round, brass-embossed shield on his left arm, and a long war spear was gripped in his right hand. A crest of feathers waved from the top of the metal helmet on his head.

The woman was at least as unusual, with hair cut severely short except for a curving forelock. Her high-planed face bore dark blue spiral designs. The body under her green tunic was long and clean-cut. She looked oddly familiar.

Behind him, Fand said hoarsely, *"Mh'athair!"*

Without removing his eyes from the riders, he asked, "What?"

Softer, in an anguished breath, Fand said, "Mother!"

The riders reined up in a semicircle in front of the great stone. All of them stared at him with an annoying mixture of anxiety and suspicion.

"Well, slow but sure," he said, smiling, "About time you got here."

With a grunt, Grant swung out of the saddle and stalked over to him. His dark face was tightly set, his brows lowered. "You stupe bastard. What did you think you were doing, jumping into the drink like that?"

Kane began a sarcastic retort, but the genuine anger in his partner's voice caused it to wilt on his tongue. Glancing over at Morrigan, he said inanely, "It seemed like a good idea at the time."

Morrigan stated matter-of-factly, "I was in no danger."

"Now you tell me." He shifted his gaze to Brigid. "What's your excuse, Baptiste?"

She swiftly dismounted. "I was pulled overboard."

She said no more, busying herself untying the interphaser case from the rear of the saddle. The bearded man, eyes sparkling as if he were enjoying a private joke, demanded, "So you're the mighty Ka'in, eh?"

"As I keep telling everybody," he snapped, "the name is Kane. Who might you be?"

"Them that bother to speak of me call me Phin, of the Clan mac Trenmor."

Kane looked over at the tall woman. She had yet to dismount, sitting rigidly in the saddle, gripping the leather reins so tightly her knuckles stood out like ivory knobs. She stared past him at Fand. The resemblance between the two was startling, yet they looked more like sisters.

The woman said, very quietly, *"Mini'on."*

Then, bringing one leg up over the horse's head, she dropped lightly to the ground and approached Fand. Kane self-consciously got out of her way. Besides, her intense blue stare made him distinctly uncomfortable.

She went to Fand and looked deeply, steadily into her face, as if trying to fathom a mystery. Bright blue eyes met molten gold. Then, carefully, tentatively, as if she feared Fand was made of spun glass, she touched the side of her daughter's face. She murmured a few words to her, tears springing into her eyes.

Kane joined his companions. Softly he inquired, "Her mother?"

"Yeah," answered Grant. "Mother Fand, they call her. Quite the woman. You all right?"

"I was thrown a few curves—"

Brigid glanced quickly toward Fand. "No pun intended."

He regarded her stonily, but she met his stare without blinking. "That's right, Baptiste, no pun intended." Acidly, he added, "Mebbe you can bring me up-to-date. I lost a day somewhere."

"I'll bet," drawled Grant.

Kane scowled, opening his mouth to say something insulting. Brigid cut him off by relating how she had been taken to the citadel of the Priory of Awen and what she had learned there.

Then it was Grant's turn to tell how he and Domi had fallen in with Phin's clan, and Brigid said challengingly, "Your turn now."

"Not much to tell," Kane replied. "Damn near drowned, but didn't. Made it to shore and damn near died of exposure but didn't. Woke up this morning with her—" he hooked a thumb toward Fand "—standing over me. She brought me here."

Grant rumbled, "Why do I have the feeling you're leaving out a few details?"

Kane looked over toward Mother Fand and her daughter. They sat on the big stone, heads together, clinging to each other. The mother appeared to be doing most of the talking. Morrigan and Phin stood apart, giving the two women as much privacy as they could in such open surroundings.

Sighing, Kane said, "All right, if it's details you want, details you shall have."

Quickly, thoroughly he told them everything that had befallen him since awakening at the standing stone, including his brief vision of Fand during the gateway transit.

"You didn't think that was worth mentioning?" demanded Grant.

"No, I didn't. How was I to know it wasn't just a jump dream?"

Brigid gave him a searching, penetrating stare. When he caught her eye, she looked away, saying, "Fand was reenacting the legend of how her Danaan namesake met Cuchulainn, right down to striking you with a staff."

"Yeah, and it delivered quite a wallop, too," he retorted. "And then there's that business with the harp—"

Brigid shrugged negligently. "In Celtic lore, magic is based on music, but it means more than song. Utilizing sound waves in the proper frequency and harmonics, heavy objects can be moved. That's one theory how the megalith sites were built. Remember the infrasound weapons?"

Dryly Kane said, "I'm not likely to forget."

"As for the staff giving you a shock, she probably uses it to channel and focus her bioelectric energy…the basis of the 'magic wand' themes throughout mythology."

"Okay," Grant interjected impatiently, "she brought

you here, you hallucinated and then you had a long chat with her. That's it?''

''Yeah,'' answered Kane, knowing how lame it all sounded. ''Pretty much.''

''Pretty much?'' Brigid repeated sharply.

''That's all,'' he said, matching the sharpness in her voice. ''Is it my imagination, or are you two suspicious of something or other?''

Brigid stated evenly, ''If Fand is linked to Strongbow as she herself admitted to you, we've got to be sure you're not psi-linked to her before we try to engage the interphase point.''

''I'm not,'' he said grimly, determinedly. ''You'll have to trust me.''

When they just stared at him, he gestured impatiently to the metal case, he said, ''Let's turn on the goddamn thing and get this over with.''

Domi piped up, ''Has anyone figured out how we get home from here?''

There was a long, uncomfortable moment of silence. At length, Grant said, ''A good point. I doubt Strongbow will allow us the use of his gateway at Wildroot.''

''Me, either,'' Brigid agreed. ''It's remotely possible that if we open a vortex, we can uplink with the Cerberus autosequence initiator.''

''You don't sound very sure of any of this,'' Kane observed.

''That's because I'm not.''

Morrigan chose that moment to cautiously and apologetically interrupt the reunion between mother and daughter Fand. She spoke to them briefly, then called the others over. Mother Fand regarded Kane with troubled eyes, but nodded courteously when he introduced himself.

"You know why we're here?" he inquired.

Mother Fand slid a protective arm around her daughter's shoulders. "Aye. What you intend could either help or irreparably harm my girl."

"Or do nothing at all," Morrigan stated.

"'Tis still a risk. Perhaps a very grave one."

"Life is a gamble, isn't it?" remarked Phin. "From the first step ye take to the last. Nothin' is certain but the final outcome."

Silence hung among the eight people. Kane felt Fand's golden gaze upon him and he steadfastly refused to meet it. It occurred to him that between the two of them, his was by far the more sterile life. He took plenty of chances, of risks, but it all had to do with the simple business of survival, of running the race. He existed; he didn't truly live.

Fand swam through primal forces, tapped into energies and emotions that verified, even justified every microsecond of her life. Maybe she was mad, deranged, walking around in a constant state of dementia. But her passions stemmed from a raging life-force, as unpredictable yet as natural as a summer storm.

"Mother explained it to me," Fand said. "I confess I don't truly understand what you hope to accomplish, but you have my leave to make the attempt."

Out of the corner of his eye, Kane noted Brigid bristling at the ingenuous arrogance in her tone, but wisely she didn't respond to it.

All of them trooped into the passageway. Aifa stood in the central chamber, disconsolately cradling the harp as she would an injured pet. Brigid looked around in wide-eyed wonder, murmuring to herself over the glyphs and rock carvings.

She carried the case to the center of the chamber and

laid it down on the floor, removing the metal pyramidion and its support systems. Fand eyed the deceptively simple device curiously.

As Brigid set the interphaser up, everyone took positions close to the opposite wall, near the passage door. She crouched over the keyboard, finger hovering above the power tab. It stayed there.

"Well?" Grant asked impatiently.

Brigid turned to face them, forehead furrowed. "Something new just struck me."

Grant groaned in exasperation.

Pretending not to have heard, Brigid said, "When we activated the interphaser in Strongbow's place, the proximity of the Danaan relics was enough to open a small rift, just large enough for a manifestation of Fand's mind energy."

"I remember," she said. "To me, it was like a dream."

"Regardless," Brigid replied, "she has a natural affinity for the quantum field at these vortex points. What if her presence here interferes with its operation?"

"What if it does?" demanded Phin. "Will we have that spatial discontinuity Morrigan told us about?"

"That seems a little extreme, but you can't be sure of anything when you're playing with the quantum field."

"If things get out of hand," Kane said, "just shut it off. Pull out the plug."

Brigid's lips curved in a wry half smile. "It's a bit more complicated than that, but it's a sound enough strategy. Okay, here goes."

She depressed the power button, and her fingers quickly and deftly tapped in the memorized numerical sequence. She rose from the device and backed away.

The gleaming pyramidion squatted in the center of the floor and did nothing. Everyone watched it in breathless silence.

A faint resonance, a nonsound, a thready pulse of vibration suddenly tickled everyone's skins. Shadows crawled over the walls, moving in fitful jerks and leaps. A hint of a breeze touched their faces, warm at first, then cool. Hair and clothing rustled.

"Something is happening." Mother Fand spoke quietly, with a forced calm.

"Yeah," Grant responded. "But what?"

A bluish, waxy light curled up from the apex of the interphaser, twisting like a finger of tepid ectoplasm. It stretched upward a foot, then two feet.

A yellow nova erupted from the tip of the pyramidion. The shock wave rocked them, slapped their breaths painfully back into their lungs, tumbled everyone off their feet. Their eyes stung fiercely, rods and cones overstressed.

Kane's vision cleared fairly fast. Through the blurred afterimage of the flare, he saw a swirling column of light, corkscrewing like the spiral patterns cut into the rock walls. It condensed, curving like a gigantic candle's flame exposed to the direct blast of a strong breeze.

It touched the largest of the spiral glyphs on the far wall and formed a funnel shape around it, a circle of spinning fire hanging against the gloom. Through it, he saw a bizarre vista of ribbons of circuitry, of distorted men in red jackets and berets. It was like looking through several hundred feet of cloudy water, body parts magnified and others weirdly diminished. The image strobed, variegated hues of color shifting over it.

Fand howled, sweat breaking out all over her face.

Her eyes rolled, and she gasped desperately for breath. A dark, thin trickle of blood issued sluggishly from her left nostril. Veins throbbed and swelled at the sides of her head.

Thrashing to a sitting position, Kane bellowed to Brigid, "Pull the goddamn plug!"

The echoes of his cry still rang when the first dragoon came bounding out of the funnel of light.

Chapter 31

The dragoon lurched to an unsteady halt, his treaded boot soles catching on the rough rock floor. His head swiveled to and fro, the barrel of the MP-5 SD-3 swinging in tandem with it. The subgun stuttered, and a short tongue of flame licked from the bore. Kane rolled as a stream of bullets raked the stone wall overhead, showering him with dust and shards.

The dragoon, still somewhat disoriented, didn't have a particular target in mind. He simply shot at the first people he saw. Sin Eaters sprang into Kane's and Grant's hands simultaneously, each framing the soldier in his sights and triggering off a 3-round burst.

All six slugs stitched the dragoon's head and shoulders, slamming him down and catapulting him through a clumsy half somersault amid a scattering of blood and tissue. He wound up lying on his stomach, with his subgun pinned beneath him.

Everyone stood, Kane shifting his attention from the pulsing funnel sprouting from the interphaser to the people in the chamber. Aifa lay crumpled in a half-prone position at the doorway of the passage. He saw no rise and fall of respiration underneath the wet bodice of her red mantle.

Phin leaned against the wall, grimacing, blood from a bullet-ripped gouge in his right biceps painting his arm crimson. By the way his arm dangled, the bone was obviously broken. The spear lay at his feet.

Putting his blaster on the pyramidion, then on the coruscating swirl of light, Grant bellowed, "What the fuck is going on? Where'd that bastard come from?"

Brigid, eyes jade hard and jade bright with astonishment, said, "Some kind of quantum conduit, between New London and here. Strongbow must have built a relay system which automatically uplinked with the interphaser when it activated a vortex."

"How?" Kane snarled out the word, feeling the steady waves of invisible energy, like a subsonic drumbeat throbbing to the marrow of his bones.

"He knew about Project Cerberus, remember, about the Totality Concept. He had a project of his own prepared long before we came along, one designed to interface with the energies here in Ireland. We opened the invasion route he'd been seeking!"

In a panicky voice, Grant shouted, "Turn it off before we're ass-deep in his snake-eyed soldiers!"

Brigid rushed to do it. Kane wondered why no other dragoon had made the quantum leap from New London, then reasoned that the first one had been a scout, and Strongbow was probably waiting for him to return with a report.

Brigid kneeled before the interphaser, fingers frantically clattering over the keyboard. The glowing funnel didn't change in appearance. With a curse, she yanked the coaxial power cable from it. Still nothing happened.

"We can't disengage!" she yelled fearfully.

Morrigan shrilled, "Fand is controlling the vortex energy now—or it's controlling her. She's keeping the conduit open!"

Kane whirled, looking with horror at Fand, encircled

tightly by her mother's arms. Her eyes rolled up in her head. Violent convulsions shook her slim body, her heels drumming on the stone floor, froth bubbling from her lips.

"If we can't break the link, *she'll* be the conduit for Strongbow's invasion," Morrigan said, terror making her voice high and unsteady.

"The only way to break the link is to kill her," Mother Fand said, holding her thrashing daughter in an unbreakable grip. "That I will not allow, unless you kill me, too."

Kane swung back toward the opening, squinting into it. The view was partially obscured by waves of lambent, multicolored fire.

"I'll break the link on Strongbow's side," he declared, stepping forward.

Grant latched on to his arm. "He's probably got a fucking army over there. Who do you think you are—this Cuchulainn stupe?"

Grant mispronounced the name and Kane corrected him. "It's Koo-kull-ayn. No, I don't think I'm anybody but me, who makes a habit of playing the one-percents."

"Not alone, you haven't," grated Brigid. "We'll all go with you."

She bent over the dead dragoon, wrestled him onto his back and pulled the MP-5 SD-3 from underneath his body. She hefted the nine-pound weapon, made sure a round was chambered and adjusted the firing-rate selector switch.

Turning to Morrigan, Mother Fand and Phin, she said tersely, "After the last one of us have gone in, and if the conduit stays open longer than you think it should, you've got only one chance to break the link." She took a breath and stated, "One of you will have to throw the interphaser into the rift."

"What will that do?" Phin asked, his voice tight with repressed pain.

"Maybe nothing at all. But if my guess is even seventy percent right, the quantum pocket we have here will be turned inside out. If there's a violent reaction, it'll be confined to New London, to Strongbow's side of it."

Frowning in consternation, Mother Fand demanded, "What will happen to you?"

Brigid shrugged, turning away. "We'll let you know—if we can."

Kane stepped carefully to the swirling funnel. It was now the color of blood. He thought fleetingly of all the blood he had spilled, all that he had shed in the service of the baron, and decided the color of the rift was appropriate. Brigid, Grant and Domi lined up behind him.

Without looking at them, he rapped, "Me first. Wait for a count of twenty, then Grant. And so on."

He tensed his leg muscles, rising on the balls of his feet. Mother Fand shouted, "Ka'in!"

He cast an annoyed glance over his shoulder, but she went on, "I want Karabatos. If you can, bring him to me. Not just for me—" she pressed her cheek against the crown of Fand's head "—but for her."

"Revenge?" he asked.

Azure hatred blazed in her eyes. "Why the damnation not?"

Kane nodded, facing the blood-tinted whirlpool. He readied himself and sprang up and forward.

His ears cracked, his vision smeared, his belly turned over sickeningly. There was no shock of impact, merely a strange, cushioning sensation, as if he had jumped into a wall a compressed air. He was conscious of a half instant of whirling vertigo as if he hurtled a vast distance at blinding speed.

Then he staggered across a solid, slick floor, slamming headlong into a body and falling in a tangle of limbs, hearing a loud clatter of metal. He had only a fraction of a second to get his bearings. He saw a cavernous ovoid chamber, crammed with catwalks, lifts, a webwork of circuitry and electronic consoles. Behind him floated a bubble of blackness. Jagged lines of energy streaked over its surface.

He had collided with a dragoon, knocking the man's legs out from under him and the air from his lungs. Kane rolled away from the gasping soldier, seeing at least a dozen other dragoons lined up in formation, on the far side of a transparent armaglass enclosure. Somewhere in the middle of his roll he heard a shrieking voice. It was Strongbow's and it came from above.

Kane gained his feet just as a pattern of phosphorescence slid over the black bubble. The pattern molded and stretched itself into a human outline, and the outline suddenly became Grant, who nearly staggered into his arms.

His head swung up and around, taking in the place, and he muttered, "Well, shit."

Then figures were running everywhere, the boots of the dragoons making hollow clanging noises on the catwalks overhead. Kane spotted Strongbow standing at the end of a catwalk on a small platform that projected out directly over the ebony orb. His hands played over an instrument panel, and he shouted hysterical, unintelligible commands. Kane couldn't understand a word he was saying.

When a trio of dragoons began unloading in their

direction with subguns, he was able to figure it out. Both men lunged sideways, away from the opening in the armaglass wall. The doorway was narrow, allowing only one man at a time to fire into the perimeter. It was defensible, but not against blasterfire directed from the catwalks above. So far, it hadn't happened.

Grant returned the fire with his Sin Eater and sent the dragoons scuttling for cover. The man whom Kane had collided with dragged a Beretta from a hip holster, and one bullet from Kane dropped him where he crouched.

The black sphere flashed and sparkled and disgorged Brigid. She stumbled, nearly tripping over the dragoon's body, then quickly oriented herself. She bounded away from the rectangular opening in the transparent barrier just as a dragoon unlimbered his weapon.

Leaning out and around, Kane shot him directly between the eyes, the shock of impact flinging the mirrored sunglasses from his face. He went down without a sound.

The orb throbbed, and Domi came tumbling out of it. Grant snatched her by the collar and bodily lifted her out of the line of fire.

Strongbow continued yelling orders, and dragoons raced to surround the armaglass perimeter. Kane understood him this time. As he hoped, he was screaming at his men not to shoot through the opening for fear of damaging the black sphere.

He inspected the pulsing, obsidian bubble, thinking it looked like the mouth of a black furnace, seething with the equally black fires of eternity.

Hoarsely Strongbow bellowed, "You down there! Listen to me! I'm not your enemy. Come out of there, and I promise you won't be harmed."

Brigid laughed scornfully. "Karabatos—"

"Strongbow!" His strident voice was a crash of fury.

"Karabatos, you're a congenital liar. You can even convince yourself that your lies are true—and maybe that's a valuable survival characteristic for a man who was in your line of business. But if you believe you can manipulate the quantum stream to your own ends, it's the biggest self-delusion of your pointlessly prolonged life."

Strongbow leaned forward, hands curled around the top rail of the elevated platform. Panic flickered on his face, showed in his inhuman eyes. "You haven't any conception of what I want!"

"Like *hell* we don't!" roared Kane. "Order out of chaos, law from anarchy, peace with honor and every other bit of self-serving dogma ever puked up by fascists who don't have the guts to admit they're fascists."

He inhaled a deep, long breath and added, "For what you did to Fand and her daughter, you should have been fried twice over in the nukestorm, Karabatos."

"Strongbow! My name is Strongbow!"

Kane laughed sneeringly. "Doesn't anybody have an idea who they really are around here? Just because you appropriated a name from history doesn't mean we're buying into your personal mythography. You're not a conqueror—you're a pathetic asshole, a failed bureaucrat, an impotent little paper pusher!"

Strongbow began shrieking again, his voice so thick with mad emotion he was completely incomprehensible. In his fury, he hopped up and down, spittle spraying from his writhing lips.

The dragoons stood immobile, seeming to be deaf and blind to the deranged rantings spilling from their lord's mouth. Kane tried to align him in his blaster's sights, but the bottom of the platform spoiled his aim.

Grant reached inside his coat. "Enough."

His hand came out gripping a frag gren. His thumb flipped away the safety pin. "Enough of this."

He lobbed the gren with an underhanded toss toward the dragoons, then ducked back behind the impenetrable cover of the armaglass. With alarmed shouts, the soldiers broke formation and started to run, but only a few of them were quick enough to get out range of the explosive charge and the effect radius of the shrapnel.

The gren bounced only once before detonating with a brutal thunderclap. A hell-flower bloomed, petals of flame curving and spreading outward. Spewing from the end of every petal was a rain of shrapnel, ripping into bodies, walls, equipment. Fragments rattled violently against the armaglass barrier, ricocheting way. Then the rolling echoes of the explosion faded, punctuated by screams of men in agony.

Grant lunged out of the opening, through the haze of eye-stinging, throat-closing smoke. He stroked a short burst from his Sin Eater, saw a wounded dragoon jerk, lurch and fall.

Kane followed him half a heartbeat later, triggering his blaster, bullets pounding through a red uniform jacket he glimpsed through the smoke. The dragoon vaulted backward, blood spurting from three holes neatly grouped over his heart.

The floor was awash with looping liquid ribbons of vermilion, adding to its already slick quality. Five dragoons sprawled across it, neat uniform jackets shredded, soaked with their vital fluids, the flesh beneath flayed to the bone.

Hefting the MP-5 SD-3, Brigid slid around the doorway. She exchanged a quick, grim nod with Domi, who double-fisted her Combat Master. Then both women rushed out into the huge, egg-shaped chamber.

Five dragoons had regrouped, firing in the direction of Grant and Kane, their weapons chattering, muzzles flashing with little twinkles of dancing flame. A couple of them bled profusely from shrapnel-inflicted wounds, but they were still in shape to fight.

A single shot from Domi's blaster drilled a hole through the jaw of one them, punching him backward with such force his head struck the floor first. A scarlet geyser erupted from his mouth and a severed carotid artery.

Brigid framed the dragoon next to him in her sights and fired a burst that opened up his chest, propelling him backward in a crimson mist. The man was dead before he hit the floor, but he kept his finger on the trigger even as he fell.

Grant staggered as the close-range bullets slammed into his coat with all the driving impact of a series of jackhammer blows. He nearly went down, feet sliding and seeking purchase on the polished floor. He coughed, and the contraction of his diaphragm muscles sparked a hot spasm of pain on the right side of his rib cage. It took an iron will to keep from clutching at his side and sinking to his knees. He knew at least one rib was cracked, possibly broken.

Blinking back tears of pain from his eyes, he looked through the flat planes of smoke for Kane. He glimpsed him racing for the latticework of girders and posts supporting the elevated catwalk.

Strongbow saw him, too, and he screamed orders to the dragoons manning the walkways to catch him in a cross fire.

Chapter 32

Grant made a rapid head count and saw at least six, maybe as many as eight dragoons on the catwalk above him. He raised his Sin Eater and raked the walkway with a deadly stream of 9 mm tumblers. They struck sparks and gonglike chimes from framework, bouncing off with angry, buzzing whines.

Only one of his targets went down, clutching at his right shoulder. His companions fired staccato bursts in Grant's direction. They had him at a lethal disadvantage, holding the high ground and establishing a triangulated firing pattern.

Grant backpedaled as fast as his legs and throbbing ribs would allow, as bullets whizzed near his head. He yanked another gren from his combat harness, snapping away the pin at the same time. With slugs humming and slashing through the air around him, he flung the metal-shelled egg. He had no particular destination in mind for it; all he cared about was creating sufficient noise and confusion to serve as a diversion. He whirled away, his Kevlar-sheathed back to the blast.

Kane felt the heavy jolt of the explosion, the sear of heat against the back of his neck. The autofire overhead stopped abruptly as the dragoons backed hastily away from the epicenter of the detonation, just in case it was another fragger.

He began climbing the framework one-handed, his

right hand maintaining a firm grip on the Sin Eater. His feet found a cross-braced girder and he sprang up from it, wrapping his hand around a steel stanchion. Swinging his legs up, he locked them around a support post. Using his knees, he shinnied up it as fast as he could. A fresh burst of fire erupted behind him. He recognized the stutter of an MP-5 SD-3 and the sharp, door-banging slam of Domi's Combat Master.

He heard a sob of pain from over his head, and a second later a dragoon pitched headfirst over the rail like an empty suit of clothes.

Domi laughed to herself that her shot had found its intended target and brought down the man who'd drawn a bead on Kane, but the laugh became a snarl when a dragoon loomed out of the smoke. He pointed a Beretta directly at her head.

She ducked and sidestepped before he squeezed the trigger, lashed out with a leg and felt her foot slam solidly against his groin. The red-uniformed man barely reacted. He uttered a faint grunt and straight-armed her. His slamming palm caught her in the upper chest, driving almost all the wind from her lungs and sending her sprawling.

She slid across the floor on her shoulders and back but managed to squeeze off two quick shots between her outspread legs. The dragoon's tunic sprouted a pair of holes, and he was knocked off his feet. Dragging air back into her lungs, she climbed to her feet, seeing Brigid sprinting low beneath the drifting veil of smoke.

Brigid had seen Grant's gren nearly vaporize a pair of dragoons, watched as their bodies, shredded and scorched scarecrows, flailed through the air, limbs flopping bonelessly.

She ran for the catwalk supports, where she saw Kane

straining to scale them. Before she covered much ground, three dragoons sprinted to intercept her. Brigid saw them coming, but she kept going, knowing a retreat back to the curving armaglass wall would only give them clear shots at her back, while leaving her friends other adversaries to deal with.

She altered direction, racing toward them, firing from the hip with the subgun. They returned fire, and she felt a bullet pluck at her hair. Wincing, she kept her finger pressed down on the trigger, directing precision bursts. A dragoon's chest broke apart in flying arcs of blood, another was thrown sideways in a clumsy, crazy pirouette, kneecaps dissolving in a fluid welter of crimson-and-white bone chips.

Then the bolt of her autoblaster snapped loudly open on an empty chamber. Stopping or slowing down meant an instantaneous, bloody death, so she increased her speed, the length of her stride, legs pumping fast and furiously.

She flung her weapon out in front of her. The metal frame smashed into the dragoon's face a microsecond before her knee smashed into his solar plexus. Carried by the momentum of her rush, she bowled into him and both of them went down, sending a burst from his subgun up toward the high, arched ceiling.

Going into a shoulder roll, Brigid cartwheeled up and over the man, using his chest as a springboard. She landed on her feet in a deep squat, then sprang up and onto the dragoon. His face was spattered with blood from a laceration on his forehead. Her right foot, with all her weight behind it, drove into his neck. She pivoted sharply and smartly on her heel, crushing his larynx, grinding it into his windpipe.

Clutching at his throat, a flood of scarlet spilling from

his open mouth, the dragoon went into convulsions, clawing at the floor with his free hand, kicking spasmodically. His sunglasses had fallen off, and Brigid, with a kind of cold satisfaction, recognized him as Lieutenant Galt.

She turned away from his death throes, retrieving his autoblaster and ignoring the distant, accusing voice of her conscience.

Kane, muscles quivering with the strain, pulled his body up to chin level with the raised lip of the catwalk. He counted six dragoons directing their fire to the floor below. The racket of the fusillade was almost deafening with half a dozen guns blasting all at once.

Propping the Sin Eater's barrel on the edge, he fired a long burst, the storm of bullets striking splashes of scarlet from the nearest dragoon's uniform trousers, stitching a red-rimmed line from calf to hip.

The multiple impacts smashed him sideways, against his comrades, starting a domino effect. Two of them fell, but they all staggered. The firing pin of Kane's blaster clicked dry on an empty magazine. Blaster barrels turned in his direction.

From the floor, Brigid set up a left-to-right pattern of fire, knocking three of them sprawling at awkward angles, their blood dripping through the openings in the floor grille.

Kane scrambled and pulled his way to the metal walkway. He kept his eyes on one of the fallen dragoons as he struggled over the railing. The wounded man caught sight of him and raised his subgun.

A hand tangled in the thick hair at the back of Kane's head and jerked him backward with neck-wrenching force. The dragoon's weapon spit flame and noise, and the bullet struck the railing where his body had been an instant before, chipping out a fragment and spinning off into space.

Kane relaxed his body, allowing it to go in the direction it was pulled. He used his legs as catapults, his head as a battering ram.

Moving with serpentine reflexes, Strongbow evaded his attempt to body-smash him. He released his grip on Kane's hair and sidestepped. Kane hit the floor grille with his right shoulder and skidded toward the edge of the platform.

He looked up just as the toe of Strongbow's boot slammed solidly into the pit of his stomach. Cramping knives of pain stabbed through him, and a second kick rolled him to the very edge of the platform.

Kane tried to use the empty Sin Eater as a club, but Strongbow was quicker. He brought his foot down in a hard stomp, trapping his wrist at the narrow lip of the platform. Numbness shot up his arm to his elbow.

Strongbow ground his heel into his wrist, the expression on his face one of venomous, delighted malevolence. Desperately Kane flung up his right leg, pounding the knee into the back of Strongbow's thigh, directly into a clump of nerves. He cried out, his leg buckled and he fell directly on top of Kane.

He began a smashing attack at once. His teeth gleamed in a snarl, steely fingers sank into the muscles of his throat while his free hand battered Kane about the head and face. The man was immensely strong, and the sour, musky stench of his exertions clogged Kane's nostrils.

Kane wrapped his legs in a scissors-lock around the gaunt body, seeking to squeeze the air, the consciousness, the life out of it. His right hand lost all feeling—the wrist bone had been shattered a few months before, and some nerve damage had occurred.

Strongbow continued to strike with a knotted fist. Kane tasted the salt of his own blood filling his mouth. He raked his nails over Kane's face, trying to blind him, but he managed to jerk his head aside. Flesh tore in four vertical, scarlet lines from temple to jaw.

Strongbow's hand tightened around his throat, cutting off his ability to breathe, to think. The man's face tilted crazily above him, swimming off into a blurry fog at the edges. Distantly, with a detached sense of horror, he heard the strange, dry sound of cracking vertebrae.

Kane reached up with his left hand, fingers hooked, and punched them into Strongbow's face. An eyeball tore loose in a pulpy spurt of golden membrane and dark, hot blood.

Strongbow opened his mouth in a thin, high-pitched howl, and the fingers loosened around his throat. Not much, but enough for Kane to drag in a raspy half lung-ful of oxygen. The pressure of Strongbow's foot less-ened on his wrist. His vision cleared a little, and he snatched his arm free and brought it up in a clumsy sweep. The heavy metal frame of the Sin Eater smashed against the side of Strongbow's head. Bone crunched, and the man's jaw suddenly hung loose.

He flailed back with an insane explosion of strength, fueled by pain, breaking Kane's weakened scissors-lock around his body. He struggled half erect and Kane lashed out with both feet. The thud of his boots' impact was dull under the sporadic crackle of autofire.

Strongbow reeled backward, catching himself on the instrument panel, levering himself to his full height and voicing a strangulated wail of frustrated fury.

The two dragoons still standing on the catwalk

looked over at him instinctively, at the raw, gelid horror oozing out of his eye socket. Only Lord Strongbow's iron voice and sacred dragon authority could restore order in this microcosmic chaos.

Even as they turned to him for guidance, for inspiration, a flying shaft of wood and metal flashed and sank deep into his chest. His scaled features twisted, convulsed and spasmed. He went lead gray to the lips. He didn't move, didn't try to touch or pull out the spear buried in his body.

Assaulted by storm squalls of agony and nausea, Kane dragged himself to his elbows and looked down, over the end of the platform. He saw what he'd expected to see.

Mother Fand stood on the other side of the pulsing rift of the black bubble. Though her form was partially distorted by the rippling bands of energy, he saw the savage, feral joy shining in her eyes.

She seemed to transmit that savage surge of energy to Kane. The pain in him gave a great surge, then ebbed away. His body was at once warm and cool, tingling with new strength, new resolve. Weariness was gone. He felt like a machine running without thought or sensation until it burned out.

He was only dimly aware of rising, rushing to his feet and securing a cross-wrist grip on the spear shaft, on his Gae Bolg. He lifted up on it.

Strongbow didn't scream, but he gurgled and his arms tried to hug Kane close. Teeth bared in a ferocious grin, his face only a few inches away from the remaining slit-pupiled eye with its crusting of scales, Kane barked, *"Fad saol agat, gob fliuch, agus bas in Eirinn!"*

Even as he mouthed the words, he wondered dully

how he knew the ancient Gaelic curse: "A short life to you, a wet mouth and a death in Ireland!"

He heaved up on the spear, hoisting the strangely lightweight Strongbow off his feet, swiveling from the hips as he swung him up and over the railing.

Kane dipped the spear down at a forty-five degree angle. Strongbow slid along it, leaving a long, wet, carmined trail in his wake. The blade made a moist, rasping sound as it came free of his chest. He dropped from the bronze spearhead and fell, with a lazy somersault into the center of the black armaglass bubble.

Kane heard a slight pop of air rushing to fill a sudden vacuum. He thought he saw Mother Fand's hands spread wide to receive him.

Hanging half over the rail, the blood-dripping spear gripped tightly in his right fist, he saw a flash of light in the black bubble, then the gleaming pyramid shape of the interphaser arced through it. The narrow tip of the spiraling energy funnel was still connected to the apex.

The surface of the bubble boiled, as if it were covered by a layer of molten lava. Lines of energy skipped over it; tumescence rose up like miniature volcanic eruptions. The bubble changed color from black to blue to red to yellow, then it expanded into a ball of white-hot fire.

For a microsecond, between one eye blink and another, Fand appeared in its boiling, throbbing center, looking as she had when he first had seen her—made of shining star-stuff, glowing and beautiful and loving him.

Her voice slid into his mind, a tender caress. *Time is a river... I am overjoyed your spirit lives still, Ka'in. There is still meaning.*

And she was gone, lost among the black gulfs of infinity.

Then came a blast that seemed to crack the Earth. He had only a glimpse of the bubble swelling savagely to a sun before breaking into a million sparkling fragments.

With a screech of metal and a popping of rivets, the support posts of the catwalk buckled. The platform sagged, and Kane felt a giant's hand snatch him, wrenching him over the rail. He braced his legs and fought the powerful, incessant suction. Mouths wide in silent screams, the dragoons flipped over the top rail.

A pillar of blinding, blazing energy fountained up from below. Thunder roared, and the column of light became a fiery whirlwind. He saw bodies, limbs flopping like disjointed puppets, swirling around the column in crazed orbits, caught up in the swirling implosion.

The platform under his feet shuddered and lurched. He toppled from it. Gae Bolg in hand, he plummeted toward the vortex, Cuchulainn diving to his doom with a cry of defiance on his lips. He would live forever in the otherworld with his beautiful Danaan princess.

His plunge stopped short with a snap that sent a streak of pain up his arm and into his shoulder socket. Brigid gripped his left wrist with both hands, bent almost double over the platform's waist-high railing. Her hair floated and billowed around her face. Eyes slitted, she clung to him, anchoring him in place. Her lips worked, mouthing words, but Kane couldn't hear her over the sucking, whistling roar in his head.

Finally he understood that she was directing him to drop the spear and grab her wrists with his right hand. He looked from the sea green color of her eyes to the incandescent furnace spinning below him, then to the spear in his fist. It wasn't Gae Bolg; it wasn't an enchanted weapon. It was just a primitive thing of blood-drenched wood and forged metal and it didn't even belong to him. Opening his hand, he watched it spiral down into the maelstrom of coruscating energy.

Then, with an anticlimactic whisper, the vortex sealed itself and the invisible fingers tugging at him withdrew. Reaching up, he grasped Brigid's wrists, only slightly aware of the sound of objects falling and crashing to the floor all around.

She backed up, heaving on him, until he was able to get a grip on a cross brace and pull himself up to the tilting platform. They stood, shaking with exertion and weakness, panting into each other's sweat-slick faces. No strength remained in either one of them.

Slowly they turned their heads and surveyed the carnage in the cavernous, hollow ellipse. A few consoles squirted sparks and tendrils of smoke. The figures of Domi and Grant rose from behind the main bank, shambling through the scattered litter of electronic parts, circuit boards and other less identifiable odds and ends. They moved slowly, stiffly as if they were in a state of shock.

Where the orb had hung suspended, only empty space commemorated its existence. But the interphaser still gleamed on the floor where it had been thrown from Newgrange, keyboard and power pack apparently still intact.

Brigid said shakily, "I guess my theory worked. Throwing the interphaser through the conduit caused a polarity reversal. I hope it didn't harm Fand."

Kane said, "It didn't."

He didn't elaborate on how he knew, nor did she ask.

Grant and Domi gazed silently up at them, then at the little pyramidion.

Finally Grant said, "The latest in a long line of one-percenters, by God."

Nobody laughed.

Chapter 33

Kane leaned his hip against a fire-blackened console and smoked the last of Grant's cigars. He had given it up willingly, saying something about having enough of fire and smoke to last him for a while.

Brigid sat cross-legged on the floor and examined the interphaser. For the past twenty minutes, she had been inspecting all of its delicate internal circuitry, micro- and subprocessers.

Grant had checked the set of locked vanadium-alloy double doors and reported they were impossible to open without a sonic key. Kane was sure only one existed, and it had vanished with Strongbow. So far, they had found no other means of exit from the elliptical chamber.

The only possibility of escape from the giant eggshell lay within the innocuous alloy skin of the interphaser.

For the time being, they were safe, and Kane was content to sit and smoke and hurt and brood. He didn't want to think about Fand or Eire or Cuchulainn or destinies or souls. But he did.

He thought, What does a man do when his entire life is turned into an endless hunt, a hunt for enemies, for meaning, for purpose?

His gaze shifted to Brigid as she hunched over the interphaser, murmuring under her breath. He owed her his life yet again, but if his life meant nothing to him, then he owed her nothing.

Suddenly she looked up, as if sensing the weight of his stare. She returned it, an almost physical force that compelled him to say, "I'll pay you back, Baptiste, in whatever way I can."

He realized he had spoken nonsense, a non sequitur, blurting out his private thoughts, and she would have no idea what he was talking about.

To his disquiet, her mouth set in a tight line. "You don't owe me anything, Kane."

He quirked an eyebrow at her speculatively, but she returned her attention to the pyramidion, closing up the side of the device. She stood up, frowning down at it. Domi and Grant looked at her questioningly.

"It seems fine," she said, "but I admit I don't know why, after channeling all that energy through it."

"What do you think happened on the other side?" Domi asked.

She shook her head, red-gold tresses tumbling about her face. "I wish I knew. I can only guess. Maybe the conduit sealed with no harm to anyone. Maybe a quantum shift occurred, sending everyone down one of the side arteries Lakesh mentioned. For all I know, it may have triggered a temporal dilation, and none of this really happened."

Grant nudged the interphaser with a foot and probed at his twinging rib cage. "Yeah, wouldn't that be nice. Can this thing get us home, or at least out of this damn place?"

Brigid lifted her hands, palm up, in a helpless gesture. "I don't know. Possibly. I programmed it with the destination codes and coordinates of the Cerberus gateway.

But it wasn't designed to act as a mat-trans unit, you know.''

"Hell," Grant said bitterly, "this piece of junk hasn't performed according to its design since the first time you turned it on."

"I know," she replied. "It's a conundrum, a mystery, and the only way to reason it out is return it to Cerberus and download its memory into the main database."

From a slit pocket in her pants, she removed a small disk. "This is it. If we use the interphaser to open a gateway, the device itself will have to remain here, but we'll have its memory."

Kane stood up, a wave of dizziness engulfing him for a moment. He waved off Brigid's steadying hand. "Let's get to it, then, and get the hell out of here."

"There's a wide—no, *enormous*—margin for error," she warned. "The field may not be cohesive enough for us to complete a full transit. And we'll have to go one at a time."

"At this point," said Grant, "I'll be glad to have a little time alone."

Reaching down, Brigid tapped the keys, and a wavering cone of light fanned up and out. There was a faint susurrus of electronic hums. "Who wants to go first?"

Without a word or a backward glance, Domi moved forward and stepped into the shimmering veil. With a swiftness that deceived the senses, she was gone, whisked away as if she had never been.

Taking and holding a deep breath, Grant strode deliberately forward, paused long enough to announce, "I hate these fucking things," and then was absorbed by the light.

Kane glanced toward Brigid. "Just me and you, Baptiste. Who draws the short straw?"

"That'll be me." She took a long stride toward the interphaser's field. She said, "See you on the other side."

Before she stepped into the glowing fan, Kane grabbed her by the arm and pulled her back. She resisted a moment. "Kane?"

That was all she said, but it was enough. He knew part of his hunt was over. He put his arms around Brigid Baptiste and held her, inhaling the fragrance of her hair. It smelled of sweat and cordite, but he didn't mind. If nothing else, he had someone to trust.

"Yeah," he whispered to her. "See you on the other side...*anam-chara.*"

Epilogue

Lakesh awoke, strapped to a bench, sweating and nauseous from the drug. From beyond the steel-riveted door came the continual sound of footsteps, faint voices, the odd scream.

He lay there for some time, staring at the damp ceiling, at its single light bulb, wondering how bad things would get and how soon they would begin. He didn't have to wait long before the door scraped open.

Two men stepped in. Without surprise, he saw one of them was Salvo. The other was a stocky, blunt-featured Mag with a moon face. Because of the poor lighting and the residual of the drug creeping through his system, he had to grope for the man's name. Finally he recognized him as Pollard. Both of them were dressed in the pearl gray duty uniforms of Magistrates.

Salvo's teeth gleamed in the gloom. "How are we feeling?"

Lakesh said, as clearly as he could, "I'll only tell that to the baron."

Salvo chuckled. "If only it were as simple as that. However, if you could bring yourself to cooperate, I might open certain avenues that would offer you a way out."

"A way out of what?"

"A death sentence for sedition."

"You've assaulted me, imprisoned me, and you dare to speak of sedition?"

"My powers are broad," Salvo replied softly, "with plenty of room for interpretation."

He paused, pursing his lips. "I am going to ask you questions, some personal, others dealing with ideology."

"I will not answer any questions unless they are put to me by the baron."

Salvo made a spitting sound of impatience. "You're a difficult man to sympathize with. However, you are worth more than even the baron imagines."

Lakesh turned his face away, staring again at the ceiling, at the feebly glowing light bulb.

Pollard said, "Why don't we make it easier for him to think it over?"

Salvo nodded. "Lakesh, you know as well as I there's an easy way and hard way of getting things done. Just for you, we'll dispense with the hard way."

Pollard leaned over him, inserting a key into the lock of the restraining straps. He opened them, flung them away and hauled Lakesh to his feet by the front of his coverall. He stood there, temples throbbing, belly lurching, heart thudding.

"Turn around," Pollard said. "Face the wall."

Slowly, unsteadily Lakesh did as he was told. "And now?"

"This."

Pollard kicked him effortlessly in the base of the spine. There wasn't enough room in the cell for him to fall, but he slammed face-first into the wall. Blood ran in a rivulet from his nostrils, over his lips.

"Again," said Salvo pleasantly. "And again and again until he understands just how valuable he is."

**A violent struggle for survival
in a post-holocaust world**

JAMES AXLER

DEATH LANDS ®

Nightmare Passage

Ryan Cawdor and his companions fear they have crossed time lines
when they encounter an aspiring god-king whose ambitions are
straight out of ancient Egypt. In the sands of California's Guadalupe
Desert, Ryan must make the right moves to save them from another
kind of hell—abject slavery.

Take
4 explosive books
plus a
mystery bonus
FREE

A deadly kind of immortality...

THE Destroyer™

#110 Never Say Die

Created by
WARREN MURPHY
and RICHARD SAPIR

Forensic evidence in a number of assassinations reveals a curious link between the killers: identical fingerprints and genetic code. The bizarre problem is turned over to Remo and Chiun, who follow the trail back to a literal dead end—the grave of an executed killer.

Look for it in January wherever Gold Eagle books are sold.

Stony Man turns the tide of aggression against the world's most efficient crime machines

STONY MAN™ 32

LAW OF
LAST RESORT

The playground of the Caribbean becomes a drug clearing house for an ex-KGB major and his well-oiled machine handling cocaine and heroin from the cartels and the Yakuza. But turquoise waters turn bloodred as Mack Bolan, Able Team and Phoenix Force deliver a hellfire sweep that pulls the CIA, international mafiosi and Colombians together in an explosive showdown.

Available in January 1998 at your favorite retail outlet.